FINALLY!

Charlie took a deep breath and faced Chase. "Are you going to act like last night didn't happen?" she dared to ask.

When he didn't answer, she perched her fists on her slender hips and stuck out her chin. "I want more."

He grimaced. "Charlie, you are the most brazen woman I have ever known."

"Are you so unaccustomed to a woman who knows what she wants and goes after it?" she asked. She advanced a step, almost pressing her chest into his. She sniffed. Leather. He had been riding this morning. There was also some spicy scent she couldn't identify. "You smell good," she whispered. "Something new . . ."

"Bay rum," he said, as he took another step back.

She grinned. A step forward. He was weakening. "I never would have marked you a prude, Chase," she said.

"A *prude?*"

"I'm old enough to know what I want," she continued. She wanted to kiss him. Touch him. She stepped forward again. He stepped back, brushing against a tree trunk.

He had nowhere else to run. Victory was close at hand. "Chase," she whispered. "I'm naked under this dress."

Moving faster than she could have expected, he grasped her shoulders, pressed his body against hers from chest to hip, then moved his hands to either side of her head, imprisoning her between his arms.

She did not speak, o

BOOK YOUR PLACE ON OUR WEBSITE AND MAKE THE READING CONNECTION!

We've created a customized website just for our very special readers, where you can get the inside scoop on everything that's going on with Zebra, Pinnacle and Kensington books.

When you come online, you'll have the exciting opportunity to:

- View covers of upcoming books
- Read sample chapters
- Learn about our future publishing schedule (listed by publication month *and author*)
- Find out when your favorite authors will be visiting a city near you
- Search for and order backlist books from our online catalog
- Check out author bios and background information
- Send e-mail to your favorite authors
- Meet the Kensington staff online
- Join us in weekly chats with authors, readers and other guests
- Get writing guidelines
- AND MUCH MORE!

**Visit our website at
http://www.zebrabooks.com**

CAROLINA
ROSE

Tracy Sumner

Zebra Books
Kensington Publishing Corp.

http://www.zebrabooks.com

ZEBRA BOOKS are published by

Kensington Publishing Corp.
850 Third Avenue
New York, NY 10022

First Printing: April, 1999
10 9 8 7 6 5 4 3 2

Printed in the United States of America

Chapter One

He clenched his fists and groaned. Was the small amount of whiskey he had consumed making him see things?

A woman? *Charlie* Whitney, a woman?

He lifted his lids, squinted. Nope. She was still sitting there, rump perched on the edge of the chair, feet barely brushing the sawdust-covered floor. Her fingers embraced a pencil; deliberate energy he could feel from across the room pushed it along the paper.

He wiped his hand across his brow and began a slow advance—hesitant, as if an angry jury was waiting on the other side. As he reached her table, he forced himself to take a deep breath.

"Excuse me."

Behind them, the saloon's doors blew open; fragrant air enveloped him. His mind raced. A faint memory beckoned: soft arms cradling him, a plump bosom beneath his cheek. Roses. The fragrance invariably recalled another life.

How appalling to recall it *now*.

With part of his mind lodged in the past, he thoughtlessly uttered the first thing that came into it: "Your nose . . . you broke it."

She tilted her head and frowned at him. Her hand rose to touch the bump on the bridge of her nose.

He did not want to be curious about her, this woman he suspected was Charlie Whitney. *Charlie?* Of course. She would have to use a masculine name for publication in a newspaper.

And, as things seemed to go in his world, she was a sweet-smelling Charlie. There could not have been some horse-faced, amazingly gifted Charlie at the helm of the insignificant *Edgemont Sentinel*. Oh, hell no.

"If you're looking for company, she's over by the piano." She inclined her head, then turned back to her work.

He followed her slight gesture, his gaze landing on a blonde slouched against the dark, startlingly varnished bar. He pulled his gaze back. She—Charlie?—appeared to be engrossed in her writing, as if he had never been there.

"I can assure you I am not seeking company."

She glanced at him then—a sharp, hard assessment. A thin shaft of light revealed sea blue eyes.

"I think I should introduce myself." He stuck his hand before her, wondering how, exactly, a man introduced himself to a woman wearing britches. "Adam Chase. New editor of the *Sentinel*."

She cast a quick, pointed look at his hand. A gasp escaped her as her palms slammed flat upon the table. She rose with an abrupt motion, her chair skidding out behind her.

Before she could move another inch, he reached across the table and captured her wrist. He had not expected such unrestrained anger.

Her pupils enlarged, darkened as she wrenched her wrist free. "I have nothing to discuss with *you.*"

She faced him like a hungry dog before a bone. Then with a sudden movement, she tore her gaze from his and skirted the side of the table farthest from him. He let her go. As she neared the door, he called out the name. The name he thought went with her.

She did not turn, but he caught the subtle straightening of her slim shoulders, the small hitch in her step. He sighed. *Charlie.*

He watched her march out of the Four Leaf Clover with a sanguine step, as resolute as a soldier journeying to combat. A soldier in britches revealing too much slender bottom.

"Damn." What a long summer it was promising to be.

* * *

"So, she was difficult?"

Adam adjusted the lever, twisted to the side for a hammer, then darted a glance at the man standing over him. A well-placed whack popped the cylinder into place. With swift efficiency, he hopped to his feet and dusted his hands on his legs. "Difficult. Yes. Definitely."

"I guess it's only to be expected."

"Hmmm ..." He did not care to discuss Charlie Whitney. Rebellious, temperamental ... *female.* He lifted his hands before his face. Ink and oil stained them, some of which he had wiped on his trousers.

Gerald Lambert, pressman for the *Sentinel* for over twenty years, walked to a crate sitting behind the press. He came back with a rag hanging from his fingers.

"Thanks." Adam took the cloth. They stood in silence as he cleaned the ink from his palms.

After a moment, Gerald laughed, perching his hip against the press. He appeared to be somewhere in his late fifties, robust and red-faced. Thin, gray hair laced with patches of blond sat upon his head in wild disarray. He had soft blue eyes and a welcoming smile. A gentle nature. Yet, he was a big man— besting Adam's six feet two by an inch or so—with a chest like a barrel and arms the width of small pine trunks.

"Her father just died, you know. Charlie's father, I mean. And ..." Gerald shifted and resettled against the press. "Selling the *Sentinel* has been hard. Really the only thing that's ever meant much to her."

Adam shrugged. "She can still work here. Jesus, I might not think it's the best idea, but I was not planning to get rid of her." He threw the rag to the floor and stalked to a desk stacked with newly delivered supplies. "Whose desk is this?" Hell, for all he knew, it was *hers.*

Gerald's gaze met his from across the room. "That was Edward's desk."

Edward. Giving name to the dead father. Gerald's downcast eyes paid tribute to *his* sorrow. What about the girl's? How would it feel to lose both your father and your business?

Adam sighed. "What, Mr. Lambert, do you suggest I do?

Beg her? Our encounter this afternoon was not one I wish to repeat.''

Gerald lifted his hands to his mouth, fingers steepled, palms pressed. He seemed to mull it over before speaking. "Charlie has been running 'round here since she was, ah, fourteen or so. She's a better writer than Edward was, more organized, too. He loved her to pieces and her''—he glanced at Adam with a faint grin—"willful nature sprouted from that, I reckon. Spoiled her, he did. But, they only had each other.'' Gerald shrugged. "She'd be interested in them things you have planned; the rotary press and that fancy lead type.''

"It matters little to me, Mr. Lambert. If she is not available, I can find someone who is.'' He would not stoop to playing nursemaid to some overgrown tomboy.

Gerald lowered his hands from his face. "You'll never find someone who loves this paper more. You couldn't get more for your money.''

"Money? Do you think money has anything to do with my decision to be here? Hell,'' Adam laughed, "I would pay a modest fortune to get *out* of this mess.''

"Then why—''

"Mr. Lambert—''

"Gerald.''

Adam sighed and slid a pencil across the top of the desk. "Gerald, I'm here to turn this newspaper around. Oliver Stokes is willing to put capital into this . . . investment. New equipment''—he tilted his head toward the worn-out press—"is first on my list. Also, we should have a telegraph in less than a month.'' He turned his attention to a pile of editorials stacked on the desk. Flipping through them with a deft hand, he noted that very few were good enough to salvage. Edward Whitney had indeed been a dreadful writer.

"Oliver Stokes hasn't done nothin' good for this town, Mr. Chase.''

Adam cast a quick glance from the corner of his eye before resuming the paper shuffle. "My experience is the only thing of significance with regard to the *Sentinel*. Oliver Stokes will simply pay the bills.'' He wadded a piece of paper in his fist and tossed it to the floor. "I know what a bastard he is. All of Richmond knows him as a miserly, hard-nosed capitalist and generally acrimonious man. Why he is interested in this burg, I have no idea.''

"He was born here.''

Adam turned. "Oh?''

Gerald nodded, apparently pleased he could provide some unknown information. "Case of the rich man coming back to his hometown and buying everything.''

"I see. Well, that makes sense.'' Once more, his gaze dropped to the editorials.

"Charlie hates him. She knew—a'course he made no hiding of it—he wanted the *Sentinel*. She and Edward tried real hard to keep it from him. Can't you understand how tough it'll be for her to work for him?''

No, he did not understand. Then again, how many times over the last few years had he been forcibly reminded of his heartless nature? "She would be working for me.''

"Yeah, but the money goes into his pocket.''

"There is not likely to be much of that.''

"Then, why does he want it?''

Adam paused. What in the world did a man like Oliver Stokes want with a small-time outfit like the *Edgemont Sentinel?* "Actually, I have no idea.''

Silence. Then an awkward cough from Gerald. "Will you talk to her again?'' He slid the toe of his shoe along the floor.

Adam grabbed the few satisfactory editorials and circled the desk. He stuffed the papers into a leather satchel resting against the back wall. He then grabbed the bag, moved to the door and paused, considering Gerald Lambert's words. This was becoming more complicated with each step he took. And here he was, acting as Stokes' right-hand man in a town that despised the man.

"Yes, I will,'' he threw over his shoulder as the door closed behind him.

Charlie glanced at the line of colorful flowers running along the path connecting her cottage to the main road. The crisp scent of pines and fresh-cut grass mingled in the air; the syrupy odor of honeysuckle was strong, too. She could see a patch of it just ahead. Vetch, clover and wild geraniums sprouted here and there, as did the rich yellow, bell-shaped jessamine, which screamed among the rest like a drunkard during a church service.

She inhaled a long breath, concentrating on the warmth in the air, the heaviness of it. Edgemont was a beautiful place. Rugged, unblemished. Fertile and green, situated between two grand rivers, the town fostered a vigorous class of small farmers, laborers and businessmen.

She looked to the mountains in the distance. Even on a cloudy day, when she could not see them, she could imagine the imposing peaks rising above rolling hills of pine and oak, above deep valleys of soil and rock. No matter what happened, they were always there. Solid, steadfast, unfailing.

"Well, have you met him?"

Charlie clutched her hand to her chest and whirled about. She stomped her foot on the dusty ground. "Hellfire. You scared the spit out of me."

Kath Lambert laughed and clapped her hands. "I had to come tell you the news. Who else would?"

No one, that was who. Only, Charlie did not want *this* news. "Did you run straight out of the kitchen?" She looked Kath over with a frown.

Kath glanced at her slightly wrinkled dress and smiled. She always smiled. She was a petite, vivacious woman with eyes the color of shiny, sour apples and a fetching, pointed nose that only served to draw attention to the lovely mouth beneath it. She looked all of sixteen, and Charlie could hardly remember ever seeing her angry or sad.

Kath grabbed Charlie's hand. "Mercy, I'm exhausted. Let's go sit on the porch."

As she trailed along behind her friend, Charlie noted that her modest home seemed to strut like a beautiful woman in the summer, surrounded by a thick carpet of green grass and wearing a necklace of roses that ran the entire length of the front porch. Charlie climbed the steps and slid into her rocker with about as much enthusiasm as she'd show at a funeral.

Kath plopped into the other one, a huge grin on her face. "His name is Adam Chase."

Charlie scrunched lower in the rocker, until her back was

resting on the seat. She closed her eyes and knocked her head back against the wooden slats.

"He just arrived in town. Yesterday, I think. He's staying at Widow Wilkin's, and I hear tell he's not married. Not too hard on the eyes either, from what they say." Kath giggled, as married women so often do when they talk about another man's looks, almost as if they're committing a transgression against their vows.

Charlie tapped her finger on the rocker. "Who have you been gossiping with?"

"Well, Myra Hawkins for one . . ."

She rolled her head to the side, fixing Kath with an irritable glare. "For heaven's sake, that one would sink her hooks into anything under eighty."

Kath leaned forward. "By the way"—she swallowed and dipped her shoulders—"he's the new editor of the *Sentinel*." The last word was a mere whisper.

Charlie laughed and added a bored flick of her hand for good measure. "Oh. I met *him*."

Kath bounced once on the seat of her chair. "Mercy. And here I've been, rambling on like a fool." She blew out an exasperated breath that lifted the fine hairs along her forehead. "What did he look like? Is he tall like Mary Ellen Rogers said? And charming like Aileen Fitzsimmons—"

Charlie stopped the restless motion of Kath's rocker with a determined grip. "You've been going to too many Beautification Society meetings. Heavens, is every woman in this town desperate?"

"From what I heard, you wouldn't have to be desperate." Kath clapped a hand over her mouth. A loud chortle burst forth, anyway.

"Katherine Hamilton Lambert. Those other prissy misses I could see spreading this . . . this babble, but you?"

Kath placed her hand over Charlie's and squeezed. "What's got you so riled?"

Charlie snatched her hand back. "Nothing."

"So, he did look that good."

"No, he did not look that good." Actually, she hadn't even gotten a decent look at the man. She hadn't even tried.

Kath's smirk turned into a full, cheek-splitting grin. "Then, why are you blushing?"

"I'm not blushing." But she was. The slow rise of heat gliding across her face felt much like a painter's gentle stroke across canvas. "I barely met the man, for heaven's sake." But his deep voice and the sharp angles of his face had created an image in her mind, even if she hadn't been able to see him clearly, and that image sure wasn't ugly.

Kath shrugged. "Oh, well, I thought you might know more since you'll be working with him."

"I am not going to work with him."

"How about going to the Beautification Society meeting with me this week? You have the time if you're not working."

A subtle change of subject. Charlie suddenly felt like crying. "No. Not now. Not ever."

"Sewing circle next week?"

"Nope."

"Fourth of July picnic meeting?"

"Sorry, can't make it."

Kath pursed her lips and rolled her body forward, until she was sitting straight in the rocking chair. "You could try, you know."

Charlie shook her head. "I went to school with those women, remember? That was enough trying for one lifetime." She saw the stubborn gleam in her friend's eyes. Kath meant well, she knew; only the girl was not her mother. Eleanor Dane Whitney had been a charming, gracious woman. Her mother's death had ended any hopes Charlie had ever had of being a lady. At any rate, whose dream had that been?

She liked who she was. So, she wore trousers on occasion. So, she was smarter than most of the men in town. So, she worked.

It was also true that she could cook and clean as well as any young woman. After her mother's death, the household chores had fallen upon her shoulders. Thanks to two years in Mrs. Mindlebright's Deportment School, her manners were impeccable. She could put her hair into any number of silly, useless arrangements; she could drink tea without spilling; she could sew a fairly straight stitch; she could walk along rutted, ragged Main Street with a book balanced upon her head.

She rolled her eyes. What more could any woman hope for?

Granted, she had never entered a cake in the annual Fair Cake Contest; never brought a basket of food to the Spring Picnic and Dance (where Mrs. Mindlebright would have you know that many a lucky couple had entered into a nice, respectable courtship); never held any meetings of the Edgemont Beautification Society at her home.

She was glad to forgo the pleasures she was *supposed* to enjoy: tittering over the cutest beau, discussing the latest kinds of embroidery, displaying if-not-new-then-very-presentable dresses and slightly scuffed kid leather boots. A room filled with aged white gloves, hairstyles marred only by the incessant humidity, dainty cups and saucers, cookies and tea.

Not that she didn't get invited to things. Well ... she used to get invited. But they always seemed to be at the most inopportune times. For instance, the Edgemont Beautification Society meetings were always on Thursdays. Thursday was print day at the *Sentinel*. The Beautification Society frowned upon inkstained fingers.

The plank floor creaked as Kath rose from the rocker. "I need to get back to my pies. You know Miles if he doesn't have a piece after supper." She slapped her leg and turned. "I almost forgot. Supper on Sunday. About five o'clock." She crossed to the decrepit, red wagon she and her husband, Miles, had been talking about replacing for at least five years.

Charlie raised a hand in farewell, watching the wagon bounce along the rutted drive, the small figure seated atop the wooden seat swaying with the turbulent motion. Kath was a good friend. Charlie knew she had won no prizes for attaching herself to a woman that most viewed as rather peculiar.

Spinster Whitney: that was what some of them called her. Hellfire, she was only twenty-four. Still, maybe life would have been different had her mother lived.

Nevertheless, she knew what she'd become: a freckle-skinned hoyden with a clearly unladylike swagger to her stride, with a fresh mouth and no respect for things proper, with a halting way of speaking, as if she was always thinking, with a too-direct way of looking at a person—even a man—and worst of all, with an abnormal fascination for a newspaper. It beat all for a woman to have a hobby like that, was all they could say. Worse yet to call it a profession.

She swallowed back any sorrow, or anger, she felt and concentrated instead on what she was grateful for. The list was not long, or complete, but it was enough.

She closed her eyes and sighed. If she could only figure out what to do about the *Sentinel*.

Adam Chase lay in a narrow bed in the small room he had rented at Mrs. Wilkin's boardinghouse. He let his gaze drift about the room. Cozy. It was cozy. And comfortable. Huge pieces of dark furniture, scuffed and colorless in spots, roosted like idle chickens. A thick green and blue afghan, waiting patiently for winter, lay atop a wooden sea chest. Moonlight from the room's lone window poured in, sliding across his legs to pool on the floor in a neat puddle.

Amazing how different it was from the other bedrooms he had occupied in his life.

His childhood room had been filled with his grandfather's furniture and books, the old man's globe, compass and rifles. A man would have appreciated the antique pieces, the significance, the history associated with each. To a young boy, they were a dead man's belongings, warm from hands he had not known and, at eight years of age, did not want to know.

Conversely, his room in his home in Richmond was practically naked of any furnishings except a bed. The house had been decorated by a man with preferences contrary to his own. On the day of his return from an arduous assignment in the West, Adam had walked into an exquisite home that repelled him. He had no one to blame but himself. The decorator, Pierre Janvier, had repeatedly asked for his opinion, but he had been especially busy those months . . . and hell, a thousand miles away.

The ladies in Richmond loved his home—Mr. Janvier was the *crème de la crème* of the society circle. Simply put, he was the most expensive. Adam could hardly believe—considering how much he had *despised* his father's home—that he was once again residing in a palace teeming with furniture he could not sit upon. One night in an inebriated frenzy, he had stripped his bedroom of everything but the necessities. His housekeeper, Mrs. Beard, had nearly had a seizure when she looked out her window the next day to see the lawn littered with the consequence of his overindulgence.

He grinned and skimmed his hand through the shadow lying across the bed, remembering the expression on Mrs. Wilkin's plump face when he had stumbled in this evening. He should go to her bedroom, knock on the door, explain he drank very little—had been inebriated only three or four times since Eaton's death, in fact. But he feared a trip down that narrow staircase would end with him resting in a broken heap at the bottom. How could he explain to her, an old woman, that sometimes it was essential to feel numb—to distinguish absolutely nothing *from* absolutely nothing?

Moreover, how could he explain his pensive mood to himself?

During the walk to Mrs. Wilkin's, a foreign, bucolic aroma and soft, lilting tunes from the Four Leaf Clover had surrounded him.

Loud couples, laughing and intertwined, women in high-heeled shoes and silk stockings, and the stink of day-old garbage and cheap perfume had comforted him.

Women prancing around in britches and ugly black boots did not. He sighed and shifted, crossing his feet at the ankle and throwing his arm over his eyes, blocking the shaft of pale moonlight streaming into the window.

If only he could block his thoughts.

"Dammit, Stokes. Couldn't you find another lackey to run this paper?" Although, it was no use complaining now—and to himself in a dark room, no less. He had accepted the position. Temporarily, thank God.

I have to get this paper on its feet and get back to Richmond. My life is there . . . my job at the *Times,* my home. A sharp flash of regret surged through him, pain he seldom felt—or seldom let himself feel. The same damn emotion had blown through him today, making him react so crazily with that odd Charlie Whitney. Imagine grabbing her wrist like he had done.

It was only . . . the past had the power to surprise him. He would forget for a month or two. Maybe six, if he was lucky.

Then, one night he would awaken with his mother's voice ringing in his ears and Eaton's blood slick upon his fingers.

Eaton. After all this time, still so painful.

A few drinks, and I am going to feel sorry for him . . . feel sorry for myself. Dammit. What more could I want? The opportunity to become a full-fledged editor is within my grasp, a beautiful home overlooking the James River is waiting for me and a few very alluring women find my company quite pleasing. One in particular shares my . . . tastes. He betrayed the pleasant thoughts as his hand clutched the coverlet.

Adam groaned, the sound hollow in the darkness of the room. Laughing blue eyes and sandy hair, dimples so like his own. Eaton had been his protector. His hero.

He had been a small boy, always the smallest in his class, but he had done his best to fight when he had to. Eaton had always been there. To fight with him—or for him—or grab him and run.

He sat up now, dropping his face to his hands. His chest felt tight and heavy, and, oh . . . what was the use in thinking about it? Eaton was lost. *Everyone was lost.* With trembling fingers he reached into his pocket and located a crumpled cheroot. He scrambled to find a match on the bedside table. As the flame flickered, shadows bounced along the wall. He felt his mask of indifference melt, replaced by raw anguish.

Face it Chase, Eaton was always there for you. When he was the one in need, you were not there. His hand shook as he inhaled. He wished for a release from the memories. *Haunting.* Memories were forever haunting him.

He pulled a pillow against the headboard and leaned against it, recrossing his legs. His head dropped back as he stared at the ceiling. A few chips of paint were missing right above his head. He felt the long-forgotten urge to cry. He *had* cried once, as he held his brother's rapidly chilling body against his.

Adam was a shell. He knew it. Hell, for all he cared, everyone knew it. Outside he was strong, charming. Inside he was empty, sullen. His brother's death had killed two in Adam's heart, for he had stopped loving his father the very moment Eaton drew his last breath. All the love in his body had poured out of him like the blood from his brother's.

Love. Bitterness welled inside him as the word circled about his mind. His cheroot dropped to the coverlet. With a muttered oath, he grabbed it, but not before a small, black-edged hole appeared.

He cursed and stood. With an angry twist, he threw the smoking stub out the window. He rested his hands on the frame and gazed over open fields awash in silver moonlight.

He needed to get this assignment finished and leave. Soon. This town—the serenity it evoked—was going to make him restless. That would make him think. He did not want to think. There were too many painful memories chasing him. It was all he could do to stay ahead of them.

Maybe a woman would help. Maybe the blond woman in the Four Leaf Clover. But there was no quickening of his blood at the thought of bedding her.

A vision jumped into his head, and he immediately experienced a warm response. Oh, no, Chase. No way, no how. Insolent. Too bold for her own good. Going into a saloon. Someone should tan her hide. Doesn't she have a man to keep her in line? His hands tightened on the window frame as he scowled.

I hope she has a husband. Or at least a fiancé.

Chapter Two

Charlie increased her pace, humming a tune her mother had sung to her as a child. For the life of her, she could not remember its name.

The day had turned out to be a beautiful one; the sun shone as bright as a brass lamp, and there was a glorious breeze that cooled the skin with ease considering the heat. It felt wonderful to escape her house. She had been lonely, and bored, this week.

She was a little late for dinner with Kath and Miles. They lived a mile away, on the main road that led past her house and into the hills. Miles had stopped offering to pick her up, though he still insisted on bringing her home in that decrepit wagon.

The experience was invariably harsh. She had to grasp the wagon's sides with all her strength just to keep from popping out like butter from a sizzling frying pan. That thing had seen better days, twenty years before.

She smiled. She felt lighthearted today. Pretty, too. For the first time in a long time. She was going to enjoy the sensation. She knew it was foolish to delight in a trifling Sunday dinner at Kath's, but there were so few things lately to rejoice about. She had decided to wear her new green day dress and, to suit her whimsical mood, had twined matching ribbon through the handle of the basket she held in her hand. The pale yellow ribbon binding her hair had fallen out as she walked, allowing strands to tumble about like long, flowing banners. The ribbon now lay in the bottom of the basket, between two jars of preserves.

As she reached the Lamberts' house, she took the porch stairs two at a time and burst through the door without knocking.

"Hello," she called from the entryway.

Charlie liked the home Miles and his father had built. They had planned for a family when designing it. The best feature of the house was the pantry. It was large enough to hold food for the entire winter. Charlie stored her preserves there, when her tiny cupboard got too cramped.

She walked to the kitchen. "Kath, thank goodness Sunday finally got here. I've been absolutely crazy in that house. I brought peach preserves, which I hope turn out better than those god-awful others." She plopped the basket on the kitchen table. "And, look at this gorgeous basket I bought from the Yankee trader who traveled through on Friday . . . imagine, I swapped a sketch of his wagon for the basket and *two* spools of thread."

Kath turned from the stove with a weak smile. "Charlie."

She followed Kath's gaze, an apprehensive tingle raising the hairs on her neck. She backed out of the kitchen and crept along the hallway, tilting her head to the side as she advanced upon the sitting room, which she had passed during her mad rush inside. Her steps slowed. If she was careful, she could just peek in.

Lean, long legs. Muscular brown arm thrown casually along the settee's back. Whiskered face. Deep, deep brown eyes, open wide and crinkling at the corners.

She stepped back and spun around, her skirt flipping out behind her. *So that was what he looked like.* Tall. An inch or two over six feet, probably. And lean. But not stringy. No, he looked . . . sturdy. A bit wild. Kind of like the sky right before a thunderstorm.

He had thick, brown chest hair.

Heat bounded across her face. The man was simply *indecent*. With narrowed eyes and a stiff back, she retraced her steps into the kitchen. "What is he doing here?" Anger, hot and heavy, pulsed through her. She couldn't stay here. She couldn't eat with him.

"Please, Charlie, do this for me. Just a simple dinner. Miles likes him and, honestly, so do I. I promise you I had no idea he was coming, but it was too late to do anything about it."

Charlie glanced back toward the sitting room. She heard Miles' deep laughter. He needed a friend, and there really was no reason to hurt anyone's feelings. She sighed. "For you, I would do almost anything. If tonight isn't proof."

Kath gave her a quick hug. "Thank you."

They filled the time with talk of trivial issues: upcoming quilting parties, sociables and sewing bees, though Charlie didn't care one whit about those things.

As the men entered the kitchen, one of them in particular seemed to suck up all the air until Charlie felt as if she couldn't breathe. She watched Miles grab a bottle and two glasses from the cupboard as Adam took a seat at the table. Turning, she determined to pay them no mind.

Adam followed Charlie's movements about the kitchen. She was a very petite woman and, for a hoyden, moved with a majestic grace—an elegant, self-confident ease. He had to admit she looked quite fetching in her simple, green gingham dress. But what had shocked him the most when she had blown through the door like a small tornado was her *hair,* wild and free, flowing about her head and down her back like some black demon. She was a fierce little piece of baggage, to be sure.

He was also sure she would be angry to know her incredibly blue eyes betrayed the capable countenance she wrapped like a heavy coat about her. All of her emotions flowed into those shockingly beautiful eyes, causing them to darken quicker than ink onto paper.

"Right?" Miles clapped him on the back and ejected a hearty laugh.

Adam nodded and joined in the laughter, having no idea what the question had been.

The women flitted and fluttered about the small kitchen, placing bowls and baskets, plates and cups, upon the table. The air was heavy with a mixture of sweet scents and gentle laughter. He felt surrounded by things foreign. He felt at once out of place *and* as if he belonged.

"Pa said the new press was delivered yesterday," Miles said, clear out of the blue.

Adam tensed and straightened in his chair. He shifted his gaze to Charlie, whose step had halted midmotion. Kath had stopped in place as well and was glaring at her husband.

"Yes, it was delivered yesterday." Adam paused and swept his glass in a circle on the table. "Um . . . it should be up and running by the end of next week." A bread basket landed in front of him with a healthy slap. He turned to find Charlie standing above him, her mouth stretched into a tight, thin line.

"Money can buy anything, it seems," she whispered, before striding back to the stove.

He reared back in his chair and turned to look at her. "What did you say?" Dammit, she was pushing him. Just like she had done in the Four Leaf Clover. It was not *his* fault he had landed in this godforsaken town.

"You heard what I said."

"Dinner's ready," Kath announced, waving her hands in the air like a frantic bird.

"Explain to me what you *meant,* then."

Charlie whipped around, a yellow dishrag twisted in her fist. "I would find it repugnant to sell myself to the highest bidder, is all."

Anger flared in his chest. "Listen, sweetheart, I am a damn fine editor. I have not had an easy ride on a political train, picking up promotions as I went along. Everything I know about newspapers I learned the hard way." He grasped the back of the chair. The muscles in his arms bulged. "I have set type and hand-inked presses, things so old and worn out the impression was illegible. I have worked as a foreman, junior editor, staff correspondent and chief confidential clerk—not in that order. I have written stories about everything from the ladies' garden club to the economic state of countries abroad, most penned on location. So save your snide looks for someone who is deserving of them."

She continued to stare at him, her eyes wide, not a flinch or a blink coming from her. He applauded her fortitude, even if her motives were misguided. What the hell had he said all that to her for, anyway? What was he trying to prove?

She looped the dishrag around her hand and pulled. "Mr. Chase, I . . . I don't know what business you've done with Oliver Stokes, but he isn't going to be satisfied until he owns this whole town. He already has the hotel and restaurant. My uncle is fighting to keep the bank. Mr. Whitefield fears losing his general store, and he has five children to feed and hardly two pennies to rub together." The rag fell to her side. "What do you think would have happened to the *Sentinel* if my father had not suddenly taken ill and had to sell?"

Her eyes closed, then flipped open. He scarcely heard her words, he was so ensnared in blue splendor.

"Mr. Chase, I've also hand-inked presses—because that was all we had. And, taken them apart and put them back together, working all night for a morning press run. I've written about everything I could get my hands on to fill a couple of pages of the cheapest newsprint, and I've read everything to stay current in an area that is severely obsolescent."

"Dinner's ready. Is everyone hungry?" Kath's voice rang in the kitchen.

"What would you have me do, Miss Whitney?"

Charlie slapped the dishrag against her leg. "Don't you realize he wants to commandeer this newspaper for his own political advantage?"

Adam quelled the urge to laugh. Charlie Whitney had done well to learn anything about the business in this place. "God, you are naïve," was all he said.

"I don't expect you to understand. My father was a good man, and we did the best we could."

"I can do better."

Kath groaned and dropped her face into her hands.

Adam watched as Charlie struggled to speak. Perhaps he had gone too far.

"Mr. Chase, you can go to hell," she finally said. Then she threw the dishrag right into his face. He pulled it from his eyes in time to see her stomp from the kitchen and out the back door.

"Mercy." Kath wrung her hands in her apron.

Adam braced his hands on the table and stood. "That went

well.'' Why had he made her angry again? He had wanted to apologize for his previous insensitivity, explain his reasons for working for Oliver Stokes and encourage her to remain with the *Sentinel* at their next meeting. Damn. He had made a mess of things.

''She is a little . . . excitable.'' Miles braved a smile.

Adam shook his head. ''No, this was entirely my fault. I was trying to provoke her.'' Provoke her? Hell, it had *delighted* him to see her blue eyes widen with astonishment, her lovely face mottle with anger. ''Maybe I should go after her.''

Miles coughed and glanced his wife's way.

''No.'' Kath grabbed Adam's shirtsleeve. ''Probably better to let her cool off.''

Adam stepped forward, rubbing the small scar on his wrist. He glanced out the glass panes, searching. A flash of green gingham was visible in the distance. He could see her inky hair bobbing along, too. The silly woman probably did not own a bonnet.

Tomorrow. He would try once more tomorrow. If that did not work, then to hell with Charlie Whitney.

Chapter Three

Charlie stood in her kitchen, bright sunlight streaming in the windows. She mentally outlined the chores on her list and decided the first order of business was to weed the vegetable garden and pick the ripe produce. She poured a glass of lemonade and walked outside, muttering to herself about the heat and thickness of the humid air.

Her house sat on a healthy plot of land a mile outside Edgemont's town center. It was a modest dwelling, comfortable and natty. Not too much, not too little, as her mother used to say.

She perched her glass on top of a wooden wash bucket sitting upside down on her back porch. Her father had added the porch two or three summers ago. There was no door connecting it to the interior of the house, but it was a wonderful place to do laundry or snap beans on a cool evening.

She had dressed for comfort for her chores. Actually, it was her favorite outfit: a pair of men's trousers—which she had fashioned from a *Godey's* pattern—and a faded, yellow cotton shirt. The shirt had come about from another trade she'd made with a Yankee peddler. The peddler had seen her sketching and agreed to an exchange. Charlie, seeing a good bargain in the making, had spent thirty minutes sketching an accurate, if slightly crude, likeness of the peddler. In return she had gotten the shirt, a couple of braided lamp wicks, some tattered hair ribbons and two precious, back-dated copies of the *Southern Quarterly Review*. Probably, in all honesty, junk the peddler did not really want.

She hummed beneath her breath as she lightly fingered the worn shirt. She shook her head, banishing any idle intentions, and with perspiration dampening her face and neck, knelt and began to pluck weeds from the dew-coated soil. She loved the feel of cool dirt beneath her fingers, in sharp contrast to the solid wall of heat that penetrated the summer air. Even if you could only immerse yourself to the first knuckle, the chore was welcome relief.

After an hour or so of weeding, her muscles began to cramp and protest from the imposing position. She paused and stretched, working her lower back with dirt-stained fingers.

And noticed him.

Her hands fell to her sides; her mouth parted. For one honest moment, the full, potent impact of seeing him struck her.

He was leaning against the back porch railing, his feet linked at the ankle, his hand wrapped around *her* lemonade glass. His hair was damp and ruffled, as if he had just drawn impatient fingers through it. The dark waves curled stubbornly about his face, clinging like small arms. She knew the innocence he projected just then was a mirage, a delusion her mind had created to lessen her dismay. He wore what she recognized as his uniform: conforming trousers, mud-caked Hessians, cotton lawn shirt—unbuttoned three buttons at the top. More chest hair, she noted, and shivered despite the extreme heat.

Trying hard to maintain her poise, she rose and brushed her stained hands on her trousers, inwardly cringing as she imagined how she must look. His expression was calm as she walked toward him, but his gaze was inquiring. She stopped in front of him. A drop of perspiration slithered from one very high cheekbone to the corner of his sensual mouth. A beautiful mouth really . . . firm and full. She quelled the urge to wipe the bead of sweat from his face.

Feeling rather defiant, and still angry over the way he had run her off from the Lamberts' dinner, she took the glass from him, swallowed the last of the lemonade, and turned, needing to hide the rosy flush creeping up her face.

She rounded the porch and entered the house without a word. She poured the remaining lemonade into two glasses. Of course he was there, having followed her, when she turned with one in each hand.

She passed him his with an indifferent stretch. "What do you want?"

Despite her rudeness, he maintained his insouciant manner as he leaned against her small pine table, his head tilted, his dark gaze resting upon her. He was too close for comfort. She felt like a deer stalked by an experienced hunter. His expression, on the other hand, was closed.

Ostensibly oblivious to her restlessness, he drank, his gaze never leaving her face. It unsettled her, the way he stared.

He placed the glass on the table. "Miles mentioned your broken fence the other night, and I thought you could use some help fixing it. Just trying to be neighborly." He flashed a smile and a pair of overworked dimples.

She may have accepted the package if the smile were genuine, but it was so different from the one she'd seen on his face when he'd talked with Miles. Too different. She eyed him suspiciously. "Neighborly? You'll have to forgive me for being . . . wary."

He coughed or *laughed* into his hand. "I think paranoid would also apply."

She jerked his glass from the table and thrust it by the side of her leg. "Mr. Chase, I must have a simple mind, because I can't see any reason for you coming here." She turned and circled back to the dry sink, placing his glass there with a firm crack.

"There is nothing *simple* in that beautiful head."

Charlie's shoulders tightened as she grasped the edge of the dry sink. Beautiful? *Beautiful?* She had heard the compliment before . . . but in a town as small as Edgemont, she'd figured it was due to poor selection. Adam Chase had probably seen lots of lovely women. Women dressed in the latest Parisian fashions, women who knew how to entice a man with a flick of their wrists. Women like her cousin Lila.

And he thought *her* beautiful?

"I guess I could use some help with the fence." Uh, oh. Had they been talking about the fence? No. She sighed and squeezed the dry sink harder. They had been talking about her mind or some such nonsense. Hellfire.

A light laugh sounded behind her. "Changed your mind so quickly? Miss Whitney, you are an unpredictable woman."

She closed her eyes. Oh, what she would like to say to him, if only she could form a clever, coherent thought. Instead, she whipped about and marched out the door.

"Faustus?" She slapped her hands against her legs and whistled.

He stepped onto the front porch. "Now, who in the world would name a dog Faustus?"

"Faustus is a cat."

Moving in front of her, he sat on the stairs, his head just about reaching her hip. "Faustus . . . hmmm, I *would* say that was Latin. But, considering it came from you, I will venture to guess it is a kind of whiskey at the Four Leaf Clover."

"Whiskey at the Four Leaf?" She glared at the top of his dark head.

He grabbed her ankle and pulled with a gentle tug. "I was only kidding. Well . . . sort of."

She yanked her ankle from his grasp. "That's the second time you've touched me. The next time you may jerk that hand back minus a finger."

He leaned against the top step and threw his head back, laughter flowing from him. Even if she wanted to, she couldn't quite quell the flood of pleasure rolling through her. She didn't know how to explain it, but she was sure laughter from this man was rare. As much as it chagrined her to admit it, he *was* appealing with his rich, masculine laugh, dark, spirited eyes . . . and dimples—overburdened though they were. She frowned and dropped to the step with a hesitant squat.

He slanted his gaze to her, his hand covering his mouth. "I must say I am flattered you've counted. I am a quick learner, though." He made a grand show of sitting straight and putting his hands in his lap, like a chastised schoolboy.

A loud meow stopped their discussion. Charlie followed his gaze to a bush by the porch, where a ruckus of some kind was going on.

His were the brownest eyes she had ever seen. They were the exact color of the dark southern soil she treasured. She rolled her head, squirmed and slid across the step, as far from him as she could get.

Despite her discomfiture, the silence between them flowed—comfortably, companionably—strange for two people who were practically strangers.

"Why are you here?" Not the fence story. She wanted to know why he was in Edgemont. Though he probably wouldn't take it that way.

He raised his gaze to the sky and leaned back. "I happened to get a position with a small Washington paper after I was so ungraciously thrown out of university. It was love at first sight. An editorship is practically all I have worked for since." Absently, he began to run his finger along his wrist. Charlie glanced down and saw a small scar, jagged and white, standing out on his skin like a firefly in the darkness. He continued, seemingly unaware of the action. "Those first few years taught me so much. I used to think a newspaper's sole purpose was to record the news of the day. Instead, I found it should be a register of the times, an objective vehicle for discerning intelligent thought. If used appropriately."

She listened, admiring his strong profile, noting his thoughtful expression. Adam Chase was becoming something of a surprise.

She lifted her hand, then let it fall to her lap. "How can you work for men who don't even begin to understand?"

The wooden step squeaked as he turned to face her. "I have fought for exceptional articles and won, and I have fought for factual, realistic editorials and lost to political influence." He laughed softly. "If I looked at every story after the fact to determine its substance, I would not have the energy or the heart to go on to the next day's edition. I have learned to be flexible."

"Flexible? Flexible regarding what? Your principles?" She looked away but could feel his gaze pursuing her. "I can't . . . I won't sell myself like that."

"It does not have to come down to selling yourself. You will never work for a newspaper in any town, in any city, where you respect every man you work for, where you like everything you write. Charlie, I did not come here to be anyone's puppet. They could have sent an inexperienced editor if that was their aim." He tapped his foot against the bottom step. "Use Stokes, use me. Learn everything you can. Who knows, maybe Stokes will get sick of the business—and who would be the first choice to be assigned the *Sentinel*'s editorship? Not an inexperienced junior reporter, that's for sure."

Which is what you are now, he could have added.

Indecision swept through her. *Learn everything you can.* His words rang like bells in her head. Could she do it?

For once she believed something without proof, without knowing all the facts: Adam Chase knew the newspaper business. But. . . .

She turned to him, intent on refusing his request, only to find his gaze locked on her. Quite without reason, she wondered how he regarded her. Why did she care? "I . . . I need to think about this." She rose and brushed off her trousers, her fingers twisting in the threadbare cloth. She climbed the steps, then threw a quick glance over her shoulder. "You're sure you want to help?"

He nodded and stood.

She sighed. What was she getting herself into?

They sat in quiet contemplation on her front porch, the newly repaired fence standing as straight and proud as a palace guard, their rocking chairs swaying in agreement. A brilliant red and gold sunset lay beyond the mountains.

Charlie rolled her head to look at him. Adam Chase was definitely a surprise. He was considerate, even congenial, when he did not monitor every action. When he spoke of things that were of great importance to him, his face softened, and emotion flowed into his eyes. Once or twice, he seemed to recognize this was happening and glanced away.

If not for the rocking of his chair, she would have thought him asleep. She wanted to thank him and better to do it while those dark eyes of his were not lighting a small fire in her stomach. "Thank you for the help today. I'm not sure why you did it . . . but I appreciate it. Sometimes it's hard to do everything yourself."

"There are so many sounds here we lose in the city. Sounds I have not heard in years." His voice was soft, low.

His eyes had not opened, so she continued to stare. He had been speaking like this all day. Not about the newspaper or anything else they could possibly debate, but normal things like rain and the exquisite color of butterflies, the unconditional love of dogs and horses, and the calming sound of the ocean as it rolled onto the shore. He shied away from discussing his childhood; she did as well. All things considered—quite unbelievably—she had enjoyed the day; enjoyed speaking to someone about subjects independent of the latest Beautification Society meeting or the best way to raise a cash crop.

His eyes fluttered open. He looked drowsy and sated. "I came to help you for a number of reasons. I was curious. Miles puts a lot of stock in you, and I respect his judgment. Also, from what I have read, you are a good writer, a little rough around the edges, but that's where I come in. And, you know this town." He covered his mouth and yawned. She watched the muscles in his neck elongate. "You would be good for the *Sentinel.* You know that. The experience would be good for you. Plus"—he closed his eyes—"I need your help."

She turned and gazed across the yard. He needed her help?

She wanted to do it. The absence of her father *and* the newspaper had left a vacant gap in her heart, in her life. She longed to hear the peculiar sound of the press, to smell the sharp scent of ink, to discuss the latest news, to decide the length of stories and to hold the finished product in her hands and know it had come from her hard work. But the *Sentinel* was Stokes' concern now, wasn't it? Or was it Adam Chase's? The questions swam in her head like a dozen fish in a half-dozen-size pond.

A loud meow pierced the silence. They jumped as if a gun had discharged behind their backs, then turned to each other and laughed.

She leaned, snapping her fingers. "Faustus is a naughty kitty, not coming home for two days." The cat sauntered to the rocking chair, rubbing his back against it. She scratched his ears, murmuring childlike phrases to the large, orange feline.

"So, this is the illustrious Faustus. He is a . . . big fellow. What do you feed the thing?" Adam grimaced as Faustus strolled to his chair and began to meow. "What is wrong with him?"

Charlie grinned. "He likes to be scratched behind his ears or under his chin."

"No, thank you. I am not, and never will be, a cat man." He wrinkled his nose in displeasure, but trailed a hesitant finger underneath Faustus' adequate chin.

"You mean you don't like animals? How could you not like animals?"

He raised his hands in mock surrender. Faustus meowed when the scratching stopped. "Hold on now, I did not say I hated animals. Only, I do not love cats. Actually, horses are my great weakness. In fact, mine should be arriving any day now. An associate from Virginia, on a round-about way to Charleston, is bringing him through."

A horseman. Charlie could imagine his fine, muscular legs astride a horse. She was glad he couldn't see the flush settling on her cheeks.

"Taber's a beautiful horse. A palomino the color of spun gold with a tail that reminds me of ivory. Pure. And fast. Some say the fastest horse in Richmond."

"Taber? What an unusual name."

"It was my brother's middle name." Why mention that? He took hold of himself as he felt his composure slip.

"Do you ride often?"

Adam found himself rubbing the puffed, crescent scar on his wrist. He pulled his hands apart. The damn disfigurement would always be a reminder. "I like to ride often. Every day if I can. Sometimes it is my only way to escape."

"Escape from what?" Her words floated to him.

Like cloud shadows on the surface of a stream, anxiety, grief and fear darkened his mind. He turned his head and looked into the twilight. Fireflies flitted around the porch. Croaking frogs sounded like booming thunder in the quiet night. He rose from the chair. It rocked silently behind him. "Do you mind?" He gestured to the cheroot he held in his hand.

"No." She shook her head.

He lit a match and brought the flame in close to his face, behind the curve of his hand.

She stopped rocking for a moment and inhaled a breath. "My father smoked. We spent many a night looking at the stars, watching for the first—sometimes the only—snowfall of the winter. And, we talked.''

He slanted a glance at her, then looked back toward the dark horizon. It sounded as if she had loved her father very much. She was lucky. God, when had he thought about his father in loving terms? Had he ever? The last time they had spoken had been a disaster.

He had tried to avoid a confrontation. God, by that time he had wanted nothing to do with his father. After Eaton's death, he had not cared ever to see him again. Adam grimaced and closed his eyes. He could *still* hear his father yelling.

''Adam, you will abandon this newspaper business. A god-damn reporter. Did I send you to the finest schools in Virginia to be a newspaperman? I am a judge, Adam, and no son of a judge will be a newspaperman. I forbid it.''

His father's tone was designed to intimidate. Low and deep, gurgling like water flowing over rocks. Frigid. Bitter.

''Forbid? It may have escaped your notice, but I am twenty-two years old, *Father*.'' He said the word scornfully, far too late to feign respect. ''I will work where I please, act as I please, bed whomever I please. And, you will not have a damn thing to say about it.''

The slap surprised him. His father was powerful in ways he had forgotten. ''You son of a bitch. I have given you everything that was in my power to give you: money, education, prestige, a chance to be someone. Things I worked damn hard for.''

His father's breath wheezed in and out of his throat. Adam almost hoped he would crumple, right there on his fancy carpet.

''Money, position, power. What about love? Did you ever tell me you loved me? Did I ever do anything worthy of a father's congratulatory pat on the back? Did you ever shake my hand in parental pride? Did you every shake Eaton's? Hell, no. But, you showed me how to be the coldest, most callous bastard I know how to be. You taught me how to hide my emotions, how to gain the upper hand, while forcing everyone around me to their knees.''

His father's face reddened. ''Love? All you can speak of is love? Your mother was the lover in this family. I did not have time for such nonsense. It's not like I had a passel of girls running around the house. I had two fine, strapping men, for

God's sake, not some milksops needing unlimited love. That was your mother's job. I taught you what you need to survive.''

Adam clenched his fists at his side. His father would never change. Why did that disappoint him? ''Mother died when I was ten years old; Eaton was thirteen. We were not men. Her death was devastating . . . and what did you do? Marry Eleana a month later?''

''I needed companionship. Abigail's death was a shock to me. I loved her, too.''

''No. You have never loved anyone.''

''You do not know what the hell you're talking about, Adam. But I know one thing. You are my only son. You will leave this profession. It was bad enough that Eaton turned out so poorly. You will not also fail me, by God.''

The few minutes after were vague. A serrated, indescribable heat suffused Adam's entire body, like the bent edge of a dull knife digging into his skin. His vision dimmed, and he lunged at his father, throwing him against a wall. They rolled to the floor, a tangle of arms and legs.

Again and again Adam screamed: ''You did not know anything about him, damn you. You did not know anything about him.''

Eleana rushed in. A crystal vase shattered at her feet. Her shrill screams worked through Adam's rage. He spun away from his father, leaned against the wall and dropped his head to his bent knees.

His stepmother stumbled over a table, tight curses peppering her words. Adam looked in time to see his father's cool, watchful gaze touch him. His father's hair was ruffled, and a thin line of blood ran from the corner of his mouth; but otherwise he appeared resolute. ''I will forget this little incident, because I realize Eaton's death has left you very disturbed. Mark my words, Adam. Now. Today. When I return home from Louisiana, this newspaper nonsense will . . . be . . . finished.'' He emphasized the declaration with a hard shake of his fist. With her slim arms supporting him, Eleana and Hamilton Chase walked through the door. Walked out of his life.

There had been no need to end his burgeoning newspaper career. The steamboat his father and Eleana had boarded hit a submerged tree three days later—a snag the riverboat captains called them—halfway between St. Louis and Natchez. The frail hull of the opulent floating palace had ripped apart like a cookie. There had been survivors, but Hamilton Fletcher Chase, powerful judge and politician—able, single-handedly, to control the most ruthless men in Washington—had never learned to swim. His form of power was worthless on the Mississippi.

Had his father spilled a harsh, bleak stain on his character that would never wash out? Unable to love after Eaton's death, Adam knew he was growing more like his father with each passing day. Relentless? He hoped not. *He prayed not.* His inherited wealth, combined with the status of his position, was bringing its own destiny. He wanted to control that destiny, but sometimes he felt like a marionette whose father was tugging the strings from above or, as was more likely, below.

A sharp pain brought him out of his trance. He dropped what was left of his cheroot over the railing of the porch. A flaming, red welt appeared on his finger.

Charlie jumped from the chair. "What?"

"I burned my damned finger." He laughed. "My God, what an idiot."

"Let me see it." She grabbed his hand and pulled him into the house.

He felt the heat from her touch all the way to the tips of his toes. To hell with the burn on his finger. None of the women he had bedded had ever held his hand as gently as Charlie Whitney was doing right now.

She put his hand under the glass lamp hanging on the wall inside the door. The scent of burning oil stung his nose.

"I see where it's red. I have some salve, just wait a minute." She removed her hand from his and walked to the kitchen. She came back with a small jar that when opened emitted a smell worse than horse dung and rotten eggs mixed together.

He put his uninjured hand to his nose. "Jesus, what is in that stuff?"

She just shook her head as she applied the salve.

He glanced at the top of her head. Sudden, unexpected tenderness rushed through him for this petite woman who was so strong in mind and spirit. His mother had been the last woman to touch him like this. To take care of him.

"For your information, this is a salve I just happen to be

lucky enough to get. It's a miracle medicine. The ingredients are a secret.''

''Well . . . it smells like one helluva secret.''

She looked at him and smiled softly, the dim light making her eyes appear just the color of the ocean where he had spent summers as a child. The lingering distress from his upsetting memory vanished.

She finished applying the ointment and closed the jar. He could feel her. Smell her. Roses and smoke, and a peculiar scent that must be her own.

She smelled wonderful.

''There. Now it won't blister as badly.'' She stepped into the kitchen and replaced the jar in the cupboard.

He wiped his hand across his forehead. It shook ever so slightly. Of course, it was the house, hot and humid, with only a slight breeze blowing through the windows. ''I . . . I need to get home. To Mrs. Wilkin's. The first test run with the new press is tomorrow. Poor Gerald has been like a kid at Christmas, waiting to get his hands on that thing.'' He pushed himself off the door frame. ''Charlie?''

She turned from the cupboard, her blue eyes flat, impenetrable. He recognized her defensive gesture; he wondered about its cause.

''Think about coming back to the *Sentinel*.'' He could not tell from her expression whether she was considering it or not. She was a stubborn woman—strong and single-minded. If he was not careful, she would have him admiring her.

''I'll think about it,'' was all she said.

He needed to get the hell out of there. He was trying to keep his eyes off her clinging britches, too revealing in their simplicity. He floundered.

During their work on the fence, her hair had come loose and was floating about her face like a dark cloud. He swallowed, struggling to gather his mutinous senses. His vision filled with sea blue eyes, taunting, challenging. He found her sufficiency both endearing and bothersome.

He would not allow his fascination with this young woman to continue.

Fascination. This thought, above all others, acted like a hand and pushed him into motion. He turned and strode through the door. The dark night swallowed him as he took the steps at a run.

"Thanks, Chase." Her voice startled the crickets in the bush into silence.

He paused. Again, her eyes swam before his. "Dammit."

He stalked off without saying good night.

Chapter Four

Adam growled and kicked a rock from his path the next day, which only served to place a nice long scratch on the toe of his Hessians. It did not matter. They had long ago lost the battle with dust.

He crossed the ground at a rapid pace. His hands clenched and unclenched by his side, muscles tightening beneath his shirtsleeves. Anyone who knew him would have recognized impatience in the firm set of his jaw, his determined stride. Unfortunately, his impatience was directed at himself. Whom else could he blame when it was his fault he had landed in this mess?

It was not enough to be an assistant editor. *He* wanted an editorship. Yesterday—not the five years he should have to wait. It wasn't that he was cheating . . . at least, not really. He was a good journalist, a good editor. Even if he did go off half-cocked sometimes. He would be the first to admit that his way of writing could be . . . dangerous. He never recommended it to anyone, especially an inexperienced reporter. Hell, he had not chosen the safest profession to be involved in during the fight for partisan control. He took great care in making sure his staff was well aware of that fact. Often, it came down to defending the accuracy of a story at the end of a pistol.

Thus far, he had managed to avoid the code duello. His editorial style was thoughtful, deliberate. His expeditious methods of research and creation were clear only to those who watched him work. His ability to relate a controversial issue in a lucid manner, all the while bringing it in line with a newspaper's policy and practices, had served him well. A talent that kept volatile issues from exploding in his face. Too bad only the turbulent issues heated his blood . . . and his ambition.

He sighed. There was nothing he could do about the situation. There would not be a damn thing to excite him in this town, no controversial issues he could foresee investigating.

Although . . . South Carolina *was* a powder keg just itching to blow—with men like Stokes lighting the fuse. The political whisperings of the last ten years were chaotic to say the least. Maybe there would be a few attractive stories. As crazy as it seemed, getting the *Sentinel* on its feet might be an adventure. It was only a small newspaper, of course, but he had the capital needed to update the equipment and get the operation off the ground. A rotary press, better newsprint and modern lead type had been necessary. Really, as much as he wished the job had gone to someone else, he *believed* in bringing the press to smaller towns. Towns just like Edgemont.

Adam laughed and shook his head. He was trapped. Trapped by one simple, yet quite irrefutable, fact.

He believed in the power of the press.

All in all, it was going to be quite an undertaking.

He had not promised Stokes much: a better newspaper than the one he had arrived to find. No miracles. Just a solid publication with a moderate following, adequate writing and profitable classifieds. From what he could tell, the *Sentinel* had never been anything but marginally profitable—a clear lack of advertising. Yet the potential was usually always there.

The *Sentinel* obviously was not a well-run business, but the caliber of writing was . . . good. Of course, many of the editorial topics were laughable: town socials, engagements, and every birth or death the region had ever seen.

Admittedly, he had been shocked to see articles on higher education for women, features regarding the agricultural movement and one particularly scathing commentary concerning newspapers underwritten by a party and used as a hired mouthpiece. That piece was impressive, which was regrettable, considering it was exactly the kind they would not be able to publish again.

A trickle of sweat rolled down the side of his jaw. He paused to pull his soaked shirt from his moist skin. He absently swatted a fly and again cursed the heat. Resuming his steps, he popped his fingers against his hand.

Two people. Three including himself.

Even for a weekly, that was cutting it close. He would need to use contributing editors on a free-lance basis. He had already contacted a few reliable correspondents he had worked with in Richmond. The next few months should be predictable: long nights, writing, proofreading, typesetting, editing.

He paused, quite dumfounded by the tremor of anticipation that darted through him, like a cold draft that catches you by surprise on a warm summer night. Was he looking forward to this? Why on God's green earth would he be anticipating such hard work—for modest compensation—that was sure to come?

He grimaced. When he had first started in the newspaper business, he had never considered compensation, never considered anything except the ethics of journalism. When had the amount of money, or recognition, begun to matter? When had the thrill of running his hands over smooth, cold planes of type begun to wane? When had the excitement of typesetting his own editorials begun to fade? A few years ago he would have felt a great sense of responsibility and determination to get this paper going. Now his mind disputed a few meaningless pieces of coin. Coin he did not, in this lifetime, need.

In part, the power struggle in Richmond had become the newspaper business to him. Wasn't he overlooking something? How long had it been since he had experienced real skin-and-bones' journalism?

A long time.

Forever.

Whether he wanted to admit it or not, he needed the opportunity to remember why he had gotten into this business in the first place. It sure as hell had not been to become a wealthy, manipulative, selfish bastard.

He dropped his head and began to walk faster, a faint sense of hope settling about him like the dust on his boots. He crossed the narrow street and entered the large building boasting Livery in red letters along the top and side.

Intense heat—from an enormous forge glowing in the back—immediately engulfed him. A stocky man, his ample middle covered with a leather apron, glanced at Adam as he stepped inside. "Just a minute," he yelled over the beating of his hammer. Adam nodded and looked for his horse, Taber, hoping the animal had arrived today.

In a moment, the hammering stopped. The portly man stepped forward and grasped Adam's hand as if they were old acquaintances. "Name's John Thomason, but folks call me Big John. I run the town's only livery, I guess you know. I take fine care of my animals, and I rent the best rigs, too." He laughed, his spirited green eyes dancing. "Truth be known, I rent the only rigs, but they're the best."

Adam smiled and returned the handshake. "Trust me, if I had not heard you were good, my horse would not be bedding down here. The name's Adam Chase."

Big John's eyebrows boosted a notch. "Adam Chase, the new editor. *And* the owner of the finest piece of horseflesh I've seen in many a year. Come on, he's in the back." He turned, his stomach rippling and jiggling under the thick apron. They walked through the insufferably hot area, into a spacious barn uniting the sweet smell of hay and the musky odor of horse dung.

Big John assumed a proud stance and spread his hands wide. "A beautiful barn, isn't it? We built her in two days, the menfolk and me. I always say you can't keep animals in a beat-up shack. You bring them in here. They don't get all frightened, because there's space, and if there's anything an animal understands, it's space. Freedom." It was a philosophy Adam was sure Big John had repeated at least a thousand times.

"Taber will be fine here."

Big John nodded, the meaty jowls beneath his neck shaking. "Oh, yes. I take good care of my boarders. I've got two strong sons who help out. Between us we make the horses real happy." A deep, southern drawl swam through his words. The intonation was unlike a Virginian's. It was harsher, but the cadence was charming nonetheless.

Adam hid a smile. It was almost as if the horses commented

upon leaving. He glanced at the ceiling. "This is an impressive
barn. Looks sturdy. And roomy."

A loud whinny suddenly pierced the air. Adam strode to the
stall where the sound had come from. A magnificent horse,
tawny gold in color, standing two hands higher than any other
horse in the barn, occupied the enclosure. The horse was restless, nudging the stall door with his nose and snorting. His
master lovingly stroked his long, arched neck. "Taber, old boy,
how was your trip?" Taber stamped a hoof in answer, and
Adam grinned. "We will see what it's like to race hell-bent
through fields again. No crowded streets for a little while." He
gave the horse one last touch behind a raised ear. "See you
soon, boy." Taber scraped the ground, his high tail swishing.
Adam chuckled. "Be patient, be patient."

He turned. Big John was gone. The man probably thinks I
am crazy, talking to a horse. Taber is my only friend in town,
though. Shouldering lonesome feelings aside, Adam walked
back into the steamy, less malodorous, area of the building. He
paused as a feminine giggle, tinkling and luscious, reverberated
through the stable. Big John's resounding baritone soon followed.

"Mr. Thomason, I know you'll be able to help me with this
tiny problem. Daddy *knew* the Fourth of July picnic and dance
was coming up, and to send the rig to be repaired right before
the splendid event. Can you imagine? Did he expect Mama to
walk to the party? In her dress?"

"What about you, Miss Dane? What about you having to
walk there in all your finery?"

Adam hid a grin as he advanced upon the couple. Big John
leaned in close to the young woman, who barely reached his
elbow and was probably younger than both his sons. They did
not hear Adam approach.

She looked to be in her late teens, twenty maybe. Her hair
was white blond and stacked high on her head, in an arrangement Adam was sure had taken all of two hours to complete.
Her attire was impeccable, a style of dress common to Richmond and Washington but not Edgemont. Her eyes were light
brown, surrounded by eyelashes the color of golden honey and
sunlight. Full lips and a pert nose set off an ethereal face. She
dressed to display her best features: ample bust and shapely

hips. She reminded Adam of the women he escorted around Richmond. Women like Marilyn. Women who liked his looks, or his money, or his talent in bed—he did not care which. When he wanted intelligent conversation, he went to dinner with a colleague.

Right now, though, this could be just what the ole doctor ordered. Taking a step forward, he cleared his throat.

The young woman's head turned, and her eyes widened just a bit. She was even lovelier than her profile suggested. "Why, Mr. Thomason, this gentleman hasn't come to rent the rig I'll be needing for the picnic, has he?" She supplied what was surely a much-practiced welcome: a shy, fleeting glance and proficient pout of her lovely lips. Adam noticed the lightest hint of rouge on them, so artfully applied, no jealous mother could complain.

Big John, unaccustomed to introductions, stumbled. "This is the new editor . . . uh—"

Adam took over. *You are no match for me, missy.* He grasped her hand in his. "Adam Chase, at your service." He lifted his eyebrows as he brushed his lips feather-light across her palm.

She performed perfectly, feigning embarrassment, jerking her hand back. Adam observed the challenging look that crossed her beautiful face. "Mr. Chase, how forward. But, because you are a stranger to our town, I will forgive you this once." She batted her long, golden eyelashes.

"Miss . . ." Adam looked to Big John.

Big John flushed an even deeper shade of red and stammered, "Oh, look at what an oaf I am. Mr. Adam Chase, this is Miss Lila Dane."

Adam pulled his gaze back to her. "Miss Dane, I am no stranger to southern customs, being a southerner myself. I just tend to ignore the . . . formalities."

She smoothed a hand down the front of her dress. "Mr. Chase, I've a bit of time this afternoon." She held out her arm, her eyes dancing. "Would you care to walk me to the mercantile store?"

Adam paused, debating the intelligence of squiring this willful young woman anywhere. The bold recklessness of her suggestion stunned him. Hell, he knew her kind—it was all he knew. If he could not control *this* situation, he was losing his touch. He turned to the livery owner with a smile. "Big John, it was a pleasure meeting you. I'll be back to ride later this afternoon. Just leave the brushes in his stall. I can rub him down." He stepped forward and took the arm Lila Dane so graciously offered.

They strolled along the boardwalk; she, pointing out landmarks of interest; he, acting as if he cared. How much did Lila Dane already know about him? He had not missed the flame of anticipation sparking those honey brown eyes.

What did it signify? He was enjoying the promenade for his own selfish reasons. He simply missed the elementary exchange between a man and woman: spicy flashes of attraction, the coy brush of skin, whispered words holding lascivious meaning. A carnal, primitive exchange that did not involve memories long dead. A conversation without eye contact that left him feeling as if he had been kicked in the gut. Enchanting pleasantries. No electricity. No midnight blue eyes. No pert little behind clothed in a pair of not-too-tight-but-tight-enough britches. No petite, feisty, dark-haired—

"Charlotte!"

The shout pulled Adam from his reverie. He turned, eyes widening as he witnessed an eager young man—a huge grin glued to his youthful face—advance upon Charlie Whitney, who had apparently just exited the post office.

"Oh, must they cause a ruckus right here on the street. Why don't they just get married and put everyone out of their misery. Lord knows." Lila sighed.

Adam swung his head around, fixing her with a cold glare. *"Pardon me?"*

"Charlotte and Tom." She glanced at him with a frown. "Oh, you haven't met her yet?" This seemed to conflict with her previous information. "She's my cousin. My *spinster* cousin. The man is Tom Walker. He works for my father at the bank. They've been buzzing around each other for two years. Or more appropriately he has been buzzing around *her*. Anyway"—she waved a hand in dismissal—"it's high time Charlotte got married. My mother said it would do wonders for her disposition. If anyone needs calming down . . ." Lila's tirade trailed off.

"Mr. Chase?" She tugged on his arm.

Adam jumped. He pulled his arm from her tight grasp and stepped back. "Sorry. Sorry. Just surprised. The Charlie Whitney I met was not the marrying kind, or so I thought." He shoved his hands in his pockets, angry with himself for thinking anything.

Lila tapped her chin and tilted her head just so. "Yes, you would have met Charlotte because of that filthy newspaper. I thought so."

She retrieved his arm and pulled him along. "Please don't call her *Charlie.* Her parents must have been mad to ever call her that. What husband wants his wife to have a man's name?" She clicked her tongue against her teeth. "Disgraceful."

"Yes, disgraceful," he said, as he tripped along beside her. Charlie obviously reserved her dazzling smiles for this Tom Walker fellow. And, once again, she looked fetching as hell without trying. Simple day dresses seemed to be her style— when she was not wearing britches, that was. Her hair was pulled in a loose knot, wisps as dark as coal bouncing about her face. She had laughed at something the boy had said. Adam felt an insane urge to run to her and . . . what?

For God's sake, was he *crazy?*

He snatched his hands from his pockets and secured his arm more resolutely through Lila's. He would be goddamned if any woman would disturb him. The best-looking one in town was on his arm and three-quarters of the way to sitting in the palm of his hand. Somehow, though, holding Lila Dane's interest only brought an odd emptiness he was unaccustomed to.

And . . . whom was he kidding? Charlie Whitney made Lila Dane look as plain as the gray dust beneath his feet.

From the corner of her eye, Charlie saw the handsome couple enter Mr. Whitefield's mercantile. Anger flashed through her like a quick rainstorm on a sunny afternoon. *Lila.* It would have to be Lila. Here I was thinking he appreciated our intelligent conversation yesterday. Ha. He probably lost interest as soon as he realized my bosom was not going to burst from my shirt.

"What are you dreaming about in the middle of the street?"

Charlie glanced into Tom Walker's pale face and presented what she hoped was a cheerful expression. "Tom, are you on your way to work?'' She ignored his question by throwing out one of her own. Please, she silently prayed, please don't talk about the bank. I'll die of boredom right here in the street.

Tom captured her arm in his and pulled her along with him. "Yes, and I'm late as it is, but I need to speak with you a moment."

Charlie's steps slowed. Lately, when Tom wanted to speak with her, the subject made her quite uneasy. "Yes?" As she tilted her head, she was surprised to see he was only a few inches taller than she. Her mind drifted to the night before; she would have had to strain and stand on tiptoes to look into Adam Chase's eyes. She searched Tom's, struggling to find a resemblance, a hint of barely concealed intensity, a shimmer of recklessness. No, the green eyes looking back at her were warm and sanguine. The only emotions inhabiting them related to bank notices and drafts.

Evidently misreading her interest, he squeezed her arm in his and smiled. "I was just wondering if you had plans for the Fourth of July picnic and dance?"

Charlie fought a hard battle to keep a smile plastered on her face. "Why, Tom, actually I hadn't given it much thought." Try no thought.

Her mind involuntarily echoed Kath's yearly admonishment: Charlie, to think of all the trouble the Beautification Society has gone through. As a graduate of Mrs. Mindlebright's, you should be there.

Oh, it would be grand. Edgemont's leading debutantes and the biggest failure in the entire history of the school at the same dance. Charlie sighed.

"Charlotte. What's wrong?"

"Um . . . it's just a little trouble at home. I mean, just a lot of work around the place. I'm just tired, I guess." She closed her mouth with a snap. Babbling had never become her.

Tom smiled an utterly maddening, arrogant smile. "I would be glad to help you anytime—do the yard work or chop wood. No one expects you to keep that place up single-handedly."

"Yes, well, I know there's help if I need it." The kind of help she should be running from. Trouble . . . in an attractive, brown-eyed package.

"How about the dance? Would you like to go?"

She glanced back at Tom. He looked so eager, like a puppy. She couldn't kick a puppy. "Yes, that would be lovely." Hellfire. She smiled, but her shoulders slumped a little.

Tom took that as a sign of her weariness. "Go home and get some rest. You look exhausted. I'll come by in a few days, and we'll discuss the dance." He gave her hand a gentle squeeze and bounded onto the boardwalk. She heard him whistling as the bank door closed behind him.

Charlie continued along, avoiding the gazes and polite nods of her neighbors. She paused at the entrance to the newspaper office. She rubbed a smooth circle on the dirt-encrusted glass pane on the door and peeped in. A lumbering figure in gray trousers and a printer's apron was hanging over a huge, sparkling metal beast. The door creaked as it swung open beneath her light touch. A lilting Irish tune drifted to her ears. She took a deep breath of ink-stained air. Returning was the right decision. Stokes was not a good man, but *she* was a capable, accomplished woman. She would fight for her principles as she fought for the good of the *Sentinel*. Adam Chase *could* teach her a lot about the business, if only she could keep from killing him.

"Gerald."

Gerald pulled his head from behind the press. For such a bear of a man, he moved quickly, and was by her side before she could speak, capturing her in a hug that lifted her off her feet.

"Put me down," she said, laughter bubbling through. "Put me down this instant."

"Your fierce words don't scare me, sweeting." He placed her feet on the floor. "It's good to see you here again. It's been lonely."

She drifted to the press and ran her hand along a metal edge. "You know, it's funny. I never expected to be forced to make decisions that were right *and* wrong. I think I'm doing the best thing and . . . this place"—she turned to face him, her eyes shining—"means so much to me. I can't seem to stay away."

He walked to her and took her small hands in his large, callused ones. His familiar, freckled face was so very dear to her. "That's part of growing up. Facing difficulties and making the best of them. Looking at both sides and choosing. Everything isn't going to be fair. Lots of areas will be all jumbled and so confusing it'll make your head spin." His gaze shifted to their linked hands, his voice a whisper in the quiet room. "Your pa would be proud of you."

She looked into his face and saw the love and pride shining in his eyes. "Thank you. Papa not being here is hard." She swallowed, struggling to say the words. "Thank goodness, you are."

"Now, who'd be here to calm down that awful temper of yours and keep you from fightin' with the editor?"

Her smile slipped. She turned from his candid gaze. "Is he a good editor? I've spoken with him, and as much as it pains me to say it, he seems to know the business." She glanced up, then down. "He even seems to *like* it."

He walked to the other side of the press and began fiddling with one of the cylinders. "Well, I've only worked with him a week or so but . . ." He paused and searched the floor before continuing, "He's very impatient, and his editorials are written kinda wildlike; but you should read them. Follow him for a day. I reckon, he stops to write every ten minutes. He says words just pop into his mind. Doesn't want to forget them."

She paused as a notion came right on the heels of Gerald's words. He *admired* Adam Chase.

"You're going to have to be open-minded, Charlie. He doesn't write like you do."

The *Sentinel*'s new editor was a force to reckon with. Dark and obsessed. A caged storm. To write like he did, he had to be hiding a great deal of himself. His light smiles and teasing gestures were deliberately misleading.

What did she care? She didn't want to see his hidden side. Maybe the man who only moments ago had his lean, muscular arm linked with her cousin's was the only one there was. The same man she'd confronted in the Four Leaf.

Charlie shook her head, denying the theory.

He *had* let her see another side of him, although it was possible he didn't realize it. The episode on her porch had been distressing—something to do with his brother—except, it wasn't her business what his personal demons were.

She snatched a rag from the page frame and began to rub imaginary dust from the press's shiny surface. She wrinkled her nose and released a sharp breath. Her heartbeat accelerated. With a slow hand, she lifted the rag to her nostrils. The scent did not wait for an invitation. It was a strange aroma: smoke, sweat and something that just last week would have been unfamiliar. She turned the bandanna—how had she thought it a rag?—in her hand. It was the one Adam Chase had used to wipe his sweaty brow the day before.

She'd known his scent. Her heart had known even before her mind.

Charlie gripped the edge of the press and slammed her eyes shut, the rag dropping to the floor. Maybe . . . maybe Mr. Chase *is transferring some of his restlessness to me. I don't know what it is, but I . . . don't . . . like . . . it.*

"Charlie?"

She snapped her head around, her teeth coming down hard on her bottom lip. She grimaced and brought her hand to her mouth. "What? What were you saying?"

"She's a beauty, isn't she?" Gerald paused, obviously waiting for an answer. "The press," he clarified when none was forthcoming.

She summoned a weak smile, nodded and walked to the two desks sitting side by side in the corner of the room. The desks were much as she had left them, except her father's looked like it had tangled with a tom cat in knee-deep water.

She frowned, settling herself into the mammoth leather chair behind the desk. The hair on the back of her neck prickled. Her skin tingled. How could she explain the odd sensation sweeping through her? *Was* there a way to explain the acute visual picture she saw? Of *him,* sitting in this chair, words spouting from his mind to paper like steam from a geyser, faster than his hand could record them.

Charlie lifted his pencil and twirled it between her fingers. The tip was dull, unlike hers, which was always sharp.

Her trenchant gaze noted papers scattered all across the desk, partial and complete, ink-stained and crumpled. How could he work in the middle of this mess?

You're going to have to be open-minded; he doesn't write like you do.

Gerald's statement banged in her mind like harsh notes from a cheap drum. She silently promised to strive for tolerance.

She had never been accused of being a conservative anything, and she'd be damned if she'd start now.

She grabbed the piece of paper sitting on top of the pile. The headline read, *Should We Use Taxation to Establish the Public Education System?* Hmmm . . . currently a very controversial issue. She scanned the page. Fascinating.

Her gaze fell to the bottom of the page and the signature: A. Jared Chase. "Why A. Jared Chase?"

"Those were my father's wishes, Miss Whitney."

Chapter Five

Charlie jumped from the chair. Adam's writing had engrossed her so that she had not even heard the office door open.

They stared, the tension between them palpable, each feeling the incredible depth of the attraction between them.

Adam gave her a long, hard look, inspecting her like a horse he thought was a reasonable purchase, just not the right purchase for him. Maybe she was right for that Tom Walker fellow. The man appeared to be even more maladroit than she, if that was possible.

Did Tom Walker know how to handle a woman? Did he kiss Charlie Whitney? Kiss her, really kiss her, with his lips, his hands *and* his passion? Did he make her writhe and moan as he tasted her, his hands settled on either side of her head, his body pressed against hers? Did she beg for more?

More. Adam thought . . . no, he *knew*, the experienced stroke of nimble fingers would never be enough for this woman. She would demand the key to free a man's soul. He could see it in the questioning tilt of her chin, the cunning turn of her lips. He recognized only what he knew to be a part of himself: the never-ending pursuit of the motivation behind the action, the truth behind the facade, the meaning behind the word.

Adam did not want her to look at him like she needed to understand him. Charlie could look all she wanted, only she would never discover anything. He would make sure of it.

Her eyes never left his, though. Not once. Damn her. He did not intimidate her. He even began to feel a little nervous as her hot gaze burned his skin.

Did she look at Tom Walker the same way? Did he run his hands along the sides of her body, lower . . . lower.

Adam swallowed. It was not Tom Walker's pale hands he imagined caressing Charlie Whitney. Did she know what she was doing to him, looking at him with those wide, pure eyes? Guileless. Seductive. Was she playing with him? Like Lila Dane would play him, if he let her? Like he would, in turn, play her? Loneliness and suspicion crept up on him.

What did it matter? Charlie was not his kind of woman—if he had a kind, which he did not. He wanted women for pleasure, needed them for pleasure. He was a man, after all. He had never wanted more than that from a woman, even before Eaton's death. Now it was an impossibility.

Adam dropped his head and drew a deep breath. A rich, all-too-comforting fragrance permeated the air about him, slashing like a sharp blade through his deep-seated defenses like no words could have. Damn, she smelled good. Not a carnal, cosmopolitan aroma like Marilyn's—and countless others' he had encountered over the years—but an arousing, earthly . . . *essence*. An honest sum and substance bottled like fresh sunshine. The rosy aroma claimed her like vines claimed a wrought-iron post.

He lifted his head, fixing her with a calm gaze he had struggled to produce. "Why did you come here?" He frowned. Had that sounded harsher than he had intended?

Charlie took a step back, her eyes glowing. "Ohhh, you will make me grovel, won't you? You know why I'm here, and probably right on schedule, according to you." Her hands shook as she closed them into tight fists. "I came back to work for the *Sentinel*. I want to make sure it isn't destroyed."

"Well, thanks one helluva lot for your exalted vote of confidence."

She lowered her voice and glanced at Gerald. He was not looking their way. "That's not . . . what . . . I . . . *meant*."

"I know what you meant." He slammed his fist on the desk in frustration.

She slammed her own right next to his. "I thought the *Sentinel* was a good paper."

With a sigh, he pushed away, rubbing his forehead. "Charlie, Edgemont is a good market for a small press. There is no other established newspaper here. But face the facts. The *Sentinel*'s revenue is suffering because it is not politically aligned. We need capital. Capital political backing will provide." Adam waved his hand toward the post office. "That telegraph is a good start."

She sighed and bounced her fingers on the edge of the desk. "Where do we start, then?"

Had he missed something?

"I'm assuming you would like a list of issues we've covered . . . to save the time of having to go through all the old copies?" She grabbed a stack of papers from the desk and began sorting and shuffling. "I'll need a day or two to make a list of the major issues from the last two years. Most of those I still remember. I'll also make a related list." She frowned as she came to a page with a large ink stain on it. "We'll meet on, say, Tuesday morning?" She crumpled the page in a ball and tossed it at him.

He caught it with one hand. By damn, she was no empty-headed female. The thought was not comforting. "Um . . . yes. Sounds great. I do not know what I would have done without you."

She rolled her eyes. "You would have been reading a lot of decaying, dusty, old newspapers, that's what."

The door closed behind them with a click. They turned at the same time.

"Mr. Chase? Oh . . . *Charlotte.*"

Adam sighed and released a breath. Lila Dane. Just what he needed right now. He glanced at Charlie, almost laughing as he saw her grimace before she could hide it.

Lila, her silvery hair glowing, her generous lips curved in a coy smile, pivoted on a slim heel as he walked toward her. Her eyes were bold and brimming with acknowledged interest. She offered him her hand as he stopped before her.

"Hello again, Miss Dane." He ignored her hand.

"Please. Call me Lila." Her eyes sharpened as she casually

tucked her arm by her side. "Charlotte." The name slipped past her lips like a lead ball.

Charlie glanced from the papers in her hand. "Hello, Lila. How are you?"

Lila's eyes narrowed. "Why, Charlotte, you're looking . . . lovely."

"Thank you, Lila. I don't try as hard as you do, but I do so hope for positive results."

Adam coughed and began a thorough search of the wood-plank floor.

"Charlotte Whitney, you're never going to learn. And to think, I just wanted to welcome you to the Fourth of July picnic and dance. It's about time you took a break from your oh-so-busy schedule. I just saw Tom at the bank. He's very excited that you've *finally* agreed to accompany him."

"Oh, good."

"Your sarcasm is amusing, as always." Lila waved her dainty, gloved hand in dismissal. She refocused her gaze. "Actually, I came to speak to *Adam*. I was wondering—since you are new to Edgemont—if you would like to accompany my family to the Fourth of July picnic and dance. My father suggested you go with us. I thought it a wonderful idea."

He did not want to go to some damn town dance, but . . . Charlie hated them, and she was going. With Tom Walker. He awarded Lila with a smile. "Why, Lila, I would love to attend the dance with your family. I thank you for the gracious invitation. Since your father and I are both businessmen, we should have a lot to talk about."

Lila clapped her hands together. "Wonderful. You may call on me sometime this week. I'll let my parents know you'll be going with us." She turned, her full skirt whisking along the floor. "Goodbye, Charlotte."

The loose pane of glass rattled as the door closed. Adam turned to find Charlie sitting at her desk, sorting and shuffling.

"I suppose this is my desk, as it has been for years. I like an organized area." She threw a handful of paper at him, sheets drifting to the floor like thick snowflakes.

"What bee is in your bonnet?" What the hell was wrong with her?

"You . . . that's my bee. I'll never get any work done with your women running in and out constantly. And Lila."

She turned to glare at Gerald, who upon hearing an argument start had mumbled a quick, "I'll go check for the mail," and hurried out the door.

Adam stalked to her, seizing her shoulders. He pulled her forward in the chair. "My women?"

"You heard me."

Had he? He tightened his grip on her shoulders. Was it possible she was jealous of Lila?

"You're touching me again."

"Do you have some aversion to being touched?"

"Yes. I mean . . . no." She shook her head.

"What do you do when Tom Walker touches you?"

"Tom?" She made it sound as if the idea of Tom Walker touching her was the strangest one she'd ever heard.

"Thanks for saving the insane behavior for me, then." Releasing her, he got as far from her as he could, by the window, where he stood trying to catch his breath. She was making him crazy.

As the front door slammed, he tilted his head back and groaned.

Myra Hawkins and her mother watched as Charlie stalked by them without a backward glance.

"Mama, do you see the way she's running down the boardwalk? Just look at her skirt, flipping around, ankles showing. It's disgraceful." Myra's youthful face wrinkled like a prune as she grimaced.

"Dear, stop looking like you sucked on a lemon. What if Chester Dole is in town today? Do you want him to see you looking like that?" Chloris Hawkins wanted her daughter to marry more than anything else in this world. To tell the truth, it was getting embarrassing. Myra was nearly twenty and without a single offer of marriage. Not even a desperate proposal from one of the Mays brothers, who wouldn't find a girl to accept them, not in a hundred years.

Not that Chester Dole was the best catch in Edgemont, either, but he did come from good stock. The Doles had a productive cotton farm, Chester had all of his teeth, and he didn't spit in public. Chloris considered him to be a fine prospect.

She was no dreamer. Her father had married her off to the first man who came asking. It certainly hadn't been love at first sight, but things had worked out just fine. Poor Myra. Unfortunately, she had taken after her father's side of the family, and extremely average looks just weren't going to get some prince—like that new editor, for instance. Chloris snorted, then shifted to see if anyone on the boardwalk had heard.

Anyway, rumor had it that Lila Dane had set her sights on that new editor. Everybody knew, what the Danes wanted, the Danes got.

"Mama?"

Her daughter's flat voice stopped her daydreaming cold. "Lord a mercy, Myra, quit screeching."

"Mama, I keep telling you, I don't even like Chester Dole. He's a big, overgrown oaf." She slapped her hands together as her lips joined in an ugly pout.

"Hush. Chester is a nice boy. You want to end up an old maid? Like Charlotte Whitney? Is that what you want?" She patted Myra's arm.

Myra glared at Charlie's swiftly moving, trim figure. "She's not really an old maid, not with Tom Walker sniffing around. Oh, Mama, it's not fair . . . he's so handsome."

Chloris shook her head in reproach. She leaned closer to Myra, and shaking a bony, wrinkled finger, whispered, "He may have a liking for her—after all, she's a pretty girl—but that's not the kind of girl any man in his right mind is gonna marry. Running here and there—in britches of all things. Doing a man's work, acting like a man, if the truth be said. And, you know your mama always tells the truth. Her parents should have known they were starting something wicked by calling her Charlie."

Chloris sighed. She really felt kind of sad when she thought about the poor girl, alone with almost no family. "Just be glad your mama is here to help guide you through life. You don't realize how lucky you are. Now smile and, heavens dear, stand up straight." She grabbed her daughter's arm and pulled her along the boardwalk as fast as she could.

In their haste, they failed to notice the lone figure standing in the open window of the *Sentinel* office.

Chapter Six

Charlie pulled a piece of hair from her face. The window caught her reflection. A clump of flour stained her cheek. She smiled and wiped it off.

Making dough was tedious labor, but it involved only her hands, letting her mind wander. The yellow kitchen curtains billowed like sails on a ship; the healthy breeze marched the scent of cinnamon about the room. She drew a deep breath. Hmmm, fresh-cut grass was in the air, too.

A sigh escaped her as she flexed her cramped fingers. Her gaze strayed to the green hills in the distance, an occasional dark peak standing behind like a big brother.

A bead of sweat rolled from underneath the kerchief tied round her head. She lifted her hand, capturing it before it ran down her neck and into her shirt.

If she closed her eyes, she could almost hear the creek gurgling. Grinning, she wiped her hands on a patched calico dish towel and headed out the door. She paused on the porch, not expecting anyone. However, with Chase's unexpected visit last week and Tom's yesterday, you never could tell. She glanced at her faded dress and bare feet. She didn't intend to get caught in trousers again—even if they were cooler than a dress. She drew the line at wearing shoes, though.

Humming, she strolled toward the creek, tall, green grass tickling the soles of her bare feet. She detected the gentle lap-splash of water against the grassy bank well before she saw it. As she entered the canopy of trees, a cool flurry of air immediately welcomed her, cooling skin that had moments ago been aflame.

Charlie stopped and dropped to her knees by the creek's edge, where she scooped handfuls of water and splashed her face. Moisture seeped through her thin dress, but she was too lighthearted to care. She leaned back on her elbows and extended her legs, dangling her feet in the tepid water. A hawk swooped above, diving into the trees.

She rolled her head back, stretching her neck until the crown of her head brushed the ground. Oh, it felt so good. Even if someone did stop by, they would never know where to find her.

Too bad I wasn't hiding yesterday.

She bit her lip. Why did she have to be so mean? She just couldn't help it. Heavens, to remember Tom's expression when he walked into her yard and saw her bending over in a pair of trousers. She collapsed on the ground—heedless of the dirt and dew coating her dress—her laughter shattering the hushed tranquillity of the thicket. His eyes had almost leaped from their sockets. He had stammered her name four times before getting himself under control. She didn't want to try and figure if it was her bottom or her boldness that had caused his reaction.

She almost wished it was the former. The bellyaching and whining from the townsfolk drained her. After so many years, one would think they would have come to accept her. Ah, hellfire, she couldn't figure what Tom Walker and his pristine self wanted with her anyway. If she tried, she couldn't think of a more mismatched pair.

Laughing again, she tried to conjure his image.

Lanky . . . yeah. Handsome . . . moderately. Pragmatic . . . of course. Predictable . . . invariably. Boring . . . yep.

Why couldn't he have eyes the color of burnt chestnuts? Or a pair of irresistible dimples? How about high cheekbones? Raven hair with red highlights?

How had *he* reacted to the sight of her in trousers? With a subtle show of male appreciation and implied respect, that was how.

Her grin shriveled like a rotten apple. Oh, her week had been brimful of him, too.

They had worked at the newspaper every day, writing, deliberating, proofreading—long after Gerald left. Despite Chase's objections, she stayed late into the night. She didn't want to tell him—it had been hard enough to admit it to herself—that the work was more exciting than ever.

It was hard not to get excited about a project working with him. He was ambitious and energetic, and painstakingly demanding, a firm believer that every story could be just a bit better. Luckily, the newspaper had deadlines, so he eventually had to let it go.

He was a good editor, encouraging her to write using her own style and talent. All the while, he calmly observed, in a way that was neither intimidating nor autocratic. It was a challenge to write a piece and have him dissect it in his sharp-edged way. He could review an editorial she had worked on for two days— one she had nursed and coddled like a baby, one as flat and lifeless as a pancake—and instantly spot the missing element. It was almost as if he climbed into her mind and helped her redirect her thoughts to paper.

He walked her home every night, the lunch basket she'd started packing for them hanging like a silent chaperone between their bodies, a deserted dirt road and bright moonlight their only companions.

She had never had anyone to *really* talk to, except her father and the Lamberts. She and Chase discussed everything: life, philosophy, religion, politics, trade, agriculture, nature, farming, Richmond, South Carolina. Everything but love and misfortune. Sometimes they didn't discuss anything at all.

Chase described his home in Richmond and the newspaper there, his travels to Europe and the West, even a little of the summers he spent along the Virginia coast as a boy—rare descriptions of his mother cropping up between the high dunes and blue sea. Personal subjects, well, were strictly forbidden fruit.

Plus, how could she ask of him what she couldn't give in

return? After her mother's death, she'd forsaken the idea of
life being fair and love conquering all.

She closed her eyes. Sunlight, obscured and scattered by the
ceiling of limbs, warmed her. She shifted, her dress sliding and
bunching about her calves.

The picnic.

Hellfire. It had been years since she'd attended a picnic.
What would she wear? Tom's evident excitement in accompanying her made her wary, too. Why in the world he wanted to
escort the town's most celebrated spinster was a mystery. She
would be the poorest specimen there. He had a veritable display
case of fetching, empty-headed young beauties to choose from.

Plus, she didn't want to socialize. She wasn't good at it, had
never been good at it. And to have to gawk at Chase and Lila
all day and night . . . that somehow seemed the worst prospect
of all.

What was he doing? Thinking? Wearing? She grinned just
imagining *that*. Of course, he would be wearing his uniform:
close-fitting cotton trousers, an unbuttoned lawn shirt of some
nondescript color and dust-caked Hessians.

She sighed and rolled to her side. As much as she wanted
to deny it, there was something special about him. Something
she hadn't yet put her finger on.

He intrigued her.

No, more than that. They shared something. Something she
had never shared with another person in her life.

She only wished she knew what that *something* was.

"Miles!"

Miles turned, leaning his ax against a maple tree. He waved
in greeting. "Adam, hello!"

Adam smiled and slid from the saddle. "Hello."

"So, this is Taber." Miles nodded approvingly. "Landsakes,
what a beautiful beast."

Adam grinned. "He is a damn fine beauty, is he not? We
have not even begun to stretch his legs today." He pushed his
hat back on his forehead and flexed his shoulders. "Do you
know this is the first day this week I have had a chance to
ride?"

"How about a drink to cool you off? Do you have a little time?" Miles hitched his thumb over his shoulder, indicating the small farmhouse behind him.

Adam shrugged. "Hmmm . . . depends on the drink."

Miles clapped him on the shoulder. "I think I have one that'll convince you to stay a'piece."

They laughed and climbed the porch steps, entering the house through a large pantry. "Go sit in the kitchen. I'll get the drinks."

Adam walked through an archway into a kitchen decorated in cheerful yellows and blues. He pulled his hat off and dropped into a wooden chair covered with a burnished gold cushion. Rubbing his eyes, he drew a deep breath and yawned.

"Tired, old man?" Miles' voice came from the doorway.

Adam turned his head. "Hell, yes."

Miles dropped awkwardly into a tiny chair that barely held him. He shoved a glass toward Adam. "This should fix you up just fine."

Adam lifted it to his nose and sniffed. "What is it?" He grimaced.

"Homemade mash. The best in this county . . . maybe the state." Seeing Adam's frown, he urged, "Go on, take a swig."

Adam took a sip and immediately began coughing. "What . . . the . . . hell."

Miles took a drink and swilled it in his mouth before swallowing. "Ah, hair of the dog."

"Sure." Adam coughed again.

Miles pounded his fist on the table, laughing. "Haven't you ever had this stuff before?"

Adam shook his head. His throat burned as though someone had taken a match to it.

"Oh, only the good stuff, huh? Well, a true southerner you'll never be until you've wet your whistle with this."

Adam licked his lips, wishing feeling back into them.

They sat a moment, the silence welcome. The late afternoon sun was setting, casting long shadows across the kitchen floor. The smell of collard greens permeated the small room.

Adam leaned back in the chair, stretched out his legs. "It feels good to . . . do nothing."

"The newspaper been busy?"

"Extremely."

"You know, maybe that's why I haven't seen my pa in a few days."

"He's been putting in long hours. Hell, we all have. It's looking better, though." He stared at the dark liquid in his glass as his thoughts traveled along the dirt road, through town and into the newspaper office.

Miles drew his finger along a scarred edge of the table. "How is Charlie doing? In fact, if you were wonderin', that's who my lovely wife is with right now. Some nonsense about a dress for the dance."

Adam started. "Charlie worrying about a dress?"

Miles chuckled. "Oh, no . . . the dress is all my Kathy's idea. Charlie, I'm sure, couldn't care less about the dress or the dance."

Adam began a fierce inspection of his thumbnail. He shrugged.

"This is the first year I can even remember her going. Charlie . . . isn't much for social gatherin's and things." He grunted.

"Well, Tom asked. What else could she say?"

"Ha. She could have said no. Just like all the other times."

"Other times?" Why was he asking? It did not interest him.

"Yeah, other men have asked her. If you haven't noticed, pretty lasses are meager pickin's round here. That fool Walker has been askin' for nigh on two years. A dance here, a church gatherin' there, a picnic. Always the same answer . . . no, no, no."

They lapsed into silence again. Adam could hear crickets outside the window, chirping and squeaking. The sun had dropped low, throwing a wide band of gold across the table. He placed his hand in the middle of the strip, moving it in and out of the light. He lifted his gaze to the window, fields that looked like they were dancing in a sea of liquid sunlight filling his vision.

He looked back at Miles. "I'm coming to know Charlie pretty well. She is for damn sure contrary to any woman I have run across." He pulled his hand from the table, letting it fall to his lap.

"Tiny-bird chairs." Miles shifted his weight. "Contrary, yep." He nodded. "That does sum it up nicely."

Adam scratched his chin. "What I cannot figure is, why does this Walker lad keep trying? Is she leading him on? Lila was telling me—''

Miles slammed his hand on the table. It was the first angry action Adam had seen him make. "Lila Dane is a bitch. Take my word for it. She's jealous of Charlie, always has been." He laughed, a wicked gleam floating into his blue eyes. "You know, I sparked her a bit, before Kathy came along. A dance or two, as I recall."

Adam fell back in his chair with a thump. Miles and . . . *Lila.*

"Surprised? So were her parents. She was sixteen or so. And lovely. But, such a spoiled—'' He shook his head. "I can't tell you what I saw in her. Probably nothin' past her bosom."

Adam took a mouthful of mash. *Miles and Lila?* "You mean—'' Coughing swallowed his words.

Miles laughed and leaned his chair back on two legs. "Oh, no, nothin' like that. We went to a few dances, and then I met Kathy—and boom. End of story." Miles' gaze slid toward Adam. "Aren't you takin' her to the dance? You shouldn't be pleased thinkin' she was . . . *intimate* with another man."

Adam snorted and finished off his drink. "I could not possibly care less." Lila meant nothing to him.

"But, you're concerned about Charlie and Tom. Hmm. Mighty interestin'."

Adam flinched. "I am not concerned. Just curious." What the hell was Miles trying to suggest?

Miles only smiled and drained his glass. "Charlie grew up . . . differently. I guess you can tell. She was allowed to roam free, write, sketch. Work at the paper." Miles' gaze caught Adam's. "Nothin' has happened with Tom because she's too damn strong for him. The milksop. And, he knows it. I don't think Charlie knows what he's sniffin' round after, although Kathy doesn't agree. She thinks sooner or later Charlie is going to come round. But, damn, how long does it take to fall in love?"

Adam dismissed a breath in a disgusted rush. "Do not even think of asking me that question."

Miles lingered, staring into his empty glass. "One day . . .

one day you'll feel for someone what I feel for Kathy. Then you'll understand.''

Adam shrugged, at an uncharacteristic loss for words. He had nothing to contribute to this topic. Nothing.

"So, how is she doin' with the newspaper?''

Again, his gaze traveled across golden fields that seemed to stretch clear to the horizon. He shifted in his chair, longing to be on Taber's back, riding like the devil. He was uneasy talking so much about Charlie. He raised his glass, only to find it empty. "She's doing fine." Better than fine. "She is very intelligent. Ten times the brains of most of the young reporters I work with."

Intellect was not all. She had talent and a sense of structure, which was often impossible to teach. Her own style. And she had instinct, which *was* impossible to teach. She also listened. Really listened. How many reporters had he watched fail because they could not stand back and listen?

Her mind absorbed everything he told her like some damn sponge. Also, God knew, she was willing to go to any length to get the *Sentinel* printed. She had even gotten on her hands and knees and tinkered with the press. . . .

Adam snapped back as Miles tapped his glass, which was full.

"More?'' He frowned but lifted the bitter mash to his lips. A coughing spasm hit him when the harsh liquor met the back of his throat. He tapped his chest and grimaced. "No more. I have to be going.'' He held out his hand. "Thanks for the . . . drink. Although I am sure my stomach will not be thanking you later.'' He rose from his chair.

Miles stood as well, thumping Adam on the back and clasping his hand. "Ahh, it'll surely help you sleep tonight.''

"If not before.''

Miles' laughter resonated through the ever-darkening kitchen.

Adam was a tall man, but he had to lift his head to meet Miles' gaze. "I will save my next sampling. For the dance.''

"Lordy. That dance. I'll be the first sorry lout there. Puttin' out food, pourin' lemonade, bringin' out chairs for the elders.'' He shrugged his broad shoulders, then winked. "Later on, though, we're bringin' out the jugs of ale and mash. Whoo-wee.''

Adam raised his hands in mock surrender. "We shall see."

"That we will."

Adam sprinted, a bit erratically, across the yard to Taber, who had begun snorting and pawing the ground. After climbing astride, he edged his mount by the porch. "How 'bout a small wager on the horse race?"

Miles' gaze traveled the length of Taber and back again. "Uh, uh." He shook his head.

Adam spurred the horse to a trot and yelled over his shoulder, "I knew you were a smart man, Miles Lambert."

Chapter Seven

Adam crossed the street with a quick, sure stride. A smile touched his face as he recalled Mrs. Wilkin's wondrous expression—glowing at him from across the breakfast table this morning—as he presented her with the bunch of jessamine he and Charlie had picked in the thriving field-of-yellow behind her house. Mrs. Wilkin had rushed to his side, giving him a childlike peck on the cheek, surprise lighting her whiskey eyes.

Actually, it had surprised Adam, too. He had picked the flowers for Lila, but the inspiration had been crushed somewhere between Charlie's romping antics as she selected the most colorful blossoms and his own chaotic emotions.

Charlie had shown no qualms in revealing the hidden patch of bell-shaped jessamine, only asking that he not tell Lila where he had picked them.

A promise easily kept.

He forced his gaze to the road as he dodged a deep, tea brown puddle. They littered the street—small and large—a gift from last night's storm. His boots were crusted with enough mud to fill a coffee mug.

He raised his hand in greeting to John Thomason as he passed the livery. People were scurrying along Main Street, tipping their hats and shouting greetings, telling each other what a fine day it was for a picnic. He wished he could steal even a smidgen of their enthusiasm.

He halted as the Dane residence rose before him like a white-peaked mountain. He gazed at the mammoth, bleached structure as a picture came to him: an impressionable young girl—sapphire eyes shining with wisdom—rejected by her aunt and uncle because her independence and intelligence had far surpassed their daughter's. Charlie had told him some of her past with the Dane family; he supposed it did not help matters that he hated them a bit for it.

He looked to the left of the house and laughed as he spied the vehicle they would be taking to the festivities. Damned if it wasn't a Jenny Lind box buggy, very similar to his own. Although his sported a fixed top, not a folding one. They were a good model, made to be easy on a horse. Fast. Sleek. Expensive. And so Lila.

Everyone else in town would arrive on foot, in dilapidated, horse-drawn carriages, or in Mr. Whitefield's wooden grocer's cart. Mrs. Wilkin was traveling that way. He would arrive with all the pomp and circumstance of a royal entrance. Well, hell . . . he was going with a princess, right?

"Yoo-hoo!"

He squinted into the sun. Lila. Perched in a white swing in the corner of her wrap-around porch. He waved his hand as he opened the wrought-iron gate guarding the walkway. This time he ignored the puddles in his path.

She had been awaiting his arrival, from the look of it. He had—in some senseless part of his mind—hoped she was going to the dance out of a sense of obligation. No. He could see her quite well as he walked up the path; she looked powdered and sumptuous. Carefully constructed. A woman with a mission.

She smiled with a gentle turn of her lips as he approached the porch. He did not return the gesture. The swing tilted as she leaned forward, her face sweeping from shadow to light. Perspiration had plastered several strands of ashen hair to her smooth forehead. Her lips glistened. Her eyes, surrounded by those incredible golden lashes, flashed amatory signals at him—signals as conspicuous as those sent by overactive fireflies.

He stopped at the edge of the steps, willing her to come to

him. It would be good to let her know he was not some groveling suitor.

They stayed like that a moment, before Lila sighed and laughed. She seemed agreeable to conceding this minor victory. With practiced poise and grace, she stood and shook her skirts. "Would you like to come in for a drink before we leave? Mama and Papa should be here any minute."

He gave her a long look, trying to decide if he liked her dress. It was a walking costume of pale pink silk trimmed in rows of white velvet ribbon. Flounces of white satin looped with pink tuberoses ornamented the simple design. Pink gloves sheathed what were sure to be hands absent of any mark of labor. She held a shoulder cape of embroidered muslin and lace. A bonnet of white crape bedecked with a large pink satin ribbon sat upon her head. She was conspicuously naked of any jewelry.

He smiled at the irony. She looked absurd *and* exquisite. He quickly reminded himself that he based this judgment on his new definition of beauty, as his old had—in the last few weeks—taken a swift kick in the hindquarters.

"Why are you smiling?" Her shadow fell across him.

Attraction and disgust battled within him. "I was just thinking how lovely you look."

"Do I really?" Of course, she had been expecting the compliment. She leaned close, injecting a teasing note into her voice. "I planned it just for you."

He forced his smile. For some reason, he wanted to tell her to go to hell.

Lila frowned. She stretched and touched his rough face, covered with day-old beard. "Did you forget to shave this morning?"

He raised one dark brow. "No. I did not."

She pressed her lips together and withdrew her hand. Gathering her thin cape—one she knew she would never need in ninety-degree weather—in a clenched fist, she looked back. No one stood in the doorway. She released an agitated breath. He wasn't going to be easy to manipulate. Then again, the exciting ones never were. This one was well worth the trouble.

Lila didn't want to spend her life lingering on the fringes of high society; she wanted to be right in the middle of it. She darted a glance at the handsome man standing below her. If what she'd heard was true, he could introduce her to the world she was missing.

At least he had dressed appropriately, if somewhat casually. Tan trousers and a white lawn shirt were not what she would have picked. A narrow, black tie was the saving grace, the ends fastened over a small knot, the crisp shirt collar standing guard. Of course, he had on that atrocious pair of *riding boots*. Thankfully, the leather was expensive. She could tell.

Her lips twisted. She would have to play this one very carefully. Adam Chase was no small-town boy to dally with. She wanted him for more serious matters.

As if he read her thoughts, his own lips lifted. A mocking smirk she was sure. Well, let him smirk all he wants. Because I want him. And what I want, *I get.*

A door slammed behind them. Lila whirled in a pink and white cloud of satin and silk. "Oh, good." She ran to her parents, after throwing a look at Adam indicating he should follow. He could not politely ignore her command.

He hesitated a moment before climbing the wooden steps. A small, balding man, with a hooked nose and dull, brown eyes peered at him from the towering height of five-foot-five. Tops. The woman standing at his side was a farcical study in contrast. She stood at least three inches taller than her husband and possessed a stately bearing no amount of money could buy. She had clear, pink skin and light brown eyes flecked with specks of green—duplicates of Lila's. Her teeth were stained with just a hint of yellow, and the skin around her lips had begun to show the slight downward pull of age. Victoria Dane's dogmatic demeanor draped upon her shoulders like a coat. A strange flash of embarrassment, as if he confronted an angry mother after bringing her daughter home at dawn, crept along the length of his spine.

He wrinkled his nose. Witch hazel. Which Dane did it emanate from? Hell, maybe all three.

The trip progressed in a sun-laden blur of gentle hills and animated fields, swimming in the brisk breeze. The sweet smell of pine and moist earth reached up and tapped his nose as surely as the wind that dabbled with his dark hair. He closed his eyes and let the sun play along his sealed lids, patterns of bright red and yellow weaving a web in his mind.

As the inane conversation between the queen and princess bounced off his ears like a child's ball, he looked to the west. He squinted at the whitewashed farm homes buried among brown pine and gray dogwood. Multicolored butterflies flitted among the variety of shrubs, doubtless looking for sweet nectar. Occasional bursts of jessamine, tulip and clover appeared among the trees, coloring the terrain. Jessamine. Again, Charlie's laughter and buoyant spirit as she frolicked among the blossoms, presenting them to him with a bow, slipped into his mind. How could he taste a memory—picking damn flowers with an overgrown tomboy—as clearly as he could taste the deep flavor of wine? He pulled a sharp breath into his lungs.

"Oh, Mama, here we are."

He turned his head. The royal carriage rounded the final bend and pulled into a wide, muddy area. He could hear the neighborly call of friends and the wild, irrepressible laughter of children. He wanted, more than anything in a long while, to leave this silly buggy.

He did not vacillate, jumping to the ground the moment the buggy came to rest. He hesitated, denying he was seeking blue eyes the color of the sea, black hair as light as spun silk.

A bony tap on his shoulder put an end to the search.

"Adam." Lila presented her hands to him as she leaned over the side of the buggy. "The mud." He glanced down and groaned.

He grunted and lifted her into his arms, all the while shifting and settling her more firmly in his clutches. He walked to the first hard, dry area he could find and rolled her out of his arms. His back issued a small tweak of complaint; Lila was not the smallest peach on the limb.

Taking her sweet time pulling away from him, she smiled. As if it was an afterthought, she grasped his hand as she turned to walk off. He now understood he was to be her toy for the day. "Lila—"

She stopped suddenly. He almost charged into her back. "Charlotte," she said, her tone dry as dirt. "How lovely to see you so soon after our arrival."

Chapter Eight

He had been so busy preparing a lecture for Lila, he had let them practically bump into Charlie. He tilted his head, to get a good look at the woman he tried to convince himself he did not even want to see. If only Lila would move a little to the left. . . .

"Lila. Chase." Charlie nodded her head at each of them. Her gaze drifted to their joined hands before darting off.

Adam slipped his hand from Lila's.

"Hello, Lila, Adam." Tom walked behind Charlie. He lifted his hand in greeting; Adam had no choice but to take it.

He noticed a slight relaxing of Charlie's shoulders as she stepped aside to allow Tom in front. Damn. I do not want him protecting her from *me*. I am her friend, a closer friend than he is, I would bet. Though, Tom's arm brushed hers as he made idle chitchat, and she didn't seem to mind. What did Miles Lambert know anyway? Maybe they *were* more than friends.

"Isn't that right, Adam?"

He shook his head. "I'm sorry?"

Tom laughed. "I was just asking if you're entering the race. Didn't see your horse come in."

He had met Tom Walker for the first time a few days before. He could not deny the man seemed to be a genuinely nice person. But, right for Charlie? Adam smiled, rather thinly, although he was happy to discuss anything that would keep him from noticing the way Charlie seemed to be leaning into Tom's side. "Miles and I brought Taber last night. Chester offered to stable him. I thought it might be a good idea." He shrugged. "Let him rest instead of riding him today."

"Anyway, we had to ride with Mama and Papa."

He flashed Lila a look of annoyance. Why did she always persist in muttering such inane statements?

"If everyone will excuse me, I promised Kath I would help set up the tables," Charlie said, not looking his way as she set off in the direction of the barn.

She was a picture of dark flowing tresses and cool peach silk. He looked to the large group of ladies assembled by the barn, arranging and rearranging tables, uncovering plates and bowls of food and squawking like a bunch of geese. Adam could not imagine she really wanted to help them. What was the alternative? Talking with Lila and Tom? Did the ladies need any more help?

Lila trailed her fingers along his arm. "I'd better go, too. There's no telling what Charlotte might knock over, clumsy as she is. Nice to see you, Tom." Lila rushed along after Charlie, awkwardly avoiding puddles her cousin seemed to gracefully float around.

"Clumsy. Why of all the . . . that woman is the most spoiled bitch I've ever had the chance to meet."

Adam turned to Tom with a surprised laugh.

Tom's eyes widened a fraction. "Oh . . . I'm . . . sorry . . . Lila—" His mouth fell open in shock.

Adam cut off any other further explanation with a sharp flick of his wrist. "She *is* a bitch; don't be embarrassed to speak the truth."

Tom snapped his mouth shut, but his gaze was steady. He seemed to be waiting for Adam to continue.

"You are wondering why I want to be with her when I know what a bitch she is?" He had answered this very question all over the states and several parts of Europe. "I understand her. I do not love her. Hell, I do not even like her at times, but I understand her. No surprises . . . no funny little"—he shook his hand for lack of a better word—"feelings."

He tilted his head and pierced Tom with a probing stare. "Sounds pleasant, does it not?"

Tom shrugged. "To be honest, it sounds pretty empty."

After a moment, Adam nodded in agreement. "Empty. Hmmm . . . not the exact word I would have used but not too bad."

A part of him rejoiced to see that Charlie seemed to have a noble champion; another part was jealous. He turned his mind from that because she—of all the people he cared to think about—*deserved* a friend. Actually, she deserved much more. It certainly would not improve her life if he alienated Tom Walker.

"Tom, how about a mug of ale?"

"Charlotte, dear, you look absolutely beautiful."

Charlie stopped, the pie she held teetering in her hand. She placed it in the middle of the table and turned. "Mrs. Mindlebright, it's so kind of you to notice." Notice? Heavens, it was kind of her to even speak.

The old woman broke into raspy cackles, a trickle of spittle settling itself in the corner of her dry, cracked lips. "I can see you're pondering my praise. Been few and far between, hasn't it?" She laughed, her head bobbing like a top. "You know, Charlotte, a long time ago, before we had horses and cows, before the sun rose each day and set each night, *I* was a young girl. A young girl full of hopes and dreams, sure that life was going to be different, wonderful, exciting. I ran around, free as the wind, and twice as fast. Didn't think about anything, didn't need to. Didn't care what anyone thought, didn't need them." She coughed and reached into the straw purse anchored on her wrist, retrieving a fragile lace handkerchief. She dabbed the corners of her lips and slipped the thin piece of material back inside as if she had done it a thousand times. Her gaze searched Charlie's a moment. The woman's eyes were as green as sour apples, though age had faded the edges yellow. "Charlotte, dear, please excuse me. What was I saying?"

"You were talking—"

"Oh, oh, I remember. Your father. A lovely man. He let you have too much rope, I always thought." She crooked her head and looked into the crowded yard. "By the way, where is he?"

Charlie took a step back. She swallowed and mouthed a few incoherent words. "Ah, he's . . . um . . ."

"He could not make it today. The newspaper, you know."

With a strange sense of inevitability, Charlie turned her head, her gaze sliding to the ground and the pair of dusty riding boots planted on the muddy ground beside her. She pushed several dark strands of hair from her face and gradually raised her gaze.

The wind whipped his hair into his face. He did not prevent it, only stared at her with sympathetic eyes.

"The newspaper. On a day like this?" Mrs. Mindlebright stepped closer to Adam and peered into his face. "Just who are you, young man?"

Adam gently touched Charlie's arm. He must have read her blank look. She spun around. "Please excuse my rudeness." Her voice was a hoarse whisper. She swallowed and tried again. "Mrs. Mindlebright, this is Mr. Adam Chase. He's the new editor of the *Sentinel*. Mr. Chase, this is my former deportment teacher, Mrs. Mindlebright."

He took the old woman's frail, gloved hand in his and touched his lips to her fingers. "A pleasure, Mrs. Mindlebright."

If he found it amusing that Charlie of all people had taken deportment lessons, he contained it well.

Mrs. Mindlebright preened beneath his flattery. Her eyes flashed with delight. Charlie had to admit he seemed fully capable of playing the part of gentleman.

"Mr. Chase, did you say? Related to the Charleston Chases by any chance?"

He inclined his head slightly. "No, ma'am, I am afraid not."

As they looked on, Mrs. Mindlebright's eyes once again took on a clouded air. "Ohh . . . the balls the Charleston Chases used to have. Glorious, simply glorious. The sweet smell of magnolias, moonlight spilling across the terrace, the most beautiful courtyard in all of Charleston." She smiled. "Just lovely."

Charlie shot a glance at Adam. Heavens, what could she do to escape this?

"We must be off, Mrs. Mindlebright. There is so much work

to be done for the picnic, you know. Again, a pleasure.'' He nodded and smiled as he grasped Charlie's elbow.

A dry whisper floated by Charlie's ear as they passed. "A fine young man, Charlotte. A fine young man.''

Adam pulled Charlie past the tables of pies and cakes, past the barrels of cider and ale. She did not object when he led her through the doors of the Doles' barn. Built of the finest timber this side of the Mississippi, it was big enough to house twenty horses without complaint. The air was thick with the odor of manure and sweat, heat mixing them together into a dense stench.

He stopped at the first wooden stall, housing a tall, golden horse. He released her arm and stepped inside, rifling through his saddlebag until he felt his leather-covered flask. He returned and thrust the flask into her hand. "Drink.''

She stared at him. "What?''

"For God's sake, you are pale as fresh snow.''

She uncapped the flask and took a healthy swallow. Her blue gaze met his.

He grinned. "No coughing? No teary eyes? Why, Miss Whitney, if I did not know better, I would say you had sampled before.''

She flushed. "So, what if I have?''

He threw back his head and laughed. "Charlie Whitney has returned.'' He sobered and took a step forward. "Are you all right?''

She nodded, her eyes glued to a point beyond his shoulder. "I had no idea what to say. If you haven't already noticed, I'm not particularly skilled at handling people. Especially Edgemont's grande dame who, sad to say, seems fairly senile. And . . .'' She blinked and glanced at the straw-covered floor.

He looked at the top of her bowed head. He lifted his hand, then dropped it by his side. She was strong. So strong. She would not want his comfort.

As if it had a mind of its own, his gaze traveled over her, taking in her peach silk gown: the short, tapered sleeves, the gently rounded bodice, the fitted waist, the tiny rosettes adorning the bottom of the wide skirt. She had even left those damn black boots of hers at home. He brought his gaze up slowly, admiring the gentle, almost boyish curves of her coltish body.

Finding her so fascinating astonished him. Her type did not usually attract him—physically or emotionally.

Stubborn. Thoughtful. Disinterested in the mores of society. Strong-willed. Intelligently passionate. Scrupulous. Mysterious.

He shook his head and released a relieved breath. It was a good thing he had this attraction under control.

She lifted her hand to her hair, pushing a stray tendril behind her ear.

He followed the movement. He loved her hair, dark as the devil's soul, cascading past her shoulders, down her back like molten lava. Had he ever noticed before how distracting unbound hair could be? "Mrs. Mindlebright spoke the truth just now. You do look beautiful."

She lifted her head, blinking as if she was not quite sure what to say. He felt her gaze skip from his eyes to his mouth. Obviously without thinking, she blurted, "You look wonderful, too."

He felt a sharp tug in the region of his chest. It was the finest compliment he had ever been paid. "Thank you," he answered in kind.

She dipped her head again, never guessing how her naiveté so endeared her to him. Questioning his sanity, he slid his palm underneath her chin and tilted her head, studying her. The heat of her skin burned into his. Her eyes were wide. So blue. What would she do if . . . ? He leaned in closer.

A voice rang out: "Charlotte?"

She drew a sharp, quick breath.

Adam stepped back, releasing her without warning. His hand shook as he shoved it in his pocket. He exhaled, then turned with a practiced expression of indifference. "She is over here."

Tom advanced into the shadows, his brows drawn together in a long, flat line. "Charlotte?" His tone clearly questioned.

"What is it, Tom?"

Adam lifted a hand to his mouth to cover his smile. He could not help it. *That* tone he was all too familiar with.

Obviously, Tom recognized it as well. He halted a few feet before them. "I just . . . I just wondered where you were. Lila said she saw you come in here."

Since this was the second time today, Adam guessed the

man made a habit of opening his mouth without thinking about what was pouring out. Adam felt the fires of anger kindle. He would like to wrap his hands around Lila's dainty, aristocratic throat.

Instead, he watched as Charlie straightened her shoulders and clenched her fists. "Is there a point to all this?" Her voice cracked as crisply as a general's.

Tom's glance shifted from her to Adam. Both stared back at him steadily. "No." He swallowed. "The picnic is beginning."

She nodded. "Thank you for finding me." She turned to Adam. "You're sure you have an extra pencil you can spare? I want to work on my editorial after lunch."

Bravo, Charlie. "Yes, of course." He went into the stall and opened his worn saddlebag, hanging high on the wall. He laughed to himself as he spied the tangle of pencils lying in the bottom of the small pouch. She certainly was quick on her feet.

He handed her two.

A sly smile only he could see lit her face. "Thank you."

"My pleasure." He stepped back.

Without another word, she spun on her slim heel and sailed past Tom, who stared at Adam deliberately before turning and following her.

Adam watched them leave, then dropped to his haunches and grasped the abandoned flask that lay in the straw at his feet. He rotated the canister between his long, lithe fingers. The amber liquid swirled and swished like an angry tide—reminiscent of his chaotic emotions. He ran one finger along the bold letter *E* burned into the leather casing. Eaton had been carrying it in his coat pocket the day he died.

His father had given them identical ones, engraved with their first initial, on their eighteenth birthdays. Of course, they had begun to drink long before that conspicuous occasion. How like their father to think he had the power to bestow the privilege upon them. Adam sighed and pushed those thoughts from his mind. He needed to forget the past. Leave it behind. It sometimes appeared to be stronger than he, wrapping him in ugly memories as binding as iron shackles.

Why had he thought so much about it lately? She brought

memories he *never* wanted to recall to the forefront of his mind; emotions he wanted to deny he could feel, into his being.

He ran his tongue across his lip. Had he been close to kissing her? When her soft chin sat cradled in his palm? He had. In the absolute pits of his brain he had been thinking about lowering his head and—

It had to stop. *Had to.*

Surely, if nothing else, he had put her reputation in jeopardy. He could not count on her to put a halt to *anything* because of that. He had never met a woman who cared less about propriety. If it was anyone else, he would be damned if *he* did. He stopped rotating the flask and stood, clutching the decanter like a lifeline. "No." He shook his head.

The barn door hinge creaked, ending his blind contemplation. Lila stood in the doorway. He thanked God for the semidarkness that shielded his expression. Unfortunately, he could see her beautiful pout from a mile away.

"What are you doing in here in the dark all alone?"

Damn. Like a hawk after a rat. "I wanted to get away for a moment. To write a bit." As if it was any business of hers.

She frowned. "You have to write today?"

"Lila, writing is my job. I do not make excuses for the time I put into it. Is that clear?" He knew his anger over her stunt with Tom entered into their conversation. He did not care to ponder if that was fair.

"Why are you hovering in the doorway like some frightened child?"

She looked at him as though he was mad. "I can't come in here with you. *Alone.*"

"Oh, I see."

"Do you?"

Ah . . . here we go. He had known she would not let the incident with Charlie pass; it would have been better for her if she had. He smiled—wanting the battle, tasting it. Slipping the flask into his pocket, he walked to her, his quiet footfalls and a horse's high-pitched whinny the only sounds occupying the cavernous structure. He stopped just before their bodies touched. A slight tremor rolled through her. She was not as brave as she let on.

She intended to push him away. Before she could, he grabbed

her wrist and pulled her into the barn, her body bumping against his. The door slammed shut behind them. She opened her mouth. He did not waste the opportunity.

Grasping her head with one hand, he dropped his lips to hers. Now he would not have to waste weeks trying to get her to open them.

She did not fight, not for a moment, but moaned and leaned into him.

Still holding her wrist in his fist, he wrapped his arm behind her back. He plunged his other hand through the stiff mess on her head. A hairpin pitched to the ground; thick strands collapsed over his arm.

She circled his neck with her free arm as he pushed her against the barn wall. The moment his lips had touched hers, he knew *she* yielded.

He knew she did not care if her hair now trailed like a wet mop down her back, did not care if they were alone in the barn, did not care that her gown was no doubt getting caked with dust and tattered by the rough timber wall. He knew what he did to her. He made sure she did not care about anything but the pressure of his lips, the weight of his body, the incredible feeling of wanting more. . . .

Adam touched his tongue to hers and felt her bow further to his seductive skill. He used what he knew. His hands, his mouth; hot and demanding one moment, gentle and coaxing the next. He pulled back and brushed his lips along the edge of her face, moving to her neck, then took a tiny bit of skin between his teeth and sucked.

Her breath leaked out in choppy puffs. "Please, again."

"Like this?" His mouth returned to cover hers. She moaned in acquiescence. All he could think was how much she tasted like strawberries.

He could not deny he wanted something from this. He wanted to frighten her; tell her without words he was not a man to be toyed with . . . or gossiped about in a muddy yard at some country dance. For reasons he refused to explore, he included Charlie in his warning.

He knew—as he had come to understand with his first sweet taste of youthful, manipulative passion—there were many ways to get a message across. He knew her kind learned much faster this way . . . and certainly with marked retention. Surprisingly, this method of persuasion embarrassed him. Though he *was* pretty good at it.

He favored talking openly . . . exploring ideas . . . exchanging thoughts, but hell, when had he ever had the chance to do that with a woman?

He felt a tremor glide across his skin. For the first time in his life he was experiencing that . . . and he found he thrived upon it, upon *her*. Upon Charlie. What was he doing in response to this new emotion . . . this new . . . friendship? Standing in some dusty barn kissing the hell out of her cousin.

He let his hand fall free of her hair and stepped back. He released her wrist and bent to gather her hairpin, then handed it to her, allowing her time to gather her scattered senses.

Lila arranged her hair as best she could and smiled at him. "My, you're full of surprises."

He glanced toward the barn door. He wanted to flee. From the smell of witch hazel, which definitely clung to her skin; from her coy smile and smug response; from the watchful, premeditated gleam in her light brown eyes. Disappointment filled him. He could not stay in the hollow, dank, odoriferous barn another minute.

He brushed past her, flinging the door open with a slap.

Chapter Nine

Charlie glanced about, hoping Tom was still occupied with organizing the horse race. She grabbed her pencil—Chase's pencil—and hurried past the groups of people laughing and joking, talking as if they hadn't seen each other in months. All but a few lived within a mile of town and saw each other on a weekly basis, at church or shopping.

As she crossed the tobacco field, she knew whispers would follow. About the scene in the barn earlier today, or perhaps her flight from the festivities. She knew they wondered why she didn't want to stay and acquaint herself with the other ladies, maybe make plans to join in the next sewing circle, or agree to attend a Beautification Society meeting. She smiled as she imagined their words: "That Charlotte Whitney. Look at her running off, with a damn pencil in her hand, to write or some such nonsense."

She looked into the distance, aiming to sit beneath the partial shade of the solitary oak sitting atop the hill. Whenever she had visited the farm as a child, she and Chester had scrambled along its thick limbs, swinging and laughing as they dropped to the ground. That was before she grew into a person too different for most of her neighbors to accept.

A chicken, obviously an escapee from the coop, pecked and

clucked its way across her path. She lifted her arms and inhaled a deep breath, admiring the poignant fragrance of wildflowers and moist earth. Damn them anyway. Damn them because they would never understand. She sighed and continued up the sloping hill, the oak just a few feet beyond her.

Her steps faltered. A hint of black stood out among the tall, green grass. A pair of gleaming, black boots to be exact. Her lips tumbled open as her arms dropped to her side like rocks. Boots. Long, muscular legs. Trim waist. Solid chest. Her travels abruptly stopped. Her blue gaze leaped to the gaping material of his shirt, unbuttoned almost all the way. Muscle and dark hair met her inquisitive stare.

She couldn't help staring. Of course, she had seen a man's chest before. Not a chest like this one, of course. Lean, firm— an inviting mix of muscled peaks and svelte valleys. And . . . tanned.

Tanned. Well, hellfire. Chase obviously sat in the sun without proper clothing. She grinned. When had she ever seen the value in being proper?

Chase had proven beyond a doubt, today in the darkened barn, that he did not live by anyone's rules. She could only respect—somewhat grudgingly—a quality so important in her own life. One so hard for a woman to employ.

She jumped as he shifted, his lips moving. His hand closed upon a pencil still locked between his fingers. The intensity with which he worked had exhausted him. She contemplated whether to wake him.

Not yet, Charlie. Just take a moment to look at him. Drink your fill, like you can't possibly do when he's awake.

He was the most beautiful man she had ever seen. His long lashes rested smoothly against his face, his broad forehead free of worry, his smooth skin painted chestnut by the sun. Patrician features: sculpted nose, with just a hint of a bump marring its surface, slender lips, square, stubborn jaw. The dimples she was gradually becoming inured to seemed to sleep with him. She missed them, missed the deep resonance of his voice. The amused twinkle in his eyes when he goaded her. The assiduous gleam in them of late which she had no idea how to define. He muttered something. She leaned closer, a guilty thrust warning her she intruded upon his dreams.

* * *

The dream was the same.

A stench. Pines, wet earth, blood. Always blood. His nostrils flared. His arms slapped at his body; pointed thorns pulled at his clothes. The sounds of boyhood games reverberated in his ears, echoing unnaturally. The sharp tang of brandy sat upon his tongue.

"Eaton? Where are you going? Wait!" He stopped among the trees. Their home sat just before him. His father was going to be angry if they were late. He started to run again, Eaton's footfalls ahead of him, loud, thundering in his ears. He placed his hands over them, trying to block the sound. He closed his eyes, and when he opened them, the sun struck his face. His feet sank into thick, hot sand. Dunes rose like waves around him. He stumbled, looking with wild eyes for his mother. This was *her* beach.

Fear danced along his skin. The water his feet kicked up coated his face; salt stung his eyes. He kept going. *Where were they?* Spiked bits of sand cut into his skin as he pumped his arms, trying, trying to run faster.

"Eaton, wait!" Adam could see him. Why could he not catch him? Panic-stricken, he glanced down to find a pair of legs that belonged to a boy. They were incapable of matching Eaton's long strides. He stopped, his breath spitting from his mouth, and watched in horror as Eaton disappeared over the horizon.

"Chase." A sharp tug on his shirt. A warm touch upon his forehead, fingers brushing through his hair. His mother? His mother had never called him Chase.

"Chase, wake up. You're having a nightmare."

Whose voice? He swallowed and turned his head. His surroundings began to come together. Without opening his eyes, he felt bark cutting into his back, felt moist soil soaking through the legs of his trousers, heard birds squawking above him. And the scent?

Roses.

He blinked his eyes, not needing them to know who was there. He had known the minute his nose joined the game.

"You were dreaming," she said, as if this explained her

presence. Black hair whipped and tangled about her face like a sooty cloud. "Would you like to talk?"

He just looked at her—could not help noticing her earnest expression, her wide, blue eyes. He intrigued her. His thoughts, his feelings. Her blue candor beckoned: let me in. He did not want to let her in. Nonetheless, he was tired. He would never find anyone more willing to listen . . . never find anyone whom *he* was more willing to tell.

He sighed, fatigued to the pit of his soul.

He patted the grassy area beside him. She hesitated, her gaze flipping from where his hand lay back to his face. Seeming to make the decision, Charlie sat. She crossed her legs beneath her, much like a child.

He smothered a smile as he noticed how wrinkled her dress was becoming, tangled about her limbs. He guessed she would rather be dressed in those beat-up old britches that looked as if they should be dust rags, but fit her like a tight, inviting glove. He took a deep breath, determined not to let his mind veer into *those* dangerous waters.

He glanced, with a forced smile, at the pencil still clutched in his hand. Placing it beside him, he drew his legs close to his body and crossed his arms on his knees. He stared at the toe of his boot as he twisted his hands around his elbows. "What was I saying?"

She shot a quick glance at his face, then lifted her gaze to the sky. "You were mumbling most of it. I did hear you calling—" She halted with a restrained gasp.

He flinched for no good reason. None of this was a surprise. "Calling to whom?" Why was he asking what he already knew? Was he so desperate to delay telling someone?

"Eaton." She cleared her throat. "I believe you were calling Eaton."

He shut his eyes, dropped his forehead to his arms. He felt a light, warm touch on his hand. He did not look up but closed his fingers over hers. "I *was* dreaming about Eaton. I was running . . . trying to catch up to him to tell him, I do not even know what. Then I look and see that my body is a boy's body, while Eaton's is a man's. Then the panic really hits me, because I know I will never be able to outrun him."

He flipped his eyes open and stared at the dirt and grass at his feet. A piece of peach fabric had gathered between the heels of his boots. "Eaton was my older brother. By three years. He was a good brother; always there for me. I loved him." He struggled to put his feelings into words. He had never talked to anyone about this. "We had to rely on ourselves more than the usual brothers, I suppose. My mother died when I was ten, Eaton thirteen. My father remarried very quickly." He heard the tremor in his voice but forced himself to continue. "Eleana was much younger and probably no more prepared to be a substitute mother than my father was to be a devoted father. At a time when you are growing up and need guidance, Eaton and I were certainly on our own."

He drew a breath. How could he describe to her the pain of losing a part of himself, losing his only remaining family, on that black, rainy day? When dirt and blood from that field *still* stained his hands? "My father . . . my father was a bastard." He lifted his gaze as he heard her gasp. "Harsh words, I know, but true." He shook his head, after all this time hardly able to believe how true they were. "He let us grow up in a cold, merciless home, no expressions of love, no fatherly encouragement. And we needed that. I guess we needed him."

A ragged sigh slipped past his lips. "You see, as a boy I was small for my age, until maybe sixteen or so. I repeatedly came home with black eyes and bloody lips. Scraped knees. A broken finger. Quite nasty fights for a young boy, maybe not so nasty if I would have realized my size, given up once in a while. Eaton got tired of cleaning my blood from the rugs . . . he finally pulled me behind our house and taught me a thing or two. Where to hit someone. How to hold my fist. He did not forget to include the most important aspect of pugilism: when to run. I seem to remember using that technique more often than not."

Adam's mind drifted. He looked directly at her, but he saw Eaton's face. "As soon as I knew he would have done it— run away, that is—it was forever after an option I considered. Although, as I grew older . . . not one I needed to use as often."

He paused, lost in thought. Then he remembered she was there. "Here." He indicated the gray-brown tree trunk. "Lean back. If you are going to listen, you may as well be comfortable." He disengaged his hand from hers as she pulled herself back to lean like he, their legs touching from hip to knee. They sat in companionable silence for a moment, not at all forced. Their position made it easier for him to avoid the changing expressions drifting across her face, but now there was the disturbing heat of her leg pressed against his to consider.

He inched his hand toward hers. "May I?"

She rolled her head against the tree trunk until their gazes met. Silently, she lifted her hand from her lap. He took it. As a safe measure, he turned from her, looking across the fields. He saw, from the corner of his eye, her gaze follow his.

He squeezed her hand. "Eaton was a sensitive person. Much more so than I ever hoped to be. My father's violent moods affected him, the verbal abuse that went hand in hand with living in that house. How I was able to shut it out, turn away from him as easily as if I had never known him ..." He shrugged. "If my mother had been alive, I . . . I do not think I could have done so." He lifted his free hand and let it drop against his leg.

"I believe it was my eighteenth or nineteenth year when Eaton began to get into trouble. Gambling, liquor, women, fighting. Not such unusual pastimes for a young man; no need for alarm, I thought. I retrieved him from jail. Minor offenses. Paid off his debts, small at that time. Rescued him from a couple of situations which could have escalated into severe trouble." He shifted toward her, then turned before she had a chance to move. "I *wanted* to take care of him. I had grown physically stronger, and for some reason—luck of the draw, if you will—I knew I was stronger in other ways. He had taken care of me as a child, and I vowed I would be there for him now that he needed me."

He swallowed. "I had been asked, rather bluntly, to leave a prestigious college, and Eaton ... well, he never went. My father was disgusted with us, dismal failures in his eyes. We were not failures. We lived in a fashionable area of town, in a rented flat. I was writing. My first position with a newspaper. And, for the first time in my life, it was exactly that. *My life.* Eaton was working in the shipping business, very profitable endeavor, or so he said. I never asked questions. But obviously, my father did." His hand squeezed hers.

"My father came to our flat one evening. Burst in without

knocking. Eaton and I had just returned from our club, and we were a bit befuddled. My father was as furious as I had ever seen him. He was a judge—oh, did I fail to mention that part?'' He laughed, but it sounded bitter even to his own ears. ''He had a contact in the shipping industry. Hell, he had contacts every-damn-where.'' He flipped his hand in small, quick circles. ''Eaton was involved in some illegal trade. I do not know how illegal, but enough for my father to have had suspicions. And, enough for a trail to be left that my father's contact could follow.''

He pulled back and raised his hands to his face. He rubbed his eyes, then dropped his hands to his lap. It would be a mistake to accept solace from this woman. She was too close already. So he avoided her outstretched hand, lying palm up on the ground beside his thigh. He began to rub the small scar on his wrist.

''That night was an awful episode. My father and Eaton came to blows. God, he was yelling; yelling that Eaton had ruined his life, ruined the Chase name, ruined everything. I wanted to kill him then. I did. Because at first I had imagined his anger was caused by fear for Eaton's safety. If I was mad at Eaton, for any reason, that was all it was. But no . . . Father was worried about the goddamned family name.'' He lowered his chin to his chest and exhaled.

She looked at him—he could see part of her face—as if she had no clue what to offer. If she only knew, as his friend, *she* was more than he had ever been offered. He wanted to enfold her in his arms and hold her close, bury his face in her neck, his nose in her rose-scented hair. He had never wanted a woman in such a way before. It was too late to start now.

She leaned in, brushing his arm with the tips of her fingers.

He stood, throwing off her hand. The last, ragged remnants of self-control pulled and snapped within him, threatening to break. His hands trembled as he shoved them into his pockets. What was he doing, telling her this? The one person he needed to stay emotionally distant from.

He stalked off, pausing to stare into the distance. He did not hear her walk behind him, but he felt the heat from her body as she halted at his back. A whisper of wind worked its way through the heavy limbs of the old oak, soothing, welcoming.

The sweet scent of roses hugged him like loving arms. He turned to face her—against his will—and found her bright blue eyes pinned upon him. No censure darkened her gaze, certainly no blame. Was that what he needed to hear, that he was not to blame? Perhaps, but he had kept it inside so long. Too long.

"Are you all right?"

He watched her lips move. A long, blue-black finger of her hair reached into the corner of her mouth.

He contained a strong urge to reach out to her, to tell her that he was not all right, that he *needed* her. To pull her into his embrace, wrap his arms around her and kiss her, letting all the emotions he wanted to feel for her overflow and fill them both. He could not do that, because he did not know what it would take from him. What would that kind of need take to survive? Love? He would never be able to love her, even if he wanted to. She deserved more than that.

He continued to stare at her, his pain and fear consorting to push him from her. In the end, all he said was, "Yes, I'm fine." He knew the response lacked conviction.

She shook her head. "I don't believe you."

Adam went very still. "Why?"

"Tell me about the scar."

He cursed and dropped his head. He threw his hands apart, but it was too late. Goddammit. Flustered, he walked around her and kneeled to gather his pencil and paper. He turned to find her standing by the tree. She searched his face. He knew what she sought to do. If she looked at him long enough, she would find some crack in his facade. Some flaw in the diamond. He had been training her to do just that. Training? She hardly needed it, from what he could tell. She had been digging beneath the surface for longer than he had.

He laughed, realizing she attempted to beat him with his own stick.

His smile died as he imagined a glimmer of awareness in her eyes, understanding in her wrinkled brow. He shifted his gaze to the ground, hunting for his neckpiece. He heard her prudent, easy footfalls compressing the grass between them.

"It's there, a little behind that small patch of honeysuckle."

He searched harder, not remembering what honeysuckle looked like.

She laughed. A light, lucid little jingle. "You are a city boy, aren't you?"

He looked, watching her walk ahead of him, her posture splendidly erect, dignified. It amazed him that people failed to see her wisdom. Her grace. It just went to show how many people neglected to seek beyond what was readily apparent. Something quite obvious, really.

Undetected, his gaze slid down her neck, along the slim line of her back, past the diminutive waist outfitted tenaciously in peach silk. He caught a tiny glimpse of ankle as she kneeled to collect the wadded strip of dark cloth. Her skirt danced with her as she rose and turned with the tie clasped in her hand. She smiled. "A little worse for the wear."

He moved closer. "Yes, well, I hate the damn things anyway. The occasion." He shrugged. Their fingers brushed as he took it from her.

She cocked her head to one side. "It's a queer neckpiece. I've never seen one like it."

He twirled it between his fingers, seeing it as if for the first time. Interesting. They were the height of fashion in Richmond. Come to think of it, he had not seen any on the men today. And he thought he needed to teach *her* to take note of what was going on around her?

A boisterous yell sounded from the general direction of the picnic. They turned in unison.

"You'd better go. The race is starting soon. You ... you must need to get Taber ready."

He shoved the neckpiece in his pocket. His gaze, against his better judgment, found hers.

She held steady, gazing at him, her face curiously devoid of emotion.

He almost smiled at that. She was learning. A thought crossed his mind, and he frowned. "Charlie, about today, the barn. It was not fair of me to place you in—"

She cut him off before he could go any further. "Don't." She raised her hand. "Don't. My problems with Lila have been going on since we were children. We've never seen ... eye-to-eye." She paused, struggling. "Blood isn't always thicker, you see. And ... I think I'll shut up, before I say too much." She threw him an adroit look that said, You know what I mean.

"Too much? What—" He snapped his fingers. "Oh, because Lila is here with me, and therefore I may be offended by your words. Well, let me set you straight."

"I don't want you to set me straight, thank you." She started to turn.

He reached for her. "Charlie, you have it all wrong." His hand encompassed her slim upper arm.

"Maybe so." She tugged her arm from his grasp.

He let her go, his dark gaze trailing her as she made her way back to the small speck of white sitting beyond golden fields.

He waited, giving her time to get back. It was not going to look good that they had once again disappeared together. Not together exactly, but who said truth was ever present in rumors?

Chapter Ten

"I wish I could have gotten you to drink more. Damn, I'm in trouble now." Miles grinned as he threw a dark blue blanket across his horse. His animal was a fine one: a dark brown pinto with ten or fifteen large, gray spots spreading from his neck to a tail as white as snow.

Adam grunted as he hoisted his saddle over Taber's back. He pulled the cinch tight and led the horse in a small circle. Reaching underneath, he tightened it a bit more, smiling as he thought of the inexperienced riders he had seen take a swift tumble because they forgot to tighten twice. Taber seemed to sense the coming ride, releasing a fierce breath. "You hear that? The sound of a champion." Taber nickered in response.

"He's not talkin' to you, you fool animal," Miles said.

Adam grinned. "Do you need any help saddling, old man?"

Miles shook his fist. "I reckon I can do it myself."

"Fine by me." Adam led Taber from the barn.

"Hello!" Aldo Friedrich motioned to him.

Adam pointed to the gray steed standing beside Aldo. "I see you are racing."

Aldo nodded, a sharp jab of his head. "My wife Rose, you know she likes to see me race a little. Like we did many times in Germany when we were younger. Good fun, no?" The skin circling his pale, blue eyes crinkled as he chuckled. "I haven't seen you around the Four Leaf much lately." A heavy accent darkened his speech. He must have been drinking.

"No, the paper has been quite busy. Maybe this week I can come by, get some writing done."

"You sit at Charlotte's table, no?"

"Yes, I suppose I could." He frowned. Since he had returned an hour ago, he had yet to catch a glimpse of Charlie.

"Excuse me." Big John Thomason hopped upon a wooden crate and flapped his arms like an angry bird. "Excuse me. Gentlemen entering the horse race gather round." The crate creaked and wobbled beneath him—surprising it had made it this far without splintering like shattered glass.

"Gentlemen, come on now, gather round. Listen, please." Big John placed a wooden whistle at his lips. A shrill call sounded. "The race starts by the northern edge of the barn, goes out into the main road, down one-half mile into Myers' woods, which is at the bend. You'll go through the creek, over the fence circling the Doles' western field, uncultivated this year, and back to the northern edge of the barn to the finish line. All of this is clearly marked, so you should have no trouble. And, as you come in, please be sure to notice the lovely finish line decorated by the Edgemont Beautification Society. That's where you will pick up your lady's bonnet."

As the men cheered, Big John yelled, "You're damn right. An old Irish tradition. The first time for us."

Several of the ladies listening giggled, blushed and whispered behind their hands. A little profanity went a long way in a small town.

Adam jabbed Miles in the ribs as they led their horses to the starting line. "What is this business about a bonnet?"

Miles swatted Adam's arm. "Keep your hands off. Do you want to injure me before the race even begins?" He flashed a white-toothed smile. "I have a pretty woman to impress today."

"*Miles.*"

"All right, all right." Miles shifted from one foot to the other. "I reckon the ladies dreamed it up. Myra Hawkins' cousin lives in Ireland, and she got a letter from her tellin' about a horse race where the men claimed a *wee* ladies' bonnet at the end of the race. Kath asked me what I thought of the idea a few weeks ago. Fine by me.'' He shrugged. ''What does it matter, anyway?''

Adam took the reins in his left hand and placed his foot in the stirrup. He paused with his knee braced against the horse. ''Sure, it is fine with you. You like the woman whose bonnet you have to take.'' Pushing from the ground, he swung his leg over. ''I, on the other hand, do not.'' He glared at Miles from atop his horse.

Miles mounted, a little slower to get settled. He glanced at his friend and laughed. ''Is there another bonnet of your choice, then?''

Adam pulled his head up and lowered his heels, the reins resting lightly in his hand. Taber always worked well on a loose rein. He leaned forward and cued Taber to a walk before Miles had the chance to say anything else. Still, he thought he heard a low chuckle behind his back.

The burnished sun, just beginning to slip from the sky, shone upon the eleven men trotting toward the starting line. Most looked to be experienced riders, mounted on sleek, solid horses. Adam had wondered if anyone would have a horse to equal Taber. Maybe not, but he *had* forgotten he was in the country. Three things these men knew well: crops, mash and horseflesh.

''Men, line up.''

Adam turned in the saddle. Mr. Whitefield was announcing. Big John had indeed entered the race, sitting two down from Adam, astride a beautiful black stallion. Big John's eyes appeared even greener than usual, surrounded as they were by his red, sunburned face. Some said his horse was the fastest in the county, but what about the rider? Adam thought he noticed a faint tremor shake the large hands gripping the stallion's reins.

''Get ready, men.'' Mr. Whitefield's deep voice rang above nervous chatter and agitated nickering. Adam leaned forward in anticipation. ''On your mark ... get set ... race!'' The whistle blew, startling horse and rider into action.

As Taber took off like a shot, Adam tucked his elbows into his sides and shifted his weight to the stirrups. As he began to move in a balanced rhythm with his horse, he urged him to a gallop. He slammed his heels farther into the stirrups as the wind began a mad dance through his hair, slapping his face, pulling at his clothing. God, he loved to ride. As if Taber understood his thoughts, the horse arched his neck, the powerful muscles beneath Adam twitching with suppressed energy.

The horses broke into a mile-eating rhythm as they sprinted down the wide country lane. Luckily, yesterday's rain had eliminated much of the dust that would usually be settling upon the riders' faces and clothes. As it was, they had only to endure slinging mud and fierce heat.

Adam shook his head as a bead of sweat rolled into his eye. He leaned lower, shouting encouragement to Taber. Glancing to the side, he saw Big John just a little behind him. They were in the lead. So, Big John's black *was* as swift as they had said.

A flag ahead signaled a bend in the road. Preparing for what looked to be a sharp turn, Adam lifted himself from the saddle, balancing his weight on the balls of his feet. He tightened his thighs against Taber's firm flanks. Big John's curses floated to his ears through the balmy air. He smiled. He must have gained a slight edge.

Hoofbeats sounded as the forest loomed ahead. He took the sharp left turn, surprised to see the path through Myers' woods was only wide enough for two horses. It would be difficult to establish a lead here—concentration and skill being much more essential than speed. Adam heard a horse's mad dash just behind him, but he dared not turn to look.

Taber stumbled in a muddy patch, slowing for one recovering instant. It was enough for Big John to pull a bit to the outside and glide past as if his black was on wings. Adam laughed in appreciation of the fine, swift animal.

A creek appeared ahead. Adam pulled the reins tighter, while letting Taber keep all he needed to retain balance. The spray of water from Big John's crossing pelted his face and chest as he bounded through the shallow, dirty brown rivulet.

Adam drew back, startled to hear cheering as the path widened to accommodate more riders. He leaned low and focused on the course ahead.

The tall picket fence grew larger, getting closer as Taber consumed the distance. Adam leaned forward, balancing himself in the stirrups. Taber flexed his legs, preparing for the jump the subtle signal had alerted him to. Man and beast knew each other well, having hurdled many obstacles while racing through the countryside surrounding Adam's riverfront home.

Big John's mount was only inches ahead. *Inches*. A fervid wave of competitiveness flooded him. He grinned and clasped the reins, trusting the powerful animal beneath him to take command.

Charlie rose onto the balls of her feet, straining to see the riders over the top of Kath's dark head. She stood with a small group of ladies, just beyond the fence bordering the western field. She couldn't see the riders yet, but the cheering she heard meant they weren't far away. Nervous, she clasped her hands in front of her, wringing them together. She searched for a glimpse of dark hair, disheveled, running with the wind. Guilt hit her hard. She knew she should be cheering for Tom; but Chase loved his horse so much, and after encountering his tormented conscience today, she wanted him to win if it would make him happy.

Pushing that aside, she placed her hands on Kath's shoulders and pushed herself a little higher. There! She could see a bit now.

"Charlie!" Kath yelled but did not turn. "What are you doing?"

"I'm trying to see. I've only just realized what a big head you have."

"And I've only just realized how short you are." Laughing, Kath pulled Charlie in front of her. "Better?"

Charlie nodded and leaned to the side. "There they are!"

"I can hear that. Quit jumping so I can see."

Charlie clapped her hands, the noise lost to the cheering men who stood in front of the fence. Due to the danger of a mount unseating its rider, they placed the women behind. In a safer place. Charlie snorted. Well, at least she wasn't stuck at the finish line. With Lila. Lila had glanced at the slimy boots of the men who had put up race flags and proclaimed herself finish line attendant.

Charlie shaded her eyes as the cheering got louder. Who was that in the lead? She stepped in front of Myra Hawkins, ignoring the prune-faced glare she caught sight of. Charlie stiffened her back. The girl was at least three inches taller.

As the riders came into full view, Charlie bit down hard on her lip, her fingernails sinking into her palm. Where . . . where?

Her breathing ceased. Her arms fell to her sides.

Dark hair whipping, covering his strong jawline and most of his forehead, Chase materialized before her. He was like a prince in one of the stories her mother had told her as a child, or at least, he would be if it was *her* story to tell. Sun-darkened features hardened in concentration, his brown eyes clear and wide. His energy all but pulsed through her own veins; his thoughts all but charged like a bull about her mind.

He *was* beautiful. She knew—as certainly as anything she had ever known—his was a discounted beauty. Beauty in his intelligence. Beauty in his honorable nature. Beauty in his generous gestures. Even beauty in his anguish for the past.

She could only stare, nervous and excited all at once, as he and Big John pulled together, side by side. They were an odd study in contrast. Maybe no one else noticed. But how could they not? Big John planted his weight in the saddle; Adam centered his on the balls of his feet, his bottom not even touching leather. Big John's elbows and toes pointed out; Adam's elbows and toes tucked in as far as they would go. Big John sat tall and straight; Adam curved like a tight arrow over Taber's thick neck.

A prickle of alarm danced along her skin. She stumbled closer to the fence, blindly accompanying her instincts.

Chapter Eleven

Adam looked back, trying to see Big John. He had forgotten to wear his hat, and sweat poured off his forehead in streams, greatly impairing his vision. The fence was getting close. He could see men standing around it. Did they realize how dangerous it was to stand so close to a jump? Hell, he would have to concentrate on clearing it safely and then try to secure the lead. The damn fools.

He automatically rested his weight on the inside of his thighs and lifted as Taber stretched, preparing to jump. He stole a quick look at Big John, seeing he had fallen a bit behind. *Good.* It was better if they did not clear the fence at the same time, especially with those people so close by.

Adam pressed his knees against Taber's heaving flanks. Later, he would think it could have been a faultless jump. He was in complete control; Taber's form was excellent.

Big John, pushing his mount hard, overlooked how close he was to the fence and increased his speed.

The horses vaulted the fence cleanly, but on the landing, Big John's horse—confused from the mixed signals—pulled to the left. Adam felt Taber take the brunt of a harsh kick. The horse's pained cry tore through him. He fought to control the bucking animal and watched helplessly as Big John pitched over his mount's head. Big John's black tumbled to the muddy ground.

"Get the hell out of the way," Adam yelled to the men standing close to Taber's flying hooves. Sitting deep in the saddle, he squeezed his legs hard and pulled on the reins, then released the pressure, hoping Taber would use his head to maintain balance. The horse seemed to understand and limped to the side of the path.

Adam wasted no time getting to the ground. He scrambled to Taber's rear. Blood soaked the horse's hindquarters, thin drops falling to the ground. He stood as still as a stone, rage, shock and grief tearing through him.

"Here, let me see him."

He turned with a sudden twist. Charlie brushed past him. She stepped to Taber's side and ran her hand along the bleeding wound. She brushed a stray lock of hair from her face, leaving a dark crimson smudge behind. She stood ankle-deep in mud, her hands and face spattered with blood, her intense gaze focused on the animal before her.

Her deliberate, confident movements calmed Taber, while igniting a frantic barrage of emotions in Adam.

Her gaze lifted to his, her face regaining color. He had not realized how pale she was when she rushed to him. "It's not as bad as it looks. A long cut, but not deep. We need to put a few stitches in, though. I can do that if you take him back to the house."

He opened his mouth to speak, but could not form the words. He snapped his lips together and pulled his hand through his hair. It shook like an old man's.

Her gaze narrowed. "Go to the house. Luckily, you're close. Sit before you fall, and I'll be right there." When he did not move, she gave him a firm nudge. "Go on. You need to get Taber off his feet." She tilted her head in the direction of the barn.

He grasped Taber's reins, all the while talking in a low voice to the animal. The horse followed at a slow pace through the thick mud. As Adam passed the crowd gathered around Big John, he paused. Miles was crouched beside Big John.

"How is he?" Adam asked, incapable of hiding the tremor staining his speech.

Miles lifted his gaze. "I think his arm is broken; but he's been talkin' a little, so I think his head is fine. Heck, it's a pretty hard head, I reckon."

Big John's ashen face contorted with pain. "Dammit, man." His eyelids flickered open, his green gaze searching the crowd. He stopped when he saw Adam. "Your horse?" He swallowed. "Your horse?" The words crawled from his throat, thick as syrup.

Adam crouched upon one knee. He patted the injured man's shoulder. "He will be fine."

"I'm sorry."

Adam shook his head. "Not to worry." He went to stand, then paused. "Your black?"

Big John closed his eyes, sinking back into the mud.

Adam patted the man's shoulder again and rose to his feet. He remembered then the sickening sound of bone splitting as Big John's horse dropped to the ground. His stomach churned as he started back to the barn.

The sun was setting, shadows and fading sunlight competing with each other. The temperature had fallen in the last hour. People hurried past him as he trudged through the field, no doubt headed to the scene of the mishap. He ignored the questions and curious looks. He felt less like talking than ever in his life.

When he reached the barn door, he turned Taber around and rechecked the wound. He released a sharp sigh of relief. The bleeding had almost stopped, although the animal's hindquarter was a filthy mess. Mud, blood and grass covered the once-shiny coat.

Once inside the barn—deserted, thank God—he found a large wool blanket and, after spreading it upon the ground, lowered Taber to the ground. He knelt beside the horse. "I am sorry, boy. I knew they were drinking. I had no business entering a race with men in that condition. Hell, I was even stupid enough to have a few myself." He sighed.

He pushed to his feet and brushed his equally filthy hands on his filthy trousers. He could just imagine Lila's face when she got a look at him. That almost made him smile. Almost. First, he needed warm water and soap. Pushing through the barn door, he strode toward the main house.

* * *

Charlie raced up the porch steps and flung the front door open. It smacked against the wall with a dull whap. Chester Dole's mother, Sue Ellen, was in the field, busy tending to Big John, but she'd told Charlie where to find her supplies. Sue Ellen had special needles and thread—the needles longer, the thread thicker. Perfect for treating horses, or so she'd said.

Halting in the comforting coolness of the small pantry, Charlie searched the area. She spied the red box sitting just where Sue Ellen had said it would be, directly under the apple preserves, to the left of the sweet potatoes. Her hands were shaking as she reached for the box.

She'd been so scared.

Terrified.

All she could see in her mind was Big John's horse veering to the left and colliding with Chase's, Big John flying off his horse's back. She'd been sure Chase was going to do the same. But, no . . . he had controlled Taber with a silent strength that had been remarkable to behold.

She thrust the box under her arm and wheeled around.

At least she had been in control when she'd reached him. Considering she had wanted only to throw her arms around him, touch him, make sure he was all right. She pushed her shoulder against the front door and drew a breath of relief. At least she'd avoided humiliating herself in front of the entire town.

A broad, hard chest. Strong arms clasped her shoulders, quick reflexes keeping her from falling. She tightened her grip on the box which had slipped into her hands.

"Sorry—"

She snapped her head up. "Chase."

He stared at her, then released her and stepped back, onto the porch. A thick lock of sun-streaked hair fell across his eye. He impatiently brushed it aside. "I came in to heat water."

Charlie looked back at the cast-iron stove so similar to her own. "I'll do it. I don't know how I thought to tend a wound without washing it first." She met his gaze. "I did get the needle and thread . . ." Her words faded as she shook the box with a slack turn of her wrist.

He smiled. A smile that held a mixture of gratitude and tenderness. And relief. "Thank you. I was . . . out of my head for a minute back there. Everything just happened so damn quickly. Of course, you were the first person by my side."

She glanced at the floor. He said this like it was *good,* but there was also a strange twist to his simple words. She pushed the box into his hands. "Go sit with Taber; he's probably frightened. I'll heat the water and bring it out." She spun around in a flutter of blood-stained, ruined silk.

Charlie entered the dimly lit barn, holding a bucket of water in her hand. Liquid dribbled over the rim as she walked, a large, wet circle forming on the side of her dress. In the deep shadows of the far corner, she spotted Chase. He was sitting cross-legged at the rear of his horse, head bent, his whispers circulating idly about the dim area. His hands gently probed the animal's injury.

She deposited the bucket on the ground, water sloshing down the side to puddle on the pinestraw-littered floor.

"You should have called me. I didn't want you to lug a bucket of water all the way in here." He got to his feet, brushing the seat and legs of his trousers.

"I'm not so weak as that."

He moved the bucket closer to Taber. "I certainly believe you."

She didn't think he was laughing at her, but his words carried a slightly amused tone. A blush colored her face. She was very glad for the protective shadows.

"Go ahead and sit." He indicated, with a quick nod of his head, the spot he had just abandoned.

She dropped onto the refreshingly cool straw, adjusting her skirts about her. Mrs. Mindlebright would be proud. Except *I'm in here alone with a man*—for the second time today. She threaded her fingers together and pressed her lips tight. Why was she restless? She and Chase spent a lot of time together. Would idle talk make the situation more comfortable? Offer protection? Better not to answer. Better not to even *think* about that.

Chase knelt beside her. "Are you close enough to have a go at it? Do you need more light?"

She glanced at the oil lamp burning by her side. "Yes, I'm close enough, and no, I don't need more light. Not yet, anyway. Just move the lamp a bit to the left, in case Taber kicks."

He stiffened as if he'd forgotten this might be a painful procedure. "Yes, of course." He moved the lamp. "I will sit up there. Talk to him. Reassure him if I can."

She nodded and turned to inspect the open box he'd placed beside her. Relief poured through her as she found a well-furnished kit: two long needles, a spool of thick, white thread, cotton, a cake of soap, several pieces of large—what looked to be clean—strips of cloth, alcohol, and a jar of ointment. "Good. This should do nicely." She tore a strip of the cloth in two and dipped a piece in the water. She glanced at Adam and managed a small smile. He looked as nervous as a new father. "Don't worry. I've done this a time or two before. We don't have a veterinarian in town. People tend their own around here, or they call someone who can." She shrugged as if that explained it.

Taber blew sharp breaths through his nose as she began washing the wound. "Take it easy, boy," Chase whispered.

"This isn't even as deep as it looked. A somewhat jagged cut. A few stitches should take care of it." She grabbed another strip of clean cloth and doused it in alcohol. As she applied the cloth to the wound, she heard only a shallow nicker in response.

Adam tilted his head, studying her from beneath veiled lashes. The insane pull of a smile threatened as he noticed her pink tongue clasped in concentration between her even, white teeth; her slim, steady hands beginning to thread the needle.

Sensing his scrutiny, she lifted her gaze to his face. "I'm going to stitch now."

He made no comment, just nodded his head.

She took a deep breath and got to her knees. Sitting back on her bottom, she glanced at him once more. She looked pale, though in the dim light it was hard to tell for sure. His gaze fixed on her hands.

Taber stiffened as she pushed the needle through his thick

skin. Pull. Push. Pull. Push. Pull. A thin trickle of blood fell over her fingers. She wiped it away with the torn cloth. Push. Pull. Push. Pull. She probed the inflamed area with her finger. Seemingly satisfied, she rolled her neck and sighed. "All done."

Adam stood and walked to her. Bending on one knee, he examined her work. He pulled a trembling hand through hair he imagined was standing in stilted clumps of disarray. He happened to glance at his boots, the black leather now wrapped in a jacket of blood and reddish brown mud. His boots had looked like this once before; except that field had not had red clay mixed in with the mud. That mud had been as black as death.

He closed his eyes and took a breath, drinking deeply of the warm, moist air, needing to distinguish one event from the other. Sounds called to him: the chirp of crickets signaling the arrival of night, the gentle hint of voices beyond the four walls of the barn, the faint breaths of the woman beside him. Her light touch slipped across his arm. Slipped into his heart. He clenched his fists and shoved to his feet, opening his eyes to find hers fixed upon him.

"Why do you do that?"

Her simple question pressed a harsh laugh from him. "*What?*"

She tilted her head quizzically, not disconcerted in the least. "Why . . ." She tapped her finger against her lips. "Why do you run away all the time?"

He groaned and knelt beside her. Like a coward, he did not get too close. Yet the distance was not enough to obscure the fragrance that was Charlie's alone. Roses and a natural, sweet redolence that rolled over him as relentlessly as waves on a stormy sea. Fighting the attraction tugging them together, he focused instead on the pinestraw beneath his boot and the way it crackled when he shifted.

"I'm not . . . running." He sighed. "No. No, I *was*. I was pushing myself away." He waited for her nagging questions. He should have known better. After all, had she not disproved every judgment he had thus far managed to bring against her? "You just get so close. I do not want *anyone* to get that close. I cannot . . ." His gaze skipped from hers.

"Chase, is it," she paused. "Is it somehow because of Eaton? This afternoon, you didn't finishing telling me."

He did not speak for a time, just twisted his hands together, wishing he had never come to Edgemont, wishing she would leave him alone and let the grief retire inside him. His gaze swung to her. His eyes began to burn. "Why do you call me Chase?" Please God, let this ruse work.

She frowned. "I don't know." She laughed lightly. "You just don't seem like an Adam to me."

His hand twisting stopped, and he smiled, a genuine, catch-this-before-it's-gone smile. Another ploy to avoid her determined intuitiveness. "My father liked the name Adam. It was his uncle's name. Uncle Adam was a hard man, my mother always said; she detested him." He laughed and picked a piece of mud from his boot. "We spent our summers at an ocean cottage when I was a boy. My father was too busy to come with us, but little did we know then how nice that made it. The first summer in my memory is of running down the dunes, sand sticking between my toes, the heat punching and shoving me toward the water's edge, my mother's strong voice calling to me: Jared. Jared."

He flicked the piece of mud to the ground. "Of course, when we returned home after the summer, my father was furious. My brother, only six or seven at the time, had taken to calling me Jared, too. Hell, I had taken to the name myself. In fact, I pitched a fit when anyone called me Adam. My father included." He met her gaze as his smile disappeared. "My father never relented. He was the only person in my family to address me as Adam after that. That is the reason for my byline, by the way. I started writing under my full name, but after my father's first eruption, he asked that I change it to A. Jared Chase. Did not want to tarnish Uncle Adam's name." He laughed and shook his head. "He seemed to have forgotten my uncle was a gambler who died a penniless drunk."

"Why do you let people call you Adam, then? I mean, if you don't like it?"

He took no time to think about this at all. "Charlie, haven't you noticed yet? I do not care. What people call me or what they think about me. All I care about is my work."

She shook her head. "I'll say it again: I don't believe you. You're a good person, better than you think."

He tapped his foot against the straw. "You only think you see it. You are the misunderstood one. This town has a goddamn angel under their noses, and they do not even know it."

She shifted her attention to packing the medical kit.

"Who's running now, Charlie?"

She plucked a soiled cloth from the ground as if he had never spoken. "I'd leave Taber here for the next day or two. I'll check on him before you move him and periodically until the wound heals. Put this ointment on daily. And keep the stitches covered. The swelling should go down in a day or two."

He shifted and moved closer. His thigh brushed hers. He captured her chin, turning her face to his. "Are you running?" A smile spread across his face.

"I'm not running." Inaudible. Uncertain.

"I did not hear you."

She licked her lips. "I'm not running." Louder.

"Yes. You are."

She flinched but did not pull her chin from his strong grasp. "No . . . I'm . . . not."

"Temper. Temper." He was baiting her. He knew it. Anger would trot her sweet, little, swinging bottom right out of the smaller-than-ever barn. Plus, some part of him wanted to punish her for knowing him so well. "You do not want to be called a hypocrite, now do you?"

She shoved him and leaped to her feet so quickly he was left holding air. Her furious footfalls rapped against the ground. *Wham.* The thick wooden door slammed behind her.

Adam brought his hands to his eyes and rubbed until bright colors collided behind his lids. He jumped up and strode to his saddlebags, grabbed the flask tucked in the side pocket and took a long gulp. The fiery liquid trickling down his throat did little to assuage the sick feeling that settled like a stowaway in the pit of his stomach, when he remembered Charlie's sincere expression as she'd tilted her head and said he did not look like an Adam.

His mother had always said the same thing.

He hurled the flask back into his bag and returned to Taber's side. His gaze fell to the neat row of white stitches, standing as straight as a picket fence. He had hurt her a moment ago.

He turned and slammed his clenched fist into the barn wall. A fleshy thunk was the only retort as rewarding pain swam up his arm.

Chapter Twelve

The night was a typical summer one. The heat had not disappeared altogether, yet it had mellowed. The breeze now had more room to move.

Charlie guessed this was why she loved fall and winter so much. It was a pale and brittle time, but a time of open spaces and the crisp, alarming sting of life. She sighed and pulled at her soiled dress. She would have smiled if it were funny. She was ten years old again. Another dance, and she was the dirtiest child there.

Conventional behavior invariably fit her like hand-me-down clothes. No matter how much they were mended and washed, they fit improperly and looked worn and old. And they were uncomfortable to boot, because you knew they weren't yours and everyone else did, too.

She stepped back as Myra Hawkins ambled by in the awkward arms of Chester Dole. Myra grimaced as Chester's foot landed on hers. Charlie hid a smile as Myra threw her mother a vicious glare. Chloris Hawkins—tight bun pinned on her head, tight smile pinned on her face—just nodded and sent Myra a tacit warning only a mother could give. Chester, his wide, freckled face split nearly in two by a crooked-tooth grin, was oblivious to the scene being performed in his own yard. The Hawkins were slipping in the proverbial hook.

Charlie waved as Kath and Miles sailed by. Kath's full, mint green skirt billowed about her. Spotless. Charlie shook her head in bewildered awe.

Jake Marston slammed his foot to the ground as a high note crept into the night, signaling the end of the spirited folk song. Breathless couples stopped in place and broke into spasmodic, raucous clapping. Charlie joined them.

Jake Marston was the best fiddle player in the county, some said the best in the state. He'd played at every dance Charlie had ever been to. Her father had delighted in dancing with her while Jake's fiddle sang in the background. There was some indefinable, rock-solid . . . security in dancing in your father's arms. Unconditional love and acceptance whipping about you like the wind. Was that the love Chase had hungered for from his father?

She turned her head slightly and shot a quick glance from the corner of her eye. He stood across the way, leaning with casual grace against a thick pine, his booted feet crossed at the ankle, his arms folded over his lean chest. She knew him well enough to recognize his boredom with the conversation going on around him. Her uncle Hubert, dressed and stuffed like a Sunday turkey, threw his hands in small circles at his sides as he no doubt explained the latest banking resolution.

The resolution concerned the assistance banks could render the state in case of conflict with the government. The *Charleston Mercury* had reported the issue, and Chase wanted to be right behind them. Would the old *Sentinel*—a newspaper not limited by political control—have pursued the story so aggressively? Was Chase's delegation of the story to her a lesson in the making?

She watched as he expelled an exaggerated breath, rolling his eyes at her uncle. He tightened his arms around his middle but said nothing. She wanted to laugh at his predicament or . . . punch him, she didn't know which. He was infuriating and . . . and his conduct bordered on boorish. But, she understood he was trying to push her away. Oh, she understood. Even if the way he was trying to do it angered the hell out of her, it was surely for the best. What good could it do to get any closer to him? For him to get any closer to her?

In the clandestine darkness of night, just to look at him . . . she could not deny her attraction. The soft, flickering lantern light complemented his tanned skin, the gentle curl at the ends of his thick hair, the strength and arrogance in his stance, and the white flash of teeth as he finally showed some interest.

She pulled her gaze from him. Lanterns hung from wooden posts, encircling the overflowing refreshment table. Two barrels of ale sat next to the table, various bottles of liquor stacked on top. Chairs for those too old or unpopular to dance littered the ground beneath the draping pine limbs like leaves tossed in the wind. The chairs faced the dance floor—a large, circular area as bare as an old man's head.

Charlie liked to observe people at night; they were visible, but muted. The half light created a watercolor portrait of sorts. They must have felt it, too, this indistinctness. They acted a little unfettered, less self-conscious than they would on Main Street tomorrow or in their homespun parlors at the next sewing bee. Of course, the spirits were helping some along quite well.

She smothered a smile as she watched Aileen Fitzsimmons flirt with Mary Ellen Rogers' beau. Mary Ellen glanced to the side just then and saw the cozy couple. She flounced to Aileen with a twisted grimace on her face and proceeded to peck her beau on the shoulder like some angry rooster, tail feathers flared and wings spread. Charlie covered her mouth and turned away as the angry woman launched into a rather heated repartee. Still smiling, Charlie walked to a lone chair sitting outside the circle of lanterns and slipped quietly into it.

A resounding shout floated through the air. Aldo Friedrich. He and the German assemblage stood around a barrel of ale, short jackets, caps and meerschaum pipes singling them out as clearly as Aldo's loud call. Toby Finn and the Irish gathering, top hats perched on their heads and the ever-present cudgels lying by their sides, congregated at an empty ale barrel. They were unconcerned. Their concentration centered upon the liquor bottles sitting on top of the barrel.

She understood these people's need to preserve their own language and dress, in some way remember what they had— not always by choice—left behind. She also understood why no one, except the Lamberts and Tom, had gone out of their way to talk to her tonight. Even Chase was avoiding her. Their gazes had met once or twice, fleeting collisions across the moonlit yard, but one or the other of them always retreated.

What did she expect, after she ran from that barn? Ran as fast as her legs could carry her, through the neat lawn separating the barn from the sanctuary of the Doles' square farmhouse. She sighed and shook her head. He'd been trying to bully her into leaving before something dreadful happened. And it worked. She should have handled the situation better. She should have called his bluff.

"Mind if I interrupt your musing?"

Charlie released an appreciative breath. "Are you joking? Pull up a chair!"

Kath handed her two glasses and went off, returning by way of a dubious stride, dragging a sturdy wooden chair behind her. She settled the chair and threw herself into it, nearly upending it in the process.

Charlie glanced at the glasses in her hand, then back at her friend. "Kath, how much have you had to drink?"

A loud hiccup. "Oh, dear me. Mercy." Kath giggled and patted her lips. "Not that much."

"Oh."

"I just saw you sitting here all ... by ... yourself. Miles *hic* went to rescue Adam from the bank vultures. I think I saw Tom there, too. How *hic* boring." She leaned her head to the side and laughed.

Charlie patted Kath's hand, smothering a smile. "Yes. I agree."

"Has Tom been a *hic* a pleasant escort?"

Charlie rolled her eyes. "Charming as always."

Kath tipped her head against the chair's back. It rolled, of its own accord, to the side facing Charlie. "Where, by the way, is my drink?"

"I spilled it. So sorry."

"But, we had two glasses." Kath waved two wide-spaced fingers.

"Yes ... there is *that* to consider."

"Don't you like Tommy?" Tom Walker hadn't been called Tommy since he outgrew short trousers.

Ignoring the question, Charlie took a covert sip of the spiked drink. Miles and Chase were laughing at something Aldo Friedrich was saying. True to his word, Miles had rescued Chase. But, spoiling it all, an agitated cloud of pale pink was descending upon them as precisely as a railcar on tracks. When Lila reached them, she slipped her arm through Chase's as if it were the most natural action in the world. Miles' smile collapsed. Adam looked down at Lila. Charlie could not see his face.

"She's a bitch, isn't she?"

Charlie snapped her head around. She sputtered and laughed. "Katherine Lambert."

"Oh, she is. You *hic* think I don't know Miles sparked her a bit? Well, I do. And now she has her claws sunk deep as dirt in Adam. Poor fella."

Charlie looked back to the three people glittering in the lamplight. "Yes, poor fella," she whispered into the night.

Adam frowned, catching Miles' stiff glance as it touched on his and Lila's entwined arms. He gingerly disengaged his limb. "I need another drink. Miles? Lila?" Miles saluted with his empty glass. Lila shook her head. He guessed she wanted his sole attention. Too damn bad. Without another word, he strode to the keg now bathed in risqué, Irish tunes. He stopped before the circle of swaying men.

"Hello, Toby. How about a couple of drinks?"

Toby Finn's eyes widened. His thick, gray hair, colored only by an occasional wild red splinter, tangled like dingy cotton about his head. It *looked* quite a bit like dirty, raw cotton, actually.

Toby slapped his hand against his bony leg. "You're empty. It's a sorry day. A sorry, sorry day." He threw back his head and laughed at his own drunken joke. As if by cue, the rest of the Irishmen followed suit.

"I would not *be* empty if you would quit your bantering."

Toby grinned. "Quite right, man, quite right." He filled Adam's glasses from the bottle clutched in his fist, then lifted it to his mouth. He took a liberal gulp and burped, patting his ample belly.

Adam turned away with a grimace and glanced halfheartedly at the glasses in his hands. He grunted. "Oh, what the hell." He took a drink from each to keep them from spilling. "Damn drunk," he muttered and walked off.

He had taken two steps before his mind registered what he was seeing. His steps lapsed. Charlie was standing by Miles, her arm outstretched. Adam followed the direction she was pointing and felt the pull of a smile. Kath, her head lying on her shoulder, her arms crossed over her stomach, was sound asleep. His gaze traveled back. Miles was bowed with laughter, and Charlie wiped at her eyes as she tried to control her own reaction. Lila stood by them, stone-faced, looking for all the world like a queen gazing upon her court.

Against his will, his gaze traveled back and forth, between the women.

Hair: indigo . . . snow-blond.

Eyes: blue-black and as turbulent as a storm-tossed sea . . . light brown and as empty as a bear's jar of molasses.

Lips: similar . . . full, yet one was a deeper, truer shade of pink.

Figure: petite, coltish, graceful . . . generous, curvaceous, sensual.

Intellect: Oh, God. Gold nuggets . . . rotten acorns.

Sadly, none of this mattered. He and Lila were the same: self-seeking, superficial, callous. They could toy with each other and survive. Survive the way he and Marilyn had, and all the others. Charlie? Toying with her would leave them *both* confused. Strange, he had never considered a woman's feelings before. God, he was even considering his own.

He brought the glass to his lips and drained half of it in one swallow. The yellow glow from the lanterns swirled and danced in the shadows as he resumed his step.

"Here." He handed the glass to Miles. "Watch out, Toby poured a good one."

"And you've finished half of yours already?" Miles' gaze pegged Adam.

"Just thirsty, old man."

"Uh-huh."

Adam paused. Powerless to stop himself, his dark gaze crept Charlie's way, his first opportunity to really look at her all night. She was watching the couples whirl about the earthen dance floor. He did not miss the agitated tap of her foot, or the tight arch of her back. What could he say to her to amend his earlier callousness?

Unfortunately, Lila solved the problem in her own tactless way. "Are you having a good time, Charlotte?"

Adam's frown deepened as he watched Charlie's back straighten, further if that was possible. He saw her fists clench as she circled to face them. Her expression looked as if she were preparing for a liberal dose of castor oil. Hell, did she hate him? He found no answer in her too-bright smile, or her focused, blue gaze, which did not slide his way.

"Well? Are you having a good time, Charlotte?"

"Of course. A wonderful time, Lila."

Lila sniffed into her pale pink glove. "Oh, well, I mean you haven't danced much . . . and that makes the party."

"Yes, I suppose it—"

"She just keeps turning me down, so I guess Tom is the only lucky fellow tonight." Finally, this drew Charlie's attention. Her puzzled gaze met his. He smiled and wagged a finger in her face. "Do not deny you have been stingy with your dances, Miss Whitney."

"Um, yes."

Lila's predatory gaze roamed between the two of them. She did not like the focus seeping away from her. Miles' sharp gaze did not miss much, either. A speak-first-think-later expression leaped into his eyes. Adam knew a comment was forthcoming unless he did something.

"Miles, don't you need to see to Kath?" A graceless hint.

Miles smiled, then chuckled. "Heck, I reckon you're right about that."

The simple reply did not fool Adam. He knew the questions would not escape him forever.

Miles bowed before Charlie. "I'll see you soon, no doubt. Lila." He nodded his head. With a wink to Adam, he strode in the general direction of his inebriated wife.

Lila clucked her tongue against her teeth. "Oh, that man is so rude. Truly a barbarian."

There was a brief silence among the three people before Adam tipped his head back, snorting, trying to hold in his laughter. Whiskey jumped from his glass to his hand. Lila's face flamed. Adam waved his arm "Sorry." He clutched his stomach, trying to catch a full breath. "Barbarian." He gave up and broke into loud chuckles.

Lila stamped her foot and clenched her gloved fists. "Adam Chase! How dare you have the nerve to laugh at me. Of all the . . . ohhh." She leveled a scathing glare at her cousin, then stormed off.

Adam got himself under control and looked to find Charlie's gaze, cold and angry, trained upon him. His amusement departed like air through torn sails.

He studied her face, moonlight casting shadows of pale, shimmering ivory across her smooth skin. His mind whirled with explanations, apologies, trite, meaningless words; anything . . . anything to erase her expression. One by one, he discarded all of his oft-used excuses. "I'm sorry," he finally said.

He released a breath of relief as she tilted her head to the side, her straight teeth beginning a studious torment of her bottom lip. She was considering his apology. Yet, he could not quite ignore his reaction to what she was doing with her mouth. He shuffled from one foot to the other and tried to visualize the ugliest woman he had ever laid eyes upon. When he recovered, he lifted his gaze to hers, avoiding her lips.

By God, if he could not almost see the wheels in her mind spinning like the cylinders on a press. She was wondering what he was doing, giving her a real apology, wondering why he cared enough to apologize anyway, wondering why. . . .

What is he up to? Apologizing like that? I didn't think Chase was the kind of man to apologize to a person, especially a woman. Maybe it's because I work for him. I mean, we do have to maintain some kind of professional relationship. Yes, that must be it. She frowned. Is that the only reason he . . . why that's downright insulting!

"You were doing fine there for a moment, but now you have gone galloping off on the wrong horse entirely."

She snatched her head up, sable locks flying about her face. She pulled a strand from her mouth. "What?"

"I said, You have it all wrong."

"Have what all wrong?"

He sighed and ran a hand through his already muddled hair. "I did not apologize because I am used to doing it. Or because we work together, although that would be a logical conclusion. I did it because—" He cleared his throat. "I did it because I was an ass, Charlie. You helped me with Taber, and how did I repay you?" He cast his gaze to the ground.

His simple words ate at her anger, her suspicion. Oh, he knew so well how to charm her. Hellfire. She wasn't going to forgive him that easily, but . . . he was trying, wasn't he?

"I'm sorry, too." Had she blurted that out? Too late she hoped his apology was sincere.

He shook his head. "Sorry? You do not have any reason to be sorry."

"Yes, I do. I *was* running. It seems we have something else in common in our inability to establish close friendships."

He stared at her, his gaze questioning.

A tingle of alarm—or was it excitement—danced along her arms, her back. The fine hair on her skin lifted. He had the power to devour a person with those eyes. Did he even realize how wonderful it was to sink into those dark depths, warm and inviting, intense and alive, all at once? They coaxed her: tell me, tell me. Your hopes, your dreams, your fears.

She blinked. She'd never told anyone—her father, Kath— about the abandonment fears that had plagued her since her mother's death. Again, she looked into his dark, earnest gaze. She almost cracked. Oh, what it would be like to share those feelings with someone.

He was leaving soon.

For a moment, she had forgotten.

Her hands crept into tight fists, peach silk meshed like prisoners between the fingers. "You . . . you finish your story, I'll start mine."

Startled surprise ripped across his face. His eyebrows rose sharply. The expressive, sincere promise in his eyes dulled. Frowning, he stepped back.

Guilt nipped at her heels. And relief. She dropped her hands to her sides.

"Checkmate, Miss Whitney. A strategically placed offensive attack. And vicious, if I may say."

Was that disappointment she heard in his voice? But his eyes
. . . the perceptive slant forced a tremor along her spine. She
looked away. "I don't know what you mean."

He grasped her chin between his warm, rough fingertips,
tilting her head. Her stomach churned as she surveyed his pale
face and the muscle tap-dancing a jig along his jaw. He leaned
in, close enough for her to smell the whiskey riding his breath.
"Do not lie to me. Run because you're scared. Push me away
with the truth. I can handle that. Use what you have to fight
me, but do not turn around and tell me I am imagining the
battle."

Closing her eyes, Charlie swallowed, her throat dry. She
could smell his skin: leather, liquor, smoke. Oh, she wanted to
lean into him.

He dropped his hand from her chin. She flipped her eyes
open, missing the contact immediately. Her heart beat a wild
rhythm in her chest. She blinked, not believing what she was
seeing: a tender smile, crinkling the skin around his eyes in an
endearing way she'd yet to notice. Is this the way it would be
with him? A new layer exposed every day like a cocoon falling
from a surprisingly beautiful butterfly?

A drunken dancer stumbled between them. Adam took a step
back and straightened. He swept his hand through his hair as
he glanced around.

"What happened?" She reached for him.

He jerked his hand, hiding the swollen, bruised knuckles by
his side. "Oh, nothing." A casual shrug of his shoulders.

"Nothing, huh?"

"Yep. Nothing." In his uninjured hand, he still held a glass
containing a small measure of alcohol. "Cheers," he toasted
before finishing it off.

She frowned.

"I thought you were partial to the stuff."

Her cheeks brightened, but again, she said nothing.

"It is no fun drinking alone. How about a small sip? I think
I even saw the scrupulous Mrs. Mindlebright, that pillar of
southern diplomacy, sampling tonight."

She blew a small puff of air from her nose and straightened
her back as she'd seen Kath do so many times. "You are a
cad, Chase."

He laughed then. "But never a barbarian."

She tilted her head to hide her own smile. "No. Never a barbarian."

"Drinks." He brandished his empty glass. "Wait right here."

She turned just after he did and walked away.

Chapter Thirteen

"Why that overbearing . . . egotistical . . . arrogant—" Charlie swung her arm at a limb hanging in her way, the thin strip slapping her skin with a sharp crack. "Ouch!"

Her indelicate thrash through the high, tangled grass was the only thing that topped her irate grumbling. "Wait right here while I get a drink. Who does he think he is? Expects me to sit and talk with him just because Lila stalks off . . . asking me to drink in front of the whole town . . . as if I don't have enough troubles already. And Tom, talking business all night. Why if I never—"

A muffled sound pierced the silent darkness.

Adam halted, coming to an abrupt standstill when she did. Her rambling speech finally dried up like an old raisin. She had reached a tall pine, its limbs overlaid with a wall of thick, gray vines. He could hear someone or something on the other side. Obviously, so could she. He watched as she leaned forward, her arm crawling along the ivy vines obstructing her view. Pushing them just a little to the side, she rose onto her toes, straining to see through the still, moonlit darkness.

He leaned in and looked over her shoulder. Oh.

They leaned back in unison. A low gasp tore from Charlie's lips. He thought she might say more. He stepped behind her and slipped his hand over her mouth before she could. When she started to struggle, he pulled her against his body. She writhed and tried to pull herself from his firm grasp. He leaned and whispered in her ear, "Shhh . . ."

She twisted without reward.

"Hush . . . do you want to ruin their rendezvous?" Adam had to control the strong urge to laugh as she stopped struggling, redirecting her strength into trying to see the couple, shrouded in faint layers of damp haze and pale moonlight. He had only to control the heat that rolled through him, settling like a rock in the pit of his stomach—and lower. A sudden reaction to the slim, delicate body pressed against his. The fragrance of roses rushed in to reprimand him for his folly. His arm dropped from her.

Charlie took a step closer to the vines, pulling them apart with a gentle tug. Faint whispers, interspersed with ardent moans, met their ears. He fought to retain his own composure as the couple's urgent fervency circled them like hungry wolves.

Run, Charlie. If you ever listened to me, listen to me now. Run, before this goes where we do not want it to, takes us places we do not need to be, lets us see sides of each other that we hide from everyone else. His mind pleaded with her even as he reached for her with unsteady hands and turned her to face him. An angry surge hammered through him as he saw guileless, childlike conjecture cross her face. Why wasn't she retreating? *You ran earlier; run now.* But, he was not about to let her go; let her slight shoulders pass through his fingers, smooth silk elude his skin. His lids fluttered, releasing him from his questioning torment. *To hell with her, then. To hell with them both.*

His hands slid from her shoulders, to her slim neck, rising into her loose bun. He pulled her hair free of its pins as he closed in on her. Her feet collided with his, and she stumbled against his chest. When she fell into him, he surrendered. With a low groan, he angled her head back and took her mouth. His tongue brushed her parted lips. Surprisingly, she allowed him inside. The blood pounding in his head and the liquor flowing through his veins made the ground tilt—a startling, marvelous, scorching tilt. He stumbled back and almost took them both to the ground.

Charlie moaned softly and gripped his sides, steadying *him*. She worked her hands up his damp back.

Who was this woman, opening her mouth beneath his? Experimenting and imitating, trailing her tongue along his lips? God, she tasted delightful. Tangy: whiskey and cinnamon.

He wanted to sink into her, was trying to as he slanted his mouth over hers, deeper . . . deeper. His hands skimmed forward to cradle her face, the heat from her cheeks searing his rough skin. Her fingers dug into his back, almost clawing, as a low moan passed between them. Had the sound come from him or her? Hell, he had no idea.

He kept telling himself to stop. Instead, he leaned in farther, the momentum building, his passion racing nearly beyond his control. Soon, they would be writhing on the muddy ground or crushed against a rough tree trunk. That would be a mistake, the biggest of his life. Irreversible. But this was exactly what he wanted to experience. With her. And, God, it was glorious. Frightening. Enslaving desire and compulsion all jumbled in one hot dream. Need was trapping him.

He pushed back, tearing his mouth from hers. His chest heaving, he gulped great breaths of warm, pungent air. Swallowing, he lowered his forehead to her upturned one, the light sheen of sweat on their brows mingling.

Her small hands gripped his shirt. The need to hold her or slither to the ground assailed him. He had never imagined anything like this existed. Was there even a way to describe it? Like wildfire roaring across dry, brittle woodland? Like the harshest wind tearing through tall, golden fields of wheat? No, no . . . *no*. This was deep . . . savage . . . frightening. Was his body even his any longer?

Her muscles rippled beneath his hands. Whether she knew it or not, he shook with tremors, too. He kept his head pressed to hers, breathing in the sweet scent of her hair. His heart thudded as the clean, fresh essence of soap and roses filtered into his brain. Why couldn't she reek of expensive perfume? God knew, he had bought enough of the stuff to flood an ocean. Just then, he realized he did not even like the smell of it.

Taking another deep breath, he drew back. The bullfrogs and crickets seemed to be screeching and squawking all about them. How long had they been . . . occupied? He glanced through the vines. The other couple had disappeared.

"Jared . . ."

Her sigh slipped to him on velvet currents. He let his gaze fall upon her upturned face. The honest wonderment reflected there was like a hatchet to his gut. "Oh, God, Charlie . . . no." He did not want her to know him as *Jared.* Jared had been dead for years—had died in two parts—with his mother, with Eaton. That carefree boy had barely had time to become a man before he disappeared. It was too late for him.

Reluctantly, the beauty of her face, bathed in silver moonlight, called his hand to her cheek. He brushed his fingers along her jaw, resting his palm beneath her delicate chin. "You are so damn beautiful," he heard himself say.

"If you say so." Breathless. Doubtful.

"You do not know, do you?"

She shrugged and pulled her chin from his palm. "I don't know *what* I know anymore. I know my heart is racing so quickly that I feel a little sick. And exhilarated. And afraid. And wonderful. And . . . I don't think you're going to help me understand this, are you?"

He could hear the anger in her voice. He deserved it. "No," he whispered. His voice sounded as hollow as the drop of a penny down a dry well.

She laughed, an awful, cold sound, and turned away.

"Wait." He stepped forward.

She stopped. A small pivot. Their gazes met. Her small fists opened and closed at her sides. "You . . . you didn't like when I called you Jared, did you?"

He closed his eyes and bowed his head.

"Answer me."

His head lifted. His eyes opened. Her blazing, blue gaze devoured his face. His gaze traveled over her high cheekbones, to the swollen, pink lips that screamed of recent plunder. If fear and defeat did not own him at that moment, he would have laughed at her defiant stance, feet spread just so, tight fists closed at her sides, probably in anticipation of knocking his head off. He should have known Charlotte Whitney was not one to cry or whine about a simple kiss.

Simple? Hell. It was the most earth-shattering kiss he had

ever confronted—the deepest emotion he had ever experienced with a woman—and all in the brief span of a minute. It was much more than he would allow himself to experience again. That seemed enough of a reason to give her the truth. "No . . . I did not like it."

The only outward indication that she had even heard him was her sharp inhalation. "Thank you for that, at least." She rotated and started back to the house.

He took two faltering steps, and asked, "Jared . . . why does that matter?" What does *he* matter?

She stopped but did not turn. He heard her sigh, the sound reverberating through the silent night like a funeral bell. He wanted to run to her, scoop her into his arms, carry her to some feathery bed. Sweep her clothes off, lie between her beautiful, protective legs. Press his lips against her slim neck, fall asleep with her steady heartbeat singing in his ears. God, it hurt to stay where he was, to not go to her. He knew he could ask nothing of her. Not unless he was willing to give. He was not.

She looked at the sky. She was not going to answer. Then he heard the words float to him on the wind. They tore through him like nothing had since that day . . . and that damn bloody field where he had died with Eaton. "Jared matters, Chase, because he's you. The real you." She dissolved into the distance before he claimed his next breath.

Disgusted, he spun around, kicking the first thing he set eyes on—the liquor bottle he had discarded upon seeing Charlie standing before the wall of vines. He reached with a violent bend and plucked the bottle from the moist weeds. He turned it between his nimble fingers, the amber liquid running about the bottle like angry ants. Why did her words surprise him? He had known there was something between them. Hell, they practically burst into flames when they were together. Before tonight, though, he was not sure she knew it.

What made him so leery? Her honesty?

Maybe.

Women of his acquaintance did not open their mouths beneath his until they knew they were getting something substantial, something more than a heated kiss, in return. Women of his acquaintance did not slide and melt into him, in a perfect, singular fit, until he had showered them with gifts and false praise. Women of his acquaintance did not lift shining eyes to his, presenting their desire as plainly as if it were on a silver platter. And women of his acquaintance never, *ever,* admitted to wanting him in the way Charlotte Whitney just had. Wanting more than physical release, more than monetary benefit, more than social gain, more than a shallow joining of . . . nothing.

She wanted *Jared* Chase.

Well, she asked for too much. With a muttered curse, he flung the bottle to the ground. He wanted to find sweet Lila and cart her home. Without a good-night kiss, thank you. He had his fill of kissing for one day.

Chapter Fourteen

The slam of the office door propelled Adam from his reverie. He twisted in his chair. Oh, only Gerald, who was bearing down upon him like an out-of-control locomotive, his gray hair leaving his head like smoke tossed into a brisk breeze. His eyes were bloodshot, his gait precarious. In short, he looked—and smelled, Adam noted as Gerald got closer—atrocious.

He passed Adam with nary a word, heading straight for the pitcher of water Charlie kept in the office. Adam grunted. He did not want to think about Charlie.

"What are you grumbling about? I'm the one dying."

Going against his sullen mood, Adam smiled. "What's that, old man?"

Gerald poured a glass of water and lifted it to his lips. He managed to hit the mark on the third try. He closed his eyes and swallowed with great effort. "A bit too much drink last night."

"Oh . . ."

"How the hell are you feeling?"

Adam's gaze dropped. "Fine."

"Fine?"

"I am suffering no ill effects from alcohol, if that's what you are implying."

Gerald tiptoed to his chair by the press and slid into it as if he were made of glass. "Don't raise your voice. Ohh . . ." Groaning, he dropped his head into his hands.

"Please. Go home. You do not look to be much help today. And, you smell terrible."

With the help of his hands, Gerald shook his head. "No. I've never left the press in need, and I never will." He rose on swaying legs. "Even if I am dying."

Adam rolled his eyes. "Go. We will not be going to press until tomorrow at the earliest. I have to finish the Fourth essay, and Charlie still owes me her bank piece." Seeing Gerald's stubborn look, he insisted. "Home."

Gerald's gaze strayed invitingly toward the door. "You're sure?"

"I would not say it if I weren't sure. If the paper needed you, I would drag you here if I had to."

"Yes, you would, wouldn't you?" Gerald clapped his hands, then grimaced. "I feel like a dozen horses have trampled on my head."

"Too much whiskey?"

"Hell, no, man. I'm German! Too much ale."

Adam grinned and raised an apologetic hand. "Sorry."

"No offense taken. And, I think I will take you up on your offer of a day's rest." He crept to the door, all the while looking as if he were trying not to move his head.

"Tomorrow, bright and early."

"Yes, bright and early." The door closed on his softly spoken words.

Adam forced himself back to his work, seizing his discarded pen and settling more comfortably in his chair. "Now, where was I?"

Six young ladies who will enter the world better prepared to meet its challenges. The graduation

"Oh, yes. How could I have forgotten such a fascinating story?" He dipped his pen and started again.

The graduation was a lovely affair

Another door slam. He jerked his arm, sending the inkwell to the floor. It shattered, showering ink along the right leg of his trousers, from ankle to knee. "Dammit—" He bounded from the chair and whirled toward the door.

Charlie stood there, her mortified gaze jumping from the dark ink stain spreading in a slow circle on the floor, to his ruined trousers. She rushed to him, grabbing a cloth from the rack of type as she passed it. "Heavens, what a mess."

His gaze fell to his cream trousers, now spotted like a leopard's skin. He shook the dripping editorial he had been working on, a few more black drops falling to the floor.

Adam drew a sharp breath as her cloth-covered hand pressed against his cloth-covered leg. Obviously not enough cloth, because the heat from her skin reached him all the way to the tips of his toes. "Whoa. *Stop.*" He grabbed the rag from her and lifted her by the shoulders. He stumbled in his haste to step away from her.

Against his will, his gaze melted over her like hot wax. It was amazing how someone so pitifully oblivious to the art of feminine enhancement could look so damn good. It was obvious she did not try. From her slipshod braid tied off by a wrinkled ribbon, to her threadbare calico day dress, she was magnificent. Even the black, serviceable boots—as ugly as any he had ever seen—well suited her petite feet.

He sighed and looked away, pulling a hand through his hair. "An old pair of trousers," he stated with a negligent flip of his hand. The detail he omitted was the ink that was fast adhering fabric to the hair on his legs. She probably would not care to know that. He sighed again and bent to gather pieces of splintered inkwell.

"Do you want this? No sense getting ink all over your hands." She waved the rag before his face.

He took the cloth without looking up. "Thanks."

"Well, um . . . I just came in to tell you that I'll have the bank story done this afternoon. In fact, I'm heading to the Four Leaf now. I thought today would be quiet with the town nearly deserted and—"

"You ought to stay out of there."

"Pardon me?"

"Charlie, the Four Leaf is no place for a woman. You can write here." Glancing up, his gaze collided with hers. He felt like an agitated bull, preparing to face off with a rival.

"Where I write is none of your business," she said, then snickered, just to anger him, he was sure.

He tossed the cloth to the floor and rose. "Fine."

She flung her hands into the air. "Why did I come in here, anyway? A waste of time . . ." Her words trailed off as she marched to her desk and began rifling around, scattering papers in an unusually haphazard manner.

He followed, stacking his fingers like straight-backed soldiers along the edge of her scarred desk. His dark gaze drilled into the crown of her head. "Why *did* you come in here?"

Her hands stilled. Her head lifted. She squinted and expelled an angry breath. "I came in here to get the revision notes for my story, as if it's any of your concern. And, for your information, I've been writing in the Four Leaf for years."

"Damn fool idea, if you ask me."

"As far as I can tell, no one is."

He gripped the desk's edge. His dark gaze clashed with her blustering, blue one across a battlefield of cluttered paper. With a will of its own, his hand inched toward hers. He drew a breath, regretting it the instant her scent registered. Regretting the temptation snapping between them like a taut wire. With false placidity, he resumed his place at his desk, grabbed his pen and began to write as if she had never walked into the office.

The graduation was a lovely affair, attesting to the wonderful care and attention Mrs. Mindlebright

He wrinkled his nose. What was that smell?

Charlie paused in her search. "I was picking jessamine this morning. I guess that's it."

His gaze jumped to her. Damn. He had spoken aloud.

She cast a catlike glance his way. "By the way, how did Lila like them?"

He tightened his grip on his pen. "Lila? Like what?"

"The jessamine."

"Hmmm?" Shit. The pen stilled. A pause. "I did not give them to her."

"Why?"

"I chose not to. Can we leave it at that?" His gaze never left the desk.

"Of course, Chase."

He restrained a rush of anger, irrational anger, he knew. Had their kiss meant nothing? Though, as he turned to face her, he knew better. Her expressive, sapphire gaze regarded him with nothing short of loathing.

"So, last night did not progress us to Adam?"

She forced her lips together before she said something she would regret. What did he want from her? She searched for a way to escape, focusing her gaze just above his head. Better to ignore his discerning, chestnut eyes. Better to ignore his thick, curling-at-the-collar mane of dark hair. Better to ignore the tense flex of his long, able fingers. Better to ignore thoughts about how splendid he looked, sitting there regarding her so calmly, intelligence and an inexplicable resplendence shimmering off him like sun rays glinting off a smooth plane of water.

Coward. Better to just speak her mind, plain and simple. But it was disconcerting ... to have only to *gaze* upon him and promptly lose her well-deserved anger. *And* an entire, prepared speech. She cleared her throat. "Regarding that incident ... well ..." How could she bungle this when she'd practiced it the whole way here? She tried again. "Regarding that ... um, well ... I think we should just forget ... forget it happened. There was drink involved, and ... and I think we should just forget it happened." There, that was simple enough. Clear. Concise. Definitive. Feeling a little bolder, she dropped her gaze to his.

With raised brows, he lifted his finger to his lips and tapped them, his dark eyes studying her in his cool, careful way. After a moment, he asked, "Did you have anything to drink?"

She simply stared, quite the rat in the trap.

"Did you?" Again, he tapped his lips.

"Not much."

"What was that?" He inclined his head toward her.

She said it again as a slow burn worked its way through her. One part anger, one part embarrassment.

"Well, that is not my excuse either, believe me."

Her bottom lip slipped between her teeth. She chewed with concentration as she resumed her frantic search, papers spilling from shaking fingers. With a quick glance to the side, she saw his damn boots perched on her father's desk, his hands laced across his flat middle. The conceited ass.

"You need to shave," she said to keep the conversation flowing until she could find her notes and leave.

He smiled, his hand rising to his face. "Do you not like it, Charlotte, dear?"

"No." A sheet dropped to the floor. She squatted to pick it up. "You look like a vagrant."

"Well, my. Miss First-Class-Show-Of-Propriety speaks. As if I would heed your pathetic counsel."

She wrapped her arms around her middle, the paper crushed between her fingers, and swallowed her hurt, hoping the pain didn't show on her face. "I know I'm not some high-bred *lady,*" she spat the word, "like you're used to knowing. I'm sorry for what my presence is liable to expose you to. And, I'm equally sorry that you're going to have to endure it." She stripped her arms apart and raised one clenched fist. She shook it at him, feeling like an overzealous minister before a pulpit of sinners. "I'm going to stay with the *Sentinel,* come hell or high water, you or Oliver Stokes."

She was glad to see his eyes widen as she leaned forward, forcing him to tilt his head to meet her gaze. Tremors skirted along her spine, threatening to race down her arms, her legs. "We tried to be friends, but maybe we're both . . . too—" She wrenched her gaze from his and walked on weak legs to the door. She flung it open. "You're just like everybody else in this town, Chase. We'll forget this happened, forget it all happened. Forget we were ever friends."

Chapter Fifteen

July left Edgemont, dismissed by an intolerably hot, dry August. Crops and tempers in the small town were suffering.

Withering corn stalks had Miles' face pinched with worry. Kath fretted about Miles. Gerald carried his concern for his son's farm to the newspaper office, where it joined the tension already simmering between Adam and Charlie. Adam buried himself in his work to avoid thinking of anything else. This only increased Lila's vile disposition. Hubert Dane went out of his way to please his daughter, becoming disturbed when he could not. He berated his assistant, Tom Walker, at every turn. Tom turned to Charlotte for solace, but she buried herself in work to avoid thinking of anything else.

Aldo Friedrich seemed to be the only happy person in town. Whiskey sales had risen for no reason he could fathom. The confounded heat was what he finally decided upon.

In the middle of the month, a raging storm answered the town's prayers, though it brought along hail and violent winds. The day after, the menfolk held an emergency meeting in the Edgemont Baptist Church to discuss the damage and organize groups to complete the necessary repairs.

The church, which also served as the town's schoolhouse, was airless and overcrowded, mingled conversations bouncing about, assaulting Adam's ears as he stepped through the door. Men stood with their backs pressed against the smooth, white-washed walls, and in small circles about the room. The gathering sounded much like excited, feminine squawking discernible at the first tea party of the spring season. It smelled like a little room full of sweaty men.

Adam pulled his rumpled hat from his head and pushed a lock of sweat-stained hair from his eyes. He had been meaning to have it cut. Charlie had grudgingly offered to do it last week, but then she would have to touch him. He knew neither one of them wanted, well . . . *needed* that. Hell, he was not sure he could endure it without pulling her into his lap and—

He sighed. He had best go to a barber. If Edgemont even had a barber.

Pushing his way through the assembly, he caught sight of Miles and Gerald standing at the front of the room. Miles grinned as Adam walked toward them. "You made it."

Adam popped his hat against his leg, dislodging a fair portion of dust and a few rust-colored strands of pinestraw. "Yeah, well. With Gerald here, and Charlie at her place cleaning up, I am damned shorthanded."

"This shouldn't last too long."

Adam grunted. He had seen meetings like these go on longer than an old man's story.

Gerald stepped forward, clapping his burly hands together. "Gentlemen. We need to call this meeting to order." He slipped two fingers between his lips. A shrill whistle penetrated the loud hubbub. Silence rolled like a wave through the assembly.

"I thought that would do it. Thank you for coming on such short notice. We're going to do this lickety-split. I know everyone needs to get back to their own homes and farms. I was asked to organize this meeting because, except for a few of the older men in town, I've participated in more of these get-togethers than any of you youngins. Hold on now, that's not to say I'm an old man, but, hell, I'm no spring chicken." Throwing up a hand to ward off the muted laughter, he continued: "First off we ought to see who needs assistance right away; I know of a few things that can't wait." He patted his shirt pockets and groaned. "Did anyone bring pencil and paper so's we can make a list?"

Adam rolled his eyes as the silence battered him as solidly as a steady drum. He just knew this was going to take more time than he could afford to spend. "Gerald, I have it."

Gerald glanced at Adam, his full, red face breaking into a wide grin. "I should have known. Good. Adam, you can be our . . . our, whatdyou-call-it?" He snapped his fingers.

"Secretary," Adam supplied.

"Secretary. Fine. Shall we begin?"

Two hours and ten pages of notes later, the meeting concluded. Adam wiped a trickle of sweat from beneath his chin and scribbled one more line. The meeting had not turned out so badly after all: he had recorded enough information for a decent write-up of the gathering, which had initially been Gerald's assignment. Strangely enough, Adam had organized the groups of men starting tomorrow morning repairing and rebuilding.

A strong nudge against his back propelled his pencil across the page in a jagged arch.

"I'm sorry, Adam. To . . . to interrupt your writing."

Adam clicked his teeth together and pivoted on a slick boot heel. Tom Walker stood there, his green gaze candid and clear, reminding Adam of the grass covering his lawn in Richmond. Did Charlie like the color? "Tom. Just putting together a few final ideas." He shook the pad for emphasis.

"You're quite an organizer, I must say."

"Lots of practice. Pulling together twenty-five stories, two hours before a thousand different press runs, must have prepared me."

"Must have," Tom replied, visibly disinterested. "Actually, I just wanted to see if I could switch groups with someone. I'd like to help with the pine tree that needs cutting down at Charlotte's. You know, the one hanging over her porch?"

Of course he knew *the one hanging over her porch*. He had spotted it this morning, while riding by her house. If he was not such a coward, he would have stopped to talk with her about it. As it was, he had told Miles, who made sure to stop by and tell her to stay off the porch until they removed it.

Strange, his riding by her house so often lately. More often than not, the neat yard surrounding her home was empty— except for Faustus, floating like a fat flame upon a green sea.

God, he wished he could ride by without looking for her. He wished he would not ride by at all.

He had even taken to wearing a wide-brim hat to hide his eyes; hide the desire he knew touched his face like a rosy blush. Every damn time he saw her, his heart twitched in his chest, his skin prickled.

Hell. He missed her.

Missed exchanging barbs with her as she angled over her desk in the office. Missed striding along the boardwalk with her, amused by one of those focused, dismissing-all-else looks she slapped across her face. Missed the way her gaze used to focus upon him when they talked, as if what he was saying was so interesting, so important. Missed her honest, deep laugh, so unlike the shallow, thin one she used of late. Missed walking her home, with the thick moonlight spilling across their path, carefree camaraderie steady between them. Of late, she took work home, leaving before it got dark, avoiding him. Avoiding those strolls he had gotten so terribly used to.

Did she miss him, too? He could not help wondering.

If she did, she hid it well. Sure, she talked to him. Hell . . . they worked together. But she was distant. He was, too. He *had* promised to dismiss her. Though it was hard. Impossible, really.

You're just like everybody else in this town, Chase. We'll forget this happened, forget we were ever friends. If he heard those words one more time, he would go mad.

She was wrong, of course. Only, explaining that would just further complicate the situation. He should be glad there was distance between them. Now there were no strong bonds to break when he left. Only Lila, which was the weakest bond he could imagine.

In a final thrust and twist of life's insidious blade, the damned dreams had started again. As vivid as ever. No age-honored tradition of time healing all wounds. The field was just as muddy, Eaton's blood just as red, flowing through Adam's fingers in nasty, wide rivers of crimson panic. Lately, he had vaulted awake too many nights, sweat binding the cotton sheets to his skin, air surging from his lips erratically. Each time, fearful he had screamed, he waited for Mrs. Wilkin to pound on his door, asking what the hell was going on.

"What do you think about making the switch?"

Adam pulled his mind back, all the while observant of Tom's expectant expression. He made a forced show of flipping to the page marked by columns of names, striking through one with an ill-tempered swipe. "Fine, consider yourself switched."

Tom frowned. "Are you angry about something?"

Adam paused halfway through his turn from Tom Walker and his sad-eyed visage. Shit. He rolled his head on one shoulder, not even trying to hide the fatigue holding him in its tight, possessive fist. "Sorry . . . just tired. The paper." He waved a hand in dismissal as he completed the turn and headed for the door.

The second round of knocking sounded. "I'm coming," Charlie called. She passed through a wide strip of bright sunlight just beginning its daily climb from the neatly swept floor to the adjoining wall. "I'm coming." She struggled to complete a hasty knot at the back of her apron. She never put it on unless she expected company.

The men were coming by to cut down that darn pine tree. She'd told Miles it could wait until they finished the other repairs in town. What did they think she was going to do—climb on the branches and swing?

Throwing open the door, she blinked, surprised to see Tom standing on her porch, an ax swinging from his hand, a wide smile settled upon his face. The faint scent of smoke drifted in after him. Of course, it was fine for Tom to cut down the tree, but she'd assumed Miles—and maybe Chase—would do it.

"Miss Charlotte! How are you?"

She shaded her eyes with her hand and leaned to the side. Oh. "Fine, Chester, how are you?"

Chester wiggled his head and shuffled his feet. "Oh, good, good. We'll have this troublesome tree out of your way in no time atall." Chester Dole was an agreeable, unquestionably dense young man. Charlie rather hoped prune-faced Chloris Hawkins did not sink her teeth into him, the perfect meal for her homely daughter.

She slid her gaze askance, puzzled by the irrational prick she felt at seeing Tom. "Hello."

"Charlotte." He moved a step closer.

She smothered the urge to step back. "I have to say, I'm surprised to see you here. Can the bank do without you for an entire day?" She smiled to lighten the gibe.

He laughed. Good-natured clear to his bones. "Oh, they can do without me today, I think. Especially after I specifically requested this assignment." His eyes danced with something she did not care to define.

"Oh?" Was this supposed to please her? Was this a special, overtly significant gesture on his part? She was not flattered. Should she fake it?

He shrugged, then told her anyway. "I asked Adam if he would switch with me. Originally, he and Miles were coming. But dog, don't you see those two enough?"

Was that resentment she heard in his voice? Did he suspect something? Had he seen anything the night of the dance? Her stomach fluttered as she recalled their stolen kiss. She swallowed hard and sputtered, "Well, thank you, thank you for volunteering to help. Adam is so busy, surely he doesn't have the time . . ." She shut her mouth to halt the stream of meaningless words that might get her into trouble if she wasn't careful.

"Oh, no. He and Miles didn't get off that easy. They're repairing Mr. Whitefield's storage shed. The roof collapsed."

"That's good . . . great. Nice of them, I mean."

"Charlotte, are you all right? Have you been getting enough sleep?" His green gaze held hers as rightfully as a mother hen appropriating a rebellious chick. "You have the darkest circles under your eyes of anyone in this town. And, at the meeting yesterday, Adam looked as if he was ready to drop at any moment." He flung his hand out. "Can that newspaper mean so much?"

Her shoulders drooped. This man would never understand her. *Never.* "Tom, I would love to have a nice, long visit, but I'm in he middle of . . . cleaning. Yes, cleaning the kitchen floor. While I have the time. Besides, you have to attend to that dangerous tree, right?"

He hesitated. "Yes, I do." He turned slowly, taking the steps with his measured, efficient gait. He glanced over his shoulder. His gaze was alert, surveying. She saw suspicion as well. "Are you sure you're feeling all right?"

She nodded, presenting him with what she hoped was a healthful, comforting smile. He smiled back, but, for the first time since she'd known him, she doubted his sincerity. As he loped off, she stepped back and closed the door, leaning her shoulder into it, pressing her face against the rough surface. She knew what she must do. This farce with Tom had gone on long enough. He was taking her to dinner Saturday; she would tell him then. She liked him, had always thought of him as a friend. Not a good friend like Miles . . . Kath . . . *Chase*. But a friend just the same.

It wasn't fair to let him wait for her to come around. She understood now—better than ever—that she was never going to *come around*. The idea of marrying Tom had, at one time, held a certain secure charm. It wasn't all her fault; he could have retreated at any time. Hellfire, there weren't many reasons she could see for him to have kept trying.

Unless he loved her.

Releasing a deep breath, she slid to the floor, dropping her chin to her knees, wrapping her arms about her legs. Had she ever—honestly, in her heart—believed she would share a home with Tom? Share a bed? She groaned.

No. No, it wasn't Tom she imagined sharing a bed with. It wasn't Tom she imagined touching, kissing, *licking,* heaven above! Did people even do such things? She prayed they did, because horribly vivid images entered her mind constantly, like waves crashing ceaselessly upon a shore. She and Chase. Images clear enough to send sharp, almost painful trails of heat through her belly and even sometimes, well . . . *below*. Nothing was exact, it was rather a mixture: the faint taste of liquor upon his lips, the silky thickness of his hair against her naked skin, the aching pleasure of his lips guiding hers. The images were indecent. Exhilarating. Frightening. Forbidden. She was quite disgusted with herself. This was something a woman dreamed about doing with her husband, for heaven's sake. Here she was, ohh . . . her face burned just to think of it.

She scrubbed her hands over her eyes, trying to erase the pictures.

If only.

If only what, Charlie? She flung her hands to the floor. If only he weren't leaving? Would that make any difference at all? She shook her head, knowing it would not. She *knew* him. He was too much like her, and so she could see through the wall he tried to hide behind. It was true, she didn't know the details of his past, but she had seen sides of him others had not. He didn't believe in love; he was *not* in love with her. Perhaps, he thought there was a mild infatuation between them, an innocent flirtation.

Beyond doubt, other women had been in love with him. With his looks, wealth and charm, how could there not? Even she, with none of those things, had managed to interest someone, in a town flooded with available, much more acceptable, much more attractive women.

Chase's women, ah, they had probably understood him about as well as a lengthy Russian novel. Of course, much of the duplicity was deliberate—sly glances and coy words meant to cloak any genuine sentiment. Those beautiful smiles and flashing dimples tended to daze a girl. Her only advantage—as strange as it was, since it had never been an advantage before—was that she thought like a man. She was as stubborn, as determined. As capable.

What about Lila, the scheming bitch, who was trying her hardest to ensnare him? Charlie couldn't even collect a deserving dose of malice for *her*. He was going to leave her, too, only the little fool didn't know it. Although, that was definitely for the best. Lila didn't deserve him. If the real Chase—the person beneath the handsome facade—walked past Lila on the street, she wouldn't recognize him. Would she think his mind, his sharp intellect, his clear, articulate speech splendid? Would she enjoy sparring with him, challenging his inestimable wit? Would she protect his vulnerability? Would she even think to search for it?

A noise. She pressed her ear to the door. Tom and Chester were riding away. Without a goodbye. Oh, well. She was going to make Tom even angrier on Saturday night.

It would have been nice—and wretched—to see Chase today. Just to take a peek at him every now and then. Maybe he would have taken his shirt off to cut down the tree. Charlie buried her face in her arms, uttering a feeble moan.

She missed him. Missed their walks, their comfortable conversations, their conspiratorial smiles. She longed for the pungent odor of his cheroots, the touch of his fingers brushing hair from her face, the charismatic timbre of his deep voice.

With that staggering kiss lying between them, could they be friends again? She wanted to be his friend—wanted to absorb everything before he returned to Richmond.

Maybe they needed to forgive each other, forgive themselves, for what they could not give.

"Lila, I cannot make it this Saturday."

Lila stiffened, the porch swing tilting as she turned to him. Her mouth settled into a flat, angry line. "What do you mean?"

"I mean: I cannot come to dinner on Saturday night." He allowed himself a modest smile, hoping to soften the announcement.

"Why, Adam, certainly you're mistaken."

"No, Lila, I am not mistaken." Still the smile.

She trailed her finger in the crease of her silk dress. Her tone was light: "May I ask, after planning this dinner for three days, what could keep you from attending?"

A ragged sigh slipped from him. "Lila, I do not have time to be sitting here with you right now. Gerald and Charlie are working this very minute, staying late to finish a press run. We are two days behind already." He shrugged as if this explained everything. "I have to *work* on Saturday night."

She shot an angry glance at him, wrinkling silk between the tips of her fingers. "Why can't Charlotte work on Saturday? Does she have a dinner to attend? I've invited ten people to my home, not including my parents. The menu is set. The replies secured. These people want to discuss Richmond. Europe. Not Edgemont." She shook her head, truly puzzled. "What will we do without you?"

Adam turned away to cover his smile. "Certainly, I cannot mean that much to your lovely dinner party?"

She laid her hand on his arm. "What else can we talk about? New marriages? No, we'll talk about Mrs. Mindlebright's upcoming class or, better yet, we'll discuss the Doles' new barn." She pinched the silk tighter. "Can't Charlotte work for you? What else has she got to do?"

He jerked his arm from her smothering touch, deciding to let his frustration show. "Lila, I have no idea *what* she has to do. I simply do not want her in the office alone at night. So, *I* am working on Saturday. End of story."

"What is it with the two of you? Do you think I didn't see you follow her into the woods at the dance, each of you trailing back, separately, twenty minutes later? I kept telling myself, 'Lila, there's nothing to be worried about, she has a beau. God help him—' "

Adam stood, pushing the swing back. "Goddammit, I've heard enough." He took a furious step forward, then thought better of it and pivoted to face her. He dropped to one knee, grasped a wooden slat of the swing and jerked it until Lila's face was inches from his own. "I am only going to say this once: I do not answer questions about my private life. Do you think what we have shared in these few, brief weeks gives you the right to dictate what I will or will not do? Or with whom?"

She did not pull her wide-eyed gaze from his, though he felt her tremble. "My family is dead, Lila. Therefore, so is my accountability to another living soul. I do not have a wife, or any illegitimate children. I do not keep a mistress. In fact, I only entertain the most discreet affairs, and those happen when and where I choose. I do not like problems, scandals, or threats. And, I do not like when my friends are hurt by unjust rationalizations, conjured by foolish, resentful people."

He released the swing and pushed to his feet, towering over her, his gaze still capturing hers. "Be careful which gossip you choose to repeat, Lila. If your sense of family is so warped that you cannot distinguish right from wrong, then let me inform you that I will not allow you to attack her any more than you already have. Do you understand?"

Lila straightened, her spine pressed like hot metal into the wooden slats. She licked her lips and tilted her long-lashed eyes at him. "Are you in love with her?" she whispered, her strangled tone clearly stating she found the prospect appalling.

He met her gaze, offering nothing. He did not owe this woman any part of his life or his thoughts. He stared for several long seconds. "Goodbye, Lila."

He did not look back, even as she called to him.

Chapter Sixteen

He needed a drink. Soon. Now. Thank God the Four Leaf Clover was right around the corner.

Something was in the air. He sniffed. Burning leaves. He could almost taste dry cinders upon his tongue. God, he hoped the damn town was not burning down. With a cough, he crossed the boardwalk and swung the Four Leaf's doors wide. They flapped behind him as he headed to the long, lacquered bar. The rank smell of tobacco and whiskey crowded the small structure. Not a sign of cheap perfume. He made a quick study, hoping the women had the night off. It was hard for an unattached man to get a drink without assistance, even in *this* town. A little sigh of relief escaped him. He did not care if he talked with another female for as long as he lived.

"She's over there."

Adam turned to find a petite, curvaceous woman, dark hair hanging well past her shapely bottom, staring hard at him. Damn if they did not sneak right up on a man. "Pardon me?"

The woman laughed then, more of a guffaw, really. Adam winced as he got a good look at a mouth full of brown teeth. "We heard about you. All nice manners and purty clothes. The one you're looking fer is over there." She hitched her head toward the back.

What the hell is she talking about? His gaze followed hers. Well, he would be goddamned.

Charlie sent him a cheery smile and bombastic salute from the dark corner, her cool, blue gaze sparkling like a child's. Something in her expression triggered a memory: her lips under his, their tongues meeting, his hand sliding along her firm back. His mouth went dry; his groin tightened. "I was not looking for her." He glanced back to the brown-toothed woman. "Really."

She smiled and put her hand against his back, pushing him toward the table. "Anything you say, mister."

He grunted, but went. Charlie, in refined fashion, whistled as he approached. "Hello, boss."

He looked back from the corner of his eye: old brown-tooth was still watching. A blush washed over his face. Scowling, he halted at Charlie's table. "I thought you had agreed to work in the office tonight."

She nodded, her face cloaked in gyrating shadows and light. "Yes, I did."

He held out his hand in question.

She glanced at her writing tablet. She was holding to her promise to get along with him. The last few days had been uneventful. No arguments, no disagreements. No kisses, either. Which was . . . good . . . bad . . . *good*. Bowing her head a little lower, she smiled. She was happier. Of course, everything was not back to normal. Never would be, she guessed. For one, they weren't walking home together. *And* that peculiar, intense pressure still vibrated between them. Still, they were sharing those lovely, furtive smiles again, as if they could talk without speaking, and they worked together like pieces of a fine pocket watch, with remarkable rhythm, precise execution. They made a good team.

The chair creaked as he sat. Affected, as always, by his closeness, she battled with herself a moment before glancing at him.

He was staring at a sketch of Aldo and his family, hanging on the wall above her head. "One of yours?" he asked in an offhanded tone.

"Yes. I drew that one, oh, three years ago. The children were just babies."

"Just another of your many talents."

Now what did that mean? The waitress saved Charlie from having to respond to his baffling statement. She carried a bottle of red wine and two glasses in her hands, which she placed on the table with a thump and a low giggle. "Just reckoned you might like this. It's one of your bottles, ain't it?"

For the first time, Adam appeared to notice her standing there. His gaze fell to the bottle. "Oh. Yes, yes . . . fine." He dug in his pocket and handed her a coin. She flashed him a smile and a wink, and walked off with a giggle.

Charlie frowned. "What was that all about?"

He stared at her for a long moment. "Oh, hell, how do I know?"

Could she trust him? After all, he came in here a lot. He knew all these . . . women. She didn't think Aldo would allow anything risqué to go on in the Four Leaf, but what about after hours?

Adam grasped the bottle, then proceeded to open it with a wooden stick with a curled metal end. He poured himself a glass, then gestured to her with the bottle. She nodded. His wrist turned, and the dark, ruby liquid flowed into her glass to a point just below the lip. He was an elegant man. Graceful: the way his fingers lightly caressed the stem; the way he cupped his palm around the curved glass, raising it slowly to his lips.

His gaze met hers across the rutted, wooden expanse. "Try it."

"What"—she licked her lips—"what is it?"

He took another drink. Her gaze dropped to his neck. His muscles quivered as he swallowed. "A French wine. The grape is called cabernet sauvignon. I tried it when I was in Europe a few years ago, but I was not able to ship it here until last month. In fact, restaurants in Richmond are just receiving it. I think it will be quite popular." He tipped his glass at her.

She raised hers to her lips and took a small sip, almost purring in pleasure as the rich, spicy liquid rippled down her throat. A smoky aroma, much like the forest in winter, met her nose. She laughed and sampled a bit more.

He smiled, one of those smiles she loved, one he shared only with her. "Lovely, is it not?"

She nodded.

A laugh from the bar drew Charlie's attention. She twisted

around in her chair. The brown-toothed waitress was pointing to them. Charlie frowned and turned back. Chase's gaze once again strayed to a point above her head.

"Did you have an affair with her?"

He jumped as if she'd interrupted a deep sleep. He jerked his gaze to her face. "What?"

"You heard me."

"Charlie." He shook his head, clearly baffled by her intimate question. "Why?" He groaned and drained his glass in one swallow.

She shifted her shoulder in the direction of the bar. "Just look at them, tittering like a pack of old women. It's not me they're after." She didn't want him to think she was crazy or anything. She didn't want him to think she was jealous, either. She knew a . . . well, a *prostitute* would never mean anything to him, but to imagine him running his hands—

She drained her glass in one swallow.

He leaned in. "That is not something you should ask a man." His whisper was harsh, his brows drawn.

"You're not a virgin, are you?"

He reared back in his chair. "*Good God.*"

"Well, old hag-tooth is cackling about something. I was just curious."

"Curious." He poured them another drink. She noticed his hand was shaking. Looking above her head again, he sighed, then shrugged. "Fine. You are curious." He moved the wine bottle in a slow circle upon the table. "They are whispering about us, Charlie. Me. You. Together." His gaze locked with hers. "They think *we* are having the affair."

Her mouth dropped open. "No."

"Yes, they do. I think part of the reason they believe that is, because . . . I"—he traced his finger along the mouth of the bottle—"I rejected their offers of, shall we say, friendship."

"But . . . but, it's not true."

"No, it is not true."

"I mean, one kiss. That isn't an affair, is it?"

He laughed, tenderness lighting his face like a full moon on a dark night. "No, a sweet, very lovely kiss would not be labeled an affair."

He thought their kiss was lovely? Sweet?

Was that good or bad? Exciting, hot . . . fierce was how she remembered it.

Were they thinking of the same kiss?

"Also, not that it is any of your business, I have not had . . . relations with any of these women. Thank you, though, for thinking so highly of me."

"Relations? Is that different than an affair?"

He squirmed in his chair. His gaze bounced away. He took another long drink, this time straight from the bottle. He tapped his fingers on the bottleneck a full minute after he finished, then finally glanced back at her. "Charlie, could you ask Katherine about this?"

She laughed. "No, I can't ask Kath. She'll be suspicious. And, she'll go off on some long diatribe about Miles."

He rolled his neck and stretched his shoulders. "Hell." A frustrated breath slipped from him. "Certainly, everyone has their own description, but I would classify relations as one time, or several times in one evening." He flipped his hand and pursed his lips thoughtfully. "While, an affair might encompass a week or a month, with flowers, small gifts. Something like that."

"Like a mistress?"

He flipped his hand the other way. "A mistress is a bit more than an affair. That relationship—without all the intricacies of a marriage—may be a long association. Some gentlemen have mistresses for years. They buy them homes, clothing, set them up, you could say. It is a good arrangement for both parties if the woman is independent. A widow who does not want to remarry, perhaps. Not that shameful, actually."

She nodded and rolled her glass between both hands. "Do you have a mistress? The one who sent the smelly letter."

He pressed his lips together. "How do you know about that?"

Was he kidding? "It's a small town. Who else would you imagine receives scented mail? Big news around here."

He took another drink from the bottle, his glass obviously forgotten. She watched as he ground his teeth together, his jaw muscles jumping. "Her name is Marilyn Elliot. And, no, she is not my mistress. Just so you know my entire life history, I have no mistress." When she continued to stare, he asked, "Aren't you going to ask why?"

She shook her head. "I think I know why."

He clapped his hands together. "Wonderful." He dug in his pocket and produced a cheroot. The obligatory "Do you mind?" followed.

"No, not at all."

He lit the cheroot with a gentle flick of the match, then leaned back to blow a deep billow of smoke toward the ceiling. A thin trail of it drifted to her. She inhaled the comforting, sharp scent. It was getting late. The press run would be finished any minute, and Gerald was coming to get her, walk her home.

She tried to catch Chase's gaze. No such luck. "Didn't you have plans tonight?"

He took a fast drag off the cheroot. "My, you are inquisitive today. Nosy, I could say if I were not so diplomatic."

"Oh." She looked at her writing tablet. "I'm not trying to be."

He threw back his head and laughed.

Arrogant oaf. She just knew her face was turning bright red.

"I know, Charlie, I know." He ran a hand over his mouth, rubbing away the laughter, but not the smile pulling hard on his lips.

"Don't tell me you and Lila had a lovers' quarrel? She is such a sweet girl. I can't imagine anyone finding fault with her."

He mumbled something beneath his breath.

They looked at each other and laughed.

This was good, because it rescued her from impossible musing. From staring at the drop of wine upon his top lip. From watching his fingers stroke the wine bottle, unconsciously she was sure. From drowning in the deep pond that was his smile, the teasing light lingering in his eyes.

Why did he have the power to soothe her, excite her, amuse her, all at once? How could her heart be beating as hard as if she'd run a mile only because he was sitting close enough for her to smell him?

"Charlotte!" Gerald's deep bellow startled them from their shared raillery.

Charlie waved. It looked as if a bottle of ink had exploded

all over Gerald. His hair, matted into black clumps, hung over his face. A long smear of ink ran from his forehead to the tip of his nose. He still wore his leather printer's apron, which had captured much of the mess. He wagged his finger at Adam as he said, "I told her not to come here. I told her that it wasn't the place for a young lady." He frowned. "She doesn't listen. Never listens."

Adam flashed him a you-don't-have-to-tell-me-about-it look.

Gerald tapped her shoulder. "Well, come on, missy. It's time we got on home. I'm tired and sore as an old dog from wrestling with that press." He shook his head. "Never will make one that doesn't have problems."

She grabbed her writing tablet and rose. She peeped at Chase, thinking maybe he would offer to walk her home.

"I—" He stood, all the while avoiding her gaze. "I thought I would work on a few editorials, since I have the time tonight."

Charlie turned away from him. His decision didn't have any effect on her. Her heart sank just the same. Hellfire. She needed to get home quickly, anyway. She and Adam had a habit of meandering along, caught in a slow current, while Gerald accomplished everything at a brisk run.

"I'll walk out with you."

Her shoulders relaxed. She hated to admit it, but Chase leaving the hungry women of the Four Leaf Clover behind relieved her.

At least for tonight.

Chapter Seventeen

Adam stood and stretched, his preoccupation keeping him from his work. The office was quiet; Charlie and Gerald had left two hours ago. Both had plans for the evening. A faint, nagging sense of jealousy plagued him. He knew she was going to be with Tom tonight. Not that she had said anything, of course.

Frustrated, he dropped his pen to the desk and let his gaze stray out the *Sentinel*'s wide front window. The boardwalk was deserted. Late afternoon was a time for dinner and family. A time to play with children or read a book while the soothing aroma of supper filled the house.

Oh, hell. I am not going to get a damn thing accomplished in this melancholy mood. He needed a few supplies from the mercantile; maybe a brief walk would help clear his mind. He had two editorials to complete before tomorrow's editing session. Charlie would skin him if he neglected to finish them by then. Sometimes he wondered just who was the boss around the place?

He closed the office door behind him and crossed the dusty, rutted street. Stepping onto the boardwalk, he saw the mercantile sign ahead, past the seamstress and a new millinery shop, run by a Mrs. J. Peters from Richmond. A sign sat in the store's window, announcing in scripted green lettering:

> *Hats, Trims, Designs.*
> *We receive new materials*
> *from Charleston every week.*
> *Come in and see.*

He bet Lila had already purchased enough materials—whatever the hell that meant—to keep Mrs. J. Peters happy for a year or more.

He pushed the door to the mercantile open with his shoulder. A shrill bell tinkled right above his head.

"Be right there," a deep voice called from the back.

"Damn bell," Adam muttered and swatted at it like he would an irksome fly. The bell rang again, eliciting another "Be right there" for his trouble.

He frowned and stepped to the front counter. The store was well stocked. And clean. Not a speck of dust to be seen. There were jars of various candies lining the neat, wooden counter and an assortment of boxes, containing ribbons and lace trim, sitting next to an antiquated adding machine. A metal box sat on the other side of the machine—what Adam assumed to be the cash box. He rolled his eyes; Mr. Whitefield certainly had a trusting nature.

"Ah, Mr. Chase."

Mr. Whitefield walked toward him, smiling as always. This was the first time Adam had actually been in the mercantile. He usually sent Gerald for supplies.

Adam watched, somewhat amused, as Mr. Whitefield's rotund body shook with chuckles as he navigated the counter area. The man's green eyes held nothing more than a noticeable amount of tranquillity.

"How can I help you, Mr. Chase?"

"Please, call me Adam."

Mr. Whitefield nodded, his smile spreading. "I want to thank you for the help repairing my storage shed. It's so hard to get things done, with a wife and five children to look after."

"Five?" Adam lifted his hand, fingers spread.

"Five. And I wouldn't trade any one of them for all the

riches in the world. No, sirree. I'm a family man. Everything I care about in this world is safe in my little apartment above the store. A few bedrooms, not much space, but, ah, we're happy.''

Adam was afraid the man might start dancing and singing if he did not change the subject. ''Well, I would love to meet them one day.'' He extracted a dirty, dog-eared list from his shirt pocket, handing it to Mr. Whitefield. ''I have a list. I've been meaning to come by sooner. As you can see, it's weeks old.''

Mr. Whitefield waved his hand. ''Charlotte tells me how busy y'all are. I'm surprised you had time to come in here atall.''

''Yes, I guess we are rather busy at that.'' Adam shrugged. ''I could have given her the list, seeing as she comes in here more often than I do.''

''Oh my, yes. If for nothing else, she stops by checking on them books near 'bout every week.''

Against his will, anything to do with Charlie Whitney interested him. ''Books?''

Mr. Whitefield pointed to the small pile of books lying upon a narrow shelf in the mercantile's window. He lowered his voice. ''She uses me as a liberry, you see. No one knows they're buying a book that has already been read. She takes good care of 'em. Not a wrinkle, not a scratch on 'em. I love doing it for her. Never seen anyone get such joy from words on a page like that one. She's a lovely girl, she is.'' He said this with a sniff.

So, Mr. Whitefield had noticed the town's treatment of the *lovely girl.*

Adam gestured to the books with a turn of his wrist. ''Has she read all of those?''

Mr. Whitefield hitched his gray suspenders through his thumbs and ambled to the shelf. He went through the pile and came back with four books. ''She hasn't read 'em. Oh!'' He slapped his forehead and disappeared under the counter. Adam feared he would have to help him get to his feet as he heard the man's knees crack and pop like firecrackers.

''Here's one she's been waitin' for.'' He straightened and slapped a book on the counter. ''I nearly forgot it was here.

Come yesterday. I thought about puttin' it in the window, but I wanted to save it for her to read first." He lowered his voice again. "Those damn Danes, buy the books for their liberry. And, you know they don't read 'em."

Adam slid the book around. *"Jane Eyre."*

"Yes, yes. She's been waitin' for that one for a long time. Took me quite a spell to get it; the Danes don't have it for their liberry yet, so—"

"I will take it. And the other four. Let's see . . ." He shuffled through the books one at a time. "Edgar Allan Poe. Emerson Bennett. Herman Melville. Augustus B. Longstreet. Hmm . . . that one is not a quick read. No matter. Deliver everything to the *Sentinel* office. Tomorrow is fine. I know you must be closing soon."

Mr. Whitefield waved his hands in small, distraught circles. "But, that one is for Charlotte. The others, well, the Danes—"

Adam interrupted him. "These are for the *Sentinel*'s library. Charlie, being an employee, has full access to the books. She can scratch them, bend the pages, anything she wants." Adam winked at him. "I am sure you can tell the Danes the shipment was delayed. Give them some of the others. Can they distinguish between Melville and Hawthorne?"

"Dis . . . what?"

Adam smiled, using charm as an inducement. "They will not know one book from the other."

"You say Charlotte can read 'em anytime she wants?"

"Of course. You have my word."

"I'll box 'em up and have 'em sent over tomorra mornin'. First thing. One of my older boys will be by. Good, strong boys."

"To be sure." Adam waved the copy of *Jane Eyre*. "I will take this one with me now."

"Sure, sure, Mr. . . . Adam."

Adam smiled. He did not even mind the annoying bell ringing as he pulled the door open. He just knew Charlie would love the books.

"I saw something at Mr. Whitefield's today . . . something strange, I think."

"Strange?" Miles pulled Kath closer to his side and yawned. He hoped the tellin' of the strange incident wasn't going to take long.

She nodded against his shoulder. "Adam was in the store, and he bought Charlie all these books ... I don't know. I just got a funny feeling about it."

"Good funny or bad funny?"

"Good, I mean ... not a bad feeling. Mercy, I don't know what I mean."

He squeezed her and laughed softly.

"What?"

"I'm just surprised you've been so blind, that's all."

She stiffened and lifted her head. "Blind? Miles Lambert, I don't know what you're hinting at."

He pulled her head back to his shoulder, smoothing his hands along her back. "Adam and Charlie are in love."

"No." She grasped his hand.

"No? Why not?"

"Why? Because of Tom."

"Ha ... do you honestly think those two are made for each other? Kathy, pull your head out of the sand."

She slapped his chest. "Tom is a nice man. Responsible. What's wrong with him?"

"That's true, but think about Charlie. Would any of those things make *her* happy?"

"Well ... I guessed maybe they would when she settled down."

"If any settlin', as you call it, was going to happen, it would have already happened."

She sighed and squeezed his hand. "I just worry about her. She's all alone now. Besides, I'm her best friend. Wouldn't she tell me?"

He shook his head. "She doesn't know it yet. Hell, neither does he."

She raised her head again. "Oh? And *you* do?"

He pulled her back against his chest and brushed a light kiss along her brow. "Now, don't go gettin' all riled. I spend a lot of time with the two of them. Landsakes, the air is as thick as a brick when they're together. They caterwaul like two cats in a sack, but you only have to see the way they look at each other. How can you explain that?''

''Charlie *was* the first person to reach him during the accident at the horse race. But I just figured . . . after all, she does work with him. They're friends. That's probably all it is.''

He squeezed her tight and kissed her brow. ''We'll see, won't we?''

A loud noise woke Adam, jarring him from sleep and a rather enchanting dream: he and Charlie, rolling around on the floor at Mrs. Wilkin's of all places, naked as the day they were born. Strange how the conscious mind was present during dreams, because instead of holding her and doing all the usual things, he had been desperately trying to get a good look at her nude body. Like he was some voyeur in his own damn dream.

He lifted his head and squinted. The office. He had fallen asleep at his desk. Again. What time was it? What had awakened him? Somewhere in his mind the putrid smell of tobacco and whiskey registered. He swiveled in his chair.

Tom Walker stood just inside the door. He had thrown it open. One pane of glass now nursed a jagged crack. Adam usually locked the door, but he could not remember if he had tonight or not.

Tom's bleary gaze roamed the office. He was leaning against the doorjamb, hanging on to it, actually. His blond hair swirled in wild tufts on his head, like an angry, frothy sea. A blue chambray shirt—probably new from the looks of it—bunched out of his trousers. Beer or whiskey, or both, drifted from him. It reeked whatever it was. Dark splotches had dried in spots, while others looked wet to the touch. His slit-eyed gaze passed Adam, then swung back. He stumbled, then righted himself, making his way to Adam's desk. Tom stopped as his knees collided with the solid wood, sliding the desk back an inch or two along the wooden floor.

Adam had not spoken or moved as Tom weaved toward him. As Tom got closer, the lantern cast enough light to discern his features. Misery, anger and betrayal twisted his face. His pale eyes were wild, his thin lips pressed together so hard that a thick, white ring appeared around them. His hands coiled in tight fists by his sides. Something about the stance struck a familiar chord in Adam: the fists, the clenched teeth, the wild eyes. He pushed his chair back. "Tom, what are you doing here?"

Tom leaned into the desk, and it slid back another inch. "You bastard."

Adam sighed and stood. Just what he needed. An angry drunk. For Tom's sake, he was glad something sat between them. "What the hell are you ranting about?"

Tom's gaze dropped; his hands clutched the wooden edge of the desk like a lifeline. He drew a deep breath and expelled it on what sounded, oddly enough, like a sob. "What did you do to her?" he asked without lifting his head.

"Do to whom?" But, really, who else could it be?

Tom's hand shot out, skidding across the desk, scattering sheets of paper and the new inkwell to the floor. The inkwell shattered, raining black drops on the desk and their trousers. Adam cast a droll glance at his legs. *I need to buy cheaper trousers if this is what is going to come of all of them.* "What the hell is wrong with you?"

Tom lunged over the desk, grasping Adam's shoulders. The force of the movement drove them both to the floor. For a moment, they were nothing but a tangle of arms and legs. Adam was the taller, more muscular of the two, but Tom's anger supplemented his strength. He connected one good time with Adam's cheekbone.

Rage and denied jealousy boiled to the surface like a pot of stew too long on the stove. Adam's heart pumped heavily, the pressure pounding in his ears. He fought to stay in control; tried not to take advantage of Tom's besotted condition. *Upset idiot.* Clearly Adam was the more sober of the two. He had to end this.

For all his good intentions, he could not deny the image that came to him: of Charlie locked in this man's arms. Tom swung at him and missed, leaving his handsome face totally unprotected. Adam raised his fist, putting all his weight behind it. A swift jolt of pain seared his knuckles. Adam heard the definite crack of bone. A nose, most likely.

Adam rolled away and pushed himself against the wall. He flexed his hand and shoved aside the guilt attacking him. He had not been the aggressor. He had not been the one to start this fight. He glanced at Tom, who was groaning, but conscious. Adam blew on his stinging knuckles. "Get up, goddamn you."

Tom slowly brought his hand to his face. Blood had begun to dribble from his nose to the floor in tiny drops. A thin line ran down his lips and his chin.

Adam huffed a disgusted breath and heaved himself to his feet. He touched his cheekbone, wincing. A knot was forming there. He grabbed one of Gerald's press rags and threw it. It hit Tom square on the forehead and flopped to the floor. Jutting his chin, Tom snatched it without comment. He dabbed at his nose, the breath puffing from his mouth in little spurts.

Adam leaned against his desk. He made a hasty, indiscriminate survey of his appearance. Torn shirt. Trousers once again spotted with ink. Face surely beginning to bruise. He hoped Mrs. Wilkin was asleep when he got home.

Tom pushed himself up, his legs spread, his hand holding the rag firmly to his nose. When he spoke, the words were muffled behind the cloth. "Don't goddamn me, goddamn *you.*"

Adam straightened with a snap and advanced on the man sitting at a crooked angle like a broken tree limb. "Spit it out, Walker. Whatever it is you came here to say."

Tom groaned as he rose to his knees. The stench rippling off him in waves was definitely the Four Leaf Clover's signature fragrance: cheap perfume, tobacco, whiskey. Adam stepped back to allow Tom room to gain his footing. Once Tom stood, he swayed like a tattered flag upon a flagpole, but his gaze was more lucid than when he had first appeared at the *Sentinel*'s door. Adam had always found a beating just the ticket to rid a man's mind of the effect of alcohol.

Tom dropped the rag from his nose, letting it flop against his stained pant leg. A crook near the top stood out on the straight—until now quite perfect—arch of his nose. A clean break, at least. The bleeding had slowed some, although a slight trickle still oozed from his left nostril. He spoke through stiff lips glazed with drying blood. "I don't know that I had anything to spit out. I just know Charlotte has been different since you and your fancy ways came flashing around this town. But I suppose it's not such a great surprise. This newspaper, and anything connected with it, has always been the only thing to matter to her." He walked to the press, brushing his hand lightly over the hard, metal surface.

Adam watched him, questions whirling round his mind. Had Tom ever stopped by the office to talk with Charlie about her work? The editorials she was writing? Did Tom even know what he was touching? Did he care? More importantly, what had happened tonight to make him behave this way?

Tom glanced at Adam, then away. "I waited for her to grow up, you know. Since she was in short dresses, I've wanted her. Something about her eyes . . . they always had that *look,* like she knew more than you did, like she was wise and pure all at the same time. Energy and life always bubbled from her, more than you could gather from a hundred different people." He sighed, a truly defeated sound. "I'm only a year older. We went to school together. I followed her, trailing after her like a lost puppy. Hoping, always hoping, she would like me. Just a little." He shook his head. "Never was interested in the things I'm interested in. I'm not interested in the things she's interested in, either. Am I?" His shoulders stiffened. "But *you* are."

Adam's mind chose that moment to recall his dream. Heat blew over his face. He turned away. He pushed the words from his lips: "If you mean the *Sentinel,* yes." He walked to the broken inkwell and bent to gather the pieces. Charlie was going to pitch a fit when she saw another stain coloring the office floor.

"I don't think the *Sentinel* is all you share. I can't say, for sure, of course. But I've watched the two of you. Looks pass between you, like you're speaking when you're not. Like a set of goddamned twins or something." Tom knocked his fist against the press. "I just hope to hell you haven't touched her, when you're only planning on high-tailing it out of here."

Adam surged to his feet with such force that a piece of jagged pottery dug into his palm. "You better shut your mouth, Walker, or I will shut it for you." A thin trickle of blood ran between his fingers.

Tom whipped around, malice twisting his lips. "Don't think I'm going to make it all better if you ruin her. I asked tonight, and she turned me down. I've waited almost my whole life to ask her that one question." He slanted his head to the side, his gaze hard, angry. "I can't get past thinking your coming here changed her answer. Changed her mind. Changed her feelings. I'm not blind enough to think she was in love with me, but I assumed she would say yes when I finally asked. I thought she would grow to love me like I love her. Forget all this newspaper business." His gaze swept the room. "The way she said no today, so final . . . I wonder if I really ever knew her at all. What have I been loving all these years?"

"Maybe you don't know her. Nobody in this wretched town seems to."

Tom's head leveled as his gaze sought Adam's. "No one but you, you mean?"

Yes. I do know her better than you do, you damn fool.

Tom clapped his hands together, mocking himself, mocking the entire situation. "Well, I'm done for. You can have her. Even if I wanted to try again, she doesn't want me to. She wants to be alone, damn her. Or with you, I don't know which. To hell with both of you."

"I work with her. That is all there is to it."

Tom threw his hand out and turned toward the door. "That's what she said, and I didn't believe her, either." He passed through the archway, his faltering gait propelling him along the boardwalk. Adam heard him stumble; soon after the irregular footfalls resumed.

Adam walked to the door. He lifted his finger to the glass, tracing the crack in the pane. They were loose, anyway. Needed to be replaced. Maybe a strong, thick wooden door would be a better idea. Someone was always slamming this one, shaking the panes. It was no wonder they were about to fall out.

I've watched the two of you together . . . looks pass between you . . . like you're speaking when you're not. When had Tom seen that?

I just hope to hell you haven't touched her, when you're only planning on high-tailing it out of here.

Adam's cheek throbbed in time with his heartbeat. The smell of ink in the office suddenly seemed too solid. He stuck his mouth near the glass. A slight draft hit his cheek. He drew a deep breath.

Was he letting emotions he was not even sure he felt show? Was Charlie in danger of being compromised by nothing?

Nothing at all. He knew the people of this town would not give her a fair trial. They would convict her—guilty as hell from the first moment.

Air clogged his throat. Were they guilty?

Were they both guilty?

Chapter Eighteen

Charlie's rapid step moved her with brisk efficiency along the boardwalk. She was eager to escape the strange glances she was receiving. Could they know about last night? About the disastrous scene in her front yard? Right out of the clear blue, Tom had asked her to marry him.

Marry him, for heaven's sake. She cringed as she recalled her awkward, inept rejection. Telling him they would always be friends. He'd laughed at that—a nasty, awful laugh. He had loved her forever, he'd said. Why, he had asked, did she think he'd followed her like a shadow when they were children?

She flushed and glanced around, as if the eyes of the whole town were watching. Only two storefronts ahead, the *Sentinel* office sign shook in the light afternoon breeze. A safe haven.

She'd skipped church this morning, another sin on a long list of sins. She was a coward. Could she ever face Tom again? The look in his eyes . . . oh, her chest squeezed up like a raisin just thinking about it. He hadn't cried, thank the Lord. Though he'd looked like he was going to. And . . . the things he'd *said.* It just did not bear repeating, even in the privacy of her own mind.

She pushed against the *Sentinel* door with a laggard sigh. She wasn't guilty of anything except a few shameful thoughts,

a wicked dream or two and an exceptional, once-in-a-lifetime
kiss. I'm twenty-four years old. Surely, most women my age
have more to repent for than that. All she'd really experienced
before you-know-who came to town were a few stolen kisses
with Johnny Appleton under an old maple tree in his front yard,
and some awkward, enthusiastic groping from her shy suitor
of *fourteen years.*

Too bad she didn't have more to be ashamed of. Tom believed
she was guilty. The town probably did, too. Maybe she should
commit the crime. Although, she wasn't sure what the crime
was. She was an intelligent, capable woman. She could find
out.

Her gaze swept the office. Deserted. She walked to the back
room. No one there. She frowned. Wasn't she late for the
editorial meeting? As she passed her desk, a note perched on
top caught her eye. Chase's bold, elegant script jumped off
the page. She picked up the sheet of paper. What beautiful
handwriting he had.

> *Charlie,*
> *I fell asleep here last night and did not leave until well
> past dawn. I left my editorials on your desk. Look them
> over and make any changes you think they need. I will
> come in later, although after the tongue-lashing I am
> sure to receive from Mrs. Wilkin, I may be confined to
> my room. Tell Gerald to start laying the type for your
> completed pieces. I will work with him on mine. Maybe
> we can get this one out on time.*
> *A. J. C.*

She ran her hands over the dry ink, imagining him sleeping
at his desk, his head cradled in his arms, his dark lashes resting
against his golden skin. She'd come upon him sleeping like
that before. It was hard not to pause and stare. To watch his
chest rise and fall with each breath. To imagine his hands,
those splendid, slender fingers gliding along her own skin. She
always took great pains not to reach those few feet and touch
him.

She smiled to herself and folded the note in half. She opened
a side drawer of her desk and slipped it in among the others.

She knew it was foolish to keep them; they weren't love letters after all. But . . . she hadn't been able to throw them away. Not one. At least this way she would have a small part of him. Not very much, granted, but it was something.

Her gaze fell to the editorials on her desk. Obviously, he trusted her to complete the editing alone. She could do it. Although, he'd yet to see the final copy for her bank legislation piece. She'd modified the perspective somewhat, and . . . oh, hellfire, who was she kidding? He wouldn't like it. It was good, but he would *not* like it. She fidgeted a moment, then snatched up the piece before she changed her mind. It might be her final opportunity to include an opinion other than Stokes' in the *Sentinel.*

She was going to do it.

Humming under his breath, Miles elbowed the door open. He thought he'd heard Adam ride into the front yard. He was only a few minutes late. Kath was setting the table.

"Adam," he said as he walked to the edge of the porch. He took a step back as he got a good look at his friend's expression as Adam mounted the porch steps two at a time. Landsakes, but the man was boiling mad and as disheveled as Miles had ever seen him. A dark blanket of whiskers covered Adam's face and jaw, his black shirt stuck to him in intermittent, sweat-stained circles, and a thin layer of dust coated his clothes and face.

Adam stopped at the top of the stairs, his gaze going past Miles, into the house. "Is she here?:

Uh, oh. "Who? Kath?" Clearly, Adam wasn't looking for Miles' wife. The crumpled copy of the *Edgemont Sentinel* clutched in his tight fist was a definite clue. The ink didn't even look to be dry, smeared as it was all over his hand. "Which way does she walk here?" Adam's hand flexed once, twice, about the newspaper.

Miles held up his hand, as if he were taming a wild horse. "Now, why don't you just wait for her ta get here, cool off a bit."

"No. I am going to kill her."

Miles forced a laugh past his lips and a smile to his face. "It can't be that bad. She—"

Adam spun around, vaulting to the ground with an angry oath.

"Adam, wait!" Miles raced down the steps, reaching Adam just as he was mounting his huge beast of a horse. Then, from the corner of his eye, Miles saw her, walking through the field of corn beside his house.

Unfortunately, Adam saw her, too.

When Miles looked back on the event, he decided it was the strangest thing he ever saw.

Charlie was looking at the clouds, clearly lost in thought, the wind throwing her hair about her face. She lifted her hand to pull a strand from her mouth, when she suddenly stopped and looked their way. They had not moved, not called to her or anything, yet she'd sensed them somehow. Surely, Adam was kidding about killing her. Although, judging from his anger, who could tell?

Miles kicked a rock from his path and turned to go inside. He wasn't going to stand in his front yard and watch them holler at each other. He got enough of that when he visited the *Sentinel* office.

He sighed and tried to conjure up a way to tell Kath her dinner party might be in a little trouble.

"Charlie Whitney! Godammit, you had better come out right now!" Adam slapped a cornstalk from his path. He was going to kill her. He really was this time. If only he could have stayed on horseback. Oh, she would be his then. As if what she had done to the editorial was not enough, now he was practically crawling through Miles' cornfield, while she hid from him like a child.

The absolute impertinence of the woman.

Just when he thought he might not find her, she stepped in front of him, emerging from the corn like an apparition in the middle of the desert.

Her eyes, a bit wild, met his. She took a deep breath and stood before him as brave as a soldier.

He reached her in three long strides, his hands going to her shoulders, shaking her. Her hair whipped around them. "Why, Charlie? Why did you do it?"

"Because . . . because, I wanted . . . I wanted it to be free one more time."

"Wanted what to be free?" He stopped shaking her, but his hands stayed, holding her tight. She squirmed and tried to pull away. He did not release her.

"The *Sentinel*. I wanted to show both sides of an issue, just this time." She searched his face with that compelling blue gaze. "Can't you understand?"

"You would be dismissed for this at any other newspaper. You must know that."

"Dismiss me, then." She flung the words at him, daring him with a quick tilt of her eyes.

He blinked, his mood growing darker with each second that passed between them. He knew he should follow Miles' advice. Cool off. Leave her alone.

Later, he would wonder why she did it, but she chose that exact moment to lean into him. It was the slightest movement, barely a movement at all, really. But he noticed, and he accepted it.

"What do you want from me?" He did not let her answer as he drew her to him. He dropped his head, seizing her lips with his, his hands tightening upon her shoulders. She sighed and lifted her arms to his neck. *If this is what you want, Charlie, I am willing.*

Making good on the threat, he stroked his tongue against her lips. Perhaps surprising both of them, she opened to him without hesitation. He wavered for a moment, then melted into her, slanting his head to capture her mouth as deeply as he could. She followed his lead, brushing her tongue along his lower lip. Groaning low in his throat, he gentled the kiss until he could feel every nudge of her body against his. Hear every breath escape her mouth, her nose. Taste sugar and lemon upon her lips, her tongue.

He lifted his head and inhaled the sweet scent of corn, earth, roses . . . *her.* His hands slid into her thick hair, tilting her head back. He wanted to touch every inch of her. Suck and lick her warm skin. He skimmed his lips down, nibbling the tender area along her neck. He considered settling her to the ground and shucking her clothes off as smoothly as he could shuck the ear of corn lying by his feet.

Oh, how he wanted to end the frustration, the pressure that had been building since the first *moment* he set eyes on her. As if she agreed, she moved her hips against him, her legs trapped between his. Stifling a groan, he sucked her skin between his teeth and bit down gently. She must not know what she was doing to him—how her movements were affecting him. He swelled a little more as he imagined her naiveté.

Only, another part of his brain reminded: This is not Marilyn, Chase. Charlie is likely a virgin.

He sighed and tensed, sliding his hands to her shoulders.

"No, don't stop," she pleaded and slithered her palms down his back. She rolled her head along his arm and slowly opened her eyes. Their gazes locked. She lifted her hands to his face, running her fingers into his hair. He could feel the vein in his temple beating a brisk tempo beneath her palm. He watched helplessly as her lids drifted shut. She pulled his head down, capturing his bottom lip with her teeth. Then, she sucked it into her mouth like a hungry dog. It was a trick he thought he had taught her.

"Jesus," he said, his voice hoarse, weak. He stumbled as he brought his hand around her back. She was going to drive him mad. She was trying to. He just needed to walk away. Instead, he twisted, leaning down to kiss her again.

This kiss was a frantic joining, a turbulent exchange of desire and longing. He was too far gone to be gentle. Too deep, too tangled in the web of passion he felt for her.

He pulled his lips from hers, raining kisses along her cheek, her neck. He was moving lower. She was putting up no borders to stop him. With his hands and his lips, he was seducing her. The lemon scent of her hair—the sweet sugar upon her lips, the soft press of her breasts against his chest—was seducing him as well.

"I need you," he murmured as he brought his hand to her breast. He touched her, a light touch. As he had dreamed, her firm roundness fit his palm perfectly. She was terrifying and so damn good.

"I need you." Did he say that again? The words filtered to his mind, and he paused, blinking hard as he gazed at her. After a moment, she flipped her eyes open, her breath rasping from her throat. He felt disconcerted, as if he had just woken up in a room he had never seen.

His heated stare traveled from his hand, still lying upon her breast, to her face, her lips. His gaze lingered there. He cursed beneath his breath and flung his arms from her, so abruptly he stumbled, just barely able to right himself.

Chase, what have you *done?*

a moment, she flipped her eyes . . . her breath rising from her throat. He looked . . . . . . had just swept out in

Chapter Nineteen

It was the first clumsy, undisciplined movement she had ever seen him make. He quickly gained control, though, and whirled around, walking a few feet from her. She drew a deep breath, hoping the embarrassing panting noises she was making would end soon. She could see his sides expanding and contracting, lifting his back up and down. He was breathing as hard as she. She watched his hands clench into fists at his sides. As if he was alone, he tilted his head back to stare at the sky.

She wanted to go to him, but her mind and body did not seem to be working together at this point. It was all very peculiar what was happening to her. The sensations in her face vacillated between tingling and pulsing with her heartbeat, and stinging and itching from the chafing Chase's beard had given her. Her breasts felt heavy and full, which they weren't. And between her . . . between her legs, she was on fire and doing a slow melt. It was the most extraordinary, most *indescribable* sensation. With a newly acquired clarity, she understood how men and women could act so strangely if this was the result.

"You are turning me inside out . . . driving me crazy."

She snapped her gaze to him. She swallowed and sucked in a gasp of air. "I don't know what I'm doing. You're the one who's experienced at this . . ." She shrugged for lack of a precise definition.

He sighed and moved his arms. She knew, without being able to see, that he was rubbing the scar on his hand. "I do not know about that," he whispered.

She searched the maturing darkness. For the first time, she noticed how disheveled he looked. He had on a black shirt she had not seen before. It was sweat-stained, wrinkled and dusty. His hair, which was shorter due to a recent haircut, was flipping about at odd angles. His hat lay on the ground; it must have gotten knocked off at some point. There was a large footprint stamped square in the middle of it.

She fought a sudden wave of guilt. Had she upset him? *Was* she twisting him inside out, like he'd said?

He glanced over his shoulder, avoiding her eyes, but said nothing, only looked away again. He began to walk, fading into the cornstalks and darkness.

She dashed forward, reaching and grabbing his hat as she passed it. "Wait!" Her words only seemed to increase his pace. She caught him, only she had to run alongside him to keep up with his long strides. "Can we talk about this?"

He grabbed his hat from her hands with such force that she jumped. She guessed that meant "no."

They left the cornfield. Adam stalked directly to Taber, who nickered at his approach. In a precise, militaristic manner, he took hold of the reins, propelled his foot into the stirrup, braced his knee against Taber's flank and pushed up, swinging his leg smoothly over the horse. Charlie felt her toes curl with hunger as she watched his lithe movements.

"Where are you going?"

Ignoring her question, he twisted in the saddle, and flipped open his saddlebag, searching. He tossed something to her. It landed in the dirt at her feet. Without a word, he clicked his heels and trotted off.

Feeling battered much like a ship upon the sea, she watched him until he was a small, bouncing dot in the distance. When she could no longer see him, she knelt upon the ground. A book. She glanced at it, but it was too dark to read the title. Her heart still raced. And her mouth felt as dry as the morning after Kath's engagement party, when she drank too much and had to be carried home.

Hellfire. Amidst all the confusion, she had forgotten to ask him about the bruise on his face.

Miles rode into town, the steady motion of his horse's gait making him sleepy. Useless, he knew. The way things were going tonight, his head wouldn't hit a pillow for hours yet. In the back of his mind, he wondered if having friends was worth all this trouble. First, he'd had to escort a silent, brooding Charlie home. And now—at nearly eleven o'clock at night— he was on his way to find Adam. Kath had pleaded with him, telling him their friend was in some kind of trouble.

Miles pulled on the reins, directing his horse to the hitching post just past the *Sentinel* office. He slid from the saddle and glanced about, not wanting any questions about what he was doing in town this late. No sounds except for the muted racket from the Four Leaf met his ears.

A gentle breeze ruffled his hair as he tapped lightly on the office door. He'd never felt the need to knock before, and he couldn't quite put his finger on it; but something wasn't right. There was no reply to his knocking, so he pushed the door open just enough to stick his head in. The front room was empty, except for shadows from the oil lamp dancing upon the walls. Surely, Adam wouldn't have left that lit if he went home. Why, it could fall and burn the whole town down around their ears.

Miles put his shoulder into the door, shoving it open. The faint rattle of glass panes and his footsteps thumping against the plank floor rang in the silence. He halted in the middle of the room as another sound reached his ears. Frowning, he tilted his head toward the back room. What the hell was going on?

"Adam?" He walked a step or two. "Are you in here?"

A loud thud, followed by a whispered curse, shattered the stillness. Miles did not go any farther. He was starting to suspect he had walked in on a *private* situation. Then, a woman's throaty, nervous giggle confirmed it. Miles swallowed and backed in the direction of the door. "I'll be leaving now. I just wanted to check to see, uh . . . goodbye!" He swung around.

"Why run now?"

Miles winced at Adam's derisive tone. He stopped and turned, an embarrassed smile on his face. Adam's activity in the back room was apparent in the tangled condition of his hair and, most especially, in the smear of bright red rouge smudged across his cheek. His shirt was unbuttoned halfway down, which was usual, but a lower button was in the wrong hole, giving the cloth an odd bulge over his stomach. Miles glanced away as he felt his face getting hot.

"Honey, do you want to meet my friend?"

Miles marched to Adam, holding up his hand. "I've . . . I've got to go. Kath was the one who wanted me—"

"Come on, sweetie." Adam's tone was remarkably cooperative.

"Let me get freshened up," a soft voice called from the back room. A giggle followed the statement. "You have to give a girl some time, you know."

Adam smiled at Miles. A hostile smile. "Oh, I know, honey. Believe me, I know."

Miles swallowed and took a step back, inching closer to the door, then glanced back as a woman sauntered into the room. She was pretty, if a bit cheap-looking. Thankfully, Miles didn't recognize her. He watched Adam smile at her, calm as could be. And she smiled back, like they were meeting for the first time at a picnic or something. Miles was the only one suffering any kind of embarrassment. What went on in big cities to make a man this . . . *worldly?*

The woman stopped as she reached Adam, laying her small hand upon his arm. Miles stared at her nails, painted as bright red as her lips, and even longer than the girls' in the Four Leaf. He couldn't stop himself from looking. Brown hair, whitish streaks running through it, hung like wet straw past her shoulders. A blue dress clung to her like a second skin, except across her bosom, where mostly real skin showed.

As he continued to stare, she lifted on her toes, placing her lips against Adam's ear. Her soft whisper floated to Miles, though he didn't understand the words.

Adam smiled, but shook his head. "No this one is *in love.*" He gritted the last two words as if a sour lemon was attached. "With his wife, no less."

She looked at Miles again, her eyes glittering, her smile in place. "Too bad." She shrugged, released Adam's arm and walked to Charlie's desk. Her small green reticule sat upon a pile of papers. As ridiculous as it was, somehow this made Miles angry, that Adam would involve Charlie's desk in this mess. Couldn't she have left her bag somewhere else? He glared at Adam, who did not seem to notice.

"Do you want me to walk you back to the Four Leaf?" Adam asked.

She shook her head. "No, my husband is there. Playing cards. He'll probably be at it all night, but he might be wondering where I got off to. His brother lives here. We're visiting, you know, and all they ever do is drink and play cards." She shrugged again, as if she had long ago resigned herself to her situation. "I wish I was staying longer, but we're leaving tomorrow on the two o'clock stage."

She leaned and kissed Adam's cheek. "It was fun." She glanced at Miles, obviously noting his angry expression. "Don't be mad at your friend, honey. A man has to have fun. And, so do *some* women." She laughed then and waved as she departed through the open door, her reticule playing a tune against her shapely thigh.

The men were silent a moment. Neither moved, only Miles angrily tapped his foot. "You're fightin' this like hell, aren't you?" Miles finally asked.

Adam turned to face him. "I do not remember calling you Mama lately."

Miles threw up his arms. "Hell, I don't care who you choose to carouse with, but in the office? What if Charlie had come here tonight? With that woman's bag sittin' on her desk? And that woman's husband just down in the Four Leaf?"

Adam made no comment. He walked to his desk, squatted on his haunches and pulled open a bottom drawer, lifting two glasses and a bottle of dark whiskey to the desk. "Want a drink?"

Miles nodded and pulled a chair over, throwing himself into it with a sigh.

Adam stood and slid into his own chair, silent, watchful. He poured them a generous amount and settled back against the soft, worn leather. Taking a slow sip, he turned his gaze toward the ceiling. It was a long moment before he spoke. "Why are you so angry? You did not get caught with, excuse the expression, *your* trousers down."

Miles laughed, embarrassed yet intrigued. He supposed it was the man in him. He coughed, not because he needed to, but because he was nervous. "Did you have your trousers down?"

Adam rolled the glass between his hands, his gaze still plastered to the ceiling. "A gentleman never tells."

"Ah."

Adam twisted and picked up a newspaper from the small table behind his desk. It landed in front of Miles. "Take a gander at that."

Miles glanced down, a headline leaping at him: *New Bank Legislation—Wrongful Preparation for Succession?* He scanned the page slowly. When he finished, he lifted his gaze. Adam was refilling his glass, his hand shaking ever so slightly. Miles considered telling Adam he'd had enough to drink for one day. No, that might not go over so well.

"What do you think?"

Miles rubbed his hand over his jaw, weary and confused. "Am I mistaken in thinking Stokes is going to be mad as hell when he sees this?"

"No, you are not mistaken." Adam laughed—a short, hard laugh. "But, by God, it is the best she has ever written." He sighed. "Hot-tempered, stubborn, strong. And talented."

"What are you going to do?"

Adam rested his head against the chair and closed his eyes. "Just the question I keep asking myself. Who knows. I am tempted to telegraph Stokes in Richmond, explain how this happened. Make up some reasonable excuse. I will take full responsibility. Charlie does not need to be involved."

"She wrote the piece and placed it without tellin' you?"

Adam nodded, his eyes still closed. "Miles, she does not have any idea how dangerous this business is. Partly my fault for protecting her, I guess. Maybe I did not tell her enough."

Miles emptied his glass and considered asking for another. He was going to kill Kathy for making him do this. "What could you have done?"

Adam rubbed his eyes, fatigue and frustration visible in the drawn skin around his mouth. "I should have told her about all the times I've spent a night, or a week, in the hospital. A stab wound here, a gunshot wound there. Broken jaw, three broken fingers." He laughed. "Those were only the times they caught me."

Miles leaned forward in his chair. "You don't think, I mean, that won't happen here, will it?"

He shrugged. "Until I talk with Stokes, I want Charlie out of here. This is the only place they would know to find her. I was going to tell her at dinner . . ."

Adam's words drifted off as his eyes opened. He stared long and hard at the cracked, whitewashed ceiling.

"What happened tonight?" Miles asked.

Adam's gaze skated to his, then away. "What are you talking about?"

Miles scooted forward until his stomach smashed against the desk. "I'm talkin' about comin' in here, findin' you in the back room with some woman, after you and Charlie have an argument in my cornfield."

Adam settled his gaze on Miles. "Who said we were arguing?"

"Well, what were you doing, then?" When Miles could see his friend wasn't going to talk, he decided to try a different path. Adam sure was a tough nut to crack. "You know what the men in town are sayin'?"

Adam's gaze grew dark. "It does not matter what anyone says."

"For you, no, it doesn't."

Adam sat forward, slamming his glass upon the desk so hard Miles glanced at it to make sure it hadn't broken. "What would you have me do, marry her?"

Miles sat back in his chair, relieved the conversation was finally going somewhere. "If you want to, I think that's a fine idea."

"I do not want marriage. To anyone," Adam said through clenched teeth.

"Are you sure?"

Why did Miles have to come after him tonight of all nights? The little piece of fluff in that clinging blue dress might have solved some of his problems. As it was, all he got to do was fondle her breasts a bit. And the whole time, all he could think of was how well Charlotte Whitney fit his palm, how perfectly her body fused with his.

Would he have been able to finish what he had started with that woman? He had doubts. Doubts he was not about to share with Miles Lambert. The meddlesome bastard.

"I do not want to get married," he reiterated.

He heard Miles chuckle. "She's gotten to you, though?"

Adam grunted, as he stood and crossed the room.

"Is it true what the men are sayin' about you and Tom?"

Adam took a vicious swipe at the dirty window. "Jesus, you just will not give up. Like a goddamn old woman."

"I'm only tryin' to be a good friend. Give you a little advice."

Another grunt.

"Well?"

Adam abandoned his inspection of the dirty window. He walked to the press and began lifting stacks of newspapers bound with string to the floor. The rest, including the copies sent by stagecoach to Stokes' office in Richmond, had left the office earlier today. Too late to stop the damn thing.

Sometimes, life had a strange way of twisting and turning.

"If these men you speak of were saying Tom Walker came into the *Sentinel* office one night, as pickled as a beet, spewing a lot of immaterial nonsense and stamping his foot"—Adam dropped a bundle to the floor and nodded—"then yes, I would have to say your gossip is accurate."

"What kind of nonsense?"

"What do you think? The same nonsense *you* have been spewing."

"Seems like quite a few of us are spewin' that same nonsense. Strange, ain't it?"

Adam glanced up, his dark gaze holding Miles'. "Charlie is my friend. End of story." Same thing he had told Tom. "That is all we can be." He looked to the stack of newspapers on the floor.

"Because you're leavin'?"

"Yes."

"You could take her with you. She doesn't have anyone here."

"You do not understand."

"I guess I don't."

He did not have an explanation he wanted to share, not this close to the time when he would be sleeping. The dreams would come too easily if he talked about it now. He spoke anyway. "I . . . I had a family once. I lost them. A long time ago—" He pushed his hand through his hair. It shook as he lowered it to the cold metal press. "You are my friend. The first one I have had in a long time. I want to talk to you. I wish I knew how." He squeezed his eyes shut. "I have not loved anyone in years, Miles. *Years*. That part of me is gone. It died with my family as surely as there is a God." He laughed, and leaned forward with his arms outstretched, his palms flat on the press. *"I want her,* Miles. Sometimes so much that I literally quake with it. That kind of wanting is not love. You're a man, you know that. At the same time, I like her too much to push her away."

Miles appeared in front of him, holding a glass filled to the lip. The dark liquor sloshed onto Miles' hand and the floor. He placed the glass in Adam's hand before he spoke. "Drink this. I've not known a man to need a drink more than you do right now."

Lifting his head, Adam drained the glass in one swallow.

"Another?"

Adam shook his head. "Mrs. Wilkin is ready to throw me out. I cannot come stumbling in on tottery feet tonight. When she got a good look at my face the other night after Tom—" He shook the glass in the air. "As bad as living with my mother."

Adam glanced back out the window, into the night. "I don't want what I have told you to go any farther. I know I probably do not have to say that." He shrugged, then added, "I do not want to hurt her, but I cannot give her any more than I have. Hell, I need to give her less."

"That may be easier said than done."

"Yeah."

Miles turned toward the door, his shoulders slumped. He paused, turned back. "My pa wanted me to tell you he's comin' in early to finish the deliveries. Said he didn't want to hear any of your bitchin' about them sittin' around all day."

Adam smiled. "I may be here when he arrives. I don't feel like going home."

"Do you want me to get a message to Charlie, tell her to stay home tomorrow?"

"No. Better do that in person. Besides, Stokes will not receive the *Sentinel* for another day or two. By then, I'll have a plan."

Miles stopped by the door. "Let me know."

"Good night." Adam walked to the window and watched Miles untie his horse, climb astride and ride down the deserted street.

Tomorrow. Tomorrow, he would tell Charlie. Damn, his head ached just thinking about it.

Chapter Twenty

Gerald rubbed his eyes, trying to concentrate on the road in front of him. His feet felt heavy as lead, but then, he had just left a warm bed. If he finished the deliveries early, he could go home before noon. The copies that went to Columbia and Charleston had gone with the stage yesterday. Oliver Stokes' copies had gone then, too. Mr. Whitefield still needed his copies, and all the businesses in town needed theirs.

Continuing to peruse his mental list, he turned left onto Main Street. He enjoyed getting up early. The calm, solid darkness just before dawn was enchanting. The crickets and frogs were sleeping, the stars not as bright as the sun was just beginning to steal the sky. It was a dull kind of darkness, but nonetheless, he liked it. He heard a rooster crowing somewhere and thanked the good Maker that he didn't have to put up with one of those harassing beasts. He'd never wanted to be a farmer. Not for a minute. How his only son, his only child, had felt the pull of that calling was one of the great mysteries of life.

Laughing to himself, he pulled his key from his pocket. Adam had taken to locking the office door. His boss was a city man, and Gerald knew he couldn't teach an old dog new tricks. Of course, it made Adam feel better, like everything was tied up safe and sound when he went to sleep at night. All the better then. The boy didn't get enough sleep as it was. Gerald told him that often.

Adam and Miles were so close in age; hell, Gerald was old enough to be the boy's father. And, like an old dog. . . .

His heart jumped when he stepped onto the boardwalk. The *Sentinel's* door was standing wide open. He crossed the short distance in three brisk strides. What was the meaning of this?

He rushed inside, but pulled to an abrupt standstill, his eyes rounding. His gaze swept past it all: papers on the floor, ripped and torn; Adam's desk on its side, the new inkwell Gerald had purchased yesterday sitting beside it in two large pieces; a puddle of black ink congealing under it. One more stain to add to the others. He turned. The press.

He raced to it, running his hands along the smooth metal surfaces. The cylinders looked to be intact, the racks of lead type undisturbed. The newspapers he'd left on the press were now on the floor. Gerald walked around and squatted, groaning as his bad knee popped. The newspapers, some still bound with string, others gaping like a raw wound, had been slashed, purposely destroyed. Why had they left the press alone? He pushed himself to his feet. It was going to be a long day. A long week.

He didn't quite know what to do. Clean up as much as he could and get a message to Adam? Thank the Maker the boy had gone home. He had gone home, hadn't he?

Gerald strode to the back room. It was empty apart from a blue hair ribbon, obviously one of Charlie's, lying on the floor. Swiveling around, he ran to her desk, shoved tight against the wall. He wiped his hand over his eyes. The more he looked at this mess, the more it looked to him like a disagreement had taken place in this office. Overturned desks, scattered papers.

Overturned desks. As a sinking feeling crept into his stomach, he walked cautiously behind the desk. The tall side stood maybe three feet off the floor. Sure enough, Adam lay next to it, on his side, pushed against the wooden legs. That was why Gerald hadn't seen him at first.

Gerald felt tears prick his eyes, thinking the boy looked lifeless as hell. Dead. *No.* Gerald could see Adam's chest rising and falling beneath a bloody, torn shirt. The shirt had once been black. Now it was a deep, dark red.

He stooped and rolled Adam onto his back as gently as he could. Gerald sucked in a sharp breath as he got a look at the boy's face, covered with blood, although his nose didn't appear broken. A wide ring of purple, the skin swollen and bruised, surrounded one eye. Gerald lifted a clump of matted hair lying like a limp rag on Adam's forehead. A nasty gash that was more than likely the source of the blood lay open, jagged. Blood seeped from it, trailing down Adam's face in a thin flow.

Gerald skimmed efficient hands along Adam's arms and legs. Performing the simple examination was second nature. With a doctor as suspect as Doc Olden, the people of Edgemont had become self-sufficient.

Gerald released a sigh of relief as he began opening the buttons on Adam's shirt; although, as he got a good look at Adam's chest, he saw a couple of enormous bruises that meant cracked ribs at the very least. The knuckles on Adam's right hand were bruised and swollen, as well. Gerald grunted. Good. The boy had given as good as he got.

Gerald rose to his feet, hoping they had fresh water in the office. Charlie usually kept a pitcher filled. He grabbed a clean rag and the pitcher from a small table. It was full. He hurried back to Adam, who lay as still as calm waters.

"I hope that bash in the head wasn't too hard." Gerald had never known someone to not wake up—although sometimes a day or two went by before they did—but he had heard of cases where people never did. Or when they did they couldn't even remember their own name. Shaking his head, he got on his knees, placing the pitcher beside him on the floor. He dipped the rag into the water and smoothed it over Adam's face. Blood immediately soaked the cloth, coloring it a pale pink. He hesitated, then pressed the rag against the gash on Adam's forehead.

Adam stirred slightly and moaned.

"Adam?"

Another moan.

Gerald dipped the rag again, squeezing the cloth over the pitcher. He ran it along Adam's chin and neck. So much blood. Gerald had raised a rambunctious, always-injured son, but . . . head wounds. Oh, so much blood. He turned and gasped, drawing a deep, clear breath.

"Do not go . . . retching . . . on me . . . old man."

Gerald whipped his head around. Adam's dark eyes were open, just barely. Pain twisted his face, but he was conscious. "Just rest easy." He touched the damp rag to Adam's cheek. "Everything will be all right."

Adam swallowed, his mouth opening then closing. He tried again. "Charlie."

Gerald frowned. "Charlie isn't here."

Adam closed his eyes and swallowed again. His voice was so faint that Gerald had to lean down to hear his words. "I know. Go . . . go check on her. They might . . . might have gone there."

"What?"

Adam lifted his hand, then let it drop to the floor. "Just go," he breathed.

Gerald jumped up, nearly spilling the pitcher of water. "I'll be back as soon as I can get to her place and back. Will you be all right?"

Adam closed his eyes, too exhausted to reply. He heard Gerald's rapid footsteps, then the slam of the door. He *would* be all right. His face felt battered and misshapen; his body ached beyond belief. God, his chest. It felt like someone had beaten a hammer against it. That was not far from the truth. Boots, hammers, what the hell was the difference? The only redeeming pain he felt was the pain in his hand. He curled it as far as he could into a fist. Due to his swollen fingers, that did not amount to much. He had fought pretty well. For two against one, anyway. It had come back to him as easily as riding a bike.

Fortunately, he had been in the back room when they came in. He was looking for an edition of the *Charleston Mercury* Charlie had stored in her files. The only problem with her filing system was, she was the only one who could find anything. Some system. He had been searching, digging, dust flying, wholeheartedly wishing he was sleepy. The front door opening had not startled him. Gerald, maybe, or another late night visit from Tom Walker.

When he walked out of the room, the men's backs were to him. Another lucky thing. Obviously, they thought they were alone. As Adam watched, one of them—the taller of the two—

pulled a knife from his boot and began slashing the newspaper bundles stacked upon the floor. Adam waited, watching the tall one finish and resheath his knife.

"You two certainly showed up sooner than I expected, I can tell you that."

They spun around. Adam catalogued everything, recognizing the opportunity as a brief one. Size, stance, facial features, clothing. He could identify them if he ever saw them again. He had no doubt. And, except for the knife in the tall one's boot, they looked unarmed. Although, there was no telling what else a boot or pocket concealed.

Obviously, Stokes questioned the *Sentinel* operation enough to have men watching. Men close enough to receive copies of the newspaper and come calling in less than twenty-four hours.

Perhaps, Stokes had miscalculated and not expected many problems from such a small press, because these men appeared to be out of their element, sneaking into an office in the middle of the night. They did not look like thugs. Hell, they looked like sons of his father's contemporaries, only dressed a little less formally. Their expressions were not vicious, either. Merely surprised.

"Could you explain to me why you are using that knife on my newspapers?"

The shorter one—who was still a rather tall man, if a bit on the skinny side—took a step forward. "Who are you?"

Adam leaned calmly against the doorjamb. His chances of escaping this predicament without injury were very slim indeed. If he did not excite them too much, maybe he could get some information before the melee began. "Seems to me, the one breaking and entering should answer the questions."

The tall one scowled at his friend. "Harry, there's only the three of them that work here. One's a goddamn woman, the other an old man. Who the hell do you think this is?" His accent was southern, but he sounded more like a Virginian than a South Carolinian. These men were probably Stokes' personal boot lickers.

Harry took another step forward. "We just came to issue a warning, Mr. Chase."

"A warning from whom?"

Harry smiled. "I don't think you need to worry about that.

Just don't print any more editorials like that bank legislation one. People are bound to get mighty upset. And, when people get upset"—he shrugged—"things tend to happen." Harry had blue eyes, a bit on the pale side. Weak eyes, but they didn't waver from Adam's as he added, "You've got a very vulnerable staff, Mr. Chase. An old man and a woman."

Adam lifted off the doorjamb. "If my staff receives so much as the touch of a raindrop, the person who caused it will be very sorry. I promise you that."

"Are you threatening us? Harry, he's threatening us." The tall one was starting to get angry. His fists were clenched, his mouth tight. He moved up against Harry, who looked calm and in control.

"Shut up, will you?" Harry said to him.

Adam tapped his finger against his lips. "Interesting name. Harry. And from Virginia, from the sound of it. That is all *very* interesting."

Now, Harry was mad, too.

"Mr. Chase, you're not very smart, are you?"

Adam shrugged. "Whatever you say, Harry. Give Stokes a message for me. You tell that bastard to come to me if he has a problem with the way this newspaper is being operated. I do not appreciate interference or advice. Sending you two is as effective as sending a runny nose."

"Why, you—"

Adam knelt, yanking his knife from his boot. He slashed it across Harry's arm as the man closed in on him. Harry released a bellow of rage and pain. Adam wanted them to go to Stokes with a scar or two. A better message than any he could vocalize.

The tall one paused, his glance jumping between Adam's face and the knife gripped in his steady hand. "Take care of him," Harry yelled, while holding his arm awkwardly against his side. Blood flowed down his wrist, over his hand and fingers.

The man Adam now suspected was a bulwark of sorts did not hesitate. Like a trained bull, he charged, heedless of the knife clutched in Adam's hand. Adam jumped to the side, the bull slamming into his shoulder. Adam steadied himself and flipped the knife to his other hand. He brought it up and around, piercing the tough skin at the back of the bull's neck. It was a superficial wound; he did not want to kill the guy, just slow him down. The bull lifted his hand to his neck, and Adam took the opportunity. He raised his knee, slamming it into his opponent's groin. The man dropped to his knees like a rock.

Adam walked toward Harry, who was glancing about, his eyes wide and alarmed. The situation had obviously gotten far beyond his control. Adam threw the knife to the floor and swung his fist as hard as he could, knocking Harry right off his feet. Harry landed on the floor with a thud. Adam realized his mistake when he heard a sound behind him.

He had turned his back on the bull.

The bull grabbed him by the shoulders, twisted him around and threw a solid fist into his face. Bright, white stars exploded behind Adam's eye; a slow pulsing commenced. Adam staggered, nearly falling over Harry, who lay stock-still on the floor like a sack of flour.

The bull came right back at him, but Adam ducked the punch and threw one of his own. The blow rocked the man's head back, and for a moment Adam imagined escaping with his face intact. Luck was not with him: he backed right into the press.

Before he could move out of the way, the bull threw another punch he could not block, and Adam ended up on the floor. He tried to pick himself up, but the bull made up for his lack of intellectual deftness with physical agility. He got to Adam first. That was around the time, Adam assumed, his head connected with his desk. He recalled rolling with the desk, coming to rest behind it. Then he blacked out. He supposed he had Harry's boots to thank for the pain in his chest. The spineless bastard.

God. Charlie was going to come running in here at any moment, and although he was not sure he could do it, he wanted to at least be sitting up when she arrived. His face felt warm and sticky. He almost smiled as he imagined what Gerald must have thought upon seeing him. That he was dead for sure.

He lifted his head. His brain felt as though it were expanding and contracting with every breath. Did the bull have to throw him into a desk, for Christ's sake? Adam groaned and tried to pull himself up, but it was no use. Tears filled his eyes as his head fell back. He gasped a full, painful breath. Blackness swirled, gradually taking him with it.

Chapter Twenty-One

"Jared Chase," she said, her breath brushing against his skin, "what have I gotten us into?" She pressed the wet cloth to his face.

He inhaled, then whispered, "Roses."

She didn't utter so much as a squeak; she couldn't just yet. His voice was so ragged. Blood smeared all over him, his lovely skin torn and bruised. She felt like she was suffocating, each breath painful. It was nothing compared to the pain he was feeling. "Gerald, where do you suppose Doc Olden is?"

"I don't know. Miles is trying to find him." Gerald sighed. "Good Lord . . . all this blood on the floor. And a knife. They brought a knife."

Charlie turned in Gerald's direction. "A knife? They were playing for keeps, weren't they?" Tears pricked her eyelids. She hadn't felt like crying in a long time.

"The knife . . . mine."

She jerked around. "That knife . . . that knife is *yours?*"

He nodded the tiniest bit, then grimaced from the effort.

She grimaced with him. "Do you want to sit up?"

"Yes." He bent his arms, placing his palms flat against the floor, then closed his eyes and pushed. She placed her hand at his back and helped him. He scooted back, leaning feebly against the wall. He swallowed and reached up to touch his chest with his fingers. "Goddamn."

She sat next to him, wringing her hands and chewing on her lip. "Do you want a glass of water?"

"No, but . . . I have whiskey. In . . . my desk. Bottom drawer."

She pursed her lips, refusing to reply. She lifted to her feet and opened the drawer, which she had to pull up because the desk lay on its side. A small, leather-covered flask was there, the same one he had placed in her hands the day of the picnic. She caught the canister in her hand, noticing for the first time the letter *E* burned into the casing. Could this be Eaton's?

She felt a frown pull at her mouth as she turned and squatted beside Adam. He had his knees raised, his arms propped on them. His head bowed against his arms. She felt an alarming, sharp pulse of guilt and concern rush through her. She had done this to him as surely as if she had thrown the punches.

"Here," she murmured, trying to keep the tremor from her voice. She touched the flask to his calf.

He raised his head slowly, blinked at her once, then let his gaze drift as he took the flask from her outstretched hand. He screwed the top off and tilted his head back. She watched his throat constrict as he drank.

"Do you think you should be drinking?" She just couldn't hold it in.

"I most . . . certainly do."

"We've called for the doctor—"

"I do not . . . need . . . a doctor."

She gasped. "Of course you do." If he only knew how he looked.

He slanted a shrewd glance her way, the purple ring encircling his eye gleaming as vividly as a radiant sunset. His face did look a bit better—she'd cleaned off much of the blood—but his head still bled, and his clothes were beyond repair. Mrs. Wilkin was going to keel over when she got a look at him.

"How is that . . . old fool going to . . . help me?" His hand shook as he took another drink.

She couldn't argue with the old fool part. She gestured to his head. "After all, you need stitches."

He regarded her with a resigned expression, then laughed. His face paled.

She opened her mouth to tell him how sorry she was. He must have seen the look. "I need to sit . . . outside. I cannot breathe . . . in here. I must look quite . . . frightening."

She couldn't argue with that, either. So, she said nothing, just helped him up. Gerald turned to watch them lumber along, Charlie's hand at Adam's back.

At the door, Adam pushed her away and teetered onto the boardwalk alone. She took a deep breath as tears threatened, pricking angrily behind her eyelids. She didn't know what to say to him. What to do. God, she had made a mess of things. An incredible mess. He had tried to tell her what this business was like. How dangerous it could be. She hadn't believed it; hadn't believed Stokes would operate that way. But he *did* operate that way. Look at what had happened.

Charlie felt a sudden burst of hate and anger ripple through her. She ground her nails into her palms. Oliver Stokes wouldn't get away with this.

Adam sat outside the office, his head drooping until his chin rested upon his chest, his back propped against the paint-chipped plank wall. He held a blood-soaked rag to his forehead. He'd folded his legs beneath him; Indian style, they had called it when they were children.

Miles approached quietly. Not soundlessly, though, stooping and dropping on his rear end beside Adam. Apparently, Miles was not limber, because he kept shifting to find a comfortable position.

"What are you . . . twisting around . . . so much for?"

"I'm not as comfortable sittin' on my rump as you are."

Adam laughed. His hand twisted around his knee. Oh, it hurt to laugh.

There was a long stretch of silence. Finally, Miles asked, "Are you in too deep?"

"Regarding . . . what?" Adam shot back. "Her"—he tilted his head in an abrupt, painful motion toward the office—"or the newspaper?" He grimaced as he pressed the rag against his torn skin.

Miles shrugged. "Both, I guess."

"I honestly . . . cannot say." Adam paused, lifting the cloth from his head. He began turning it round and round between his fingers, absorbed in the light pink mix of blood and water that dripped to the ground between his feet. "All of this . . . is certainly more . . . than I bargained for. I can tell you . . . that much."

"Jared."

He pivoted at the sound of his name, paying for the hasty movement with a searing shaft of pain that nearly cut his brain in two. Charlie stood in the doorway, looking anxious and timid. So unlike her. Did she know what it did to him to hear that name coming from anyone, especially her? It made him sad and weak, and sick inside. *Jared.* He had made a mistake telling her any of it.

Turning back, he squeezed the rag in his fist, a puddle of bloody liquid pooling between his boots.

Miles pushed to his feet with a slight nod to Adam and a small smile to Charlie in answer to her own. His heavy footfalls reverberated against the plank boardwalk, the sound straying as he entered the *Sentinel* office.

Charlie stood looking at Adam—her gaze dug like a needle in his back. She ignored reticence and settled beside him, in the spot Miles had just vacated. He looked at her then with a slight tilt of his head, then sighed and returned to his inspection of the bloody rag.

She looked a mess, disheveled and dirty, his blood staining the bodice of her plain, blue shirtwaist. He felt a tremor of riotous fear course through him. Fear not for himself but for the woman sitting beside him. Fear that what she had done— a stupid, naive, careless act—would bring her grief. More than he had been brought. He knew well enough what had happened here would not intimidate Stokes. It was only likely to make him angry.

She curved her head, staring at his fingers as they pressed the bloody cloth, again and again. He felt her gaze follow his hand as he lifted it to wipe a fresh trickle of blood that was running down his face.

"Oh, Jared—"

His hand shot out, his blood-slick fingers encircling her wrist. "No. Do not call me that!"

Her expression was contrite. He looked down, glancing at the small wrist completely enclosed by his strong grasp. He dropped her hand as if it were a hot coal.

"I'm sorry," she said.

He laughed, the sound hard and cold even to his own ears. "You would be." His breath hitched as a sharp stab of pain twisted through him.

"What is that supposed to mean?"

"I suppose you . . . would rather . . . have taken that beating. For journalistic . . . integrity? For the good of . . . the *Sentinel?*" He released a harsh, aching breath.

Charlie stared at him. "Why—"

He cut her short. "Is any of . . . that blood yours?"

She glanced at the front of her dress. "Of course not."

He only grunted.

The silence hardened between them. They had just been getting back to being friends. The kiss last night in Miles' cornfield had blown that to pieces. Once again, the longing and wonder they had been trying to bury lived.

"Did anyone . . . come to your house?"

She traced her finger in a crack in the wood. "My house?"

"For God's sake . . . Charlie. Did they come . . . to your house?"

"They?" She looked at him, her eyes wide and probing. "The men who . . . did this to you?" She shook her head, sable hair flying. "No. Oh, no!"

He nodded. That did not mean they would stay away.

"I'm sorry."

"Stop saying . . . that." He swallowed. "Had . . . worse."

"I'm sure you have, but not because of me. Not because of an inexperienced reporter's perfectly inane mistake. I should have been the one there. It was my editorial . . . and I placed it there without your—"

He turned on her, grasping her shoulders in his hands. "Shut up." He shook her as his head pounded in a slow, dull rhythm. "You have no idea . . . what they could have done . . . to you. Forget killing you . . . if that is what you are thinking. They could have done things to you . . . worse than death. Do you know . . . did anyone ever . . . oh, hell.''

He released her so quickly that she rocked back. Lifting to his feet with a movement too sudden, he leaned his shoulder against the wall and ran his tongue across dry lips. Black spots swirled in front of his eyes. He gulped a breath, pushed off the wall and began a laggard pace in front of the *Sentinel* office. He could not correct his hesitant, feeble stride.

The sun was just beginning to lighten the sky. He was glad he did not have to sit in the darkness with her anymore. Darkness created some kind of fictitious intimacy. He ground his teeth together and felt a hot flash sweep his face. Fictitious? The time of day had nothing to do with how he felt when she was near. Dammit. He kicked the hitching post anchored outside the office as he passed it, which only served to exaggerate the pain in his head and chest.

Charlie turned on her fanny to face him. The indelicacy of the movement almost forced a smile from him. *Almost.*

"Why are you so mad at me? I know it was thoughtless. I know it was—"

He crouched in front of her, their eyes level. "You know . . . nothing," he wheezed and shook his finger in her face to prove he really meant it. He cautiously lifted to his feet to resume his pacing.

"Would you please sit down. You look like an old drunk on a two-week binge."

"Shut . . . up."

"You shouldn't say that to a lady."

His response was a short, hoarse bark of laughter.

"You know, I'm doing everything I can to make this up to you. Apologies are not accepted, explanations not permitted. What else can I do?" She threw up her hands in surrender.

He sighed. God save him from naive women. "Charlie, do you not realize we are in a hell of a predicament?''

She rubbed her eyes. Obviously exhaustion from the long morning was beginning to set in. "Predicament?''

"Stokes has crossed the . . . line here. I cannot give in to him, be . . . defeated by this. The situation is more . . . volatile than I understood it to be. And, here you are . . . a female reporter . . . right in the thick of it.'' If only he had had more time to think before all this happened.

"It's only because of my editorial. We'll be careful. This won't happen again.''

He stopped pacing and glanced beyond her to the mountain ridges rising in the distance. They sat, dull gray, in the chaste, misty morning light. If only he could be sure of that. Only, he was not sure of anything. Most of all, things connected to Charlie Whitney.

"Charlie, I told you this business was . . . more dangerous than you knew. You are a skilled writer . . . improving every day . . . but you have been . . . so damn sheltered. You had no idea how a real newspaper operated.'' He closed his eyes and drew a deep breath, harnessing his anger, fear and pain. He needed to stay calm. She was just a child in so many ways.

She assumed there was good in people. She reserved her cynicism for town biddies, who did not accept her eccentric ways, and her family, who did not love her for who she was. What did she know of men who tortured and killed to get their way? Men who ruined lives in a single moment.

"What do you want me to do?'' Her voice wavered like a string tossed to the wind.

He opened his eyes and found himself drawn into her beautiful, blue, honest gaze. "I want you to quit.''

"No.''

"Charlie—''

"No. I won't write editorials for a while. I'll show you everything I scribble on a piece of paper, any piece of paper. I'll discuss my ideas before they even hit paper, but I . . . won't . . . quit. You wanted me here. I'm here.''

Her words tore through him and increased his guilt tenfold. She was in jeopardy because he had allowed brilliant, blue eyes, a few passionate kisses and the most innocent, seductive flirtation he had ever encountered to lull him. He had been lulled into thinking her genuine goodness, and the goodness of the people of Edgemont, would make a difference. Lulled into feeling secure and invincible in this small, peaceful setting.

He now understood this town's hatred of Stokes. He turned on his heel and groaned as a sharp pain shot through his chest.

Charlie jumped to her feet. "What's wrong?''

He gasped and leaned weakly against the post. Black blots were floating like clouds before his eyes. He had better tell her. "I think I have . . . a broken rib . . . or two."

"Broken ribs?" she squeaked. "Miles!"

He wanted to tell her to forget it, but he did not know if he could limp back to Mrs. Wilkin's all by himself. Hell, he was not going to be conscious much longer.

Miles came running from the *Sentinel* office quicker than Adam would have thought possible for such a massive man. He had only to look at Adam slumped against the railing to know why Charlie was causing such a commotion. "Back to Mrs. Wilkin's place for you, my friend. Pa!" Miles looped his arm around Adam's back, supporting him under his arms.

Charlie stood by, wringing her hands like an old woman. "Be careful, he thinks a rib or two is broken."

"Son?" Gerald appeared in the *Sentinel* doorway.

"Doc Olden is supposed to be coming by here any minute. Send him to Mrs. Wilkin's place, then close up the office and go home."

Adam shook his head and whispered, "No . . . doctor."

Charlie glared at him. "Shut up."

He glared right back at her as they began to make their way along the street toward Mrs. Wilkin's boardinghouse. Adam choked back a weak grin. It was obvious Miles was trying to ignore the looks he and Charlie cast at each other like sharp daggers.

Before they had even gotten to the steps leading to Mrs. Wilkin's front porch, the old woman was throwing open the door, waving her arms, and proclaiming in a shrill voice, "Oh, oh, what happened here? Mr. Chase, you are injured."

Adam shook his head. He spoke as forcefully as he could. "No, just a slight accident with the . . . printing press. Nothing to . . . concern yourself with." Charlie threw a quick, amazed look at him. He furtively captured her gaze and winked. She blushed and glanced away.

Mrs. Wilkin bustled and motioned. "Be gentle, be gentle. Has anyone called Doc Olden? Not that he'll be fit to see anyone this time of the morning. Oh, my, Mr. Chase, you just work yourself to death." Mrs. Wilkin continued to chatter like a nervous bird as they took him up the stairs. She had practically wrung her pink, lace-trimmed apron off her ample stomach. She turned to Charlie as they reached the first landing. "Charlotte, dear, go fix yourself a cup of coffee. I have some gingerbread on the kitchen table, fresh made." She lowered her voice and whispered behind a curved hand, "It just isn't fitting for you to go inside his bedroom, dear."

Of course, he heard every word.

Obviously he was listening, because Charlie swore she heard a muffled, all-too-male chuckle. Albeit, a weak, pain-filled chuckle. She felt her face flame, but she did as Mrs. Wilkin asked, grumbling as she made her way down the stairs and into the kitchen. A thick block of sunlight lay in the center of the cozy room. Charlie poured a generous cup of coffee and went to stand by a window that looked upon a neat, well-tended garden. Mrs. Wilkin's squash was ready for picking. Her potato patch was already empty, the ground turned and fluffy. She had quite a few nice cucumber plants that for such a small number were producing pretty well. Charlie made a mental note to ask what kind of cucumbers they were; hers hadn't done well this year at all. She took a hesitant sip of coffee, grimacing as she swallowed.

"Too hearty, is it? Mr. Wilkin liked it strong enough to kill fire ants. I guess I got used to it like that, too."

Charlie turned as Mrs. Wilkin bustled to the dry sink. "How . . . how is Mr. Chase?"

Mrs. Wilkin began to wash the meager amount of dirty dishes in a bucket by her dry sink. "Oh, he's in a great deal of pain, I think. I don't know how any accident with a printing press could break your ribs, blacken your eye and cut your head, but it's not any of my business. He's a nice young man, that's all I know; and any trouble he's in, well, I can't help but think it comes from working for Oliver Stokes. Nothing good has ever come from his association with this town, and nothing ever will."

She flipped her dishrag Charlie's way. "You should be careful, too. A young girl, mixed up in all this work business. Never did work when I was your age. It was unheard of. Just not done. I know you're a smart girl, Charlotte. Always have been.

Sometimes, I think you're too smart for your own good. I'm not sure if being too smart helps a person or hinders 'em. Especially a woman.'' She clicked her tongue against her teeth.

Charlie rolled her eyes. A mother hen giving advice. ''Is Doc Olden up there?''

''Oh, yes, he came weaving in just as I was leaving. Making excuses for his red face and bleary eyes. Up late birthing a baby, he said. Posh.''

''Oh.'' Charlie turned back to the window, not really seeing anything, seeing only what she had created in her mind: Men throwing Chase to the ground and hitting him with their thick fists. She shook her head and tried to brush past the twisted feeling lying like stale bread in her gut. ''I'll just wait to see what Doc Olden says; then I'd best be getting home.''

''Of course, dear. As for me, I need to pick my squash. I think I'll make a special dish for Mr. Chase tonight. Hmmm . . .'' She wiped her hands on a frayed, blue dishcloth and walked to the back door. Her ample body swayed and jiggled with her. ''There's some apple pie in the cupboard if you'd like a piece. Gingerbread on the table. Just make yourself at home.'' The slight, wooden screen door slammed behind her. Charlie heard her humming and mumbling to herself as she walked away.

From her place beside the window, Charlie watched Mrs. Wilkin walk to the small area in the garden designated as the squash area, a big wooden basket hanging from her arm, a black and gray cat clinging to her bulky legs. She waited until the old woman had gotten on her knees before she made her move. She looked back once just to make sure. Yes, still on her knees in the dirt. And how fast could the woman make it back in here? Not as fast as Charlie could make it up to Chase's bedroom and back.

She placed her cup in the dry sink and ran from the kitchen. She tiptoed up the stairs leading to the bedrooms, holding her breath for fear someone would hear her. She stopped outside the room she assumed was his. Right one. She could hear Doc Olden's raspy voice droning on as he prescribed bed rest and liquids, no heavy lifting for a month and no horseback riding for two weeks.

''Two weeks . . . off my horse? Are you . . . insane?'' Chase's voice groggy. She wondered what Doc Olden had given him.

"No, Mr. Chase, I am in full control of all my faculties, thank you. You, on the other hand, have cracked ribs and a gash on your head that, if you weren't such a stubborn fool, I'd be stitching up right now. Not to mention the various other abrasions mighty peculiar for a fight with a printing press. But, what do I know? I'm just an old drunkard." She heard Doc Olden snap his bag shut.

"Call me if there are any complications, and for God's sake, keep the bandage around your chest for at least two weeks. Tied tight. Feel free to change it as often as you wish, but keep it on."

Charlie rolled her eyes as Doc Olden finished his tirade. Obviously, Chase was not the most complacent of patients.

"Miles, walk me down, and let's let our injured editor get some sleep. Good day, Mr. Chase."

Charlie jumped behind the corner as they left his room. She heard Chase mumble something about there being no way in hell he'd let a man with such shaky hands stitch up *his* head. She smiled and turned back toward his room as Doc Olden and Miles lumbered down the stairs. She'd found out what she needed to know, now she had to get downstairs before Mrs. Wilkin discovered her duplicity.

As soon as the front door slammed, she crept from her hiding place and skulked past the partially closed door.

"You did not sneak . . . all the way up here . . . just for that . . . did you?"

Charlie stopped cold, expelled a disgusted breath and pushed open the door to his room. She walked straight to his bed, all the while daring him to say more to her than he already had.

He was half sitting, half leaning against the wooden headboard in what she would call a crouched, indisposed crumple. Dr. Olden had tied a thin bandage around his head and a thick, ugly one around his naked chest. She couldn't help noticing the dark hairs that peeked from the top of the glaringly white dressing. Jerking her gaze up, she ran directly into his mocking stare. His white teeth flashed as he smiled, and then he actually had the audacity to laugh—a diluted, painful laugh that nonetheless provoked her.

"Stop it." She shot a quick glance over her shoulder. "Do you want Mrs. Wilkin to come up here and find me?"

He shrugged carefully. "Might be interesting." His head slumped back on the pillow behind his back. Like wax dripping down a melting candle, his words blurred. He looked worn and bruised. He needed sleep.

She leaned and swept her fingers along the side of his face. He closed his eyes as a sigh escaped him. "I'll see you tomorrow, Chase." She turned to leave, her heart thudding in her chest. Oh, how she wanted to stay with him, hold his hand and watch him sleep. Make sure he didn't wake in the night, dreams of his brother tormenting him.

"Charlie?"

Damn. She wanted to keep walking, but his tone of voice was so soft, so different than usual, so . . . *warm.* She couldn't stop herself from swinging halfway round, but she did not retrace her steps to his bed. His eyes were open just enough to distinguish their color. Warm, liquid brown. They shifted to her face; then his head sank back against the pillow.

"The editorial was . . . excellent. Would not have pulled it . . . it was good enough to run. I just wanted . . . you to know." A silly smile crossed his face, as if he had not just given her the most indescribable compliment anyone had ever given her.

Before he could say more to confuse her, she mumbled an abrupt, "Thank you, Chase," and disappeared like a puff of smoke from his doorway.

Chapter Twenty-Two

Charlie stood on her back porch, staring into a dark sky full of sparkling, tiny dots of silver-white. How had her life gotten so tangled with Adam Jared Chase's?

She jumped as something brushed her leg, then laughed as Faustus plopped down at her feet. She stooped to scratch him beneath his chin. "So, someone is lonely tonight? I guess your acquaintances have deserted you. Well, don't let it upset you; they don't really know you." He purred and stretched in response.

When would Chase go back to the *Sentinel* office? Miles had stopped by her house the afternoon of the incident to tell her not to go there alone. That had been two whole days ago. Gerald was staying away until he got word, as well.

She didn't know what it meant—this absence from the office—and she was too big a coward to face Chase again to ask him. With only bandages and a quilt between them, it would be tempting fate. For all she knew, he'd been naked underneath that quilt, which was more than she needed to *imagine*, much less come face-to-face with.

With a final scratch for Faustus, she retraced her steps to the front of the house. As she walked inside, she noticed the aroma of dinner—beef stew and corn bread—still lingered in the small enclosure. She grimaced as she looked at the table, covered with dirty dishes. With a sigh, she picked up a plate and cup and carried them to the dry sink. A knock on the door startled her, and she dropped the cup into the dry sink with a loud clink. Wiping her hands on her apron, she ripped it off and tossed it into a chair before throwing open the door.

"Miles?"

"Charlie. You should ask who it is, before just openin' the door."

She frowned at him. "What *are* you talking about?"

His mouth turned up, somewhere between a smile and a grimace. "I'm sorry. Landsakes, it's just that Adam is worried over this whole"—he waved his hand in the air—"thing."

She moved to the side. "Do you want to come in?"

He eyed her—slightly embarrassed she thought—before glancing away. "Yeah, I'd better come in because . . . you have to pack. To come stay with Kath and me."

"Are you serious?"

He nodded.

"But—"

"Adam is worried. You stayin' here alone right now. I think he has reason to worry. We don't know who did this, or if they're comin' back."

She shook her head, but could not deny the logic of his simple statement. "But . . . my things. I can't . . . what—"

"Miles, is she giving you trouble?" A bellow: from the general vicinity of her yard.

Chase. Charlie's eyes widened, then narrowed.

She turned, her faded brown skirt whipping, and stalked into her bedroom. She cursed as she threw a dress into the scratched, leather case that had been her father's. She'd never really had any use for it before.

Of all the low, domineering—governing her like a child. Who did he think he was?

She closed the case and flipped the clasp with a furious swat, imagining Chase's head inside, then grabbed it from the bed and marched out of the room, out the door. She threw the case into the back of the wagon—adding another dimple to the scarred covering, she was sure—before climbing up to sit against the rough wooden siding. Damn him, anyway.

She didn't turn to look as she heard Miles close up her house.

After a few fruitless, inane attempts—by Miles—at conversation, they rode the mile between the Whitney and Lambert homes in silence.

When the wagon stopped in the Lamberts' front yard, Charlie was prepared for flight. She pulled the case to her side and managed a quite adroit vault from the back of the wagon to the ground.

"Always the lady," Adam muttered.

"She's a pistol, ain't she? Thank heaven Kathy hasn't the stubbornness of that one."

Adam's gaze traveled the distance, through the dark night, to the petite, dark-haired woman who was banging on the Lamberts' door like there was no tomorrow. "Yes. Thank heaven for that."

"Do you need help gettin' down?"

Adam shook his head. "No. I am somewhat used to the dull ache, actually. Although those sharp, swift pains are sometimes a surprise." He could not quite suppress the groan that slipped past his lips as his feet hit the hard-packed earth.

As they walked to the house, Miles glanced at him with a frown. "You should be in bed, not out here like this."

"There is no time for rest right now."

"Why?"

"Because production of the *Sentinel* can only be suspended for another day or two. We have a newspaper to print. I cannot ignore what happened here the other day. I have decided the only solution is a meeting with Stokes. In person. That bastard is going to see who he is dealing with." Adam laughed. "The man does not even know me. More the fool."

"He hired you. He must know a little about you."

"He did not hire me. More of a business exchange between my editor and him. Stokes wanted a good editor. That is all he asked for." He smacked his fist against his open palm. "Does he think I am such a weak man? That I would let him do this to me? That I would let him threaten her?" Adam tilted his head in the direction of the house.

Miles stopped before they reached the porch. He turned his

head, his gaze searching Adam's face. "Those men . . . they threatened Charlie?"

"They said in so many words that"—Adam glanced at the house, feminine laughter luring him—"that I was vulnerable because I employed a woman." He sighed. "They're right. They used their fists, and their boots, as it went, on me. They would punish her in *other* ways. Much more brutal ways."

"Are you sure?"

"Dammit, Miles. How can I be sure? What can I do? Wait for them to hurt her?" He glanced back with a frown. "They would have raped her if I had not been there. Oliver Stokes would never condone that behavior—he cannot be that much of a bastard—but how would those men have viewed a woman like Charlie? Like the rest of this town does? She works, she wears britches, she swears. Hell, she would have been swearing at them that night like a sailor."

Adam balled his fists up by his sides. "What do you think? Am I wrong to be fearful of the consequences when I leave Edgemont? She wants to run this newspaper, and with a bit more training, she could do it. That mind of hers . . . you cannot believe." He struggled to contain the anger that rushed through him at the anticipation of Charlie in danger. "To let this go unpunished . . . leave her here with this mess. Stokes has to understand this is not going to happen ever again. Not to me, not to her, not to your father."

"They brought my *pa* into this? Where is Stokes? I'll go with you. We'll beat the shit—"

Adam grasped his friend by the shoulder. "No. That is not the way to handle him. He would only have another set of thugs after us next week. Plus, he is in Richmond right now; he only spends the winter months in South Carolina." He patted Miles' shoulder. "I need you *here*. Helping Gerald run the newspaper in my absence."

Miles nodded, although it was clear he would rather solve the problem the way he knew how. "When are you leavin'?"

"As soon as I can ride a horse comfortably. I can rent a mount and ride to Wilmington. Take the train from there."

Miles was silent a moment before he asked, "What about Charlie?"

"What about her?"

Miles looked at him as if he had lost his mind. "Do you want her workin' at the *Sentinel* while you're gone?"

"Absolutely not."

Miles' look changed to one that plainly stated, *And you think I can stop her?*

"Dammit man, are you afraid of her?"

"Of course not. She's my friend; Kathy's dearest friend. But I can't stop her from doin' what you know she'd be hell-bent on doin'. Just think what you're askin' if you want me to watch over her. Just think about *her.*" He gestured to his house.

Adam shook his head, denying what Miles was saying. "No. Oh, no . . . I have another life in Richmond." He could not take . . . oh, no. It was an impossible suggestion. An impossible idea.

"Another woman, you mean?" Miles' grin flashed in the darkness.

"I don't *have* any women."

"What about Lila?"

Adam frowned. Lila? "Lila Dane means nothing to me. I told you that little flirtation was finished."

"What about Charlie?"

"Why do I feel like a horse being led to the watering trough? Charlie is my colleague, *my* friend."

A knowing grin crossed Miles' face. "Do you honestly believe that? Do you think I look at Charlie the way you do? You'd punch me in the face if I did, I'll tell you that."

Kath's entrance onto the porch halted his rebuttal. "Miles, Adam, I've made a huge supper, so come in while it's hot." She leaned forward, squinting her eyes to see them clearly. "Good gracious, Miles, bring him in; he looks dead on his feet."

"We're coming, love."

"Miles?" Adam stopped him with a hand on his sleeve. "Let's wait and discuss this after the women have gone to bed. God knows, I do not want to get Charlie all riled up."

"Oh, Lord," Miles whispered as they entered the house.

Adam sat at the Lamberts' kitchen table later that night, reading through his mail. The house was as still and quiet as a hidden pond. It was good to be alone. No need to struggle to make conversation with a woman who was, at the moment, angry and confused, or try to calm the nerves of friends who had only the best intentions at heart.

He reached up to rub the back of his neck, stiffening when the stretch produced a sharp hitch of pain in his chest. With a sigh, he let his arm drop and turned his attention to the letters sitting on the table before him. There were two from his solicitor in Richmond—the same one who had handled his father's affairs—apprising him of the gains and losses of his many investments. Mostly gains, it seemed.

There was also a short note from a colleague who had recently been hired as a correspondent for the *Richmond Examiner*. Adam had worked with the man years ago during his tour of the West. He remembered a jovial man, tall and lanky to the extreme. A bit of a drinker, if memory served, but all in all an entertaining sort. Adam slid the note, with the man's Richmond address, into the leather saddlebag beside his feet.

He straightened slowly—his injuries pained him more than Miles' potent mash could disguise—and picked up the last letter, staring at the flowing script on the front a full minute before turning it in his hands and breaking the seal. A scented page drifted from the envelope; Adam sniffed derisively as he picked up the sheet of yellow parchment. Her neat, familiar script reached out to him.

Adam, dear,
    How dreadfully boring Richmond is without you. Don't laugh, but with Father gone, this entire month has been nothing but one trial after another! The only joy is the look on men's faces when they realize they must deal with a woman. You know, I may become a proponent of women's rights yet.

Adam smiled. He missed her. Only, neither of them missed the other in any way that mattered.

How is the newspaper in your small town doing? I hope, for your sake, that it is more exciting than you had imagined. Certainly, there are women and saloons, no matter

*the size of the place. And a newspaper. What more do
you need?*

He chuckled and filled his glass with Miles' potion, which
he was afraid he was developing a fondness for.

*There has been a flurry of activity here since the last
time I wrote. A new hotel is being built at Franklin and
Third streets. There is also talk of the city buying some
property just on the western edge for development of
a state fair park. Land covered with scrub pines and
blackberry bushes! Lucky devil that owns the property.
William Clifton Thomas, if I'm not mistaken.*

He doubted she would overlook any issue involving money.

*I wish I had more time to put what I am thinking to tell
you to paper, but until Father returns, I'll be lucky to
find the time to purchase a new gown. Also, the words I
want to say may not be appropriate for a lady to record
for others, perhaps, to see. So I shall leave you with what
I assure you are benevolent thoughts. Be sure to drop a
note when you return to the city. Maybe your busy schedule will allow for a short letter to me as well.
With warmest regard,
Marilyn*

Adam sighed and dropped the letter to the table. His gaze
wandered out the window to the vast fields surrounding the
farmhouse. He should have gone back to Mrs. Wilkin's tonight,
but he and Miles had not finished discussing this mess until
well past midnight. Besides, they had extra bedrooms, and what
was one bed versus another when neither was your own?

It scared him to death to realize how attached to Charlie he
had become in these last weeks and how responsible he felt
for her. Their indescribable, passionate encounter in the cornfield had only intensified the attraction between them. How
could it not, when he knew what she smelled like, tasted like,

felt like? Knew how perfectly she fit the curve of his body. Knew how sweet and tender the skin along her neck tasted, and how silky and soft her hair felt trapped in his hand. Knew how damned erotic the scent of roses was, clinging to his skin *hours* later.

How, how dammit, could he not want more?

He shook his head, trying to conjure Marilyn's beautiful face, but the image that leaped into his mind was one of Charlie—sitting by the window, her head bent in deep concentration as she helped Kath mend clothing. The shimmering, bright moonlight from the window streaming down upon her, bathing her in pale radiance.

He groaned, scrubbing his hand over his face.

He and Miles had decided Charlie should go to Richmond. There seemed to be no other way. Fear nipped at him. He knew she would only get into trouble if he left her behind. She had him trussed up as tight as a turkey.

If he was honest with himself—which he had not been with Miles—there was a small part of him that *wanted* to take her. To show her his home on the James and his office at the *Times*. To share in her excitement as she watched paper fly through what would be the largest press she had ever seen. To behold her brilliant, blue eyes widening in surprise as she looked down the river, flour mills spewing smoke, crowding the sandy banks like kittens at their mother's teats. To witness her excitement as she encountered the bustling, noisy streets of Richmond.

In the morning he was going to tell her. She needed time to pack, time to prepare. They would be gone for two or three weeks. There was also the dilemma regarding a chaperone—a dilemma that was, as yet, unresolved. It was out of the question to travel alone with her. Her reputation would be utterly ruined. *And* . . . he did not want any more temptation than he could handle.

The train, thankfully, would be fast and *spacious,* with enough room for him to avoid being in her immediate proximity.

Unquestionably, when they arrived in Richmond, he would be far too busy to do much more than tour her around the city for an afternoon or two. A pile of correspondence as high as his head was no doubt waiting for him, plus household affairs to organize, investments to monitor, meetings to attend. He was not going to neglect any of those things to play nursemaid to a woman who could not seem to keep herself, or *him,* out of trouble. She could occupy herself. He did not particularly care how.

He smiled. For the first time in weeks his life was back in his control.

Chapter Twenty-Three

Charlie pulled her hand to her mouth and yawned behind it. Even in the darkness of her bedroom, she could not infringe upon Mrs. Mindlebright's ingrained preachings.

She glanced at the ceiling above her bed. Actually, it wasn't her bed; better to say the bed in Chase's guest bedroom. No, that wasn't right, either. He had six or seven bedrooms. If you had that many, were they all for guests? She had no idea. Even Lila's house—the biggest in Edgemont—only had two extra ones. They called *theirs* guest bedrooms.

Her gaze rolled along the ceiling, though it was hard to see the far corners, shrouded in early darkness. No chipped paint, no spider webs. She didn't think she'd ever seen a ceiling without a single spider web in sight. For heaven's sake, Chase's maid or housekeeper—whoever cleaned the place—must work hard. What was the woman's name, the housekeeper who had greeted them upon their arrival? Mrs. Beard.

Charlie yawned again and turned on her side. Her slight movement created a ripple in the thick mattress, much like a wave upon the ocean. The bed was so big, she could stretch out full length and her feet would not hang over the edge. She did it then, just because she could, stretching as completely as Faustus did on the comforting wood of her porch. She hoped

Miles wouldn't forget to go by and feed him. Faustus could certainly survive on his own on field mice and a bird or two, but she didn't want him to think he'd been abandoned.

Her gaze lit on the four-poster bedstead rising high above her head. Surely, all the furniture in this room couldn't be mahogany, but she knew that it was. The dark wood gleamed and glistened, dim reflections layering its surface. The entire house—as large and grand as it was—shone like a new penny. Neat and orderly—without a trace of character or personality. Her own home was dingy in comparison, small and cluttered, everything looking very . . . homespun. But it had a personality all its own. You could tell a lot about her by looking at the sketches hanging on her wall or the trinkets sitting on her shelves.

Chase's home was just the opposite. It was tastefully decorated—for all she knew of furnishings, which wasn't much. Yet, it was stylish to the extreme, furnished with pieces too daunting to actually sit upon. She hadn't seen every room, of course.

The second floor, where she was, consisted of four large bedrooms and a small parlor with windows overlooking the river. The third floor had *more* bedrooms—she had counted three—only these were modest ones, for the household staff, she guessed. There were also two vacant rooms tucked into the corner of the top floor. Sealed boxes and furniture covered with white cotton sheets occupied those.

The room she assumed was his was at the far end of the hall. Her own was just at the top of the stairs. He had put her there on purpose, as far away as possible. What did his bedroom look like? She would love to know, but she couldn't just snoop. He'd locked the door, anyway.

She shrugged, trying to come up with an exact description for the house and finding none. It just lacked . . . feeling. Whoever had decorated it didn't know Chase well, she'd be willing to guess. The house *looked* nice . . . elegant and attractive, but it felt indifferent and cheerless.

Charlie stretched a little farther and pulled a fat pillow to her chest. She hugged it, discarding the reasonless homesickness that plagued her. She wanted to be here. In Richmond. In Chase's home. To see a new city, a different part of the country, excited her. So, why was she homesick? They had only arrived this afternoon.

She just had not expected to feel so alone.

She would stay busy, of course. Chase told her they would go into Richmond proper in a day or two, after he had concluded his meeting with Oliver Stokes. Charlie had asked to go with him, but his negative response had brooked no argument.

Her chaperone—of all the idiotic baggage for a twenty-four-year-old woman to have—had pleaded exhaustion from the trip and gone directly to her room upon their arrival.

The older woman had complained much of the time they were on the train, but every aspect of their journey had enthralled Charlie. She wasn't sure when Chase had come up with the grand idea of asking Mrs. Peters, who had recently moved from Richmond to open a millinery shop in Edgemont, to accompany them.

Mrs. Peters was a rather nice woman really, petite with the lightest blue eyes and short, curling gray hair. The only wall to climb when sharing close quarters with the woman was that she seemed to have an opinion about everything and everyone, as older people tend to.

Mrs. Peters had two daughters in Richmond; Charlie assumed she would spend a great deal of time visiting her family.

The only doleful element of Charlie's journey north was her interaction with Chase. She blew a frustrated breath toward the ceiling. An adventure, like one she had always dreamed of— the chance to travel beyond South Carolina's borders. The chance to experience life. Except, *he* was crushing her idealistic expectations as flat as a flower beneath his stiff heel. Just like his damn house: cool and impersonal. Why, he had not looked at her closely, not so much as touched her with his *little* finger. Not once.

Most of the trip had consisted of reflective musing, absorption in the landscape and people they encountered, and reading *Jane Eyre*. She had tried to thank Chase for the book, but he'd only shrugged it off with a casual flick of his wrist.

So like him that damn gesture was.

Still, she had to admit he seemed to be concerned about her. At least in a courteous, respectful way. Charlie didn't know what to think of his behavior. He was distant and detached, yet he seemed to be acutely aware of her. For the first time in her life, she felt spoiled. Pampered.

Although, it presented a problem when the person doing the pampering was barely speaking to her.

A soft knock at the door drew Charlie from her light, restless slumber. She had tossed and turned all night, kicking and pulling the sheets about her. Deranged dreams had drawn together like vigilant warriors to keep sleep from her. She shook her head groggily and turned to her back. A quick glance at the window showed the sun up, high and bright in the sky.

"Miss Whitney. Are you awake?" Mrs. Peters whispered from the other side of the thick wooden door. "Miss Whitney?"

Charlie frowned and sat up, clutching the sheet to her chest. The dutiful chaperone come to wake her recalcitrant charge.

"Yes, Mrs. Peters, I'm awake. You may come in if you like."

The door swung open slowly; Mrs. Peters' small head peeked around it. When she saw that Charlie was indeed decent, she pushed the door wide and walked in. What had she expected, to find her naked?

"Miss Whitney, I know how tired you must be from our arduous journey." She patted the tight knot at the back of her head and sniffed in a thoroughly ladylike fashion. "We have tasks to complete today, so I suggest you rise, wash up and eat something light to settle your undoubtedly nervous stomach."

Charlie shook her head. "My stomach isn't nervous." It wasn't anything but empty. Nothing light would fix that.

Mrs. Peters clicked her tongue. "Well, it will be. With all the travel and excitement, any well-bred young woman's stomach would be apt to become a bit restless."

Well-bred? What had Chase told the woman? Mrs. Peters obviously had not lived in Edgemont long enough to hear the facts. Also, what tasks could *they* possibly have to complete?

"Tasks?" Charlie asked as she twisted the cool sheet between her fingers.

Mrs. Peters nodded and strolled to the window. The yellow silk curtains danced, influenced by a gentle breeze. Sun poured in around her chaperone, casting her in dark contour. Charlie supposed this was a gesture to allow her—in all her maidenly, well-bred modesty—to crawl from the bed and slip into whatever a well-bred young maiden slipped into upon rising. Mrs. Peters threw her a quick glance, suggesting she should get on with it.

Charlie slid from the bed and just missed the stool placed next to it, her feet hitting the floor with a dull thud. She grimaced and hurried to the wardrobe, where Mrs. Beard had insisted upon placing her meager possessions. As Charlie opened the doors, she noted her dresses, looking rather pathetic dangling there, taking up so little space. Peeling off her nightdress, she slipped one of the two clean dresses remaining—the blue one— over her head. She was pulling the sleeves into place when Mrs. Peters executed a graceful rotation.

She approached Charlie, her scrutinizing gaze sweeping from head to foot, at last falling to the nightdress puddled upon the floor. She sniffed for the second time that morning. "Thank goodness I have connections. Mrs. Follette will be here within the hour, and I must say"—with another look thrown to the rumpled nightdress, then one to Charlie's simple attire—"she is desperately needed."

Her chaperone's disdain did not trouble Charlie. She had endured that practically her entire life. "Who is Mrs. Follette?" She picked up her nightdress and began to fold it, something she never did at home.

Mrs. Peters frowned, took the nightdress from her and folded it with quick efficiency. "Only one of the finest seamstresses in Virginia. I will have you know that she had a waiting list for appointments. She is a *personal* friend. I can assure you an appointment without my reference would have been impossible. Even *with* Mr. Chase's adequate funds."

Charlie took a step forward. "A seamstress? Mr. Chase's funds? I don't need a seamstress, and I don't need Mr. Chase's funds!"

"My dear, he is being most generous sponsoring a mere employee of his. Why, you are not even distant family."

"I don't—"

Mrs. Peters thrust the folded nightdress into her hands, promptly cutting her off. "Miss Whitney, for a two-week visit, your apparel needs are simple. But, my dear, you have *three* dresses, if I am not mistaken, hanging in this wardrobe. Three basic, inappropriate dresses.''

''Those dresses are fine. I made them, thank you very much.''

Mrs. Peters' eyebrows lifted at that. ''Well, they are indeed suitable for Edgemont,'' she amended. ''Richmond, though, requires a finer level of attire.''

''I don't know what Chase, um, what Mr. Chase told you . . .'' She felt her temper rise, just thinking of Chase's high-handed tactics. Oh! She had reminded herself again and again that Chase believed he was doing the right thing. No matter how foolish it really was.

While she was at it, she might as well set her chaperone on the straight and narrow. It would certainly simplify matters for the remainder of their stay in Richmond. ''Mrs. Peters, to put it plainly, I'm here because Mr. Chase was afraid to leave me alone in Edgemont. With the newspaper. He feared I would cause trouble. More than I have already, I mean.''

Charlie watched a faint smile slide across Mrs. Peters' face. Either her chaperone had heard the gossip and didn't believe it, or she discounted someone's motives. Chase's? That was impossible, considering his conduct during their travel. It was obvious, from his stiff smile and distant manner, he wished she were anywhere but where she was—with him.

Her chaperone continued to stare at her, as if Charlie had never spoken. Didn't the woman understand? ''The dresses I have are quite suitable, I'm sure. There will be no parties or social gatherings. I avoid those as studiously as possible in Edgemont; why would I attend them here? Besides, Mr. Chase has no intention of taking me anywhere but to his office one afternoon. Oh, and a short tour of Richmond, at best.'' Chase could hardly stand to *look* at her. She was sure soirees were not on his list of events.

''You must be mistaken. It makes no matter''—Mrs. Peters nodded toward the wardrobe—''your clothing is not appropriate for even a simple tour of the city.''

''I cannot possibly let Mr. Chase furnish my clothing. I will not.''

Mrs. Peters softened her tone and smiled, obviously hoping this tactic would work. ''My dear, I am arranging this affair; there is absolutely nothing improper. Plus,'' she lowered her voice to a whisper, "for Mr. Chase, this small expenditure amounts to mere pocket change."

Charlie had nothing to say to that. She had known, of course, from the way Chase lifted a glass to his lips to the way he held a pencil, that he was a refined man. His education and breeding spoke for themselves, as they tended to do, but perhaps she hadn't realized how very *wealthy* he was. His house certainly spoke volumes. "I can't accept, Mrs. Peters. Really. I don't want to cause you to worry. It's not the impropriety." She laughed at that. "It just feels wrong to me somehow."

"Well"—Mrs. Peters patted her shoulder—"go and have breakfast. We can talk later."

Charlie watched as Mrs. Peters left the room, as cautiously as she had entered it. Could Charlie have won the argument so easily? If so, then why did she have the feeling she was being outmaneuvered? By her elderly chaperone, no less.

Only moments later, another of Mrs. Peters' soft knocks sounded on the oak double doors leading into the library. Mrs. Beard had told Mrs. Peters she would find Mr. Chase there, as he refused to use his study as a study. He conducted all of his business in the library, the housekeeper had said.

Mrs. Peters, after years of owning a business that served an aristocratic clientele, could attest to the strange behavior of those with money. Like Mrs. Beard, she observed—often with great interest—but never commented. Which she advised Mrs. Beard, who was not too happy to hear it, to do in the future.

"Mr. Chase? It is Mrs. Peters. May I have a brief moment of your time?" He did not answer, so she knocked again.

Papers shuffled, then his deep voice called, "Please enter."

She opened one of the massive doors a bit and peeked in, but halted as she encountered his cool expression. The room, a magnificent mixture of dark wood and leather, lit by bright sunlight spilling in from two tall windows, fit ideally such an imposing man. "I am sorry to disturb you. You must be very busy. Yet, I have run into a small problem."

Adam sighed and rubbed his eyes. "Yes, Mrs. Peters, I am busy. In fact, I have to leave in less than an hour for the city. Let's get this over with. What has she done?"

She blinked in the sharp sunlight, which for a moment obscured Adam's face from her vision. "How do you know—"

He leaned back in the chair and laughed quite sourly, to her ears anyway. "After spending even one hour with her, how can you ask that?"

Mrs. Peters stepped into the room, stopping just behind the chair sitting closest to his desk, resting her hands on its back. "She *is* a . . . willful young woman, I will concede that."

He laid his pen on the desk, still smiling. He appeared to be waiting for her to continue. She cleared her throat, trying to avoid the strength of his dark gaze. "Actually, it is just that"—she squeezed the leather chair and rushed into her prepared speech—"Miss Whitney needs proper clothing, which she does not have. She has no dressing gowns, no walking dresses, no morning dresses, no evening dresses. Not to mention a bonnet, gloves, slippers. And"—she sighed long and hard—"those shoes of hers. They are, without a doubt, the ugliest things I have seen since my dog had the mange."

He laughed. "Those shoes *are* hideous."

"Mr. Chase, this is hardly amusing. How can you possibly present her in public looking like a ragamuffin?"

His smile softened. "Miss Whitney has her own sense of style."

Mrs. Peters sniffed and pursed her lips. "Yes, I suppose. But she must have—"

He held up his hand. "I told you, do whatever is necessary. Just send the invoices to me."

"That is the problem."

"The invoices?"

"Miss Whitney does not think it is *right,* as she terms it, for you to pay for her clothing. I told her it was entirely proper. Apparently, that was not the aspect of the situation she was concerned with. I believe it is a matter of principle." She rolled her eyes. The idea of a young woman reflecting upon her integrity was an absurd notion. An absurdly masculine notion. "I have already sent for the seamstress."

Adam shifted in the chair, his head falling back as he ejected a grunt of laughter. "You mentioned propriety? To *her?*" He laughed again and wiped at his eyes with the back of his hand.

She straightened her back and glared at his desk as she gripped the chair. "I fail to find any humor in this situation."

He unsuccessfully tried to contain a smile. "When is this esteemed seamstress supposed to arrive?"

Mrs. Peters nodded her head. Mr. Chase was finally going to cooperate. "In less than an hour."

He frowned. "Too late to cancel the appointment, then."

"Cancel the appointment?"

"How about this? I will talk to your charge"—he laughed a bit as he said this—"on my way out. You handle the rest. I have too much to do to play nursemaid." He gave her a look beneath raised brows that clearly said, *That is what you are here for.*

She nodded. "I will handle everything from now on." She leaned forward. "Miss Whitney is just so," her words fell to a whisper, "resistant. More so than I would have imagined."

He shrugged and turned his gaze—and his attention—back to the work upon his desk. "I warned you."

Mrs. Peters circled back, cleanly dismissed. Pulling the library door shut behind her, she marched toward the staircase. Mr. Chase *had* told her Miss Whitney was headstrong, determined. That her upbringing had been . . . exceptional. But he had omitted a significant ingredient of the recipe. That she, Mrs. Jeffrey Peters, formerly Alice Fripp of the Richmond, Virginia, Fripps, was in attendance not only to play chaperone to an impulsive, spiritual young woman, but to act as a barrier between two people she suspected were in love with each other.

She sighed, picturing a wearisome two weeks as she trudged up the stairs.

Chapter Twenty-Four

Adam strode from his bedroom, tugging impatiently at his dark neckpiece. God, he hated the damn things. He longed for an unbuttoned shirt and a pair of trousers that did not chafe. He had conveniently forgotten the impracticality of Richmond's formalities: appropriate dress for morning and evening, parties and socials, meetings and appointments. Now here he was, off to recruit another helpless soul into the world of tasteful fashion and refined protocol.

He paused at the bottom of the staircase as warm laughter met his ears: Charlie's laughter. He would recognize hers in a room filled with a hundred others'. Not to mention her scent, her smile, her body, her walk. Shoving aside a strong pulse of longing, he followed the sound.

The dining room was empty, he noted as he passed through the archway. The nut brown sideboard, filled with a vast array of muffins, juices and pastries, looked undisturbed. He turned his head as another burst of laughter cut into his skin as sharply as sand in a driving wind.

Pushing himself forward, he walked into the kitchen, the door propped open with a large, red brick. Again he paused, catching sight of Charlie, her round bottom indelicately planted atop a huge wooden chopping block. His kitchen staff of two surrounded her.

Mrs. Beard and Miss Cameron stood there smiling and laughing as Charlie told some undoubtedly captivating tale. She flipped her hands as she talked, eager and free. Her feet hung far from the floor. Her legs swayed in a two-rhythm beat, to her own music as usual.

He laughed—he could not stop it—and came into the room. *This* was the young woman Mrs. Peters hoped to reform with a few scraps of silk and a bonnet.

Charlie looked up as he crossed the room. She smiled, forgetting for the moment that they were trying to keep a healthy distance between them.

He stopped before her, returning the smile. Her knees brushed lightly against his hips. He lifted a hand to wipe a stray crumb from her chin. Her skin burned his fingers. He made no move to withdraw. She made no move to withdraw.

"We made flapjacks, Mr. Chase," Mrs. Beard said as she pulled a tray of biscuits from the oven. A brawny, strapping woman of sixty, Mrs. Beard had been the cook for his family since he was a small boy.

Adam dropped his hand and stepped back, tearing his gaze from Charlie's. So much for firm resolve. His heart felt as if it was near to bursting from his chest. And all because she had brushed her knee against him. Pathetic. He made a mental note to send Marilyn a message that he was in town. Perhaps she had time to see him tonight.

"Miss Whitney likes flapjacks for breakfast. Not all those fancy pastries. No breakfast trays for *her.*" Marilyn always insisted upon a breakfast tray.

He sent a frown Mrs. Beard's way, though it was difficult to intimidate a woman who had seen you in short trousers. He glanced back at Charlie, but she was staring at the floor. He shifted from one foot to the other, the heat in the kitchen suddenly soaking through his crisp cotton shirt. A bead of sweat trickled down his back. "Mrs. Beard, if I could just have a moment with Miss Whitney."

Mrs. Beard smiled and nodded, whisking her assistant into the dining room with her.

Wondering why he was going to touch her again, Adam

placed his hand beneath Charlie's chin, tilting her head up. Her eyes revealed a mixture of confusion and an odd little glimmer he did not care to define. "You do not have to hide in the kitchen with my staff."

She puckered her brow, a thoughtful expression entering her eyes. " I have more in common with the kitchen staff, Chase, whether you comprehend that or not."

He dropped his hand and sighed, realizing all at once that she wanted to keep herself from him as much as he wanted to keep himself from her. She was even desperate enough to bring up class distinctions, for God's sake. He supposed he should be grateful. "In regard to this seamstress . . ."

Charlie scooted forward and hopped off the chopping block. Her ugly, black boots slapped against the floor. She walked past him to the cast-iron stove where corn pone lay in a tin pan. She broke off a small piece and popped it into her mouth. Chewing, she mumbled, "No. You've spent too much money already. Besides, I don't need any clothes. What are you and Mrs. Peters trying to do? Turn me into Lila?"

She looked over her shoulder, her gaze catching his as he looked over his shoulder. He spun around. "This is ridiculous. I have two women in this house, two more than I *need,* and I am trying like hell to please them both. Just order the damn dresses. Mrs. Peters is right. We may go to dinner in town one night." He threw up his hands in disgusted resignation. Did he imagine the calm reflection in her expression? He pushed a little harder. "I forced this decision on you. You would still be in Edgemont if it were not for me. Think of it that way."

She shrugged and took another bite. "I don't know much about seamstresses."

"You just stand there with your spine straight and your arms raised. They measure; you pick colors and fabrics and styles."

She did a slow turn, her bright blue gaze centered upon him. She brushed her fingers against her side, looked down, then up, then back at him again. "How do you know?" she finally asked.

Ah, she was much more courageous than he. She did not need him. He was not even sure she wanted him. But she was curious. Curious about the emotions that constantly jumped between them. She was courageous enough to explore. He was not.

He turned from her and walked through the kitchen, the dining room, and across the entrance hall to the door. She followed. He heard her. There was no way to be quiet in those boots of hers. He smelled flour or cinnamon—not the usual scent of roses—following him, too.

"Wait," she whispered from behind.

He stopped and tilted his head to the ceiling, then drew a breath and half turned, still facing the door, ready to flee at any moment.

The sight of her in his home, surrounded by possessions he neither loved nor coveted, shook him. He coveted *her,* her body, her mind, her soul. If only he could devour her, then cast her aside when he was appeased. No. He liked her too much. Besides, he had never been the kind of man to do that to a woman. Better to stick with the ones who cast *you* aside.

"Thank you," she mouthed across the few feet separating them. Her lips opened and closed, her tongue peeking for a moment between her teeth.

He felt his heart lift and drop with her simple words. He felt himself lift and harden as he watched her. Did he imagine her short, shallow breathing? Her ever-darkening gaze? He swallowed and shook his head. "Nothing," he mouthed back, "it's nothing." His gaze swept over her before he shook his head again and pushed through the door.

Adam ambled along the deserted passage from stable to house. The path meandered through a dense copse of pines, azaleas and the ever-present, boisterous kudzu vines, which attached themselves to every square inch of available bark. The moonlight, dim from a quarter moon, lit the path enough for him to see. He did not really need any light—he knew the path well—though his footing was less than sure, less than graceful. This was due to a lack of sleep the night before and one too many glasses of whiskey in the early evening.

A thick branch lying in the middle of the path twisted beneath his foot, and he stumbled, falling to his knees. Instinctively, he placed his hands in front of him, thereupon wrenching a ragged hole in the sleeve of his jacket, which he clutched in one fist. With a curse, he pushed himself up with the other hand. His head ached, and he smelled like a trollop. One had taken every opportunity to rub herself against him during the course of the evening. He had accepted only her aromatic gift.

He should have known better, should have refused Pete Stewart's offer to share a few stories. A few drinks. After his abysmal meeting with Oliver Stokes, and the hard, irrefutable truth that Charlie Whitney was sleeping—no doubt curled in a sleek little ball—in a warm bed in *his* home . . . it had just been too much. Anticipating her there, waiting for him, made something shift inside him, something indisputable and fervid. Something he hoped had more to do with his penis than with his heart.

He halted as his house came into view. It was dark except for a faint light glowing from the library window. His fists bunched. *She was still awake.* After he had avoided her tonight like the coward he was rapidly becoming, left her to her own devices, left her alone with Mrs. Peters, chaperone; after confronting enormous guilt because her first full day in Richmond had been spent cooped up in his house, all the while denying he wanted to spend the evening talking and laughing with her . . . after all that *she was still awake.*

Was there no mercy for the weary?

He shoved his hand through his hair, groaning. He wished he could not remember the taste and feel of her so well. Wished the swell of her breast was not stamped upon his palm like permanent lines. Wished the softness of her lips was not drawn like a map upon his tongue. He groaned again, his heart picking up speed as his long legs propelled him forward. He stumbled up the front steps to the door. He wished, with his whole heart, that he could *not* close his eyes and breath in the distinctive scent of her. He wished he did not know her so well, like her so much. Respect and trust her.

Because it was hopeless. As of this afternoon, their lives were detached. For reasons he could neither disavow nor disregard.

He grasped the round, metal doorknob between his shaky fingers and turned, expecting the door to be locked. He breathed a silent sigh of relief. Mrs. Beard, for all her inquisitiveness and motherly admonitions, ran the household quite shrewdly and appropriately for a confirmed bachelor. She would never have left him out in the cold, so to speak, upon his own brick steps.

He held the heavy wooden door next to him as he eased inside. He did not want to release it and have it slam against the wall from a sudden gust of wind. He closed the door behind him and from habit turned the lock. The noise reverberated through the hallway; he put his fingers to his lips, suggesting silence. Realizing how absurd, and drunken, the action was, he scowled and flung his hand away.

He turned his head this way and that, seeing no one. Then, forgetting his promise to leave Charlie to her own devices, he stepped quietly to the door of the library. It was open an inch or two, the small distance more than enough to weaken his resolve and provide just the right amount of temptation for him to act upon. He did. Soundless, the door swung open. Mrs. Beard was rather adamant about oiling hinges, he seemed to recall.

His gaze roved over his desk and the two leather chairs sitting before it. Nothing. He scanned the shelves of books to his right. No disarray as far as he could tell. He took a step into the room, turning his head to the left, in the direction of the fireplace. A large sofa, covered in gold and black satin damask, sat in front of the fireplace, its high back facing him. He walked toward the sofa, thinking someone must have left the lamp lit for him, because there appeared to be no one in the room. Then he spotted a petite, satin-clad foot hanging over the sofa's arm. He stopped and looked down, upon Charlie Whitney.

She was fast asleep, not curled in the tight ball he had imagined, but rather stretched out on her side. His gaze floated with languid ease from the top of her dark head to the tips of her feet. It was the first time he had been able to look his fill. The first time he had seen her sleeping. Sable hair loose and spread like a pillow beneath her. Lashes lying softly, darkly against smooth, tanned cheeks. He smiled and leaned forward a little. She had glasses on—round wire frames perched jauntily upon her nose. He had never seen her wearing those before.

A slight smile curved her mouth, puckering her lips just so. Her right hand curled under her chin, her fingers clutching a charcoal pencil. A pad of paper lay beside her, upon the floor.

He tried, unsuccessfully, to keep his gaze from resting on her chest, which rose and fell with her even breaths.

She had dressed inappropriately as usual, in a dressing gown of pale green silk she should have worn only in the privacy of her bedroom. He could see the lace edging of a nightdress, made of the same green material, peeking between the valley of her breasts. The silk hugged the curve of her hip snugly and, for his viewing pleasure, had gotten twisted at her knees, exposing the rest of her legs to his hungry gaze. His eyes widened as he noticed how very dark her calves were. Evidently, she sat in the sun with her dress pulled up. Or those damn trousers rolled up.

Against his better judgment, he walked around the sofa and knelt to pick up the pad of paper that had fallen to the floor. Resting on one knee, he flipped it open. One page contained a list of editorial ideas. Another recorded the comforts and grievances of train travel. A recent one. He turned another page and stopped cold. It was a sketch. Of him.

She had caught him unaware, of course. He was smiling, a soft, gentle smile, one he certainly did not recognize but feared she had seen much too often. It was a smile reserved for his mother and Eaton. A smile that displayed the buried, forgotten side of him. Godammit, she had drawn *Jared Chase*. Adam Chase was absent from the sketch he held in his hands. He flipped pages, finding more: asleep at his desk, gazing across rolling fields, leaning upon the press with Gerald, stacks of newspapers at their backs.

What could this mean? Could she possibly think about him as much as he thought about her? Did she lie awake at night asking God why he had thrown them together when it was far too late? Did his gaze burn into her skin like hot coals? Did she lick her lips and taste him, lift her hands to her face and smell him? Did she know the instant he walked into a room? Or walked out of one?

He dropped the pad of paper and covered his face with his hands. He wanted to make his yearning for her disappear. He wanted to destroy what he felt for her, before it destroyed him. He wanted emotions that had been dead for years to suddenly possess nourishment and grow. *No.* He shook his head. He could not love anyone ever again. He *would* not.

"Chase?"

The sleepy whisper jarred him as effectively as a swift kick to his stomach. He jerked his head up, his heavy, stinging eyes meeting her drowsy, muddled ones.

"Chase . . . what are you doing?" She glanced at the pad of paper on the carpet beside his feet. A rosy flush crept up her neck and settled on her face. "Oh . . . my sketches. I needed someone to sketch. I didn't think you would mind—"

"I do not mind. Only . . ." He pulled his gaze from her face, training it on the pad of paper as if his life depended upon it. "They frighten me."

She lifted herself to her elbow as a frown plucked at her face. "Frighten you?"

He swallowed past a dry throat. "I am frightened to the depths of my soul, Charlie. I am losing control of myself, my thoughts, my actions." He clenched his jaw tight and began to rub the scar on his hand. "I dream about you . . . *about us* . . . and wake up gasping for breath, my hands reaching for someone who is not there, my goddamn heart pounding hard enough to burst from my chest."

He continued, lifting his gaze, focusing on a point just beyond her shoulder. "I can close my eyes and see you, smell those damn roses and . . . I tell myself I will forget. I will get past this. Just loneliness . . . thinking about Eaton and my mother. Wishing for what is not possible." He lowered his head.

She sniffed, then stood with swift anger. "You're drunk."

"That changes nothing I have said."

"Why *are* you saying these things? Why? Why are you doing this?"

Her breath unwittingly teased his hair. "God, you smell wonderful. Like roses and sunshine, and that damn dirt you love so much. It invades my dreams like you would not even believe."

She shoved against his shoulder. He lifted his head and watched her walk to the window behind his desk. If he could only touch her. Just once. Would it be possible to satisfy his hunger with one passionate, fleeting encounter?

She turned slowly, her arms wrapped around her stomach. Her breasts, propelled by her defensive gesture, peeked from the lace-edged neck of her nightdress. He saw her shiver. Not from a chill, he guessed.

He crooked a finger at her. She did not move, only stared at him. He was close to vaulting to his feet, anything to get to her, when she dropped her arms and came forward. Instead of fleeing as she should have, she slipped her glasses off, laying them on a desk as she passed it.

He pulled her to her knees when she reached him, not giving either of them time to think, to argue. He looked into her face, losing every bit of reasoning he possessed as the blatant desire reflected on her face rolled like a wave of heat over him. Exhaustion, hunger and loneliness battled within him. He could not deny them any longer. He thrust his hands into her hair and brought her to him. She did not fight. Rather, she opened her mouth when she felt his touch. Then she flicked her tongue against his lips, then against his tongue. She was learning so quickly—exactly what he liked.

He groaned deep in his throat and clutched her tighter to him. He had to get closer to her. Slanting his mouth over hers, he deepened the kiss. He ran his tongue along her soft lips, explored the inside of her mouth. She tasted of cinnamon.

She tangled her tongue with his, and his heart jumped, hammering so hard in his chest that he guessed he might collapse. He tightened his arms as she swayed into him. Or, perhaps he swayed into her. It did not matter. He was not going to lose contact with her. At that moment, he did not give a damn if everyone in the house came tumbling in upon them. He wanted her more than he had ever wanted anyone in his entire life. No, that did not even begin to explain the sensations rocking through him.

He had never *imagined* anyone could want the way he wanted her. Taking control, he circled her waist, his other arm wrapping around her shoulders. In one deft movement, he turned her to her back.

Suddenly, she was lying under him, warm skin and cool silk pressed against him. Her body blended so well with his; peaks and valleys resting within each other. She arched her back and squirmed beneath him, all the while murmuring meaningless words.

He laughed softly, kissing his way down her neck, nipping

the tender skin with the edges of his teeth. "Slowly, love, slowly," he whispered as his hand settled upon her breast. His laugh had been in part because he was afraid. In some dark corner of his mind, he was afraid she was going to abandon him, although the groans she emitted and the adventurous way she pressed herself against him were the actions of someone whose need was as great as his own.

"Your legs. Open your legs." With his finger, he drew a small circle around her nipple. She moaned, hardening as quickly as he.

She did as he asked, and he settled himself between her legs, his throbbing erection pressed to her, heat joining them. Two thin layers of silk and one slightly thicker layer of linen separated bare skin. Too much separated them.

Purely on instinct, she wrapped her legs around the back of his knees, locking him to her. She arched against him, her hands sliding to his waist where she jerked twice, wrenching his shirt from his trousers. He sucked in a breath as her warm hands scurried inside his moist cotton shirt. He should have known better than to think he would frighten her. She was the most daring person he knew. As if to prove that declaration to a further degree, she sucked a piece of cloth-covered skin between her teeth, a sensitive spot just below his collarbone, biting and groaning as her hands clutched his back.

His mind spinning, his control slipping, he lowered the neck of her dressing gown past her shoulder. He gazed at her. Her breasts were so beautiful, the nipples erect and jutting proudly. He dropped his lips to one, sucking it through the thin silk nightdress. He moved his hand to the other, stroking the puckered tip.

She was writhing and moaning so much that he was having trouble staying on top of her. Honestly, he had not known she wanted him this much, or that she would like so well what he could do to her. He *wanted* to do everything. Taste her everywhere. Lick. Suck. Bite. Kiss. Feel. Only, he did not know how much longer he could last. Clothing still covered them, and he felt like a schoolboy about to burst.

She tugged at his waistband. "Take off . . . your trousers."

He blinked, placing his palms flat on the floor on either side of her head, lifting himself enough to look into her face. Her eyes were bleary, wide, the pupils small and swimming in a sea of deep, deep blue.

"Trousers?"

"Your trousers," she panted, her breath rasping in and out, her chest rising and falling. "I think . . . I can get . . . your shirt off. You'll . . . you'll have to do . . . the trousers."

"The door is not locked." He said this as calmly as he could despite his own excitement. Said it logically, too, like he had not been thinking about stripping her clothes off only moments before. "We are on"—he looked up before glancing back at her—"the *floor*."

"You mean you haven't ever done this on the floor before?"

"Well, no, I did not mean—"

"Or that we can't do this on the floor?"

"No, I did not mean that, eith—"

"You mean we aren't going to . . ." She sounded very disappointed, heaven love her.

He smiled, and his mind started a slow tilt again. "No. I most certainly did not mean *that*."

She gazed at him, her face flushed, her sapphire eyes wide, expectant.

He laughed and shook his head. "I do not know what I meant. I just never expected you to come right out and ask me to . . . take off my trousers."

She frowned. "Does this have to do with the etiquette problem? I didn't know I had to act the lady with a man sprawled on top of me."

He leaned and kissed her, sucking her bottom lip between his teeth in a gentle caress. "Charlotte Whitney, I can honestly say that you never have to act the lady with me sprawled on top of you," he whispered against her lips, then he levered himself on his elbows. His usual gracefulness thankfully restored, he rose to his feet. He extended his hand, which she refused with a quick shake of her head.

"No."

"Get up."

"No. I want to finish." She met his direct gaze with one of her own.

Soft laughter bubbled from his throat. Kneeling, he slipped

his arms beneath her, lifting her high against his chest in one swift motion. "I can promise we are going to finish."

She smiled, shyly for her, as a blush crept up her face. "Nothing is going to leave, is it?" She directed a pointed look at his crotch.

He kissed her soundly upon the lips. "No, nothing is going to leave."

He walked through the entrance hall and took the stairs two at a time, holding her tight against his chest. Striding along the hallway, he stopped at his door and slid her from his arms, slowly down his body. She wrapped her hands around his and lifted up on her toes to touch her lips to his.

He groaned, shoving her against the door. Bringing his tongue into her mouth, he lifted her hands high above her head and pressed them into the wood. In response, she rubbed her pelvis against his. If he did not know better, he would have judged her a very experienced woman.

"Wonderful," he said.

He touched with enthusiastic abandon. Her breasts, her stomach, her hips. Crumpling the silk material in his fingers, he laid his palm on her bare hip. She let her arm fall from high atop the door and grasped the silk from his hand. In an action he would remember his entire life, she jerked the dressing gown and nightdress over her head, leaving herself completely naked in the hallway in front of his bedroom door.

"Jesus." He placed himself in front of her. He looked in the direction of Mrs. Peters' room—the only other one occupied on the second floor. "Jesus," he said again.

He glanced back to find her face turned up to his, a small smile turning her lips. Her desire did not scare her. Or his apparently. She was *enjoying* this. He dropped his head, letting his gaze roam freely the length of her, like a child in a candy store who had not expected to be in the candy store quite yet. She was lean and muscular. Marilyn's voluptuousness flashed through his mind for just a moment. He found it hard to believe he had ever found Marilyn attractive.

The woman standing before him was perfection: breasts, petite, upturned, well-formed; stomach, flat and full of shadowed hollows; hips, straight, boyish, with a gentle curve at the widest point; thighs, sleek, tight, athletic; calves, small and curved. To have those legs encircling his again, while he thrust. . . .

He reached behind her, his arm brushing against her bare skin and opened the door with a savage twist of the knob. He grasped her shoulders and pushed her inside the room, slamming the door behind them with a swift kick of his heel. She stumbled. He held her steady as he captured her lips beneath his. His hands were everywhere at once, caressing, pinching, rubbing. She met the challenge using her fingers, her lips, her teeth. He could barely hear their moans over the blood pounding through his head.

"Your clothes," she murmured.

He nodded and released her, tearing off his shirt, buttons flying every which way. He hopped on one foot, pulling his trousers off, mindlessly throwing them to the floor.

She drew a fierce breath as she got a good look at him. Her first look. Maybe her first look at any man. She followed the trail of hair down his body, her eyes widening as they reached his arousal, erect and jutting at a sharp angle. She did not pull her gaze from him, her eyes hot and smoldering.

As he watched her watch him, he actually felt himself *blushing*. Her look was not that of a modest virgin, or one of a courtesan, which Marilyn sometimes employed. Charlie's look was gentle, lustful, honest . . . awe-struck.

"Come here." His voice was low and hoarse.

She came forward with her hand extended, her palm sliding up his chest as she got close to him. She stopped at his nipple, her fingers teasing it as he had done to hers. He groaned and pulled her into his arms, lowering his head and kissing her hungrily, savagely, releasing all the emotion he felt for her in that one kiss.

He stepped back, meaning to pull her toward the bed, but she stopped him with a soft touch to his cheek. As she looked up at him, she whispered, "No, let's stay in the light. I want to see you. I don't want to cover up with sheets and darkness."

He closed his eyes. He actually got harder, if that was possible. He was so desperate for her that her simple words were enough to make him lose control. Her goddamn *words*. But who loved words more than he and Charlie? Who wanted to experience life more than she did? Hell, she did not even want to move to the bed.

She stepped into his arms. "I don't want anything to stand between us tonight."

"No." He placed a soft kiss upon her hair, then lifted a thick lock to his nose, inhaling the clean, earthy scent of her, running the silky strand across his lips. He bent and nibbled her neck, moving to the hollow between her breasts. He captured her nipple with his finger, then with his teeth. She gasped and arched against him as he drew it between his lips. He sucked one, then the other.

Her hands gripped his shoulders, tighter and tighter. "Please."

She began thrusting in a natural rhythm. He thrust back. They could make love standing, but no, this was her first time. With a final taste of her nipple, he sank to his knees and rolled back, pulling her to the floor with him. He could not wait much longer. He had waited much too long already.

She spread her legs, allowing him full access. He intensified the kiss, beginning a slow grind against her. Up and down. Up and down. She groaned, writhing, asking him in soft, gasping mewls for *more*. His mouth left hers, his lips finding and locking once again on her raised nipple.

She bowed her back, running her hands through his hair. "Chase."

Her hips began to imitate his movements until he was burrowed quite snugly between her soft folds. She was wet. He knew they were close, so close to *finally* discovering what it was going to be like between them.

He lifted up, so he could see her face. Her eyes were closed, her skin flushed, her lips swollen and so beautiful. He trailed his hand between their bodies as he gazed at her. His thumb found the part of her that he knew, if he touched, would send her over the edge. He wanted to make sure she felt pleasure. He knew this could be painful, and he also knew he would not be able to last very long once he was inside her.

She snapped her eyes open as he dipped his finger there, moving his thumb deliberately back and forth. She looked bewildered and impatient all at once. Her mouth fell open, and she stretched her neck, tilting her head back against the thick rug. She shut her eyes, her tongue running frantically along her lower lip.

"Let it come."

She did not reply, just moaned.

He felt her pulse about his finger. Her breathing picked up until she was making continuous, low growls, almost catlike, deep in her throat. "Let it come, sweetheart, let it come," he said again.

Her hips lifted to meet his hand. "Ohhh . . . Chase . . . please."

She wrapped her hands round his arms, digging her nails into his skin. He welcomed the pain that would, for the moment, separate him from the enticing scene of Charlie Whitney, wild and naked, beckoning. He could not tear his gaze from her. She was quivering and shaking, her body betraying her, leaving her for him. He was holding all the cards, manipulating her with his hands, his mouth, his warm body.

As her climax began to consume her, she pushed her head into the side of his neck and whispered against his skin, "I . . . don't know . . . what . . . *it* . . . is."

"You will," he said as he fit her nipple between his lips.

Her body tightened, and she moaned, allowing the wildness to take her.

Chapter Twenty-Five

The room was spinning, the floor beneath her suddenly as soft as cotton, the air entering her lungs as thick and ambrosial as syrup. She let her mind reject conscious thought, until she was simply a mass of nerve endings. The tender skin along the side of her breast tingled from the nip of his teeth; her nipple puckered from the brush of his thick hair against it. But, oh . . . the triangle at the juncture of her thighs—a place of mystery to her before this night—burned and throbbed. Really throbbed. From the stroke of his thumb and the repeated plunge of his finger.

She squeezed her eyes shut, as tight as she could. Colors swam before her. The scent of liquor and smoke invaded her nose. She moved her mouth to his neck and licked, tasting soap, salt and a light tang she could not define. Him.

He pulled away. As she opened her eyes, he settled back and it was then she felt him probing at her entrance. He was incredibly, indescribably hard. He rubbed against her, then captured her lips as he guided himself in. Slowly, deliberately. She felt herself enfold the tip of him. Would he fit? Did it hurt him, this tightness?

As if in answer, he groaned against her mouth. ''Finally, by

God, I am going to make love to you.'' He lowered his mouth to her ear, kissing her earlobe tenderly. ''Trust me.''

She did, bringing her hips up to meet his as he thrust forward. The discomfort was short-lived, totally overwhelmed by the reality of him sliding into her. She wanted all of him: in her, on her, around her.

His firm, warm weight pressed her into the floor, his hard length sliding, inching, ever so slowly until their hips met. She rubbed against him then, welcoming the crispness of the hair on his groin and chest.

Curiously impatient for movement, she urged him, arching and commanding him in whispered demands. His thrusts increased in speed and depth. She met him each time, running her hands restlessly along his back, his buttocks.

The rug underneath them rippled, pulling the bedside table from the wall. A vase fell to the floor where it shattered into a thousand small crystal pieces.

She scarcely noticed. She was concentrating on following his lead, nothing more. Lifting herself to meet him, hanging on to him as he hung on to her. She was opening, accepting, clenching, allowing room for nothing else. They were a perfect fit.

He had begun to murmur words to her, words she neither wanted, nor needed, to understand. *He* was finally with her. Jared Chase was with her, and she wanted to shout with wonder.

''Let it come,'' she whispered his earlier command to him. ''Let it come.''

His arms quivered. He shuddered and panted above her. ''Dreaming of this. Of you. Of us.'' He groaned, and his back stiffened. ''Sorry, I cannot, cannot . . .''

She pulled his mouth to hers, twisting her hands in his hair. She did not want to hear his apologies. Not now. Not ever.

He shuddered and lowered himself to her, plunging into her, she suspected, as far as he could go.

Vaguely, as their gasping breaths mingled, she wondered if their lovemaking was unusual. To her it was truly incredible. If she lived to be one hundred, she would never hope to experience anything like it again.

''Am I too heavy? Can you breathe?''

She shook her head weakly.

Obviously not sure how to interpret her response, he rolled
to his side and gathered her against him. She sighed and snuggled her face in the crook of his neck, lazily stretching her
arms around his back. He rested his head on the top of hers.
She was thankful he was quiet, because she could think of
nothing to say. What could augment the most stimulating, energetic adventure she had ever encountered? She didn't want to
explore the reasons; she just wanted him to hold her. She wanted
to smell the faint scent of soap in his hair, feel his skin cooling
next to hers.

As her heartbeat slowed, she relaxed. He kissed the top of
her head and lifted her arms from around him. Sitting up, he
picked her up from the floor. She curled into him as he walked
to his bed. He lowered her to the soft, thick mattress, then
pulled a sheet over her and climbed in behind her. He dragged
her into his arms.

She snuggled against him and closed her eyes, hoping for
dreams of unbridled passion.

Charlie sat up, her hair hanging in a damp mass in front of
her face. She flipped it away with an impatient pitch and glanced
about, dazed and a bit confused to see she was back in her
room, in her bed.

What had awakened her?

The window swung back against the wall with a bang in
answer to her question. As she slid from the bed, her nightdress
bunched around her waist. She tugged it down, glad she was
wearing it. Obviously, Chase had dressed her and placed her
in bed, as if she were a small child. Her sleep had been as
restful as a child's. No. As restful as if she had been thoroughly
made love to, then allowed to fall asleep in her lover's arms.

She laughed softly. Was she actually embarrassed by being
put to bed? By a man she had been so intimate with? What
about lying naked with him? What about? She shook her head
and walked to the window. Her toes curled against the cool
floor as she leaned forward. A dismal, gray day looked back
at her. She sighed. Somehow a sunny day would have been so
much better. She was afraid the drabness would match Chase's
mood. Was he going to want to talk with her? She honestly

did not know. Neither of them had planned this; neither of them was willing to let it go too far. But . . . *she* wanted it to go farther. Heaven help her if last night was the final taste of him she was going to have.

She turned her head left, then right, searching along the riverbank for a view of the hills or factories Chase had described during one of their few conversations on the train. The thick layer of mist hovering over the water obscured her vision. A flash of black near the river's edge caught her eye. She froze, her breath stalling in her chest.

It was Chase, dressed in his favored attire: tight trousers, lawn shirt, Hessians. He walked along, slowly, his head bent, his arms crossed behind his back. A large, brown dog trotted in circles around him, trying to gain his attention.

She watched as Chase curved from the bank, taking a path which led into a patch of dense pines on the far reaches of his property.

She ran to the wardrobe and threw open the doors. After pulling off her nightdress, she slipped one of her cotton dresses over her head.

She stopped at the door and threw a quick glance at her bare feet. Mrs. Peters had taken her boots and done heavens knew what with them. Now all she had was a pair of flimsy satin slippers. She would probably ruin them, trudging along a muddy riverbank.

She made her way along the hallway, pausing at the top of the staircase. No chaperone in sight. With a whispered sigh of relief, she hurried down the stairs and through the door as quietly as possible. As she crossed the yard, she looked ahead for Chase, but he had disappeared into the trees. She skirted the bank and entered the path where he had, threading her way along the narrow trail that twisted and turned, aimlessly it seemed.

She stepped neatly over a large puddle, then grimaced as a sharp piece of pinestraw pricked her foot. Damn Mrs. Peters and her meddling.

Upon entering a small clearing, she stopped, startled to see the river once again. The path had wound right back to it. On a sunny day, this would be a lovely spot. A silent sanctuary sitting along the water, thick pine branches providing the perfect canopy.

Chase was there, crouched upon his haunches, tossing a stick to the dog who dashed after it with a joyful bark. The animal grabbed the stick between his teeth, then flung himself into the river, where he yipped and splashed before returning, soaking wet and shaking, to Chase.

"Whoa, boy, are you trying to get me all wet?" Chase laughed and threw the stick again, farther this time, into the edge of the water.

She had not noticed it last night, but he had been to the barber. His hair was much shorter. He looked different ... more aristocratic if that were possible. More beautiful. She stood there, observing him, as he laughed and tussled with the dog, whom he referred to only as "boy." Her gaze captured him: the wind-driven dance of dark hair, the flex of muscle in his arms and shoulders, the curve of his firm buttocks outlined by the tight cotton trousers. And those beautiful hands, those long, lean fingers. Fingers that had touched her, *inside*. . . .

She must have made a noise because Dog looked up, barked once and ran to her, clearly delighted to have another potential playmate.

Chase paused and dropped his head. She watched his chest expand as he took a breath. Then, in a sudden movement, he stapled his fingers upon the ground and pushed himself up, brushing his hands on his trousers as he turned.

Her gaze met his—a searing, ardent glance as thick as summer air. She flashed him a quick smile, which he did not return. Sighing, she bent and picked up the stick Boy had brought to her, throwing it into the trees. He loped off after it.

She looked up to find Chase had come closer. "Is he yours?" she asked.

He turned his head, an impassive expression set upon his face. She would have given a half eagle to know what his mind was creating like a little factory inside his head. But the look he presented to her was the same old look: aloof, restrained. Inexplicably disappointed, she glanced away. She would damn well hide her emotions if he was going to so blatantly hide his.

Think nothing, nothing, nothing.

"The dog is not mine, not really anyway. He just shows up

from time to time, stays at the stable. Mrs. Beard is sneaking scraps to him, I gather. The mutt feels quite welcome.''

Charlie took a deep breath and glanced back at him, forgetting her promise of a moment ago. ''Are we only going to talk about that dog?''

He grimaced. ''Charlie, you are the most brazen woman I have ever known.''

''You seemed to appreciate my brazenness last night.''

''Good God.'' He threw up his hands as he pivoted from her. He stalked to the river's edge and angrily kicked a rock into the water.

She followed him, desire and frustration building inside her. ''Are you going to act like last night didn't happen? Can you dismiss what is between us so easily?'' She stopped as she reached him, her shoulder brushing his arm as they stood looking at the water. ''Is it always like that?'' she finally whispered.

''No . . . it is not always *like that*.'' His voice was thick, hoarse.

''I''—she perched her fists on her slender hips, stuck out her chin and turned to face him—''I want more.''

He threw her an incredulous look while making a poor attempt to contain his laughter. ''Oh, Charlie,'' was all he managed to utter.

Her face burned with embarrassment, but something deep within made her continue. ''This is not funny. I'm here to offer you an . . . arrangement, of sorts. Yes''—she nodded—''an arrangement.''

''What kind of . . . arrangement?''

She cleared her throat and swallowed. How did one *propose* this? ''Well . . . I . . .'' she shrugged. ''I am not planning . . . I mean Tom Walker is . . . when I get back.'' She shrugged again. ''There *is* no one there . . . oh, hellfire.'' She threw up her hands.

His gaze dropped, and he struggled to appear apathetic. He really did. But she could see the hint of a smile tugging on his mouth.

''You know what I mean,'' she said and stamped her foot. He wanted her! She knew that. Maybe as much as she wanted him. He just seemed so hesitant. Which was not a sentiment she associated with him.

"Chase?"

"Hmmm?"

"Quit rubbing that scar."

His gaze flew to hers as he flung his hands apart.

"You don't have to worry," she said, a perceptible note of strength snaking through her words.

When he continued to stare at her without uttering a word, she struggled to think of a delicate way to state the obvious. Honesty, as usual, won. "My virginity," she blurted, "I think you're worried . . . me being alone after this."

He stretched and picked up a rock, then stood and twisted as he skipped it across the water. Tap, tap, tap, plop.

She followed suit, jerking her wrist as she snapped the rock from her hand. Chase's gaze traveled from her to the water. Tap, tap, tap, tap, plop. He grinned as he cast her a sidelong glance.

She smiled, trying to deny the warm tingle his silent, trifling flattery sent her. "I have a creek behind my house, remember?"

He nodded and sighed. "I am not going back to Edgemont."

She was silent for a moment as she bent to gather another rock. "I know."

He turned to her, his eyes as dark and wide as the muddy river bottom. "How?"

She shrugged and flicked her wrist as the rock flew from her hand. Tap, tap, tap, plop. "Last night . . . I just knew. I could see it in your face, hear it in your voice. You were drunk and"—she flipped her hand in a small circle—"I just knew."

"Why, then . . . why did you let me—"

She took two steps forward until they were nose to nose. Or nose to chest, actually. She glared up at him, her face hot. "I did not *let* you. Is it so difficult for you to imagine that I may have done what I damn well wanted to?" She jabbed a bony finger in his arm. "You let *me!*"

He took a step back.

"Are you so unaccustomed to a woman who knows what she wants and goes after it?"

"No. I am not."

She clenched her jaw and squeezed her nails into her palms. "What is it, then?"

His gaze dropped from her eyes, to her lips, to her chest and back again. He opened his mouth, then shut it with a frown. An image of his hands on her breasts jumped into her mind. Was he thinking about that, too? She swallowed. Her composure was slipping.

Losing patience, she advanced a step, pressing her chest into his. She sniffed. Leather. He had been riding this morning. There was also some spicy scent she could not identify. "You smell good." She sniffed again. "Something new."

"Bay rum," he said as he took another step back. His flat expression revealed nothing, but she noticed his eyes darken as his gaze crawled the length of her.

She grinned. A step forward.

"An arrangement. Just like the ones you described." She reached out, skimming her palm over his chest. She hoped he was going to relent soon. She wasn't sure if she could physically overpower him, but she was willing to try. "You won't even have to buy me flowers. An even exchange. My enthusiasm for your experience."

He coughed and stumbled back. "Are you *insane?*"

He was weakening. His uncharacteristically awkward movement told her so. "I never would have marked you a prude, Chase." That should get him.

"A *prude?*"

"I'm old enough to know what I want," she continued, "and I'm old enough to take care of myself." She noticed a light sheen of sweat glazing his skin. Had that been there before?

"But—"

She wanted to kiss him. Touch him. Her fingers itched so badly that she had to curl them tight into a fist. It would be wonderful to have him touch her the way he had last night, too. She took a step forward. "I want this. I want you. I can't help it." Maybe *she* was a fool to think what was between them was mere friendship. She brushed speculation aside. To think she had made it twenty-four years without making love, and then come to realize how amazing it was!

He stepped back, brushing against a fat tree trunk. She smiled. He had nowhere else to run.

She stepped forward. "I never would have taken you for a man to reject a serious offer."

The pulse at his throat was tapping against his skin. Beautiful skin. Soft lips. Firm chin. Wide chest. Flat stomach. *Oh.* He looked as hard as the tree trunk he'd shoved himself against in his mad rush to escape.

She smiled. Victory was close at hand. "Chase"—she placed her warm palms on his chest—"I'm naked under this dress."

He snapped his head around, his eyes blazing with hunger, anger. "Stop playing with me."

"I so want to play with you. That's what I am trying to tell you."

Moving faster than she could have expected, he grasped her shoulders, turned and pushed her up against the tree. The rough wood bit into her back as he pressed into her from chest to hip. He moved his hands to either side of her head, imprisoning her between his arms.

She did not speak, only stared up at him. *Finally.*

Chapter Twenty-Six

Defeated, he sighed and leaned in to kiss her. She issued a breath of relief as his lips settled upon hers. He almost smiled. Obviously, she had been running out of ideas to get him to touch her.

She reached for him, wrapping her arms around his neck. She tried to pull him closer, but he resisted, digging his fingers into the rough bark. Her taut body was so inviting . . . he wanted to lose himself in her, sharpen himself against her like a dull knife, but the wood had to be biting into her tender skin. She had not voiced a complaint, though. She had, in fact, begun to stir. Especially, it felt, against his erection. He groaned. Christ, he wanted her. If only she had not mentioned her lack of underclothing.

Had she lied? Running his hands down her body to her waist, he pulled her dress up in fistfuls. With the material wadded in a sloppy roll at her navel, he slid his hands to her buttocks. Skin and muscle, smooth and tight, met his roving fingers.

Oh . . . she had not lied.

He seized her hips, lifting and nestling her against his hard length. Instinctively—she was a damned intuitive creature with respect to lovemaking—she wrapped her legs around his waist.

"Yes," she whispered against his lips, "I like this." Of

course *she* would. He did, too. Her skin was warm and the air between them thick, just like the night before. A kaleidoscope of colors had begun to spin before his closed lids. Everywhere he touched her, his skin tingled. He slanted his head, inviting her tongue to engage his in play. After all, this was what she wanted.

Her arm dropped from his neck and trailed between their bodies. He sucked a sharp, surprised breath into his lungs and tore his mouth from hers as he felt her reaching for him. Her fingers carefully undid his trousers. She released him from a tangle of cloth and surrounded him with her fingers.

"Does this hurt?"

He lifted his head from her shoulder, where it had dropped when she had first touched him. "No . . . no." Corrupt contemplation he knew, but he hoped she left the scent of roses upon him.

He glanced down. Bare legs tied like a string about his waist, the dark triangle of hair between her thighs mixing intimately with his own. As he stared, incapable of speech, barely able to breathe, she placed him at her entrance.

Before she let go of him, she ran her hand along him. An inquisitive touch. Gentle, arousing. He literally pulsed in her hand.

He threw his head back and closed his eyes as he raised her hips and slowly, slowly eased into her. She arched in an impatient movement, drawing him in with a hard, long thrust that left them both gasping.

"Charlie." He lowered his head and kissed her.

She moaned against his lips as he began a vigorous rhythm. He wrapped his arms around her, to protect her back from the rough trunk. Each thrust chafed. But the hot points of pleasure coursing through him, her soft skin surrounding him, were more than enough to defeat the small dose of pain.

Her sweet breath caressed his neck, his ear. He squeezed her bottom as his tongue moved in rhythm with his thrusts. He could not get enough of her. He had never been with a woman and experienced so much. Her sharp scent roosting in his nostrils; her shudders striking his fingers; her salty taste seducing his mouth; her enticing, low moans chiming in his ears.

Strangely a mental picture, far different than what he was actually seeing, sprang to his mind.

He saw her hunched over her desk in the *Sentinel* office, her pink tongue tucked between her teeth. He saw her striding along the boardwalk as though President Fillmore was awaiting her arrival. He saw her snapping her fingers and clicking her tongue, talking to that damn orange cat. He saw her running through a cornfield, her sable hair whipping like smoke.

He lifted his face to the side of hers as all those images intertwined in his mind, in his heart. He squeezed her as he drew closer to his desire.

She shivered and twisted, asking him to help her, telling him she was burning up.

He kissed her neck and whispered, "Close your mind. Do not think. *Feel.*"

Her muscles clenched. She must be close. He turned with her in his arms and laid her gently upon the ground, sinking on top of her. Her arms flopped behind her, thrusting her chest up. Her eyes were shut, words slipping from her lips in an incoherent flow.

He lifted his hands, placing one at the juncture of her thighs, the other at her breast. He began to caress her. Even through the cotton cloth of her dress, her nipple hardened, puckered.

"Jared . . . I'm dying."

He groaned and shuddered above her. "Then I am . . . dying . . . too."

They moved together, sweat from their bodies mingling, the tangy aroma of sex settling upon them like a sheet.

A tide of fervent response consumed him. She curved against him as his name slipped past her lips in a loud cry. Her muscles clenched like a brace about him. It was more than he could take. He thrust into her, then held himself still as everything he had, everything he felt, flowed into her. He shut his eyes, allowing the world to fade into nothing but his strong heartbeat.

He drew a breath and lowered himself to her. Her harsh, quick breaths lifted the hair from his neck. He heard her swallow.

He rolled, pulling her with him. She did not resist, descending like a feather against him. As he flung his arm over his forehead, he wondered if he would be able to stand without collapsing and walk from the secluded clearing. Damn. It had been even more phenomenal than last night. And more frightening.

She tilted her head slightly; then he heard her giggle. He had not heard her giggle before. Not once. Charlie Whitney was not a giggling girl. Helpless, he rolled his head toward her and flicked his eyes open. Hers were wide and blue. So blue they brought an ache to his chest. "Why are you laughing?"

A mischievous glint entered her gaze. "I was thinking about writing an editorial on the public school system."

"School system?" She had been pondering an editorial while. . . .

She lifted her hand to her mouth and laughed behind it. "No." She shook her head. "I was imagining the places a resourceful person could find to make love. I mean, if it works so well with clothes *on.*"

His mind flipped through a vast array of locales suitable for just such a passionate encounter. Charlie was there, in all of them—under him, over him, beside him, in front of him, bending, pulling, licking, sucking. He sighed and squeezed his eyes shut. "Charlie . . . you are killing me."

She touched his face. Helplessly, he leaned into her touch. "I've never been a modest, prim model of correct behavior. It used to upset me that everything I did was perceived as being so"—she paused as she searched for the right word—"wrong. So inappropriate."

Adam opened his eyes, mindful of the sincere expression that would be shining like a bright star upon her face. He had never known anyone to be so damn sure of themselves and, at the same time, be able to understand—even laugh—about the way the world perceived them.

"My mother once told me she was amazed she had been a part of creating a child so very different from herself. She was *pleased.* Can you imagine? Such a wonderful, wise, elegant woman . . . and here *I* was, lagging along her side, barefoot often as not. Dirty face, torn clothing. She allowed me to do too much, I suppose, to make my own decisions. Even then. She wanted me to be able to think for myself." She smiled and trailed her hand down his chest, stopping when she came to the patch of dark hair that showed through the open neck of his shirt. She slipped her fingers through it, absently, never imagining how even this very simple touch upset his equilibrium.

"I know who you are, Adam Jared Chase."

He pulled away and rolled to a sitting position. He slung his arm upon his raised knee and glanced back at her. She was regarding him quite calmly, as if she had expected his abrupt movement. He supposed she had. *Damn her.*

"You mustn't think I'm being insincere. I'm sure you have known many women who have been. Who wanted more than they said they did." She lifted herself on pointed elbows, which only served to advance her breasts to the front of his mind. "I'm telling you *exactly* what I want. In definite terms, as a matter of fact."

Insincere? Was that what she thought? Her honesty scared him senseless. He should have never touched her, never kissed her, never laid a damn finger on her. Because he was not going to change. Even for her. But letting her go back to Edgemont after making love to her like this was probably going to kill him.

Just look at her: lying there, dress pulled up to her waist, blues eyes glowing with passion. So beautiful. He urged his gaze from her. "Oliver Stokes has contacted an editor to take over the *Sentinel.* Temporarily at least. Benjamin Folkes. I have met him a time or two . . . been in the business for years. Well-respected. Conservative. A good front man for Stokes." He shook his head and traced a pattern in the pinestraw lying between his feet. "He is an ethical man, but he will not buck Stokes. Actually, I figure he has to be close to retiring. Would be a good way to leave the business." He shrugged. What the hell did that matter? "Anyway, I have scheduled a meeting with Benjamin next week. Stokes wants you to meet with him, as well."

"Stokes knows I'm in Richmond?"

He nodded. "News travels fast. By the way, the bastard is very happy with the progress of the *Sentinel.*"

"Why is he bringing in a new editor, then?"

"My editor in Richmond wants me back. Stokes has agreed. He figures the hard part is completed. The *Sentinel* has been reorganized. The press is in place. He has a very capable pressman and a promising reporter. Also, after the incident with his thugs . . .'' He stopped tracing circles in the straw and tilted his gaze to hers for just a moment before sliding it back to the area between his feet. "Let's just say I was not obliging."

"What did you do?"

"I told him I would kill him if he tried anything like that again. Miles will keep me informed." He did not mention he had said this to Oliver Stokes as he shook the man by the collar of his brown linen jacket. "Stokes also mentioned the gossips around town are very interested in the female reporter residing in my home."

"Hmmm . . . you may have some explaining to do."

"There will never be any explanations." He understood what she was implying.

"Oh."

"She is only a friend."

"A friend you're *intimate* with."

"Yes."

"Why can't we do that?"

"We *are* doing that." Dammit, she was the most eccentric woman.

"I want to know today isn't going to be the last time. I want to *share* this with you. I don't want you to feel so bad every time. I want you to know that I accept you for who you are." She paused, then said, "I want to call you by the name I say in my head when we're together."

"No." He pushed his fingers through the straw.

She continued as if he had not spoken. "I'll stay until next week. After we have this meeting, I'll go back with Mrs. Peters. I'm not going to deny what I want any longer. And I'm not going to help you deny what you want any longer, either."

His gaze migrated to her. Her face was tilted to the sky, her blue eyes wide and clear. Was she so sure she could do this and leave? She seemed sure. Did Charlie realize how absurd it was to compare what he felt for her to what he felt for Marilyn?

It was no matter, really, for he could not deny he wanted her, even if he was able to deny the depth of his emotions. Besides, he could no more leave her alone—while she slept just down the hall from him—than he could make it snow in

July. Next week, though. He would send her off next week. With enough memories for a lifetime.

He sighed. "All right. I give up."

She smiled, with a noticeable suggestion of relief.

Perhaps this was what he needed. What he had needed since Eaton's death.

Rain began to pelt them as he pulled her on top of him.

With the storm acting as a shield against the rest of the world, their swift desire propelled them.

The arrangement commenced.

Chapter Twenty-Seven

"Ow . . . my back is stinging. I think I scraped it on that tree. Maybe I should ask Mrs. Peters for some—"

"No! I can put something on it tonight. Give me a reason to undress you."

Charlie grinned and flipped her gaze to him as they walked along the path to the house. "Do you need a reason?"

Adam grinned back at her. "Nope, guess not."

They laughed and continued along, their linked hands swinging. The grass was slick with rain and shiny green, like a wet emerald. He pulled her to a stop as they reached the edge of the woods. He leaned, kissing her softly. "We cannot go back together. I'll sneak in through the pantry door. Mrs. Beard is at the market this morning, so the way should be clear."

Charlie's gaze dropped, and she grimaced. "Mrs. Peters is going to scream if she sees me like this."

"She was going to visit her daughter today. You should be safe." He gave her a soft nudge.

"Thanks," she said as she trudged away.

He could not help laughing as he watched her make her way to the house. She was a sight, all right: Brown dress soaked and muddy, grass and pinestraw clinging to it. Dark hair plastered to her skull in a soggy mass. Best of all, her dress was a little too short, revealing delicate, dirty ankles.

He sprinted across the lawn when she rounded the corner of the house. Should he have let her go in through the pantry and taken the main door himself? Oh, well, too late for that.

Slipping inside, he closed the door. All was silent. Mrs. Beard and her trips to market were fairly predictable.

"Charlotte Whitney, what in the world?"

Oh, no. He tiptoed to the doorway leading from the kitchen to the entrance hall. Leaning a bit to the left, he saw Charlie standing just inside the door, Mrs. Peters settled directly in front of her like an enraged bull. The old woman's back faced the kitchen.

"What were you doing out in this rain?"

"Well—"

"I hope that dress is one of those old rags you brought with you."

"Actually—" Charlie's gaze narrowed as she caught sight of him hovering in the doorway.

Mrs. Peters tapped her toe with an angry rhythm. "Are you listening to me?"

He winked and placed a finger to his lips.

"Yes, Mrs. Peters, I'm listening." Her eyebrows lifted and her lips parted, and for just a moment he thought she was going to give him away. Then the corners of her mouth lifted, and he knew she would not.

Mrs. Peters sighed. "I just cannot imagine what has happened to you."

Adam sent Charlie a jaunty wave, stepped silently around the corner and started down the hallway leading to the back staircase. The last sight he caught was Charlie rolling her eyes at her chaperone and saying, "Well, Mrs. Peters, the truth is . . ."

Charlie looked north, up the broad, deep river. The sun was fading, but she could still glimpse Richmond's dappled, clay hillside. Those hills—she had learned—held a melange of shops, factories, foundries, churches, hotels, warehouses, banks and mansions. She had passed the incredibly wealthy and the indescribably poor on Richmond's crowded streets.

She and Chase spent the days in the city, eating ice cream on the grassy expanse of Capital Square, visiting City Hall, buying plums and grapes from the town market and feeding them to each other between laughter and kisses; stopping by the *Times* office, where Chase showed her a printing press the size of a mountain, and a supply closet she would always remember with a warm glow.

They spent the nights exploring—mind *and* body—hungrily, feverishly. They took walks along the river, talked of life and philosophy, love and religion, politics and wealth, as bells pealed and smoke from the tobacco factories and flour mills swirled thick in the air around them. They visited small, dark restaurants, whispering to each other across a table as the world around them faded into the background. They sat in companionable silence in his library: he, working on one of his assignments; she, sketching him with broad, sure strokes.

She observed the pass of time with a silent eye.

Chase had become her best friend. Her closest friend. He voiced her thoughts before she did, shared her interests, supported and challenged her ambitions, ignited her temper *and* her passion. He smiled when she muttered something scandalous, debated social issues with her till she was blue in the face, and made love to her tenderly and with spirited abandon.

She drew a deep breath, smiling as the sharp aroma of tobacco met her nose. It was a wonder she could detect a scent as entrenched as this one was. Glancing toward the house, the pale light shining from her window beckoned.

She walked at a slow pace, sidestepping muddy puddles and downed limbs from the storm the night before. As usual, her thoughts jumped to him, as they had for so long now. What seemed like forever. He had finally let her in. A bit, anyway. It felt good, so deep and sure.

Only . . . another part of her denied their closeness, pushed it away with a cold, swift hand. She felt strong and independent for doing it, even as a hard knot formed in the pit of her stomach.

Last night, a sharp crack of thunder had woken her, and she'd turned to find him twisting and mumbling, tangling the sheets around his legs, sweat covering his face. One name passed his lips. Eaton. She knew his were fierce nightmares.

She'd shaken him, all the while murmuring soft words, not expecting his violent reaction. It was obvious from his startled expression he was not used to sleeping in the same bed with anyone.

His past had bubbled from his lips, from his soul, like hot lava spewing from a volcano. She had been foolish to think the circumstances affecting them were similar. Her mother and father had loved her, had willingly offered love *to* her. Chase and Eaton had turned to their father for love, only to find a harsh man who was unwilling or unable to offer more than money and a name. They had survived simply because they had each other.

How awful it must have been for him. To hold the person he loved most in the world in his arms, his brother's life spilling on the ground like whiskey from a broken bottle. His memory was still vivid. He said he sometimes woke to find himself wiping his hands upon the sheets—trying to wipe away Eaton's blood.

A warm breeze blew off the river, lifting strands of hair from her face. She increased her pace to a light run, throwing a quick glance at her window. Sure enough, Mrs. Peters' pinched face was peeking from between the curtains. *Hellfire.*

Charlie hopped up the steps and pushed through the side door, the inviting warmth of the kitchen rushing to greet her. The distinctive aroma of cinnamon hung heavy in the air like a thick, comfortable quilt.

"Miss Whitney, you'd best get up there."

Charlie flashed Mrs. Beard a weak smile. "I know, I know."

Mrs. Beard clicked her tongue against her teeth. She kept her gaze trained on sticky biscuit dough as she said, "That old nag has been here at least ten times asking after you. I told her you had taken a short walk." She sniffed and frowned. "None too pleased to hear that, I tell you."

Charlie only grunted and continued through the kitchen. She glanced around and, seeing she was alone, lifted her dress past her ankles and took the stairs two at a time. She wasn't looking forward to the evening, damn Mrs. Peters and her meddling.

She stopped before the door to her bedroom and smoothed a hand over her tangled hair. She tugged on the sleeves of her dress, hoping to settle some of the wrinkles. She looked a mess as usual, and *she* knew it. Mrs. Peters just had not yet learned to accept this as fact.

The door flew open, and Charlie gasped and took a step back.

"Young lady, where have you been? Do you have any idea what time it is?" She grabbed Charlie's elbow and yanked her—quite forcefully—into the room. The door slammed shut behind them.

"Mrs. Peters, the dinner guests won't be arriving until—"

"I *know* what time the guests are arriving. I planned this evening."

Charlie grimaced. Yes, she knew that as well.

"Two hours is not enough time to dress for the evening."

Two hours?

Mrs. Peters hauled Charlie to the bureau like a recalcitrant child. "Oh, dear, I sometimes forget you have been without female influence for so long."

"Really, this is just a simple dinner."

Mrs. Peters glared at her before turning to the wardrobe. "Charlotte, dear, you minimize the evening I have planned. Mr. Chase is a man of means and reputation in Richmond. His father was a well-respected judge; his family is associated with the very best people. He has just recently returned from an assignment. One of interest to many of his friends." She opened a drawer and lifted a pair of gloves, stockings and a small box of hatpins from within. Walking to the bed, she deposited them carefully before returning to the wardrobe.

"Also, and I am surprised Mr. Chase had not thought of this, he has a visitor, a colleague, staying with him as a guest in his home. Due to the fact this visitor is a woman, there has been a great deal of curiosity and speculation. My presence lends a certain amount of credibility to the situation, but there has to be some kind of formal introduction. Otherwise it looks, well . . . suffice it to say that it does not look good."

Mrs. Peters opened another drawer and removed a turquoise fan and a pair of dainty slippers the same shade of blue as the fan. "Although, this evening is certainly not a *formal* evening of any sort. It is a modest dinner party. Hardly appropriate, if you ask me."

Charlie couldn't help asking. "What would have been . . . appropriate?"

Mrs. Peters waltzed to the bed, depositing the other items as Charlie looked on with perceptible dread and a small flicker of fear. What the hell was she supposed to do with those things?

"Appropriate? A ball for no less than one hundred guests. Or an evening at the opera followed by a late dinner for at least fifty friends and acquaintances. Certainly not this . . . this"—she flung her arm in exasperation—"affair."

Charlie turned, hiding a smile at Mrs. Peters' choice of words. If she only knew how appropriate they really were.

A full hour and a half later, Charlie stood before the mirror, spit-shined as an old shoe—as presentable as she ever would be. Mrs. Peters had finally left to attend to her own toilette, proclaiming Charlie "tolerable."

Her chaperone was perturbed because Charlie had refused to don the hideously wicked corset, a mass of stiff bone and ties she was having none of. It looked like some contraption used to keep a prisoner from escaping. She'd be damned first.

There had also been the small argument about the hat. It had a ridiculous blue feather jutting from the top of it which kept flopping down, resting on the top of Charlie's nose every time she put it on. So, that was that.

She *had* agreed to the stockings, which actually felt light and mysteriously thrilling against her skin; the gloves, which she planned to discard as soon as possible; and the fan, which she intended to hold in her hand but never open. She had, in fact, completely ignored her chaperone's quick lesson about how to use it. What did she need a fan for if not to fend off heat?

Even though she was wearing a preposterous amount of clothing—unnecessary layers and adornments—Charlie could not quite suppress the small spark of excitement that skipped through her as she gazed at herself in the long mirror.

She'd never worn her hair in this kind of twist before. A chignon, Mrs. Peters called it. Of course, she'd seen Kath and Lila wear their hair this way many times, but she had never tried it herself. There wasn't much to doing it once you knew how. Mrs. Peters had even intertwined a blue velvet ribbon in her dark strands.

Charlie ran her hands along the sides of her waist. Admittedly, the turquoise silk dress fit well. Her needlework simply could not compare to this. Now she understood why women paid a seamstress great sums of money. She was very handy with a needle, but this dress was a work of art. Small, perfect stitches—not a bit of thread showing.

She gave a quick pull to the neck of her dress. It was round and showed a hint of cleavage she had not known she had—one she wasn't sure she wanted to expose—and just the barest trace of shoulder, too. Mrs. Peters had noted her surprise and assured her the dress was all the style. Quite modest. Too modest, too blue, too plain was what her chaperone had actually said.

Charlie's gaze dropped once again to the dark valley between her breasts. A hot flush lit her cheeks as she imagined his lips there.

The sound of laughter drew her to the window. Three men were there on the lawn, their red-tipped cheroots glowing in the darkness. She noticed Chase immediately. The familiar tilt of his head, the line of his shoulders. He leaned his head back, glancing into the star-filled sky. He was bored. She knew him well enough to tell.

Smiling softly, she placed her palm flat against the glass. *She loved him.*

Surprisingly, this was not the startling denouement she might have expected. Love had crept up on her as peacefully as the aroma of fine wine on the senses. She had respected him from the start. How could she not? He was brilliant—observant and so remarkably diligent that she felt a fierce surge of forbidden pride every time she worked with him. It was true he could be harsh and demanding, but she'd come to believe this was only because his mind sliced through topics as rapidly as an oar through water.

Liking him . . . well, that had taken a bit longer. Although, it was inevitable they would like each other. They shared a comparable sense of humor and an incredible number of common interests. They agreed on most political issues, argued about religion, debated the necessity of philosophy, differed on the issue of ecology, promised never to discuss fashion and acquiesced enthusiastically with respect to intimate relations.

In truth, that aspect of her relationship with him had begun almost immediately. She had not liked him the first time she laid eyes on him, but she had never been able to deny his attractiveness.

Her gaze followed him as he walked to the house, pulling a hand through his hair in an impatient gesture. She loved watching him. It was crazy, the fancy of an obsessed lover, she knew, but he *moved* with a feline grace and agility that never failed to crowd all thought from her mind and propel hot blood through her body.

He could be stooping to gather a fallen penny or brushing dirt from his boots. Irresistible . . . that's what he was.

She lifted her hand from the glass. Too bad. It had been too dark to see what he was wearing.

Mrs. Peters knocked lightly and, without waiting, entered the room. "We should make our way downstairs, Charlotte."

Charlie circled to face her chaperone, her dress dancing through the turn with her.

"Do not look as if you have swallowed a pit. This is going to be an enjoyable evening."

"Humph."

Mrs. Peters sighed and slipped her arm through Charlie's as Charlie passed her on the way to the door. "Now remember, head held high, shoulders back. Walk slowly. You have a lovely figure. No need to ruin it with an ugly curve in your back."

"Mrs. Peters, do you realize I am twenty-four years old?"

Much too reasonably, her chaperone said, "Of course I do, dear. Guidance is what you have been missing. Age means little."

Charlie clamped her jaw tight, refusing to discuss the matter any further. What was the use?

"When it comes down to it, a newspaper *is* a commercial venture."

Adam nodded and exhaled a gray wisp of smoke. His fingers caressed the thin cheroot. "I only ask, does ethical journalism have to be sacrificed for the sake of fiscal concerns?" He turned, flicked ashes into a bronze urn sitting on the table next to his chair and recrossed one outstretched leg over the other.

Tanner Barkley, one of the best newspapermen in Richmond and an old friend of Adam's, only smiled.

Adam relaxed his rigid posture and laughed, realizing Tanner's game. "I know. I need to bury my idealistic tendencies. Who would think I still had any after so many years in this business?"

Tanner lifted his glass to his lips. "Legitimate press must take its place in political society."

"Yes, but who benefits from the shift from independence?"

"It would seem to me the press may then cease to be seen as the dangerous and revolutionary force it is currently viewed as in some circles."

"I think the view is deserved to a certain extent, and so do you. Furthermore"—Adam stubbed his cheroot in the urn with a forceful twist that followed through in his words—"there are no benefits for anyone from a newspaper's alignment with political society, as you so graciously christened it."

Tanner's pale blue gaze skipped from his empty glass to Adam's frown. "You—"

The sound of the library door opening and closing suspended all conversation between the men. They swiveled around in their chairs in time to see a whirlwind of turquoise sweep across the room. "Shush! Don't tell her I'm in here," the whirlwind hissed before disappearing behind a heavy velvet curtain.

The library door sounded again, this time with a great deal more force.

"Is she in here?"

Adam tried to eradicate any trace of surprise from his face and turned to regard Mrs. Peters with a practiced expression of indifference. "Excuse me?"

Mrs. Peters, her face drawn into a tight pinch, glanced at Tanner, then at Adam. Her face reddened. "I am . . . I am sorry to interrupt, Mr. Chase. It is just that," she struggled, "that . . . *young woman* is giving me a difficult time. Again."

Adam frowned. "She will turn up. Try the kitchen. One of her favorite haunts."

Mrs. Peters nodded, a small bob of her head, apologized again and backed from the room.

Tanner laughed as they settled back in their chairs. "What was that all about?"

Adam glanced at his friend and shrugged. How could he explain the inexplicable? Better to let her speak for herself. "Come on out, chicken."

"Is it safe?" A petite foot shifted beneath the curtain.

"Yes. I think I glowered harshly enough to keep her away for at least ten minutes."

"Thank heaven." Charlie released a breath as she emerged from the folds of the curtain. As if nothing remarkable had taken place, she shook her skirt and strolled toward them. "You didn't have to tell her about the kitchen. Now I will never be able to escape there again." She sighed and waved her hand in the air. "Just continue your discussion. Pretend I'm not here." She walked leisurely, looking at the book-lined shelves.

"For God's sake, sit," Adam finally said.

She glanced up, a teasing grin curving her lips. A feral light entered her eyes.

She looked beautiful tonight, and unlike the usual, doubtful Charlie Whitney, this Charlie Whitney knew it. With a flip of her long, blue skirt, she walked to the chair behind his desk and sank into its warm, leather depths.

Her gaze locked with his across the width of the desk. Was she remembering what they had done in that chair two nights ago? They had been so energetic, the chair had flipped over backward, pitching them to the floor. The floor had served quite well, too, as he recalled.

He pulled his gaze away and glanced at Tanner, who looked at him, then Charlie.

Adam cleared his throat. "So, what did you do?"

Charlie leaned forward and placed her palms on the desk. Her chest thrust forward with the movement. Adam watched Tanner stir in his chair. He suddenly felt the insane urge to jab his friend in the ribs. Hard.

"What did I do? That woman . . . bless her heart, is making me crazy. It is just too much for her to chaperone a woman like me. Ridiculous, anyway . . . as if I were a young girl. She just wants to drag me from one introduction to another."

Adam started, belatedly remembering his manners. "Miss Charlotte Whitney, Mr. Tanner Barkley. Miss Whitney works for the newspaper I was with in South Carolina. Charlie, Mr.

Barkley's an old friend of mine who works for the *Times* as a traveling correspondent.''

"How do you do, Miss Whitney?" Tanner nodded his head, then laughed as she presented her hand. He leaned forward, clearly hesitating, then shrugged and shook it.

Adam took a deep breath and made himself refocus his attention. He did not own the woman sitting across from him. No matter how much he wanted to in the darkness of the night.

Tanner laughed again and Charlie joined in.

Adam's blood bubbled beneath his skin.

"What could you possibly mean about your chaperone . . . not knowing what to do with a woman like you?" Tanner asked with a grin.

"She wants a woman who follows the rules. I do not follow anyone's rules but my own."

"Hmmm . . . interesting."

Adam grabbed his glass and stood. Be damned if he'd sit and watch Tanner Barkley flirt with his . . . with Charlie. "Another, Tanner?"

Tanner nodded and extended his glass.

"Me, too."

Adam rolled his eyes. "Of course."

"Miss Whitney, Adam and I were just discussing politics and the press. The old man over there thinks it doesn't benefit anyone for a newspaper to go in that direction. What do you think?"

Adam felt her gaze skip to him. He turned, balancing the three glasses in his hands, avoiding her eyes.

"But . . . that's—"

Adam placed her glass in front of her, then sat. "I never said I agreed with a partisan press. I said *you* had to learn to accept it."

"Yes, well . . . I suppose you did." She shifted her gaze to Tanner. "My opinion is very likely biased, Mr. Barkley. The owners who are making these decisions know nothing about the people who produce the newspaper. They have no concept of the values and convictions that those people bring to their work." She lifted her glass with both hands and took a small sip. "In essence, they make decisions based more upon increasing the fundamental consciousness of the working class in the direction they want to increase it. Manipulation, plain and simple.''

Tanner's teasing smile slipped a notch. ''I can't argue with that assessment, ma'am.''

''Newspapers are only going to grow with the growth of the news agencies. Paper costs are getting lower; the literate population is increasing. If only . . .'' Adam pulled his gaze from her, focusing on the noise of a carriage arriving outside.

''If only?'' she prompted.

How could he answer a question that *had* no clear answer? If onlys served no purpose in life, except to make you feel like manure in the bottom of a livery stall.

If only Eaton had lived. . . .

If only Charlie needed him more. . . .

If only the two of them were alone in a world free of complications. . . .

If only they had more time. . . .

He had purchased the train tickets this morning. Charlie was leaving in two days. Mrs. Peters had practically yelled with relief, glad to be fleeing a confusing situation. Charlie, besides a slow, sad smile, had shown little emotion about his announcement.

While *he* felt like someone had kicked him in the gut.

''If only?'' Again, she tried.

He looked back at her, smiled and shrugged.

''You're going soft, Adam,'' Tanner said.

''Maybe so,'' Adam concurred. ''Maybe so.''

Charlie pursed her lips and rose from her chair. ''I should go find Mrs. Peters.'' She sighed. ''She's probably dredging the river bottom for me.''

Adam slipped his watch from his pocket and flipped it open. Closing it with a snap, he got to his feet. ''Guests are arriving, and I have neglected my duties as host long enough. I will walk you out. Tanner?''

Tanner stretched and yawned. ''Please, excuse me. I had a long night; awake till dawn waiting for a contact. I may just stay behind and finish my drink, if you don't mind. Hate the formalities, introductions and all, you know.''

Adam did know. This was not his, or Tanner's, affair. Why had Tanner been invited? He socialized with him, of course, at their club and a few other places he would just as soon forget. But neither of them were dinner party men.

Just who would be at this damn thing?

Charlie passed him on her way to the door, her long skirt whispering against the polished floor.

She was angry with him. All right. He *was* trying to keep his emotions from her. He was trying to deny the incredible *vulnerability* he felt when he was with her. He could not be as honest as she. He just could not. Because if he was, then he would never be able to let her go. And loving someone again was much more than he was willing to risk. It was too *late*.

He caught her, though, slowing her with a light touch to the back of her neck. Her skin burned his fingertip as surely as a flame. "Wait."

She stopped but did not turn. "I need to go."

He moved closer until he pressed against her. Remembering Tanner was in the room with them, he fought the urge to kiss the soft, bare skin exposed by her neckline and upswept hair. "You look beautiful. More beautiful than any woman I have ever seen." He inhaled, catching her scent at once: roses and something earthy, like fresh grass and pinestraw.

She half turned, blue eyes wide, surprised.

He smiled. "I do not lie."

"You don't tell me everything, either." She sighed, and he saw her shoulders tremble just a little. "Jared . . . you're my best friend."

He swallowed and took a step back. "You are mine. You know that." He nearly choked on the words.

"Then, why? Why lock me out?"

"Sweetheart . . . *two days*. You are leaving in two days." He balled his hands into fists at his sides. "Why make this any goddamn harder?" He could not keep the anger from his voice. Damn her. She wanted him to share his whole life, then casually say goodbye. Was he allowed to keep some things from her? To save himself?

"I don't think of what we've shared in the same way that you do. I never have."

"What the hell is that supposed to mean?"

He watched her force a smile. "I'm sorry. I'm just nervous."

She fluttered her hand, an insouciant movement unnatural to her.

He noticed, felt a moment's frustration, then shook his head as it occurred to him that the little sneak was turning his own tricks on him.

Hiding behind smiles.

She moved forward and grasped the handle to the library door.

His gaze followed her, the sleek cut of her dress in harmony with her slim build, the blue silk curves inviting his touch.

She laughed and snapped her fingers. "Ahh, yes, I meant to tell you . . ."

He blinked, forcibly separating himself from the hunger that was tightening his stomach and enlarging things elsewhere. "Tell me?"

She pulled the door open and half turned on the ball of her foot. "Mrs. Peters wanted me to mention that Miss . . . Miss . . ." she scratched her chin with a gloved finger. "Elliot! Miss Elliot called at the last minute to say she would accept the invitation to dinner."

"Damn," he whispered beneath his breath as the door closed behind her.

Marilyn.

Chapter Twenty-Eight

She was attractive. Charming. Intelligent.

Her attractive, charming, intelligent hand was resting lightly on Chase's arm.

He was the height of elegance tonight, in a black linen suit, complete with silk waistcoat and snowy white collar shirt. His dark skin glowed in contrast to the crisp color.

Charlie looked away. She smiled and nodded to the man seated to her left. He had made a comment she supposed she should reply to, but she'd not been listening. Something about the performance. She smothered a yawn and joined in the applause.

At least she had made it through dinner. Too much food. Mindless conversation that interested no one. Meddling disguised as polite questioning. What fun was it to eat when so many people were hawking your manners and the amount of food you put into your mouth? She'd felt like she was having dinner with thirty Mrs. Mindlebrights.

She glanced around the room, one she had never been in before. A parlor, Mrs. Peters had called it. It was a comfortless room, full of stiff furniture and belongings she was afraid she would break: ballerina figurines and crystal vases full of fresh flowers, and miniature portraits of people she guessed had no relation whatsoever to Chase. Chairs from other rooms sat in a half circle before the piano. Luckily, she had been a late arrival and sat on one of the sofas behind the chairs. Chase and Marilyn Elliot sat on the other.

The woman had cornered him, obvious for everyone to see. Imagine Mrs. Peters' embarrassment if she ever realized she had invited Adam Chase's mistress to her little soiree. Perhaps, though, polite society allowed this, if prudently handled. She didn't know. All she could tell that mattered was the mistress chewed with her mouth closed.

Charlie wanted to understand. She wanted to deny the hot flash of jealousy she felt. But she couldn't quite accept another woman *touching* him. As liberated as she wanted to be, the sight of Marilyn's hand on his arm ripped a gash deep inside her. It made her think harsh, ugly thoughts.

It didn't help any to know Marilyn would be here when she left. Hellfire, she didn't expect him to live the life of a priest. She knew . . . recognized the reality of their situation. But still, it hurt.

"Miss Whitney? What do you think of Miss Cameron's musical ability?" The man seated by her on the sofa leaned forward in expectation of her answer.

"I'm sorry?" Had he been talking to her for long? She hoped not.

"Miss Cameron . . . she is quite good. I love to hear her play." He tapped his hand on his knee. "Absolutely divine."

She nodded. "Yes, she is." Apparently, Miss Cameron had an admirer, and *Charlie* had been lucky enough to get the seat next to him. "You know, I feel a slight headache coming on. I think I may take a moment to catch my breath. On the verandah." She had a porch. Chase had a *verandah*.

Miss Cameron's admirer—she couldn't for the life of her remember his name—assented with a curt tilt of his head and stood with a slight bow as she swept by.

"I hope I don't miss much. She *is* divine," she added because she thought she needed to.

Across the room, Mrs. Peters' stern gaze followed her. Charlie winked and flicked her fan against her head in salute. Her chaperone frowned and sighed. She couldn't hear it, of course, but she did see the deep inhalation and release of breath she had come to know so well these last two weeks.

She took a sharp left as she entered the hallway. She wanted to escape Miss Cameron's *musical abilities*. Escape the sight of Marilyn Elliot's hand on Chase's arm.

The verandah was just the place.

Marilyn Elliot's light gray gaze lingered on the man sitting beside her as he watched Miss Whitney exit the room. Against her best efforts, Marilyn liked the young woman, who had approached her, introducing herself with an outstretched hand. As pretty as you please. Marilyn had never shaken a woman's hand before and was not sure how to do it. Grasp and squeeze? No squeeze with just a shake?

Charlotte Whitney had definitely been a surprise. Intelligence, spirit and a refreshingly straightforward manner, wrapped in a freckle-specked, sun-blistered package.

Marilyn smoothed her hand down the front of her emerald silk dress. She and Adam had never had any more than a friendship that certainly went beyond the proper bounds of friendship. But she was a woman after all, competitive and rancorous at times. She admitted to being saddened to see him so entranced by another woman. She'd assumed what they shared was the most any woman was ever going to share with him.

Yet it took only a moment, to witness his gaze lingering upon Miss Whitney's face—at once hot and smoldering, the next warm and lovingly amused—to know what he felt for her in his heart.

Marilyn had to admit they were a well-matched pair. Intelligent to a fault, beautiful in a disinterested way, aggressive, honest, and of course, infatuated with a dusty old newspaper. Wouldn't you know it?

Jared. Miss Whitney had called him that today, when they walked into the dining room together. *Interesting*.

Marilyn knew only a little about Adam's family. Of course, she had heard the gossip: the mother's demise at a fairly young age, the indifferent, tyrannical father, the elder son's death during a duel. Other than that she did not know much. Adam did not speak of his family. He used his middle name when he wrote, but she had never known anyone to address him by it.

As he shifted with a restless twitch, she felt a heavy pull in her chest. Leaning over, she whispered near his ear, "Go have a smoke. This is dreadfully dull, but Kate's a friend, and I have to stay."

He turned to her, his gaze tight and calculating as if he expected her to say more. Dared her to almost.

So, he had not admitted to himself that he loved the girl. Marilyn almost smiled. That was more like the Adam Chase *she* knew.

"Go on." She settled her hands back in her lap and straightened her spine. "Kate will probably only play another song or two. We can take a stroll later."

He nodded and rose from the sofa. As he walked behind it, he patted her shoulder.

Marilyn Elliot turned her attention to Miss Katherine Cameron, who was arranging her skirt and flexing her tiny hands in preparation for another piece. Marilyn swallowed and tilted her chin, head held high. Adam's gesture was meant to comfort, she was sure, but it had felt so very much like a farewell.

"Hello, stranger."

Adam turned at the sound of her smooth murmur. He had been peering through the darkness, looking for her. As it was, he could barely see her, hidden in shadow, the moon providing only a feeble remnant of light.

"Looking for me?"

"No." He turned away from her and released a small puff of smoke.

She laughed, a seductive laugh, low and throaty. His hand shook as he lowered it to the balustrade. She was becoming a woman before his eyes, beneath the persuasive stroke of his fingers, changing in ways that excited him, made his blood dance beneath his skin.

He heard her walk toward him. Her shoes thunked against the floor as she dropped them from her hands. She slid her arms around him and pressed her face against his back. "I think you *were* looking for me."

Of course he was, but there was no need to give her more ammunition. "Whatever you say, love." He denied the callousness of his words as he laid his free hand over hers, which were clasped together across his stomach.

They stood in silence, the darkness isolating them from the noise of the party. A light breeze carried the scent of roses, honeysuckle, tobacco and the spicy scent of cologne. Somewhere a night owl called.

Adam extinguished his cheroot and turned in the circle of her arms. She clung to him, her head pressed against his chest. He leaned, burying his nose in her silky hair. She had loosened the chignon.

Waking in the middle of the night, when the horrible dreams threatened, was nothing new. With sweat rolling down his face and neck and the force of his expelled breaths shaking his entire body, finding her there *was*. Lying on her side often as not, touching him with her hand or her foot or her hip, for it was too hot to hold each other as they would in the winter.

Winter.

She would be long gone by then. He closed his eyes, turned his head and kissed the top of hers, her hair clinging to his lips. The strands smelled faintly of lemon. "Your hair smells good."

Charlie giggled and twisted to look at him. Her sapphire eyes were wide and clear, contentment and pleasure flowing from them. He envied her. Envied the absolute assurance she projected. Envied the happiness she felt, which she seemed to be able to protect from events beyond her control.

He was struggling to protect his. At least until she left.

"Jared . . ."

His gaze settled on her mouth as she slid her tongue deliberately along her bottom lip.

He groaned low in his throat and lowered his head, touching his lips to hers. She quivered and sighed and swayed into him, rubbing her hips back and forth against his hard ridge of desire.

My, she had learned well.

"Let's"—pulling her lips from his, she kissed the side of his mouth—"go down"—her lips trailed along his neck—

"by the"—drawing his skin between her teeth, she sucked—"river."

He wanted to; oh, how he wanted to. He wanted her on her back, her thighs spread, her legs wrapped around his waist. Her savage, urgent little breaths commanding his attention as completely as a herd of buffalo trampling over him. He wanted to delve so deeply into her that he could not climb out. Disappear without a trace.

Except, he would take her with him, of course.

He frowned and pulled away from her. Now where had *that* come from? Was it a fantasy? It was a rather insufficient one compared to the others he had produced before *she* had come along. Where were the lacy undergarments and crude propositions? The full breasts and round hips? Now he fantasized about being deserted like some bewildered pirate on a lone isle with Charlie Whitney?

Disgusted with himself and his pathetic daydreams, he thrust her aside. "Ow." He lifted a hand to his neck.

She stared at him a moment, then spit a short laugh. "You shouldn't push a woman away when she has your skin between her teeth."

"Go inside, Charlie."

She stopped laughing and narrowed her eyes. She stared at him for a moment; then her brow flattened. He hated the comprehension he saw reflected upon her face.

"You torture yourself for emotions no one could help feeling."

"*I* can help them."

She stepped forward, her chest brushing his. Her eyes burned in that noble, persuasive way that made him believe what she said. Or want so badly to believe. She would have made a damn fine politician.

"No. You cannot. You will have some relief in this life when you realize that." She squeezed her hands into tight fists by her sides. "You are not God, Jared. You cannot control everything. You cannot control my feelings *or* your own."

"*Go inside, Charlie.*"

She rocked onto the balls of her feet and back again. Sighing, she bent to gather her shoes. She walked past him, then paused before entering the hallway. Half turning, she smothered a yawn against the back of her hand. The lamp hanging by the door revealed a wicked glint in her blue eyes. "I think I may go up to bed. It's so *hot* . . . too hot for clothes, don't you think?" She winked and turned. "Night, Chase," she threw over her shoulder.

He waited until she sashayed inside before he let his laughter come. She was the most incredible woman he had ever known. The most incredible he had ever dreamed of knowing.

For two more nights she was his.

Charlie woke with a start. She opened her eyes. The place next to her in her bed was empty. She sat, bringing her knees to her chest and hugging them close.

Where was he?

They had spent the day walking along the river, fishing poles tossed over their shoulders, a basket of food in his hand, a can of worms in hers. It surprised him that she knew how to dig for worms. Or maybe, it only surprised him that she *would* dig for worms. Virginia soil was firm and cool, a little browner than South Carolina's, but good and fertile just the same. Plenty of worms, anyway.

She slid from the bed, neglecting the stool, reaching feet first until she touched the floor. She padded with silent steps to the window. A puff of wind blew in, pressing his fine cotton shirt against her. The last few nights had been dark, the moon small and dim. There was no chance that she could see him. All she could hear was the rhythmic slap of water against a sandy bank.

Where was he?

A faint noise sounded. Removed from the house, near the woods. She stuck her head through the open window and looked to the right. Hoofbeats. He'd been riding at this time of the night?

Taber had been delivered yesterday, much to Chase's pleasure and relief. He'd been worrying like a mother hen about the horse getting hurt on the trip north.

However, the sight of Taber in his stall had hit her like a brick in the head. A sharp twist of pain had centered in her stomach, and she'd turned to him, ready to tell him they were making a mistake. That leaving, living a life without each other, was a mistake.

Then he'd turned to her with a soft smile and a kiss, and she just couldn't tell him.

Dear God, the irony, to realize she had made a promise to protect herself, protect him, from the kind of hurt she'd felt at that moment. A thousand times since then, she had opened her mouth or touched his sleeve, intending to tell him.

This is wrong, Jared. Wrong. We belong together. Don't you see that? We are glass broken in two. The pieces fit together perfectly. Don't you see?

There were two truths as far as she could tell. One was he *didn't* see. Whether this was because he refused to see, or because he really was too far gone to love someone again, she was not quite sure.

The second truth was she loved him.

She loved him with a depth of feeling she had never imagined, never even realized was possible. Loved him more than she loved herself, she guessed, if the sheltering, lioness-watching-over-her-cub protectiveness was any indication. It went beyond lust, infatuation, even the respect and awe that had started this whole mess in the first place.

She sincerely cared about him enough to get on that train tomorrow morning and ride out of his life and back into hers. She wanted to protect him . . . from herself. Because she had decided that perhaps he *was* past being able to love someone again. At times, their closeness seemed as painful to him as alcohol in an open wound. He flinched and pulled away, dodged questions and contact, concealed his feelings and his thoughts with false smiles and laughter.

She thought she had gotten past a point with him, crossed a fence, a fence *he* had never meant anyone to cross ever again. So here she was, past this fence, but he was *never* going to let her go any farther.

She could not go back.

He struggled with this. She watched him being pulled back and forth as she bounced against his self-constructed barrier, trying in her honest, straightforward way to jump over it or break it down. Sometimes, he had an almost fearful look in his eyes, like he imagined she might get past his defenses. The fear in his gaze hurt her more than anything had in a long time. More than all the nasty taunts thrown at her while she was growing up. More than her parents' deaths.

She had not been the one to blame for those events, but she *was* the one causing this pain.

She had promised him she would leave when the time came.

She took a deep breath and turned toward the bed.

When the door opened a few moments later, she was curled on her side, her eyes closed, her lips pressed together.

His footfalls ceased as he neared the bed. The heat of his gaze sliced her like a sharp edge of glass. The heavy scent of leather and horse radiated from him. It was the hardest promise she had ever fulfilled. To lie still and quiet when she wanted to grab him, pull him to her and smother him with all the love she felt.

But dear heaven, she did not want to make life any harder for him.

She wound her fist into a tight ball under the pillow as he placed his hand on her face. His skin was moist with sweat. He sighed and ran his finger along her eyebrow, the curve of her nose. He brushed his thumb across her lips, so slowly, as if he were trying to memorize the feel of them.

Leave, will you! Go, dammit, go!

He turned as if he'd heard her. The door closed with a firm click behind him.

She guessed he never heard her weeping, curled in a ball in the middle of the bed.

Chapter Twenty-Nine

Miles kicked a pile of leaves from his path as he crossed the dirt drive leading to his house. He loved the intensity of fall. Crisp, raw colors. Colors you couldn't create if you tried. But darn if the amount of leaves didn't damn near kill him. He'd raked and raked. 'Bout raked himself into an early grave. And still, leaves and pinestraw everywhere.

Thank goodness Charlie hadn't accepted his offer to rake her yard. He really would be a dead man.

As he neared the house, the front door slammed back against the wall. Kath ran down the steps, launching herself at him. He grinned and dropped the rake, opening his arms to her.

"What's this, my girl?"

Kath kissed his mouth and pulled back. She was nearly out of breath.

"Whoa, hold up."

"Oh, Miles, I felt it move!"

"What move?"

She laughed and slapped his shoulder. "The baby, you ox."

Swinging her around, he laughed and hugged her close. "My son is a strong boy already."

"It may be a strong girl, you know."

"Ah, Kathy, I know that. But I'm thinkin' this one's a boy. Strong and fit. Kickin' already."

She sighed, but smiled, and took his hand, leading him up the stairs and into their house.

The baby was due in late winter. Kathy and Charlie had been busy knitting and sewing, getting clothes and booties ready. Charlie was almost as excited as her best friend.

"Do I smell apple pie?" Miles patted his stomach.

"Yes, and you'd better enjoy it. We don't have many good apples left. I need to preserve some for the winter."

He sat at the table and poured himself a glass of tea. He needed to wash up before dinner, but a short rest wouldn't hurt anybody. Sipping the tea, he noticed a letter sitting in the middle of the table. He glanced at the front of the envelope before breaking the seal. "Another one?"

Kathy glanced at him and rolled her eyes before turning back to her pot of beans. "It's absolutely ridiculous, if you ask me."

He smiled. "Obviously no one is, my girl."

"They're both stubborn mules."

"If you say so." He overturned the envelope. A piece of paper slipped to the table. Bold, black script covered the cream-colored sheet.

"How many letters have we gotten?"

He lifted his gaze and sucked his lip between his teeth. "Hmmm . . . three or four, I guess."

"Mercy. Charlie looks at them like they're lost treasure, yet she wouldn't touch one if you paid her a quarter eagle."

He shrugged and returned to the letter. "What does that matter? You tell her what's in 'em."

She banged the spoon against the stove. "She says it doesn't matter what they say. That he's writing to you. Not to her. Like she doesn't care or something."

"Kathy, we don't know what went on in Richmond."

"No, but I have my suspicions."

"Landsakes. Just ask her what happened and put us all out of misery."

"I don't know, Miles. She's changed so much since she went up there. It's like she's older . . . wiser."

Kathy was right about that. Charlie *was* different. Not different in a physical way. Not in any way a casual acquaintance could detect. He couldn't quite put his finger on what it was. The before-Richmond Charlie—as he'd come to think of her—had been a bit like a firecracker, hopping around with energy. Restless, eager.

The after-Richmond Charlie was calm ... mature. He wouldn't describe her as unhappy, though. He really didn't know how the hell to describe her, and he was frankly sick to death of his wife asking him about it.

Charlie Whitney was *her* best friend. The best friend *he'd* had in a long time was sitting in Richmond, writing him letters. Miles had even written a few back, which was surely a first for him. He supposed he couldn't chastise Kath for not asking Charlie what had happened. He hadn't had the guts to ask Adam a damn thing, either.

"What does he have to say?"

Miles flattened the page on the smooth wooden table. He squinted, then glanced at Kathy to see if she'd noticed. She'd been bugging him for the last month or so to go see Doc Olden about getting spectacles. All he could think of was his father, rubbing his tired eyes and slipping on his lenses, gray hair ballooning about his head.

Surely, he wasn't old enough to need spectacles.

"Do you want me to read the whole letter?"

"Of course, read the whole letter."

He sighed. Women.

> *Dear Miles and Kath,*
>
> *I hope you received the cradle. A man in Richmond has been making them since I was a child. You can count on having it for your grandchildren, as well.*

"Miles, did you thank him in your last letter?"

He sighed again. "Yes, but I only sent it two days ago. Landsakes, he won't have it yet!"

> *I hope the* Sentinel *is progressing under Benjamin Folkes' charge. I get copies here when I can, although Stokes is suspicious regarding my intentions. Miles, let me know immediately if anything happens. As I no doubt mentioned in a previous letter, I talked with Mr. Folkes before he*

left for Edgemont. He seems like a nice man. A very
competent editor. He should be able to teach Charlie a
lot about the business.

My work is going well, except for a minor incident
last week researching a story. Due to my editorial duties,
reporting is a role I had not occupied for two years or
more. I found I missed it. I guess I forgot that it is not
as easy as concocting an editorial while sitting at a desk.

The weather here is beginning to take a definite turn
toward winter, I think. The air is cool, quite chilly at
night. I am making good use of the fireplace in my den.
Likewise, Miles, a bottle of your liquor warms me on
those cold nights.

Miles laughed loudly. His smile fell as he caught Kathy's
frown. He coughed and continued.

I wish you good health and a mild winter.
    With thoughtful regard,
Adam

"Hmmpt . . . he didn't even mention her name."

Oh, Lord. "Yes, he did. He said he thought old Ben Folkes
could teach her a lot."

"That is *not* what I meant."

"Kathy—"

She slammed the spoon against the stove for the second time
that night. "Don't Kathy me, Miles Lambert. I'm not just being
nosy. I thought Charlie and Adam were in love with each
other before she went to Richmond. So did you, if I remember
correctly."

He smiled and turned, not mentioning that that had been his
idea almost from the start. He'd brought Kathy around to thinking it.

"Mercy. I just want them to be happy. Why isn't that possible? I feel like, with a little minor tweaking here and there, I
might be able to push them in the right direction."

"Oh, Kathy, you—"

She went to him and sank to her knees. Grasping his hands,
she tilted her head so she could look into his face. Her green

eyes were shining, wide and clear. His Kathy had a heart of gold, she did. She did pry, but earnest intentions propelled her prying.

"Miles, wouldn't you want someone to help us if we had been . . . um, misdirected?" She squeezed his hands and smiled. "I've got an idea. It's harmless. Truly."

He groaned and rolled his eyes. "What do I have to do?"

She bounced to her feet and threw her arms around his neck. "This will help them. I promise it will."

He lifted his gaze skyward, all the while saying a prayer.

"Missy, I do not like the lead from the first paragraph to the second. Not tight enough."

Charlie lifted her head from her arms and groaned. "You must be joking."

"No, missy, I'm not joking."

"Hellfire."

Benjamin Folkes popped the knuckles on his right hand and gave her a bland look. He was always popping his knuckles, even the knuckle that only had an inch of finger attached to it. The first time she'd shaken his hand, he'd looked her dead in the eye and said with a terse nod, "This is a tough business, missy."

Had he expected her to flinch and pull her hand away? Instead she'd stared right back at him, straight as a new arrow, and said, "Yes sir, I guess it is."

That had earned his grudging respect.

Grudging because he believed journalism was no place for a woman, of which he reminded her daily. What did she care? He knew the business like the inside of his pocket, even if he was too old and tired at times to share the contents of his pocket with her. His experience, his insight, was what she wanted from him. Vindication she didn't give two apples about.

Chase had been right about Benjamin Folkes. He wouldn't take a chance on angering Oliver Stokes, not because he was timid or believed in the partisan system, but because he was older than dirt.

"Missy, I think I may go home early today. My back, you

know." He placed his hand along his side and stretched. The cracking sound that followed was enough to convince her.

She nodded. "Yes, go. I'll work on the lead."

He lifted his finger.

"I know. The other editorial needs work, too."

"Until tomorrow."

She released a ragged breath as she lowered her head back to her arms. She barely heard the sound of the door opening and closing. She was so tired. Bone-tired. Exhausted. Overworked.

Gerald did all he could. So did Benjamin Folkes. But, due to their age, they couldn't stay up all night printing a newspaper or work two days straight to make a deadline. Every week that was. Therefore, *she* was doing what had to be done to get the *Sentinel* out on time. Of course, the deadlines had become a bit ambiguous. The paper had gone from weekly to about every ten days.

She shrugged her shoulders. She did the best she could.

The work did what it was supposed to. It kept her from thinking about *him*. Well, it kept her from thinking about him all the time.

He was never very far away. Yesterday, she turned in the bright sunlight, and dizziness swept through her. As the patches of black filtered through her vision, she could see him, standing there in the *Sentinel* doorway as he had so many times, dark hair glistening in the sunlight, eyes flooding with anger or impatience, or as it was later . . . desire.

At night, she curled her fingers around his hand, touched his lips with her own, caressed his warm skin. At night, when she lingered in that place between dreams and reality, those were the only moments she felt truly content.

She could close her eyes, run her tongue across her lips and *taste* him. Tobacco, red wine and a scent all his own. Spicy and sweet all at once. Somewhat like cinnamon.

A smile played upon her lips as she imagined his reaction to being compared to cinnamon.

"Charlie?"

She groaned and snuggled deeper into her arms.

"Charlie, wake up."

A slight nudge. She shook her head, resisting. Who was calling her? Was it time to get up already? Where was Jared? Was he still sleeping?

"Jared?"

A soothing touch along the top of her head.

"Charlie, wake up, honey."

Charlie lifted her head. It felt as heavy as lead. "Kath?" She squinted and blinked a couple of times. Yes, it was Kath.

"You need to go home. It's getting dark."

Charlie sat, pushed her hair from her face and yawned. "I . . ." She stretched and yawned again. "I can't. Paper due in two days." She rubbed her eyes. "Got to finish a few editorials."

Kath flung her reticule down and shoved a wooden chair by the desk. "Mercy. Should I sit in this or just rest my handkerchief on it?"

Charlie frowned. "It's stronger than it looks."

Kath didn't look like she believed it but settled down anyway.

"Why are you in town so late in the day?"

"Miles had to run by Mr. Whitefield's. Something he couldn't wait until tomorrow to do. I thought I would ride in with him. The weather's so pleasant." Kath smiled. "Almost like a summer day."

Charlie looked away. The summer had ended years ago.

"Charlie?"

She turned back to find Kath watching her with a sympathetic look. *Oh, no.* She knew that look.

"Don't you want to talk about it?"

Charlie shook her head. "No, I don't."

Kath laid her hand on the desk and leaned forward. Her chair squeaked and wobbled, but thankfully, did not dump her upon the dirty floor. "I don't know how to talk to you right now. I don't know what, I have no idea how . . ." Kath drew in a deep breath and released it with a slow push. "I want to be your friend again."

Friend. Kath would always be her friend. A dear friend. A lifelong friend. However, her best friend was in Richmond. That would always be. Until she was ninety. Until she died. Forever.

Charlie lifted a hand to Kath's face, capturing the tear that was tracing a path through the light coating of dust on her face. Charlie dropped her hand, patting Kath's reassuringly. "The baby is making you awfully teary-eyed. Poor Miles."

Kath laughed and grabbed her reticule from the desk. She dug around, producing a cotton handkerchief. Her initials were stitched in blue in one corner. She blew her nose—delicately, of course—then pushed the handkerchief back into its place.

"I stitched those letters onto that handkerchief the day after Miles asked me to marry him. Actually, I made five. That's the only one left." Kath swallowed and licked her lips.

She seems nervous, Charlie thought. Now why is that?

"I was so in love with him. He made the moon shine brighter . . . the sun shine longer. He was, and is, the very air I breathe. I don't think I could live without him."

Charlie clenched her jaw and drew back. "Adam is not Miles, Kath."

And I'm not you.

Kath's face reddened. "I *know* that."

Charlie lowered her face to her hands and pushed a rough breath past chafed lips. "I'm sorry."

Kath scooted along the seat of the chair until her elbows rested against Charlie's on the desk. "Talk to me. I want so much to help you. I don't even know that anything is wrong." She tapped her fingers on the desk. "You just seem so different. So preoccupied. So troubled."

Charlie lifted her head. The look in her eyes, whatever it was, brought a fresh wave of tears to Kath's.

"For heaven's sake, get your hankie out."

Kath sniffed and wiped at her nose with the back of her hand. "You look terrible, by the way."

Charlie smiled at this. Kath was losing more of her polite social behavior every minute. "Why, thank you. I'm feeling quite well, as a matter of fact."

"No, you're not. You stay in the sun too long. Your lips are dry and chapped. You have hideous dark circles. You've lost weight. How much sleep do you get?"

Charlie wrenched her gaze from Kath's sharp-edged one. "I sleep. Some nights."

"*Oh, Charlie.*"

"Leave it be, Kath. Please."

"You stay locked in here. Sometimes at night. Alone." She waved her hand around the office. Sunlight was creeping down the walls as shadows began their daily acquisition. "Is this all you want from life?"

Charlie pushed her chair back and vaulted from the seat. She strode to the window. Squinting against the glowing dark orange light, she stared at the distant mountains that were turning shades of black and gray with the sinking sun. "How can I convince you that I'm happy?"

"You could start with the truth. Not all these smiles. Hiding your feelings. You never used to do that."

No, she hadn't, had she? Not with Kath, at least. Why *was* she guarding it all so closely? Was it so painful to remember him? To recall the gentle touch of his fingers, the soft whisper of his hair upon her skin? The feel of his bare skin next to hers? To summon the features of his face into her mind, as clearly as if he was standing before her? She swallowed. "He's not like Miles. He's not like you *or* me. There are circumstances in his past. Horrible things. He couldn't, he can't." She shrugged. *"He can't."* The words were almost inaudible.

"If you love him, how can you stand to be apart?"

Kath, with all her romantic ideals and experience with "true love," would never understand what she knew to be the truest form of love: to accept someone for who they were. Or, who they weren't. "Maybe it's not so . . . *important* to be together," Charlie said at last.

"You honestly believe that?"

"I understand him, Kath. I accept the way he feels." She did. But it still hurt like hell to remember. Missing him was near to driving her mad.

"He's a worldly man. Those letters he received this summer. Mercy, they were scented of all things."

Charlie's slow smile widened. She could see it reflected in the dust-covered glass.

"I am not in love with her," Chase had told her the night of his dinner party, as they lay in bed—naked, drowsy and remarkably satisfied.

"I know that. I know you." And she did; nonetheless it had felt good to hear him say it. Somewhat surprising he had felt he needed to.

His only reply had been a grunt and a kiss upon the top of her head. Then he'd whispered, "Too well, I think."

Charlie shook her head to clear the memory. "It's unjust of you to blame him. Those letters"—she laughed and wiped her knuckles across the window—"have nothing to do with this. She has nothing to do with this." She rubbed two fingers in a deliberate circle through the dust.

"Are you sure?"

Charlie laughed, knowing this would shock her conventional friend. "Of course I'm sure. I met her."

"Met her?"

"She was very nice. Pretty, too."

"But she, she and Adam . . . they . . . "

Charlie lifted her hand from the glass and idly circled back to face her friend. "I know him. Better than anyone will ever know him. Except for two people. Who are dead. And for that he has no peace." She steepled her fingers and popped them together. Once, twice. "He was honest about the limitations of any relationship we might have, Kath. I didn't want any more than he did. I *agreed* with him."

"Do you still agree?"

No. She did not. The day she'd seen Taber in his stall in Richmond had affected her like a bolt of lightning in the middle of a clear day. Finally, it had occurred to her that leaving terminated any connection between them—except for a few faded memories. He would not be there to help her repair her fence; or stand behind her, squeezing her shoulders, as he encouraged her to write; or hold her, stroking her skin with his nimble fingers, when she was tired and lonely. She missed those things so much. So damn much that she filtered the world through gray glass most of the time now.

A wagon arrived outside. Charlie turned. Miles. Good. This subject drained her.

"We're taking you home."

"Kath—"

"Enough of this. Walking home in the dark! Gerald should be here with you."

"Gerald is not my chaperone, dammit." Mrs. Peters had been enough to last a lifetime.

"When did you start cursing so often. Just like—" Kath

pursed her lips and walked quickly to the door. "I'm not leaving you here." She pulled it open and perched against the side, waiting.

"Oh, for heaven's sake." Charlie stalked to her desk and grabbed a stack of papers. "This is only because you're pregnant, Katherine Lambert. I just don't want to be the one to upset you. I'll let Miles do that."

"Yes, dear, whatever you say."

"I don't know about this. It's interferin', it is." Miles slid into bed and pulled the covers up. Kath turned and rolled into his arms, laying her head on his chest.

"If you'd talked with her today, you would know some interference is needed. I don't mind doing it."

"Well, I do," he said as he wrapped his arm around her.

"I need your help."

"Now—"

"It's just one little letter. Simple. Honest. What harm can that do?"

"One simple, honest, manipulatin' letter."

"Oh, Miles. Where is your sense of romance?"

He grinned and took her hand beneath the covers. "I'll help you find my sense of romance."

She laughed as he pulled her on top of him.

The letter could wait until tomorrow.

Charlie scrubbed her hands on her trousers and emerged from the shelter of trees next to the stream. She drew a deep breath. Woodsmoke was heavy in the cool air. She pulled to an abrupt standstill as she spotted her cousin on the porch.

Lila waved and smiled.

Charlie released a frustrated sigh and advanced forward, rubbing a spot of dirt from her palm. Her footfalls echoed the crunch of leaves and pinestraw. She paused on the bottom step as Lila came forward with outstretched hands.

"Charlotte, how are you?"

"I'm fine, Lila. How are you?" It surprised Charlie that her cousin wasn't fretting about her trousers. Other than a brief glance, Lila seemed unconcerned.

After a moment, Lila dropped her hands. "I'm doing quite well, thank you for asking." She gestured to the door. "May I come inside? I wanted to talk with you."

Charlie nodded and climbed the steps.

"What are *these*?"

Charlie laughed and picked up one of the honey-colored shells Lila pointed to. "They're locust skins. You know, they leave them sticking in the pine tree bark when they shed."

"Why in the world are you saving *those*?"

Charlie shrugged. "I don't know. I like them."

Lila grimaced and promptly stepped inside.

Charlie grinned and followed, shoving aside a strong urge to stick one of them in her cousin's plentiful hair.

Lila slid her hand over the mantel, then flicked her fingers. Dust drifted in a slow swirl to the floor. "I guess you're wondering why I'm here. We haven't been exactly friendly for a long time, have we?"

"Not too friendly since we were, oh"—Charlie rolled her head as if she were tallying a figure—"seven or eight years old."

Lila giggled. A distinctly nervous giggle. "Surely, it hasn't been that long."

It had been *that* long.

When Charlie made no effort to comment, Lila's face reddened. "Charlotte, I wanted to tell you. Be the first to tell you that—" She twisted her hand in her lovely yellow skirt. "I'm going to marry Tom Walker."

The rag in Charlie's hand slipped to the floor.

Lila's gaze jumped to the cloth. Her tongue whisked across her lips. "I'm marrying Tom Walker."

Charlie laughed and snatched the rag off the floor. "Why?"

Lila snapped her head up, glaring. "What do you mean why? I'm pretty and . . . and my father's arranged a nice dowry. Tom will have an even better future, working at the bank."

Charlie pulled a chair from the table. Finding this all very strange, but knowing she had to say something, she said, "I'm happy for you, Lila.'' She walked into the kitchen and poured two glasses of tea. "Sit. Quit acting like a tense fox.''

"I'm not tense.'' Lila didn't argue with sitting, though.

Charlie set the glasses on the table and settled across from her cousin. "Why tell me in person?''

Once again Lila's gaze danced away. She drummed her fingers on the table. "Because Tom loved you. Or thought he did. He told me so. And . . . *I* wanted to tell you . . . that, that he loves me now.''

Charlie stared at her, wondering why she felt such pity for this woman. Her cousin was beautiful, and she would never have to worry about having enough money to buy food or material for clothing.

Charlie had spent the last two weeks preserving vegetables and fruit, in hopes of having enough for the winter. When Lila showed up today, she'd been at the stream, submerging the last of her butter in the chilled water. Next week, she and Kath were salting meat and storing their remaining vegetables in the Lamberts' root cellar. So much to do just to survive. While Lila had never had to lift a finger, had never wanted for anything her whole life.

And Charlie felt sorry for *her*? Yes. She did. With all her heart. She would never, *ever* want to trade places with Lila Dane.

"Mrs. Peters said your trip to Richmond was very pleasant.''

Charlie blinked. "I'm sorry?''

Lila frowned. "Mrs. Peters said your trip to Richmond was pleasant.''

Charlie smiled. "It was." She wondered what else Mrs. Peters had said.

"Tom loves me, Charlotte.''

"I'm happy for you, Lila.''

Her cousin scooted her chair as close as she could to the table and peered into Charlie's face. She squinted and tilted her head to the side, quite obviously trying to see if Charlie was telling the truth.

Charlie contained the laughter that threatened. "I never loved Tom, and I'm glad he's found someone. What he felt for me was simply a childhood infatuation, nothing more.''

"An *in* what?''

She did laugh then. Heaven's Lila was dumb. "A crush. Just a silly little thing."

Lila nodded with a quick jerk. "Of course, I *knew* that. I just thought I should tell you because you might be upset."

Finally, the pearl in the oyster.

"I mean, coming back from Richmond *alone*. We all expected, the town I mean . . . him to come back, too."

"Well, as you can see, he didn't."

Lila casually brushed a lock of blond hair off her face. "That's not a surprise, you see. He told me before he left that he didn't want any woman here. Liked those big city women better. No morals, is what I suspect." She shrugged her shoulders in accordance with a swift shake of her head. "You're better off without that, I say."

What a bitch Lila was. Interesting, too, that it had taken her all these months—and the procurement of a fiancé—to secure the nerve to hound Charlie for what she believed was the theft of Adam Chase. Thank goodness her cousin was not a surprise any longer.

Charlie glanced out the window. "It's getting late. I know you have to be running along. You brought your carriage, didn't you?"

Lila threw her a harsh look, then with great dignity, stood and shook her full skirt. "Yes, of course."

"Tell Tom I said congratulations, will you?"

Lila squinted again; then her face cleared. She smiled. "I will, Charlotte. We're having a large wedding. I'll let you know when I set the date."

Charlie nodded and practically pushed Lila through the door. "Good night. It was nice of you to stop by." She waved and closed the door with a snap. Lila's skirt had barely cleared the threshold.

She walked to the table, pushed Lila's chair in and took the glasses to the dry sink. The laughter bubbled from deep in her throat, and she bent over, wrapping her arms around her stomach.

Lila and Tom?

The image of an angry hen frantically chasing a small, scared rooster came to mind. Charlie gasped for breath as she slid to the floor. Leaning back against the stove, she covered her face with her hands. This was the first time in two months that she'd laughed. *Really laughed.*

It felt good.

Lila and Tom? Tom and Lila?

What strange happenings there were in the world.

Chapter Thirty

Adam pressed against the wooden crates. As the men walked by, he prayed the darkness concealed him.

Goddammit. He had not imagined they would walk this way.

"We meet a' Shockoe Creek tomorrow morning," one man said, his words distorted by a thick German accent.

The other merely grunted in reply.

Adam released a tight breath as the heavy warehouse door slammed shut behind them. He pushed off the crates and turned hastily on one heel, running straight into a tall, muscular obstacle.

"Shit!"

A hand grasped his shoulder. "It's me. Tanner. Come on. There's no time." Tanner did not release him, merely yanked him along toward the front of the warehouse.

"Why are we walking away from the door?" And, what the hell are you doing here, Adam wanted to ask.

Tanner must have realized he was leading Adam as if he were a child. He dropped his hand. "There are three men outside the back entrance. They're waiting for the German, I think."

Adam swallowed. The German was going to be in trouble.

He would have walked right into the mayhem if not for Tanner's interference.

"Thanks."

"Not now. We still have to get out of here."

They crept along as quietly as possible, yet their footfalls rang like church bells in the deserted structure. The stinging odor of raw tobacco and sweat pervaded the warehouse, one of many along Kanawha Canal.

"Want a smoke?" Tanner gestured to a huge burlap bag, open and overflowing with shriveled, yellow-green tobacco leaves.

"Funny."

As they reached the front entrance, Adam stopped Tanner with a tap on the back. "They may be at this door, as well. Let's go through one of the windows running along the canal."

"What about your arm?"

"I can make it."

They turned and made their way to the row of windows ten feet above the dirty plank floor. Dim shafts of moonlight struggled to penetrate the grime-coated glass, landing in ser-rated patches at their feet.

Tanner tilted his head. He pointed. "There's an open one. I'll pull a crate over and check to see if the way is clear."

Adam glanced behind him as the sound of the crate being dragged across the floor filled the area. He could scarcely see Tanner in the darkness; then the muted light flowing into the window brought his profile into sight as he climbed atop the crate.

"All clear. Thank God. Climb up, if you can. I'll help you over."

Adam nodded, cursing his stupidity. What would have hap-pened if he had gotten caught? With his injured arm, he was as helpless as a child.

He pulled himself onto the crate, trying to protect his arm as much as possible. Every contact with the wound acted like the thin edge of a knife upon his skin. He stood, brushing against Tanner.

"Hey, no free feels."

"Shut the hell up."

Adam grasped the window ledge with his good arm and

swung his left leg up. Tanner supported him as he worked to place the other.

"Got it?" Tanner asked, breathing hard.

Adam nodded as he swayed, squatting precariously on the ledge. He looked at the ground for a moment, then closed his eyes and jumped. Luckily, he hit the ground on his feet. Momentum forced him forward. He pitched to his unharmed side, but rolled twice before coming to a stop. For a moment, he thought he was going to heave his dinner into the dark canal.

The slap of Tanner's feet hitting the ground sounded behind him. Adam groaned and rose onto his elbow, every movement clumsy.

"Do you need help?" Tanner asked from above, his dusty boots coming into Adam's line of vision.

"No." He pushed himself to his feet, ignoring the proffered hand.

"Stubborn ass."

"I want this story."

"Adam—"

"All right. All right." He lifted his hand in mock surrender. "Let me put this another way. I am taking the story. How about that?"

Tanner shrugged with practiced ease and sauntered to the sidebar and the open bottle of whiskey.

They had been lucky enough to find a private room in their club where they could talk; Adam had refused to discuss anything at dinner.

Pouring a drink, Tanner turned to regard his friend with a cool, calculating eye. Adam knew what he was doing. Tanner had been in the business long enough to get all the information he could in one sweeping glance.

"Looked me over closely enough?"

"Yes, sir." Tanner saluted. "No business of mine what you do with your life, sir."

"Damn right," Adam agreed and raised his glass to second it.

Tanner tilted his back, draining it in one swallow.

Adam pushed away from the wall, his negligent stance somewhat painful under the circumstances.

"What about your arm? That gonna hold you up?"

Adam glanced at the sling. It was bloody and dirty from his rough landing on the canal's boardwalk. "Hold up? I write with my right hand."

Tanner slammed the glass down. *"You fool."*

A bored smile was the only response Adam would allow.

"Dammit, man, you're taking too many risks. What could you be thinking? You got out of that storage building last week just before the cussed thing collapsed."

Adam shrugged.

"Your clothes were on fire, or has that little fact escaped your memory?"

"Trust me, flames licking at your trousers is something you never forget."

"What about tonight? Sneaking into that warehouse with a useless arm. It's a damn good thing I followed you." Tanner poured another drink and swirled the amber liquid around in the glass.

Adam blinked and turned away, resting his good arm on the window ledge as he looked out over Bank Street. Carriages of all shapes and sizes crowded the passage. The hoarse bellow of street vendors and the gentle cry of horses floated to him. The wind brushed the velvet curtain against his face. He flicked it away and drew a deep breath. He grimaced. The smell of rotting fish and garbage was rich in the air tonight.

Strangely enough, he missed the calm of Edgemont. The sweet scent of honeysuckle and pine. The tranquil magnificence of a balmy night, when every star in the sky, hundreds and hundreds of them, could be clearly seen. He longed to savor the wind, whipping across the open fields, caressing his skin, bringing with it the essence of every living being it had touched.

"My decision is a sound one," he whispered, overlooking disturbing recollections. An intoxicated man stumbled from a saloon; Adam observed his faltering progress along the street with a discriminate eye.

"No. You're too careless. Something is distracting you."

Tanner was correct. Distractions were everywhere. A dark-haired woman in a crowd of people caught his eye like never before. The soft sound of feminine laughter sparked so many memories, memories he cherished *and* abhorred. And oh, the scent of roses had the power to bring him to his knees. He shook his head to clear it of things that were beyond his reach.

"Quit worrying, Tanner. I found I missed the investigative aspect of the business. Simple as that. The editorial side is not quite as challenging. I had forgotten that until . . ."

"Until South Carolina?"

Adam gripped the ledge, his shoulders stiffening.

"Why don't—"

Twisting around, Adam threw his hand out. "Stop. Whatever it is you were going to say. It is none of your business."

"You made it my business. *I'm* the one who took her to the train station." Tanner frowned and shoved his hand in his pocket. "Try explaining to a woman why her . . . *friend* isn't there to see her off."

"Thought you said she did not ask."

Tanner lifted his shoulders in a half shrug. *"She* didn't. But the old bag couldn't stop talking about the 'utter boorishness of such an act.' Made me feel damned uncomfortable, it did." He walked to a chair and threw himself into it. "Coward."

Adam rubbed his eyes and sighed. He was a coward. He would never forgive himself for letting her leave without a word or a note. *Nothing.* The worst part, the part that ate at his gut like buzzards to prey, was she understood why he had not been able to come to the damn train station.

He knew she did.

And she would never be angry with him for it. No matter how furious he was with himself.

Tanner pulled himself to his feet. "I'm going home. I'm too damned tired to try to talk you out of this idiocy." He crossed the room in three strides. The door slammed behind him.

Adam rotated back to the window, allowing the memory of blue eyes the shade of a dazzling twilight sky to surge through him in agonizing waves.

The morning air was sharp and frigid, as brittle as an old woman's cackle and just as inviting. Crisp sunlight, reflected off the river's surface, bounced into Adam's eyes as he stooped to grab a rock sitting between his feet. He turned the rock in his hand as he stared blindly into the water.

"I have a creek behind my house, remember?" she had said to him. He smiled, remembering the strange way she skipped rocks, with that peculiar curl of her wrist. Surprisingly, the damn rock had gone flying, tapping along at least three or four times.

So much about Charlie Whitney had been a surprise. Her intelligence, her strength, her courage, her startling wisdom. Her passion, which lay so close to the surface.

He should not have tapped that passion. Because, like a miner who discovered a wide vein of gold, he was greedy. He wanted more.

She had said that to him, too.

He laughed and tossed the rock into the water.

Unpredictable. Never had he met a woman so unpredictable. So candid. So impertinent. She was the poorest excuse for a southern belle he knew.

She was the best lover he had ever had.

Of course, the desire that lay between them was extraordinary. The mechanics of the act faded into the distance when you wanted someone that much. When he remembered being inside her, images assaulted him as mercilessly as an angry soldier: heated skin, lips touching, seeking, roses and the musky smell of sex, moist warmth, breathless cries.

Security. Contentment. *Love.*

He growled low in his throat and wrenched around. With angry steps, he walked deeper into the woods edging the river.

He could not love her. *Would not love her.*

Oh, God. It frightened him to consider that the matter had been decided without his consent.

Frowning, he kicked a limb from his path and climbed the gentle slope that lay ahead of him. At the top, a bare area, free of pinestraw and twigs, stretched beneath a large pine tree. He shifted his gaze about the space. A flash of color in the dirt caught his attention. Falling to one knee, he trailed his hand upon the ground. Imbedded most of the way in the soil— with just the tip exposed—was a pencil. Adam swallowed and extracted it as if it was crystal.

She must have come here to sketch.

His neck muscles tensed as a picture of her sitting beneath the tree came to him: tongue stuck between her teeth, head tilted to the side in concentration, feet more than likely bare, skirt hiked to her knees as she wiggled her toes in the cool dirt.

The crack of the pencil snapping in two tugged him from the vision. He muttered and threw the pieces to the ground. Then, pitifully, like a beggar after a few coins, he gathered them and slipped them in his shirt pocket.

He turned his face into the cold wind blowing off the river and tried to remember his mother's voice. Sometimes he could not remember her face, much less her voice. What would she have told him to do? His mother's heart had been pure, her love for her family genuine. Even his father, the bastard, had received only her deepest respect. He had never talked with his mother of life and love. After all, she had died when her children were still children.

He sighed and ran his hand through his hair. It shook as he lowered it to the ground.

He would have liked to talk with her now. Ask her why she had stayed with his father when love was absent. Ask her what he should do with his own life.

She would have liked Charlie.

He sighed again and pushed himself to his feet with his good arm. He had stopped using the sling, although the doctor had grumbled, saying the blisters would heal quicker if he did not stretch the skin.

He turned and headed down the slope, his breath racing in a white cloud ahead of him. The sun was sinking in the sky, the night air getting colder by the minute. He hoped Mrs. Beard had a fire lit in the library. Sleep would not come easily this night.

As he approached the house, he noticed a light in the kitchen window glowing brightly. The side door would be open. Pausing before the pantry entrance, he kicked dirt and straw from his boots. When he opened the door, warm air and the spicy scent of pepper encompassed him.

He closed the door behind him and walked through to the kitchen. Mrs. Beard stood at the stove, moving a wooden spoon in slow circles about a huge pot.

"Smells good."

"Vegetable soup. And corn bread. I'm trying to use all the food that's fixin' to go bad. Should be ready soon." She banged the spoon against the side of the pot and turned to him. "Should I set the table?"

He shook his head. "No. The library is fine."

She turned back, clicking her tongue against her teeth. Mrs. Beard believed that only food eaten at a well-set table digested properly. "Whatever you say. I put your mail in there just a little while ago."

"Thank you," he said as he left the room. Mrs. Beard was a diligent butler, cook, housekeeper, and mother all mixed into one.

His footfalls echoed in the silent hallway as he strode to the library. He threw the door open, pleased to see a small blaze fluttering in the fireplace. Tossing his coat onto the nearest chair, he began unbuttoning the neck of his shirt as he walked to the desk. Damn. He hated having a shirt buttoned all the way to his neck. He had once told his father a buttoned shirt was the reason he had decided against becoming a lawyer. Needless to say, Judge Chase had not been amused.

He sank into his chair and pulled off his boots. They hit the floor with a thump, a bit of stubborn straw still clinging to them.

Comfortable and ready to do battle, he reached for the stack of letters sitting in a neat pile on his desk. Flipping through them, he sighed. Solicitor Bailey. Solicitor Jameson. Nothing but correspondence from—

His hand stilled.

He dropped the other envelopes and held one in both hands as if it were a newborn babe. Then he sucked in a breath and ripped it open. He could not halt the rapid acceleration of his heart, nor the slight quiver in his hands. Miles always mentioned Charlie at least once or twice in his missives. Nothing personal—nothing interesting that was, he thought with a twisted smile—but Miles did manage to relate a few events in her life.

Adam was grateful for any news. He worried about her. She was alone, with a home to take care of and a job to perform. The town ostracized her because she dared to want a career. A career she *needed*. Which was the concern at the top of his list: she was as poor as a dirty orphan. He often wondered if there was a way to send her some money, although he knew she would not take it.

He pulled the sheet of paper from the envelope and frowned. Only one page. Oh well, better than nothing. He held the letter in the light coming from the oil lamp at his side and skimmed the words; his head moved left to right as his gaze trailed across the page.

He threw the letter to the desk and grabbed the envelope, which he had torn in two in his agitation. "No." He held it open and looked inside, thinking Miles must have made a mistake. "She would *not* do this."

The envelope was empty.

He grabbed the letter again. As he reread it, his anger grew. Had she been lying to him all along?

He kicked back from the desk and jumped to his feet. With a muttered curse, he propelled his arm across the top, sending pencils and paper flying. Rounding the desk in two strides, he stalked to the fireplace. Crumpling the letter into a tight ball, he flung it into the hearth. His gaze never left the paper as it sputtered and caught fire, turning into a pile of black ashes.

Much like his heart.

Chapter Thirty-One

Adam pulled the heavy coat close about his neck as he traversed the street. The faint scent of smoke and whiskey emanated from the coarse wool. At least the material had absorbed the *pleasant* odors from the train. If it was not so cold, he swore he would have come on horseback.

Hell. He did not even know why he was here. In this town. *Again.*

Shifting the leather satchel he carried from his right hand to his left, he pulled his hat lower on his head and hunched his shoulders into his jacket. The last thing he needed was for someone to recognize him.

Freeing a visible breath, he increased his pace. He was almost there.

Leaving the whitewashed buildings of the town and the few people traipsing about behind, he pushed his hat up on his forehead. The sun had set only moments before, transforming an ordinary cloud-filled sky into a brilliant exhibition of red and gold. As he walked along the dusty road, he catalogued the seasonal changes.

The underbrush running along the edge of the road was stringy and brown, lying dormant till spring. The long, willowy grass was golden yellow and dry, bent by wind's nimble fingers.

The shrill bird's call was weaker than before, but the weather must have been warm enough for some to remain.

He followed the road as it curved to the left. The way was familiar. Many times he had passed by, on foot or astride Taber. He had never been able to pass her home without glancing over, hoping for a glimpse of her.

A taut breath rushed from him as he came to the end of her drive. Unable to check the action, he turned his head, his heart coiled tight in his chest. Her cottage looked harsh compared to what he remembered. Probably due to the withered azaleas and naked, gray dogwoods standing guard in front. The wealth of welcoming red and pink azalea blossoms was absent, as were the velvet rose petals that had once littered the ground.

Maybe she was at the *Sentinel* office. He had not checked when he was in town. Maybe she was not even—

The screen door swung open, ending his conjecture. At first, all he could see was a large wicker basket piled high with wet clothing. Then a flash of jet black hair amassed atop a down-turned head emerged. She let the door swing shut behind her as she struggled with the basket, walking stiffly, bouncing the laundry from side to side as if she were about to drop it at any moment. She leaned back, resting it against her stomach as she negotiated the stairs.

He stepped forward, automatically going to help her, but a nervousness dissimilar to any he had felt until that moment kept him from following through. What would he say to her? His anger had not disappeared, although seeing her again acted upon his senses much like a rainbow on a cloudy day.

Her hair evaded the pitiful knot on her head, trailing down her face and neck in disheveled thatches. She wore a tattered, brown sweater that looked older than Gerald's teeth and a pair of ragged black trousers. She had never looked more beautiful. Even from this distance, her blue eyes shone brilliantly in a face alive with intelligence and emotion.

As she teetered around the corner of her house, hoisting a burden that was surely as wide as two of her, he decided enough was enough. He would help her with her damn laundry and they would talk. His mind filled with questions, images, accusations. What Miles had written in his letter could not be true.

Starting forward before he lost his nerve, he rounded the

corner of her house just as she stopped at the foot of the clothesline. Dropping the basket of laundry, she pushed her hands against her lower back and stretched.

A strong stir of sympathy flooded through him as he watched her reach to gather a wet towel. After wringing it, she flipped it across a length of thick rope tied haphazardly between two trees.

How hard it must be for her, alone in the world. *He* was alone, yet unlike him, she did not have money—which, awful truth that it was, made life much easier. *And* she was a woman. No one expected a woman to be able to take care of herself. In fact, people resented it like hell when they witnessed one who could.

A leaf crunched under his boot as he stepped forward.

Charlie paused and cocked her head to the side. She dropped the shirt clutched in her hand and turned cautiously.

When she completed the turn and stood facing him, he stopped, stunned to realize just how much he had missed her. He searched her face, looking for any indication of how she felt to see him. Had she missed him? Did she lie awake at night thinking about their time together? Did the taste of him, the smell of his skin, haunt her every waking moment?

He frowned as he noted the dark crescents, almost bruises, beneath her eyes. Her mouth was pinched, her skin pale.

She looked remarkably young and exceedingly frail.

She shook her head once, still staring at him, then closed her eyes. A moment later she flicked them open. They seemed to climb from her face, pulling forward and widening. A gust of air rolled in from behind her, kicking black tresses into her face.

He watched her throat tighten as she swallowed.

"Jared?" She licked her lips.

He took a step forward.

Lifting her hand to her head, she closed her eyes again and said softly, "You're back."

He dropped his satchel to the ground and rushed forward, but before he could reach her, she swayed and slipped to the ground as weightlessly as a piece of parchment in the wind.

* * *

Adam pressed the damp rag to her face, gently wiping the dust and flecks of blood from Charlie's forehead. She'd bumped it when she had fallen. *Dammit,* if he had only been closer, he could have caught her. Once again, the sight of her dropping to the ground like a broken stick flashed in his mind. He cursed as he dipped the rag in the basin of water sitting upon the night table.

Was she sick?

When he'd picked her up to bring her inside, her slight weight had shocked him. She had always been petite, but now she was gaunt. He lifted her hand from the coverlet, wrapping his fingers around her wrist. The steady rhythm of blood flowing beneath her skin calmed him. He glanced down. Her small hand was tucked securely between his fingers. The bones of her wrist protruded at harsh angles.

What had happened to her since she had left Richmond? If she did not awaken soon, he was going to find Doc Olden. With a ragged sigh, he placed her hand upon the bed.

"Charlie? Wake up, sweetheart." His heartbeat and her frail breathing were the only sounds in the room. How he wished for her infectious laughter and audacious wit. Her smile that was at once rebellious, then seductive. The quick, bold thrust of her sapphire eyes.

What was he going to do when she roused?

Scream like hell? Hold her? Make love to her?

He dropped the rag into the basin with a dejected groan. No. He had come to Edgemont for a reason. No doubt the rationale behind it was asinine. But dammit, he wanted an explanation. He *needed* an explanation.

He had never had one from his mother, or from Eaton. Their deaths had not been mysterious, but the manner in which each existed just before death was still an immense mystery to him. Why his mother had stayed with his father, he would never know. And Eaton. Why, oh God why, had Eaton not come to him with his problems? Adam would have done anything in his power to help his brother.

Perhaps he had been a child, not yet the man who could have helped.

It was too late to know. Moreover, he was so damned tired of guessing.

It was *not* too late with Charlie. He refused to live the rest of his life wondering why she was making such an inconceivable mistake.

"Jared?"

He jerked his gaze to her face, a swift exhalation of relief escaping his lips. Her eyes were tiny slits, barely open, but she was awake. "Charlie, sweetheart." He lifted her hand and placed it against his face. "You scared the hell out of me." The smell of ink and freshly printed paper lifted to him in a light wave as he caressed her palm with his lips. "I think I should fetch the doctor."

She blinked, forcing her eyes open. "No. No." She flicked her tongue across her chapped lips. "I'm fine."

He frowned. God, she was stubborn. "Do you have something for your lips?"

She rolled her tongue across the top one. "My lips?"

Dropping her hand, he braced his on his knee, leaning in until his face was only inches from hers. He was quickly losing patience. "Your lips look like charred wheat."

Pressing the chapped lips in question together, she glared at him. "Thank you for the lovely compliment."

He quelled a smile. Her voice was as weak as a baby's, but her spirit was as strong as a mule's.

"I have balm in the top drawer of the night table."

"That putrid stuff?" he asked, remembering the stuff she had put on his finger so long ago.

She rolled her eyes. "No . . . this is different."

"Thank God." He turned to open the drawer: a pair of spectacles, a book, two pencils and a small tin that must be the balm. He grabbed the tin, closed the drawer and turned to her with a resolute manner. Her eyes had closed.

Powerless to do anything but stare at her, he found himself lost in a slough of emotions. On one side of the fence were the protective feelings, the feelings that made him want to hold her, take care of her. On the other side were the lecherous feelings, the feelings that made him want to strip his clothes off and slide into bed with her. Of course, there were feelings sitting *on* the fence, too. Those were the ones whispering, "Get the hell out of here."

"Are you going to put the salve on or not?" She sounded resigned and cross.

Smiling then, because she could not see it, he opened the tin, pleased to note the salve emitted no *bizarre* odor. Dabbing the ointment on his finger, he then smeared it on her lips.

"Not too much," she grumbled.

"Hush." He tapped his finger against her mouth. As passion interfered, he softened his touch, smoothing the pad of his thumb across the soft swell of her lower lip, pronounced by her stubborn pout.

She raised her lids, and their gazes collided. Blue and brown, each turning darker by the second.

Charlie, stop looking at me like that, he warned, even as he leaned in to her. *Stop, or I do not know what I may do. It has been so long. Too long.*

A limb slapped against the window, reminding him where he was. What he was about.

Abruptly, he pushed the chair back and rose to his feet. He dropped the tin on the night table and ran his hand through his hair, then lifted it before his face. It shook as wildly as an old man's. He shoved his hands in his pockets. "You need to get some sleep. We can talk later." He raised his brows to bolster the command.

"I don't need to—"

"Just do it."

She frowned and snapped her mouth shut. Closing her eyes, she flounced to her side, away from him.

He waited until her breathing slowed, then walked to the bed and pulled the edge of the coverlet over her. It did not cover her completely, but at least she was sleeping. The dark circles beneath her eyes suggested rest had not come freely to her of late. He could sympathize. Some nights a bottle of red wine had been his only champion.

Forcing himself to leave her bed, he walked with stiff strides from the room. He shut the door behind him, sighed and leaned against it. He closed his eyes and clenched his fists, fighting the strong sensations running wildly through him. His shoulders lifted with a deep breath as he struggled with himself, struggled with his anxiety and the torment of his memories. He recognized the thick taste of fear in his mouth.

Charlie Whitney *was* frightening when she looked at you dead in the eye, her gaze relentlessly absolute.

It unnerved him as much as a ruler against his knuckles had in grade school.

He shivered as a chill skipped along his skin. It was dark, and a fire needed to be lit in the hearth. With a low groan, he pushed from the door. They could settle everything in the morning.

If he only knew what the hell he was going to say.

Adam flipped the eggs in the iron skillet and reached behind him for the loaf of bread. He had forgotten what good bread Charlie made. After slicing off a couple of pieces, he placed the loaf back in the wooden bread box. He glanced at the table. Salt. Pepper. Bacon. He had not been able to find the butter. Shrugging, he took the eggs off the heat and slid them onto a plate beside him. Placing the plate on the table, he then grabbed the threadbare dishrag hanging on a hook by the dry sink and wiped his hands.

As he lifted the knife to cut a piece of cheese, a knock sounded on the door. Frowning, he walked to the window and moved the lace-trimmed curtain aside. Miles' broken-down wagon was sitting in the drive. He could not see who it was knocking on the door. Having spent the night in Charlie's house, he could not open the door to just anyone, although her sofa had not been a *pleasurable* experience.

Hell, he was here because of Miles' letter. How surprised could he be to see Adam standing there?

Adam swung the door open just as Kath lifted her hand to knock again. Her fist froze in the air as an expression of outright panic crossed her face. She tried to compose herself, tilting her head down and lowering her hand to her waist, brushing wrinkles from a dress that looked as if it had just jumped off an ironing board minutes before. "Adam . . . what are you . . . um, it's nice to see . . . you." Her gaze skipped to the knife in his hand.

He smiled, feeling much like a cat stalking a mouse. What was making Katherine Lambert so nervous? He intended to find out. *Now.* "Thank you for your sincere welcome. Come in, come in." He grabbed her arm and pulled her inside, shutting the door with a snap.

She laughed and placed her hand upon her chest as she stumbled along behind him into the kitchen. "Mercy, I really ought to be going. I was just stopping by to see if Charlie needed a ride into town. The *Sentinel*—"

"She is not going into work today," he assured her as he waved the knife in the air like a conductor's wand. "But, I am glad you stopped by. Charlie is still sleeping. Since yesterday evening, I might add."

Kath threw a quick glance at the closed bedroom door. "She hasn't been getting much sleep lately."

"Why?"

Kath turned to him with wide eyes. Her gaze once again dropped to the knife in his hand. "The newspaper . . . Benjamin Folkes . . . is an old man." She smiled uneasily and cleared her throat. "He has a bad back. Charlie is left with the bulk of the work."

Adam gripped the knife with tense fingers. Damn Oliver Stokes. Was it impossible to find an editor young enough to stay awake during a press run? However, the idea of Charlie, spending days and nights working beside a young man—a handsome, talented editor perhaps—rankled. Frowning, he shoved the image aside. "What about Gerald?"

"Gerald does what he can, but he's no spring chicken, either."

"What about Tom Walker? He can help her do some of the chores." Until she moved into the man's house. He could not force himself to utter that sentence. Charlie and Tom in the same house, the same bed; just the thought made him want to put his fist through a wall.

Kath's neck muscles jumped as her gaze roamed the room. She swallowed and patted her chest with her hand. "Mercy . . . would you look at the time." She started for the door. "I really must be going."

"*Katherine Lambert.*" Adam tossed the knife from hand to hand as if it were a rock.

Her footsteps slowed. She turned to face him. He forced himself to remain silent as she closed her eyes, folding and unfolding her hands in her cotton skirt. "Tom Walker won't be helping Charlie with this place," she said with a shaky laugh. "He may be helping Lila, though."

Adam glanced over her bowed head, lifting his gaze to the patch of sky he could see through the curtain he had left open. Gray clouds prevailed, promising rain on a frigid winter day. He stroked his chin with the dull edge of the blade and contemplated her response. Lila? Why would Tom be helping Lila? He would only help the woman he was to marry, right? The picture of what was really happening here began to form in his mind. His hand fell to his side as he swung his gaze to her face. "Is Tom marrying Lila?"

A blistering pink flush spread across Kath's pale face as she lifted her head, meeting his gaze. She nodded, a meager movement he took to mean yes.

He blinked and fingered the edge of the blade. The rational part of his mind felt swift, certain fury at being played like a marble pawn on a chess board. But his heart, irrational and weak, thumped against his ribs in what he feared was extreme relief. And fear. Fear that this barrier—one he had been prepared to respect at all costs—had disappeared. The fury checked back in as he realized he was once again tangled in the Whitney web. He was not sure if he was happy about that or not.

"Did Charlie know about the letter?"

Kath shook her head, a brilliant red stain coloring her cheeks and the bridge of her nose.

He marched to the door, his arms swinging in rhythm with his angry stride. He looked back at her, his gaze following hers to his hand. The knife, clutched in his fist. He walked back to the table and slapped it alongside the food. "Wake Charlie and make sure she eats. She is too damn skinny." Before she could respond, he was halfway across the yard.

Chapter Thirty-Two

"Oh, my God!" Charlie dropped her fork into her lap.

Kath coughed and spread her palms along the table, not quite meeting her friend's gaze. "I know. It was a crazy idea. Mercy. I only wanted to help."

Charlie snatched the fork from her lap. She swallowed the eggs sitting on her tongue; they tasted like sawdust. "Help?" She waved the fork in the air. "Help?" She could hear her voice rising. Help? "You sent him a letter saying *I* was marrying Tom." She jabbed the fork into the eggs on her plate. "How in the hell could that help?"

Kath sighed. "I want you to be happy. You love him and he loves you. It's so obvious."

"I told you before. He is not Miles."

"I know he isn't. Believe me, I know."

"Where did he go?"

Kath shrugged.

Charlie clicked the fork tongs against her teeth. "Probably to punch Miles in the face."

"Oh, mercy. Do you think so?"

Charlie smiled into her breakfast plate. "He did write the letter, after all."

Kath jumped from the table. "I have to find them."

"Sit." She pointed to Kath's chair. "I'm joking." That was not altogether true; she didn't know what Chase was likely to do. He was angry. Justifiably so. What could they have been thinking? To manipulate him—telling him she was going to marry Tom. Surely, he had known that could not be true.

But he *had* come.

A warm tingle charged through her. She had been dead inside for months, writing articles and washing clothes, printing newspapers and darning socks, setting type and pulling weeds. While trying to survive, she had pushed all those forbidden memories to the back of her mind. The sensation of a man inside her. *No . . .* not any man. Only one man would ever do that to her.

He was all she would ever want, and seeing him again had swept those memories before her eyes, her mind, her heart: the salty taste of his skin on her lips, the sweet smell of him lingering on crisp cotton sheets, the gentle touch of his fingers, caressing, seeking, exploring. Thank you, God, she thought with a nod to the heavens. Thank you for letting me see him one more time.

Charlie sat on the porch stairs, a thick sweater draped over her shoulders, a worn-out hat swinging from her fingers. Watching Chase walk up the drive, she took a deep breath, hoping to calm the wild thump of her heart. As he drew closer, the early evening sun fading behind him, he dissolved into shadow. His eyes, his face, his body, all eluded her penetrating gaze. She leaned back on her elbows as he reached the bottom step, waiting for him to emerge from the darkness.

"You were waiting for me."

She nodded. Of course she was. "Where have you been?" She twisted the mangled brim of the hat into further disarray.

He hesitated, then glanced over his shoulder toward the fading sun. The meager light illuminated his profile, his strong chin and elegantly curved nose. "I was at the newspaper, finishing Benjamin Folkes' editorials."

"Oh."

He snapped his head around, lifted his gaze the length of

her, then said with barely concealed anger, "You should have let me know."

She laid the hat by her side, looking away. "I don't know what you mean."

"I talked with Gerald."

She shrugged. What did he expect her to say? That she needed him? That she had started a hundred letters telling him how desperately she needed his help with the *Sentinel,* only to remember her promise by the riverbank? She refused now, had then, to tangle him in a web of her making.

"Goddammit, but you are stubborn."

She turned then, her anger sparked, her gaze fixing on him. "Why did you come here?"

He sank to his knees on the bottom step, his face level with hers. Their gazes locked in a silent contest of wills. She did not move an inch, refusing to be intimidated.

Sighing, he lifted his hand to her face, touching the tip of his finger to the bruise on her forehead. Lowering his hand, he stroked the ridge of her cheek, the skin beneath her jaw. "I came here because I could not stand the thought of another man loving you," he whispered hoarsely. Sliding his hand into her hair, he pulled her closer as he leaned in.

She moaned low in her throat before his mouth ever touched hers. The anticipation of touching him again, of having him touch her, was enough to make her crazy. She struggled to catch her breath as his tongue began to trace her lips. Oh, God, she thought, her mind remembering and recording all at once, was he this wonderful before?

She trembled and pressed forward, opening her eyes when she encountered only cool winter air. He had retreated, a pensive expression on his face. Was she imagining the naked fear she saw reflected in his dark gaze? She knew intimacy scared him. Where would it lead? Didn't he know by now she would never hurt him?

Rising to her feet, she offered her hand to him. He hesitated only a moment before taking it. She opened the door and pulled him inside. The house was dark, except for a fire flickering in the hearth. The crackle of burning wood and the acrid aroma of smoke filled the small room.

Charlie closed the door and stood behind as he walked for-

ward, watching as he glanced about the modest structure. He
turned his head toward the fire, the warm glow from the flames
revealing a quilt and two pillows. A bottle of wine sat on the
floor beside the pillows, two mismatched glasses next to it.

He glanced at her, then back to the makeshift bed, as a lazy
smile spread across his face.

"That's the bottle of wine you gave me last summer."

"I thought it might be."

She walked around him, turning until they stood less than a
foot apart. Lifting her hands to the buttons on his shirt, she
released one, then the others, until the cloth hung open from
neck to waist. He made no move to help her, but if his tight
gaze and rapid breaths were any indication, he liked what she
was doing.

Encouraged, she pushed the shirt from his shoulders, forgetting it as it slipped to the floor. Her gaze devoured his chest.
She wanted to memorize every crest and hollow. Noticing the
wide bandage on his left arm, she looked at him questioningly.

He shook his head as if to say "not now" and stepped
forward. Grasping the sides of her face with both hands, he
lowered his head and pressed his lips to hers. She parted them,
not wishing to play the part of a chaste woman when she was
not. Nor did she wish to be. To act as if she had forgotten the
incredible passion that flowed between them, or to act—even
more absurd—as if she didn't want him, would be impossible.
She was sure he could see the stark need in her eyes, hear it
in the immodest beat of her heart.

Laying her hands on his shoulders, she tore her mouth away
and bent her knees, planting kisses down his neck and chest.
She slanted her head and circled his tight brown nipple with
her tongue.

"How . . . I have missed you, sweetheart," he said, his chest
rising and falling with each quick breath. He let his hands fall
to his sides as her mouth moved lower. The taut muscles of
his stomach clenched in what she hoped was anticipation.

She kissed until her lips met the cotton cloth of his trousers.
As she worked the buttons loose, her knuckles brushed against
his hard shaft. She heard him groan, then felt his fingers grasp
hers in a tense grip. She paused and glanced at him through

dark lashes. Was he stopping her now? When she desperately wanted to see him again, touch him again?

She recognized the expression on his face: pupils darkened so they appeared black in the dim glow of the room and lips pressed into a thin line. No, there would be no stopping now.

He did not speak, simply dropped her hand. Bending, he tugged his boots off and threw them to the side. She watched his stomach muscles bunch and tighten as he straightened and faced her. Without a word, he pulled her to her feet, grabbed her shoulders and shoved her against the door, sinking into her from lips to toes.

"Nights, I have lain awake. So many nights, wanting you. Wanting this."

The whispered words rang in her ears as he rubbed against her, his long body angled so their waists were parallel. She groaned and stretched, searching for his mouth. "Please," she said. Her body—especially the tender area below her waist—began to hum in response. Every part of her remembered this. Remembered *him*.

He obeyed her appeal, his mouth falling to hers as his hands stripped her of her clothing. Crisp air lingered on her skin but a moment as he slipped his arms around her, wrapping her in his warm embrace.

They stood, she pressed against the door, he pressed against her, writhing and touching, tasting and licking, their moaning louder than the pop and shift of the logs in the hearth.

She felt cool air upon her face and opened her eyes to find his slowly traveling the length of her. He paused in two places before meeting her gaze. "Beautiful." He lured her to the makeshift bed by the fire.

She sank to the blanket, surprised by the sudden shudder that shook her. She rolled to her back and looked at him as he took off his trousers. The dancing flames threw scarlet light along his chest and legs, along his arms as they flexed and straightened. Her mouth felt dry from exertion, her mind dazed with the knowledge that he was hers once again. *Jared.* She must have whispered it aloud, because he nodded before dropping to his knees beside her.

He placed his palms against her nipples and kneaded them in small, tight circles. She moaned and twisted her head to the side, shutting her eyes so tightly that colors collided behind her lids.

"Open your legs." She felt his knee brush between her thighs.

She submitted. Without hesitation.

Probing fingers, lips on the back of her knee, teeth nipping the inside of her thigh. She was dizzy with anticipation, longing. She lifted herself to his mouth as she clenched the blanket in both fists. Oh, yes, it was delightful, sensuous . . . vulgar. She loved it.

She wrapped her fingers in his hair and pulled. All at once his weight settled upon her. She tilted her head and flicked her eyes open. His face loomed inches above her own. He was struggling to contain his rapid breathing. She was glad to see he shared her flustered state.

"I want to look at your face while I make love to you, Charlie Whitney," he said and slid into her, his arms pressed flat on either side of her head.

She opened her mouth to respond, only to hear a groan slip out.

He pulled back, then pushed his hips forward, inching into her. Their gazes did not stray as he governed the deliberate rhythm. He only laughed as she urged him—with her hands and her hips—to go faster. He whispered in her ear, "Patience, sweetheart. Patience." But he could not hide the tremor that laced his words.

She smiled and moved her hands to his hips, guiding his movements. "Slowly, then. I'll close my eyes . . . think of your lips kissing me there, your tongue inside me."

He stopped, staring at her, his eyes as wide as she had ever seen them. And as dark. She was sure this time they had made the full run to black.

"Goddammit, you make me crazy." He thrust into her. Hard. He seemed incapable of softening his movements. She heard an apology mixed in with his moans.

She didn't want his apologies. She didn't want to make love to him like a lady. Her body and her mind felt not quite hers as they moved together, sweat and heat binding them. Were those her teeth biting his shoulder? Her hands pinching his damp skin? Her voice imploring him to go faster? Her legs tightening around his?

As they strained and stretched, their bodies shifting much like a wave upon a stormy sea, she imagined herself a wild animal, panting and clawing, desperate for gratification. For sustenance.

He knew. He paused, drawing his hand between their bodies.

Yes. She remembered. He closed in upon the small bud of skin she had come to recognize as being the center of her pleasure. He had, of course, known it all along.

She twisted her head, burying her face in his hair as he settled deep inside her. The spicy scent of him flowed through her nostrils, so solid and memorable that she could all but taste it. She clutched him, her hands curving around the rounded muscles of his back. Not able to control herself, she writhed under him, lifting her hips.

Move dammit. *I need it.*

"Charlie." His voice was ragged, his breath hot upon her skin. "No. Do not move. I cannot—"

"I ... don't ... care." She sucked a soft patch of skin between her teeth and angled her body, up, then down, drawing him in and out of her.

He rolled to his back, holding her about the waist to keep them joined. "Do it, then."

She rose until she was sitting, her legs bent, her knees pressed along either side of him. Flinging her hair from her face, she stared at him. His face was red; a vein in his temple pulsed. A trickle of sweat rolled down the side of his neck, much like melting wax. She captured it with her finger, then brought it to her lips. He groaned and closed his eyes. She felt him twitch inside her.

She was amazed she could do this to him. Level-headed, stubborn, inaccessible Jared Chase lay sprawled beneath her, his lips pressed together so hard the edges were white, his fingers digging into the skin at her waist.

He wanted her.

Moreover, it seemed as if he had missed her as much as she had missed him.

"Are you trying to ... kill me?" His eyes opened, an almost angry expression reflected in them.

She laughed and lowered, brushing her face against his. She placed her palms flat on the blanket on either side of his head. "Whatever do you mean, Mr. Chase?" But she proved the question pointless by lifting the length of him, then down. Then again and again. "Like this, Mr. Chase?"

"Crazy," he said and pulled her mouth to his.

Pleasure, intense and determined, was so close to the surface that little more was needed to secure it. She hoped it was the same for him. It was hard to think, so she merely reacted: Jared surging beneath her, his hands guiding her hips; the taste of his sweat, salty and distinct, upon her tongue. The scent of sex, roses and the combination of them, lingered in the air.

As heat tore through her, a stinging, white wave of bliss, she pulled her lips from his and tucked her head into his shoulder, fighting to hold back her whimpers. Her fingers crawled through his hair; she pulled as needlelike pricks danced along her neck and back.

He dragged her hips down, and she felt him, really felt him, jerk inside her. A hoarse cry fell from his lips. His hands stilled her as he thrust into her, grinding his hips back and forth.

"Oh, heaven." She collapsed on top of him. His heart thumped as heavily as a hammer beneath her ear. They lay sated and silent for so long, the frigid air began to nip at her moist skin. For a moment, she had doubted she would ever be cold again.

She sighed and rolled off him, leaning back and pulling the edge of the blanket over them as well as she could. Settling her head on his chest, she threw her thigh across his and stretched the other leg along the side of his body.

"Cozy?"

"Umm, very." She snuggled into him and kissed his chest.

"Did you find any of my hair tangled in your fingers?"

She tilted her head. His eyes were closed, a lazy smile upon his face, those damn dimples of his dug as deep as a well in the ground.

"I think you removed a sizable hunk of my hair." He yawned and pulled her closer to his side. "Getting older, may need that hair."

She smiled. He sounded content. Thank goodness, he hadn't

abandoned her or tried to deny what had taken place between them.

A sharp gust of wind rattled the window above them. The occasional crackle of burning wood lulled her. She snuggled deeper beneath the blanket, moving gently so not to wake him. His breathing was calm and even. She wiggled her nose and sniffed; his chest hair tickled. His distinct scent mingled with smoke on his skin.

She experienced not an ounce of contrition for lying naked in a man's arms. A man who was not her husband. There was not a lick of shame, not a spot the size of a grain of sand to be found in her.

He was not her husband, but he *was* the man she loved.

"I love you, you know."

She closed her eyes. It felt good to finally say those words. Even if he did not hear them.

Adam slipped through the door, shutting it as softly as possible behind him. Charlie was sleeping like the dead, which was about the shape she had been in when she'd fainted the day before yesterday. Still, his stomach knotted when he remembered her pitching into the dirt at his feet. He shook his head and slipped a cheroot from the pocket of his shirt. The wind and his fingers, which quivered ever so slightly, kept him from lighting it on the first try. "Dammit." He tucked it tighter between his lips.

Resting his shoulder against the wooden porch post, he observed the tranquil morning. The sky was still dark, but a glimmer of red was beginning to show on the horizon. He tipped his head into the cold wind. Did they get any snow here? Being so close to the mountains, he supposed they got some.

He wished like hell Charlie had some of Miles' whiskey in her house. He needed a drink right about now—hell he needed a whole bottle.

I love you, you know.

She had said it as if he should know. And, of course, he should have. Charlie would never give herself to a man without love being the active force behind it.

Why, why did she have to *say* it?

And how could he leave her? With two old men to help her with the *Sentinel?* She needed help. It looked as if it was about time for a new roof for her house. How could she possibly afford that?

He kicked the toe of his boot against the step.

He had awoken this morning with dreams in his mind and Charlie tangled about him like a vine. The dreams brought the past into his heart, before his eyes, reviving his mother and Eaton. So much so, that he woke thinking they were there in her house. *With* him. He realized in an instant that was not possible, would never be possible, and turned to find her there. Solace, for the first time in years. To know he was not alone.

He lowered himself to the step, placing his elbows on his thighs, dropping his hands between his knees.

Their faces had dimmed in his memory, his mother's and Eaton's. Even in his dreams the images withered like an aged daguerreotype. His mother's hair had been a lovely shade of auburn, had it not? And Eaton had spoken with a slight lisp, had he not? He smothered the cheroot and threw it to the ground. How could he have forgotten his own family?

His mother's voice came to him then, almost as if she stood behind him. Words she had spoken long ago during one of their summers at the seashore. Advice he had forgotten. *You carry them always, in everything you do. In everything you are, they are alive.* He had asked about her parents, who had passed away long before he was born. *The way you hold a fork, Jared, the color of your eyes, the places you will visit with your children and say, I remember when. These are the things which make a person complete. Death cannot take them.*

His mother. Eaton. Charlie.

I love you, you know.

He dropped his head into his hands, fighting a powerful urge to cry. He had never considered himself to be an emotional man, never expected to feel so much for one person as to be overpowered by it. Overpowered. What he felt for Charlie Whitney *did* knock him quite completely from his feet.

He supposed it was love. Dammit.

A soft nudge against his back had him swinging around. She stood by the door, wrapped from neck to ankle in the blanket they had slept under. He caught sight of a slim, pale shoulder.

He presented his back to her and swiped his hands across his eyes. "Do you have anything on under that?"

"Nope." She shuffled over and plopped beside him.

Have you no decency, woman? he wanted to ask. But this was Charlie. His Charlie. He liked that she had no shame concerning him.

"Fire in the sky." She pointed to a sun steadily rising, tinting clouds that sat just above the horizon a blustering redgold. "We're like a fire in the sky. Defiant, passionate . . . then we fade away."

He turned, controlling his expression, betraying none of his earlier thoughts. "What are you talking about?"

She shrugged and tugged the blanket to her neck. His gaze followed, lingering on the soft swell of breast he had glimpsed.

"I guess I was just wondering. I mean, well . . ." She swallowed and shrugged again. "When are you going back to Richmond?"

He glanced away, then returned his gaze to her. She was staring at her toes, wriggling them like a small child. He suppressed a smile. "I am not going back to Richmond. At least, not permanently."

She jerked her head around. The blanket slipped from her fist. "Not going back?"

He raised the blanket to her neck, lifting her hand to hold it. "I want you to marry me."

"But . . . our arrangement?"

"The arrangement be damned! You need help with the newspaper, and your roof needs to be repaired. Maybe replaced. Would not support heavy spring rain, I can tell you that much."

"Roof . . ."

He grasped her shoulders and turned her to face him. "Will you quit repeating what I say in that odd tone."

Her brow furrowed. "Roof?"

"Charlie."

"Roof!"

His hands fell from her shoulders. He had a sinking suspicion he had committed a blunder here.

She jabbed her finger against his collarbone. "You want me to marry you so you can fix my roof?" Jab. "And help with the *Sentinel?*" Jab. "Are you daft?" Jab.

He grabbed her wrist, lifting her bony finger from his chest. "You could be pregnant. Have you ever thought of that?"

"Of course I've thought of that."

"How would you manage? You barely have enough money to survive as it is."

She jumped up so quickly that the blanket became tangled in her ankles. She almost fell. He reached to steady her. She flung his hand aside.

"Who is talking to me? When did Chase get back in town?"

He frowned at her, genuinely bewildered by her response. She loved him, right? Did all women not want to marry the man they loved? "I have no idea what I have said to make you this angry."

"You are a fool," she threw at him, then stumbled into her house, slamming the door behind her.

He sighed and leaned his head back against the post. What the hell had happened? The door opened, and before he could react, his shirt smacked him in the face. The sound of his satchel hitting the porch boards was followed by the slam of the front door. Again. This time she threw the rarely used lock into place.

Chapter Thirty-Three

"Quit laughing."

Miles wiped his eyes with the back of his hand. "You asked her to marry you so you could fix her roof? Landsakes, that's a good one." He covered his mouth with his hand, but it did not help; the chuckles sprang forth anyway. "And ... you didn't even ask her, you *told* her."

Adam stood up with such force that his chair toppled over. "Why did I come here?"

"Because"—Miles straightened his lips—"because she threw your satchel out, too. Here or Mrs. Wilkin's, I figure." His mouth crumpled, and he dipped his head as he lost the battle with laughter.

Adam ran his hand through his hair and went to get his bag, which sat by the door. Mrs. Wilkin's it would be, then.

"Wait, Adam."

He paused and turned. Kath stood in the doorway leading to the pantry. She wiped her hands on her apron and came forward. "I'm sorry. I was eavesdropping. Come and sit back down." She gestured to the overturned chair. "Please."

Well, what the hell. He shot Miles a hot glare, righted the chair and seated himself.

Kath walked to the chair opposite Adam's and slid awkwardly into it. Obviously, her pregnancy was beginning to make some activities difficult. She frowned at Miles, who was still trying to compose himself, then turned to Adam with a smile.

"You just need to go talk to her." She laughed and pulled at the apron stretched tight over her middle. "Don't you understand why she's upset?"

"No, I do not."

She shook her head and glanced at her lap. "Mercy, men can be so dumb."

"Now, wait a darn minute—" Miles thumped his hand on the table.

"Pardon me?"

Kath raised her head, leveling her gaze on Adam. "Do you love her?"

Of course he loved her. But he had only realized that this very morning.

Adam shifted in his chair as she continued to stare at him, her jaw set as stiffly as a pastor's in a room full of sinners. He threw a quick glance at Miles, who was studying his fingernails as if they could solve the world's problems. Thanks, friend.

"Well?" Kath's green gaze drilled into him.

Adam shoved his hand through his hair, avoiding her eyes. As his sleeve brushed his nose, he caught the faint trace of roses. A vision of Charlie sleeping by the hearth popped into his mind: her dark lashes resting against her smooth skin, her lips parted, her fist snagged in his shirt. He wanted to take care of her, protect her. Did *any* of them understand that?

"Charlie is a woman, Adam. She needs to hear that you love her. Mercy, I'll be the first to admit she's a mite . . . unusual. But a woman, still." She reached across the table and touched his hand.

He raised his gaze to her.

"Go to her. Tell her that you love her. Need her." She laughed softly. "Then you can fix her roof."

"That was not the best way to ask, was it?" Adam lifted his head.

"Damn foolish, if you ask me." This from Miles.

"No one is asking you." Adam stood. He paused when he reached the door. "Can I take your wagon? No need causing any undue gossip.'' He shifted from one foot to the other. ''I will bring it back tonight, if I can stay, that is.''

''You stayed last night; why would tonight be any different?'' Kath said, as she rose from the table. ''Dinner's at six. We'll expect you and Charlie. See you then.''

Adam smiled and stepped through the door, laughing as he heard Miles ask, ''Now, what did you mean about men being dumb?''

Charlie sneezed and wiped her hand across her nose. It was cold in the office, even colder on the floor. Not to mention the dust. The press had been acting up today; a loose cylinder, Gerald said. He was getting too old to crawl around on his hands and knees, so here she was, lying on her back, covered with ink, under the press.

She heard the door open and close. She almost called to Gerald, asking what he'd forgotten, until she caught sight of black polished leather. Hessians. She took a deep breath, fighting the urgent quickening of her heart. Hellfire. She'd tell him what she thought of a new roof!

He stopped alongside the press, on the side closest to the door. Surely he could see her legs poking out. Why didn't he say anything? Cautiously, she rolled her head his way. It was definitely Chase. No one in town had boots like that.

Why doesn't he say anything?

A piece of paper slipped to the floor, landing right next to his boots. She lay there, barely breathing for trying to be quiet, and stared at the sheet. She sighed, grabbed the sheet and jerked it under the press. She frowned. Had she heard him laugh? Oh, the *nerve* of the man.

She moved the paper this way and that, attempting to find enough light to see what it was. She squinted. *Deed of ownership. Transferred November 29, 1850,* Edgemont Sentinel, *Charlotte Elaine Whitney.*

She reared, banging her head on the underside of the press. ''Ow!''

He grabbed her ankles. ''Put you head down.'' She could tell by his tone he was laughing. Oh, would she tell him a thing or two.

He gave a firm yank, and she slid on her bottom across the floor. Merciful heavens, she hoped no one was strolling by along the boardwalk. She glared at him, the deed wrinkled in her sweaty fist. She jumped to her feet.

He dropped his gaze, then lifted it to her face. ''You bought another pair of those god-awful boots.'' He pulled a handkerchief from his back pocket and began to wipe her nose and forehead.

She ripped the cloth from his hand and tossed it in the air. ''What is the meaning of this?'' She waved the deed beneath his nose.

''Do not crush the damn thing.'' He pried her fist open and extracted the deed, which now had a crease running along its center. Grasping her hand, he pulled her to the closest chair and pushed her into it.

She wanted to grab him by the shoulders and shake him as hard as she could. Or shove him to the floor and cover him with kisses. Heavens, he smelled good. Like soap and tobacco. He must have taken a bath, and *she* looked like a hired hand on a cattle drive.

His feet shifted as he squatted in front of her. She lifted her gaze along his long legs, stopping when she came to his waist.

''This goes with it, I suppose.'' He dropped a small velvet-covered box in her lap.

She threw a quick glance at his face. His gaze was fixed on the far wall. Her hands shook as she reached for the box. The hinge looked old, a little rusty, but it popped open on the second try. She flipped the cover back. A ring winked at her from faded, red velvet folds: a glowing, round sapphire perched amid a circle of diamonds. She lifted her gaze as she ran the tip of her finger over the blue stone.

''Chase . . .''

He met her gaze then, his brow drawn together. She felt her heart flutter in her chest. He was *nervous*. ''Jared, remember?''

She laughed and looked at the ring again. ''What . . . this is beautiful, but—''

He tilted her head so she could see his face. ''The ring was my mother's. Her mother gave it to her.''

''But—''

He stalled, the finger beneath her chin trembling. He swallowed and pressed his lips together. "I love you, you know."

"You heard." *Oh.* That explained this morning. She had scared him once again.

His shoulders lifted with a deep breath as an impatient glint flashed in his eyes. He dropped his hand by his side. "How about it?"

Why, I should make him squirm. He really is *terrible* at this. Truly awful. "How about what?"

He frowned and gestured to the ring with his shoulder. "The ring, you know. Do you want to . . . get married?"

"No, I'm afraid I've hired someone to come take care of my roof."

He sputtered a laugh and grasped her knees with his hands. "Charlie. Dammit."

"And we already have such a lovely arrangement."

He dropped his head to her knee. "You want everything. You want me to open my soul to you. All right." He sighed. "I missed you so much after you left Richmond. God, I could barely endure spending time in that house. The scent of you stuck to the sheets for weeks. I finally realized it was in my brain, not on those damn sheets." He rolled his head on her lap and squeezed her knees. "I would sit on the porch, looking at the river, imagining us there together. And your voice. Your voice would come to me on the wings of the wind some nights. I would turn, expecting you to be there."

She lifted her hand to his head and trailed her fingers through his dark, curling hair. A tear drifted from the corner of her eye, making a slow path down her cheek.

He continued as if he did not feel her touch. "I drank too much, could not sleep. Tanner's still mad at me for one stunt I pulled. I could not go, that house was not, I wanted . . ." He raised up and seized her by the back of the neck, lifting her from the seat of the chair, bringing her mouth to his. The kiss was one part anger, one part desperation, one part passion, one part love. It was the first kiss they had shared with love admitted between them.

He slid his hands to her back, grasping her cotton shirt in both fists. "I'm scared," he said against her lips, "scared to love you."

"I know," she said against his.

He withdrew, releasing her so abruptly that her bottom smacked against the seat of the chair. "Actually"—he laughed softly—"this is the first time I have known that to be true and not been frightened to death of it."

"Frightened?" Of what?

He lifted his hand to her cheek and rubbed his thumb across her lips. "That you know me so well. For a man who is not looking to suddenly slam head-on into his other half." He smiled. "Fairly frightening."

His other half? For heaven's sake, she had thrown him out of her house this morning, and he thought she was his other half? She tilted her head to the side, leaning on his hand. Her bottom lip disappeared into her mouth as she began to chew. "About this morning—"

He laughed and pulled her into his arms. She slipped there easily, comfortably, as if they were two distinct parts that fit into a perfect whole. She was starting to believe he was truly hers. Heavens, she wanted to run down the street, shouting that she loved him. "I love you, I do," she said against his rough wool coat.

"Oh, sweetheart. I am sorry. Sorry it took me so long, sorry I let you leave Richmond. You knew . . . that I was dying inside? You knew why I could not go to the train station."

She nodded against his chest.

He kissed the top of her head and gathered her close. The occasional shout from the boardwalk, the sound of a passing carriage, the cold air in the newspaper office, all ceased to exist as they reveled in the knowledge that they finally belonged to each other.

"The *Sentinel* . . . it's ours?"

"Yes. The bastard drove a hard bargain, but I was very persuasive."

"Richmond?"

"Tanner is staying in the city for a few months. He needs a place to stay. We will travel back often. Special assignments for the *Times.*"

She pushed him away with a hand to his chest. "You left your job?"

"I sent a telegraph today."

"Today?"

He threw his gaze to the floor, as a red tinge colored his cheeks. "I told you, I just figured all this out."

She suppressed a smile; he sounded like a recalcitrant child caught leaving muddy tracks on a freshly mopped floor. Should she be irked that he'd been intending to depart again?

He *had* brought the ring with him. He must have been planning something.

"I sent for Taber, too. He likes it here. Open fields. Clean air."

"What about my roof?"

He glanced up with a half smile, his dimples digging into his cheeks. "Miles can fix the damn roof, after all the trouble he has brought me."

"Trouble? You think I'm trouble?" She touched a finger to his nose. "You haven't seen anything yet."

He laughed and touched his forehead to hers. "Just go slowly with me, Miss Whitney. I'm a novice where this love stuff is concerned."

"I'll keep that in mind, Mr. Chase."

Epilogue

"Papa!"

A small body plowed into his legs. Adam turned from the counter of the telegraph office. He bent and scooped his son high against his chest. The scent of his son—leather, dirt, horses and child—was enough to make his knees weak. Enough to make him say his prayers twice a day and three times on Sunday.

"Papa, you have to come to the office."

Adam nodded to the clerk behind the desk and walked through the door. Looking at his son, he was amazed, as always, to see a tiny version of himself looking back. Except for the startling blue eyes, his son looked like he had been spit from Adam's mouth.

"Piggyback, okay?"

Adam smiled and swung his son to his back. "Hold on tight. No dropping off like last week."

"Oh, Papa, my hands were slippery."

Yes, from dipping them one too many times in the horse trough. Come to think of it, his son smelled rather horsy today. "Eaton, have you been messing with the horse trough?"

Vigorous shaking burst forth against his back. "Nope. Been down at the livery."

"Ah."

"Taber gets lonely, Papa."

Adam tipped his head to Mrs. Whitefield as they met crossing the street.

"Hold on." He hopped onto the boardwalk, tightening his arms across the plump legs wrapped around his stomach.

"She's doing it again." His son sighed, an age-old sigh he and Charlie often laughed about. Sometimes, Eaton seemed wiser than his parents.

Adam paused at the door, curbing the urge to glance inside. After all this time, his heart still thumped with heavy strokes if he saw Charlie walking toward him along the street or heard her voice coming from the back of a store. As each day passed, he loved her more. She was his best friend, his lover, his wife, his confidant. And, though it had been surprising when it happened, the mother of his child.

He dropped Eaton from his back and squatted until his face was level with his son's. The boy was tall for his age, only five, and growing as fast as kudzu.

"Remember what I said? Your mother's more tired than usual. You did the right thing by coming to find me." He winked at Eaton and patted his shoulder. Eaton beamed like he'd won a medal.

"Your mother is a stubborn woman and resists letting the Chase men take care of her."

"Yes, Papa, I know." Eaton sighed again.

Adam laughed and planted a quick kiss on his son's cheek, which Eaton promptly wiped off after looking to make sure no one had seen it. "I'm not a baby to be kissing on the street."

Adam smothered a grin. "So sorry, I forgot."

They entered the office, grinning and holding their fingers to their lips. Adam glanced at her desk, the same scarred one from years ago. She would not let him replace a damn item in the office. He supposed she never would.

"See, Papa."

"Yep, I see." He stepped to the desk and brushed his hand along the smooth skin of her cheek. Tanned as always.

Her eyelids fluttered, and she tilted her head, regarding him with a warm smile. "Jared."

He dropped to his knees beside her. "You were supposed

to stay home today.'' He lifted a strand of hair from her face and tucked it behind her ear.

She shrugged as if that was explanation enough.

''I thought we agreed that when the weather got warmer, you would stay home part of the week.''

She laughed and laid a hand on his arm. ''You worry too much. Heavens, I'm hardly showing. We have four months to go.''

He took her hand in his. ''I just worry. Will you, for once in your life, let me take care of you?''

''Papa, Papa, look!'' Eaton ran to them, sliding to a halt just before he plowed into the desk. ''There's a fire in the sky! Just like the one you showed me before!''

Adam winked at his wife. ''Hear that, sweetheart? A fire in the sky Imagine . . . it has not even begun to fade.''